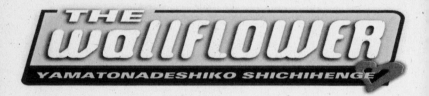

THE WALLFLOWER
YAMATONADESHIKO SHICHIHENGE

♥ 1 ♥

Tomoko Hayakawa

TRANSLATED AND ADAPTED BY
David Ury

LETTERED BY
Dana Hayward

DEL REY

BALLANTINE BOOKS • NEW YORK

A Del Rey® Book
Published by The Random House Publishing Group

First published in Japan in 2000 by Kodansha Ltd., Tokyo
as *Yamatonadeshiko Shichihenge*
This publication rights arranged through Kodansha Ltd.

Published in the United States by Del Rey Books,
an imprint of The Random House Publishing Group,
a division of Random House, Inc., New York, and simultaneously
in Canada by Random House of Canada Limited, Toronto.

www.delreymanga.com

Library of Congress Control Number: 2004095918
ISBN 0-345-47912-2

Text design by Dana Hayward

Manufactured in the United States of America

First Edition: October 2004

3 4 5 6 7 8 9

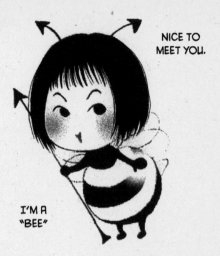

NICE TO
MEET YOU.

I'M A
"BEE"

I'm going to talk a little bit about how this series was created. My original idea was to write a "how to" book, about a girl with low self-esteem and her journey to becoming beautiful. Hey, what happened to that idea? Will the main character, Sunako, really become brighter and happier? Even I don't know the answer to that question. Anyway, this is Volume 1. I hope you'll check out the other volumes, too.

Contents

Honorifics

Throughout the Del Rey Manga books, you will find Japanese honorifics left intact in the translations. For those not familiar with how the Japanese use honorifics, and more important, how they differ from American honorifics, we present this brief overview.

Politeness has always been a critical facet of Japanese culture. Ever since the feudal era, when Japan was a highly stratified society, use of honorifics—which can be defined as polite speech that indicates relationship or status—has played an essential role in the Japanese language. When addressing someone in Japanese, an honorific usually takes the form of a suffix attached to one's name (example: "Asuna-san"), or as a title at the end of one's name or in place of the name itself (example: "Negi-sensei," or simply "Sensei!").

Honorifics can be expressions of respect or endearment. In the context of manga and anime, honorifics give insight into the nature of the relationship between characters. Many translations into English leave out these important honorifics, and therefore distort the "feel" of the original Japanese. Because Japanese honorifics contain nuances that English honorifics lack, it is our policy at Del Rey not to translate them. Here, instead, is a guide to some of the honorifics you may encounter in Del Rey Manga.

-san:　　This is the most common honorific, and is equivalent to Mr., Miss, Ms., Mrs., etc. It is the all-purpose honorific and can be used in any situation where politeness is required.

-sama:　This is one level higher than "-san." It is used to confer great respect.

-dono:　This comes from the word "tono," which means "lord." It is an even higher level than "-sama," and confers utmost respect.

-kun:　　This suffix is used at the end of boys' names to express familiarity or endearment. It is also sometimes used by men among friends, or when addressing someone younger or of a lower station.

-chan: This is used to express endearment, mostly toward girls. It is also used for little boys, pets, and even among lovers. It gives a sense of childish cuteness.

Bozu: This is an informal way to refer to a boy, similar to the English term "kid" or "squirt."

Sempai: This title suggests that the addressee is one's "senior" in a group or organization. It is most often used in a school setting, where underclassmen refer to their upperclassmen as "sempai." It can also be used in the workplace, such as when a newer employee addresses an employee who has seniority in the company.

Kohai: This is the opposite of "sempai," and is used toward underclassmen in school or newcomers in the workplace. It connotes that the addressee is of lower station.

Sensei: Literally meaning "one who has come before," this title is used for teachers, doctors, or masters of any profession or art.

[blank]: Usually forgotten in these lists, but perhaps the most significant difference between Japanese and English. The lack of honorific means that the speaker has permission to address the person in a very intimate way. Usually, only family, spouses, or very close friends have this kind of permission. Known as *yobisute*, it can be gratifying when someone who has earned the intimacy starts to call one by one's name without an honorific. But when that intimacy hasn't been earned, it can also be very insulting.

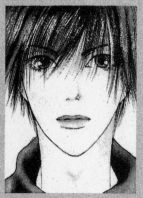
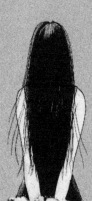
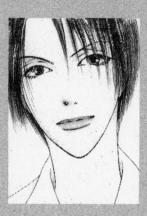
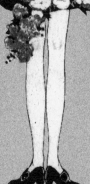

THE WALLFLOWER
YAMATONADESHIKO SHICHIHENGE

Chapter 1
A Ray of Light in the Darkness

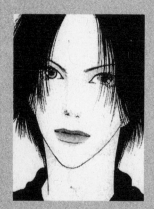
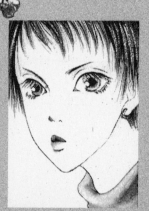

Tomoko Hayakawa

Chapter 1:
A Ray of Light in the Darkness

Chapter 2:
Behind the Iron Curtain!

Chapter 3:
The Bright Bright World ♥

Chapter 4:
The Good Old Dark Days of Youth

Chapter 5:
Go Into the Light

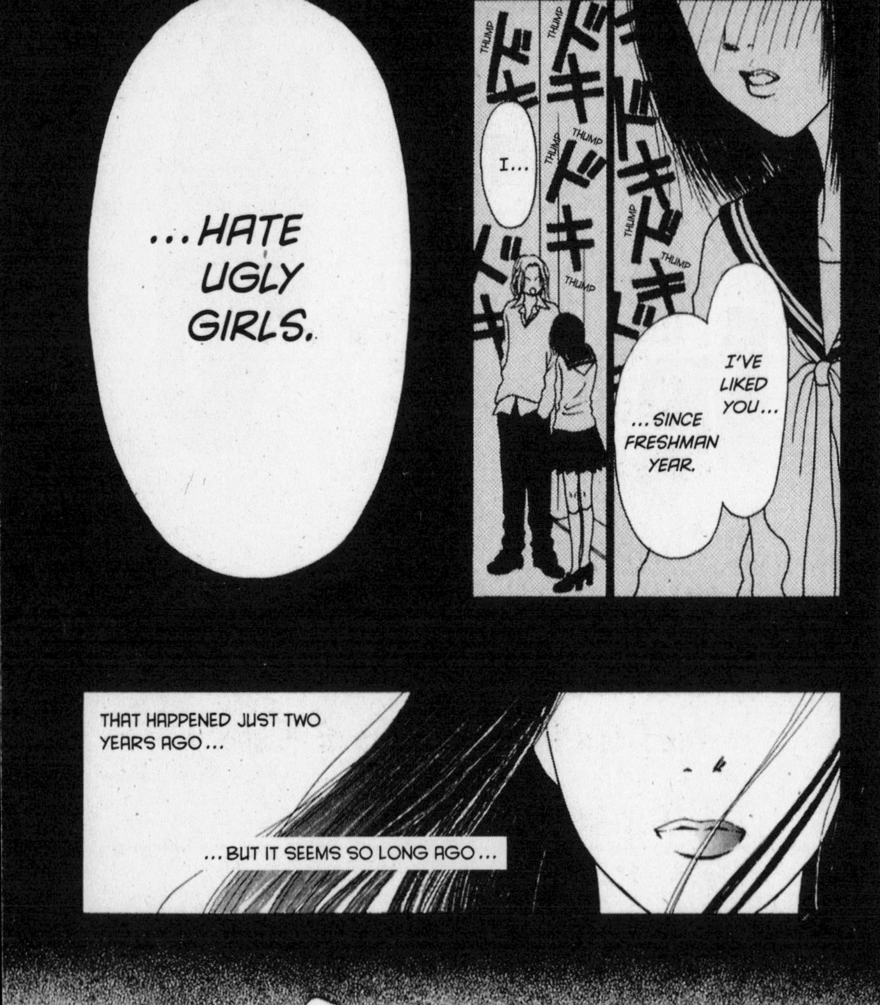
I'VE LIKED YOU...
...SINCE FRESHMAN YEAR.
ドキドキ
THUMP THUMP THUMP THUMP THUMP THUMP
I...
...HATE UGLY GIRLS.
THAT HAPPENED JUST TWO YEARS AGO...
...BUT IT SEEMS SO LONG AGO...
"...SO ANYWAY
...PLEASE TAKE CARE OF MY NIECE."
IS SHE SERIOUS!
After being widowed at such a young age...
a new love...
leaving on a trip...

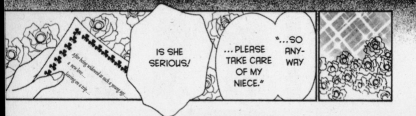

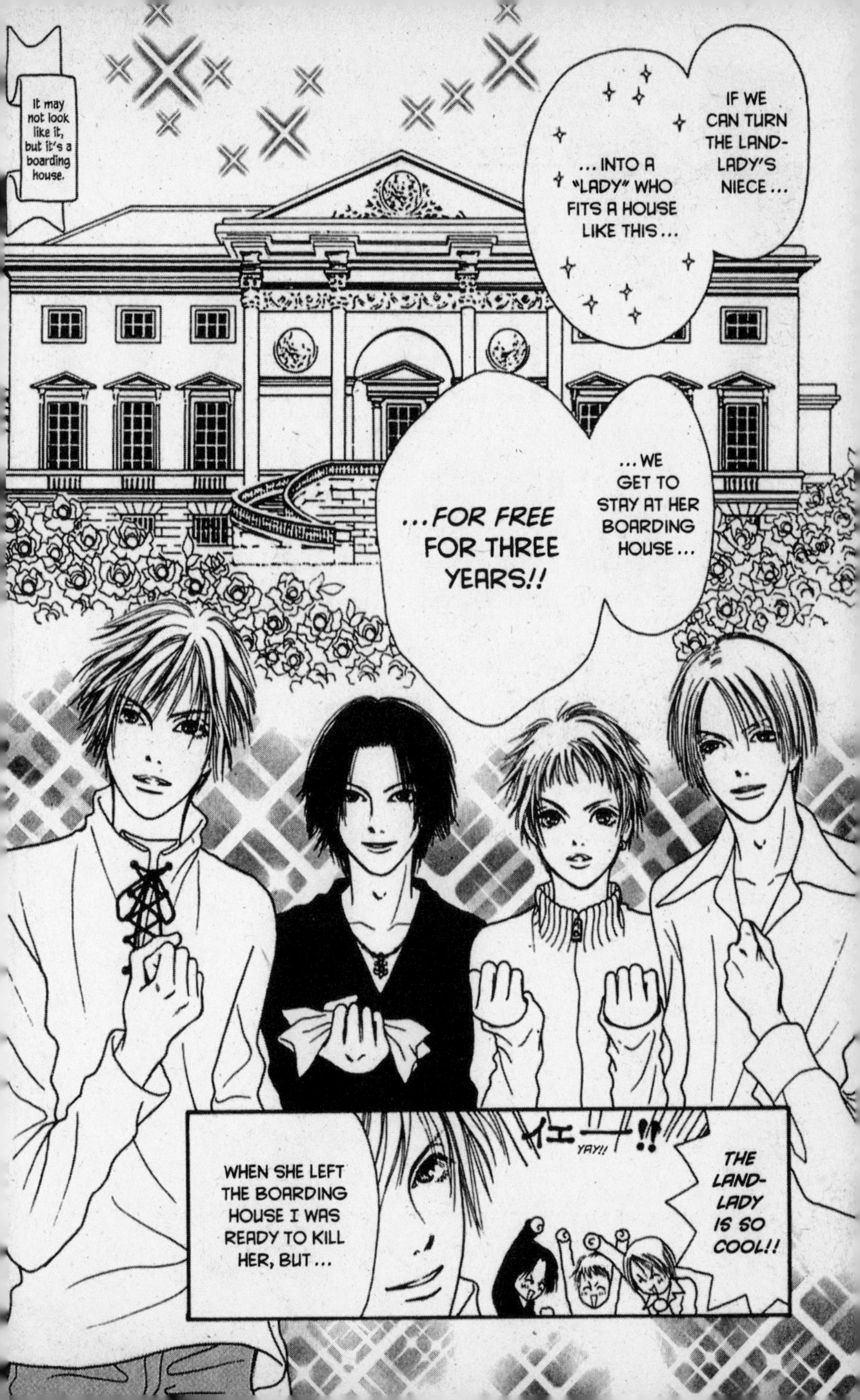
IF WE CAN TURN THE LAND-LADY'S NIECE...
...INTO A "LADY" WHO FITS A HOUSE LIKE THIS...
...WE GET TO STAY AT HER BOARDING HOUSE...
...FOR FREE FOR THREE YEARS!!
It may not look like it, but it's a boarding house.
THE LAND-LADY IS SO COOL!!
イエーー!!
YAY!!
WHEN SHE LEFT THE BOARDING HOUSE I WAS READY TO KILL HER, BUT...

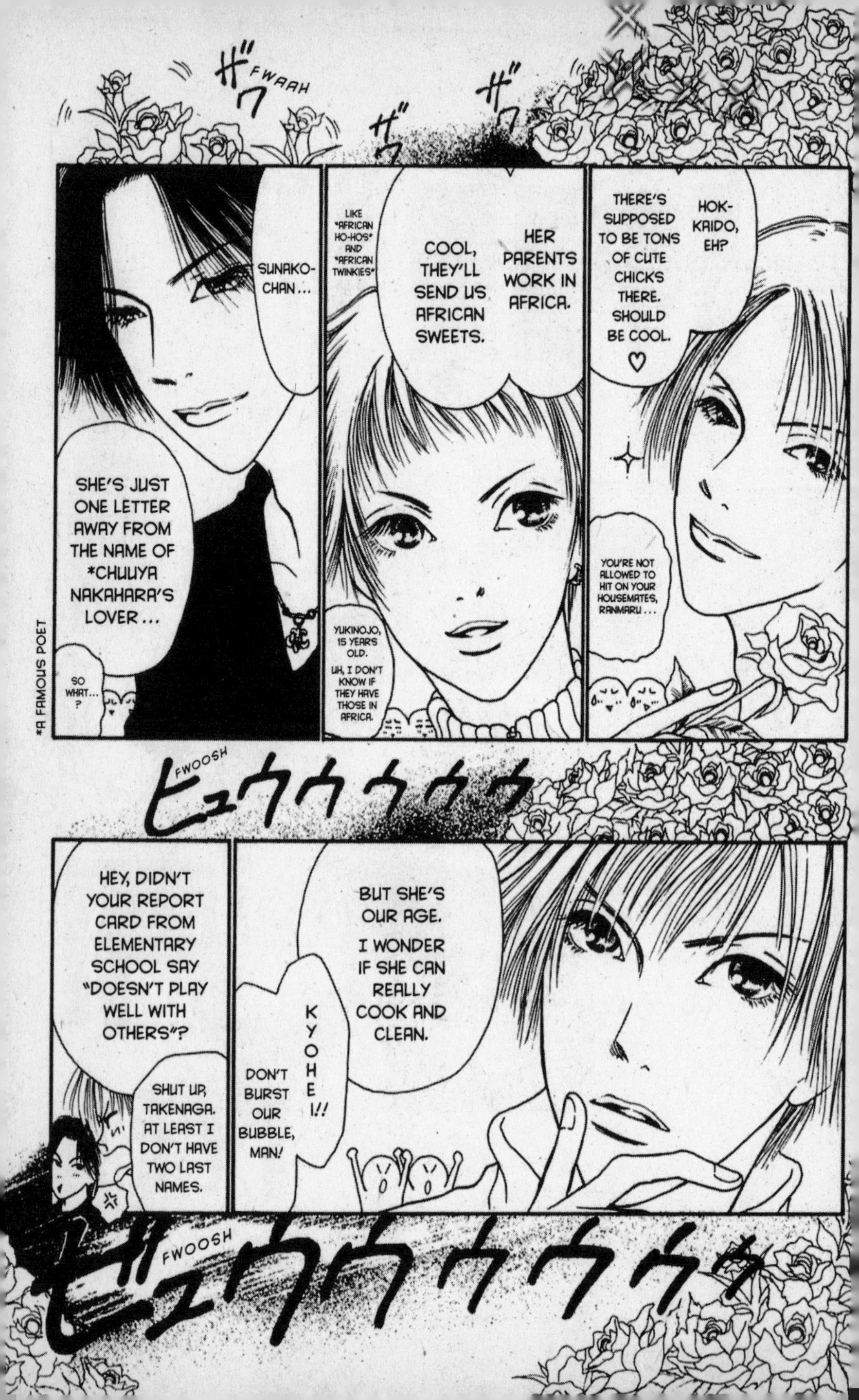
ザワ
FWAAH
ザワ ザワ
HOK-KAIDO, EH?
THERE'S SUPPOSED TO BE TONS OF CUTE CHICKS THERE. SHOULD BE COOL. ♡
YOU'RE NOT ALLOWED TO HIT ON YOUR HOUSEMATES, RANMARU...
HER PARENTS WORK IN AFRICA.
COOL, THEY'LL SEND US AFRICAN SWEETS.
LIKE "AFRICAN HO-HOS" AND "AFRICAN TWINKIES"
YUKINOJO, 15 YEARS OLD.
UH, I DON'T KNOW IF THEY HAVE THOSE IN AFRICA.
SUNAKO-CHAN...
SHE'S JUST ONE LETTER AWAY FROM THE NAME OF *CHUUYA NAKAHARA'S LOVER...
SO WHAT...?
*A FAMOUS POET
FWOOSH
ヒュウウウウウ
BUT SHE'S OUR AGE. I WONDER IF SHE CAN REALLY COOK AND CLEAN.
KYOHEI!!
DON'T BURST OUR BUBBLE, MAN!
HEY, DIDN'T YOUR REPORT CARD FROM ELEMENTARY SCHOOL SAY "DOESN'T PLAY WELL WITH OTHERS"?
SHUT UP, TAKENAGA. AT LEAST I DON'T HAVE TWO LAST NAMES.
FWOOSH
ヒュウウウウウウ

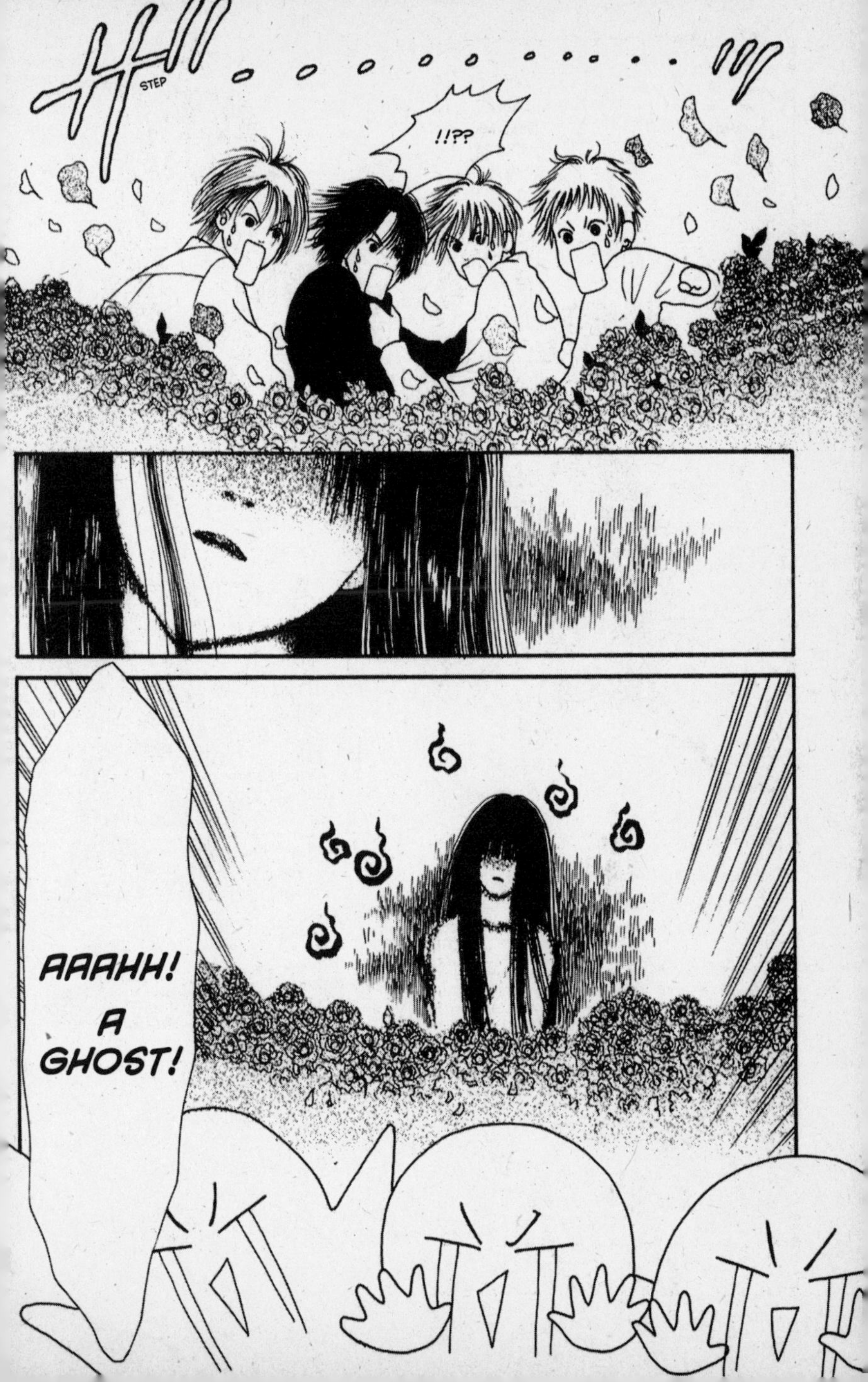
STEP
!!??
AAAHH!
A
GHOST!

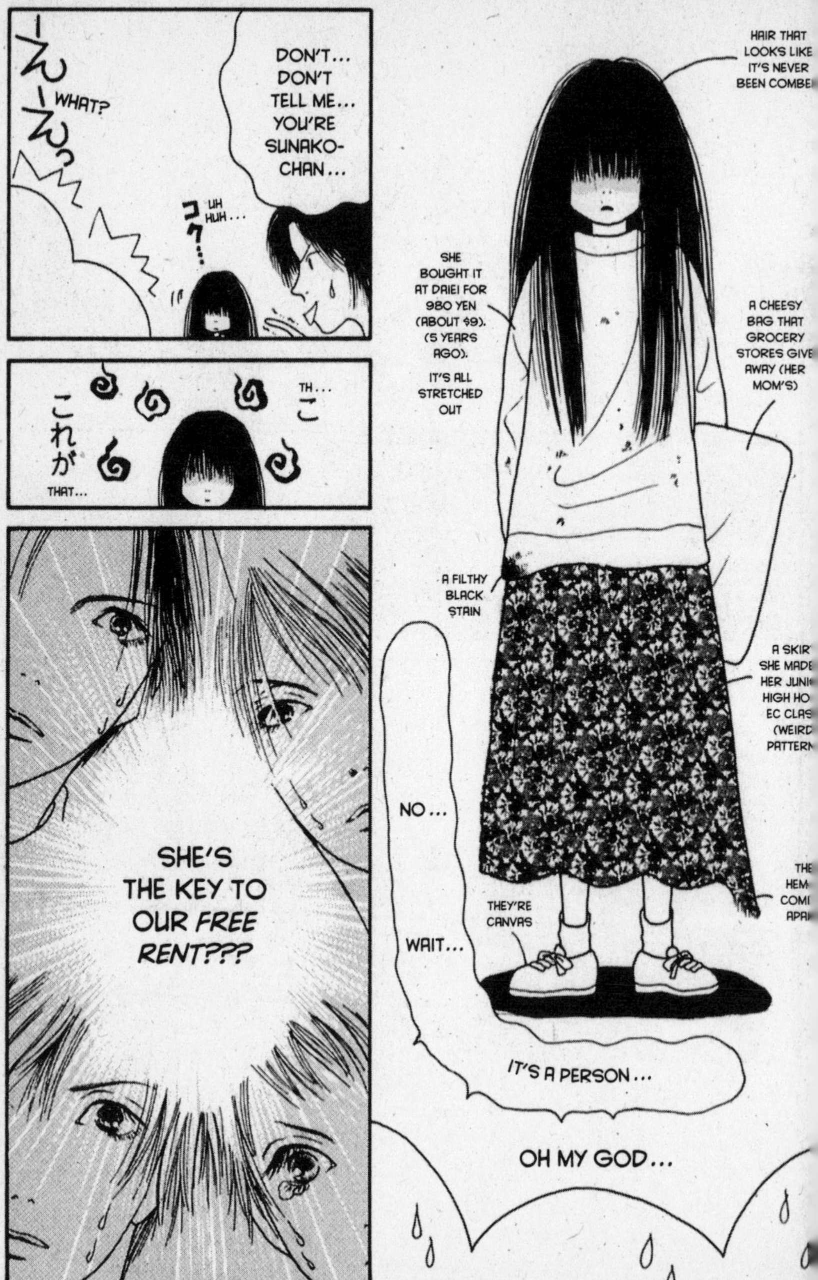

HAIR THAT LOOKS LIKE IT'S NEVER BEEN COMBE
A CHEESY BAG THAT GROCERY STORES GIVE AWAY (HER MOM'S)
SHE BOUGHT IT AT DAIEI FOR 980 YEN (ABOUT $9). (5 YEARS AGO).
IT'S ALL STRETCHED OUT
A FILTHY BLACK STAIN
A SKIR SHE MADE HER JUNI HIGH HO EC CLAS (WEIRD PATTER
THE HEM COMI APA
THEY'RE CANVAS
NO... WAIT... IT'S A PERSON...
OH MY GOD...
DON'T... DON'T TELL ME... YOU'RE SUNAKO-CHAN...
コク… UH HUH...
えーえっ WHAT?
こ TH...
これが THAT...
SHE'S THE KEY TO OUR FREE RENT???

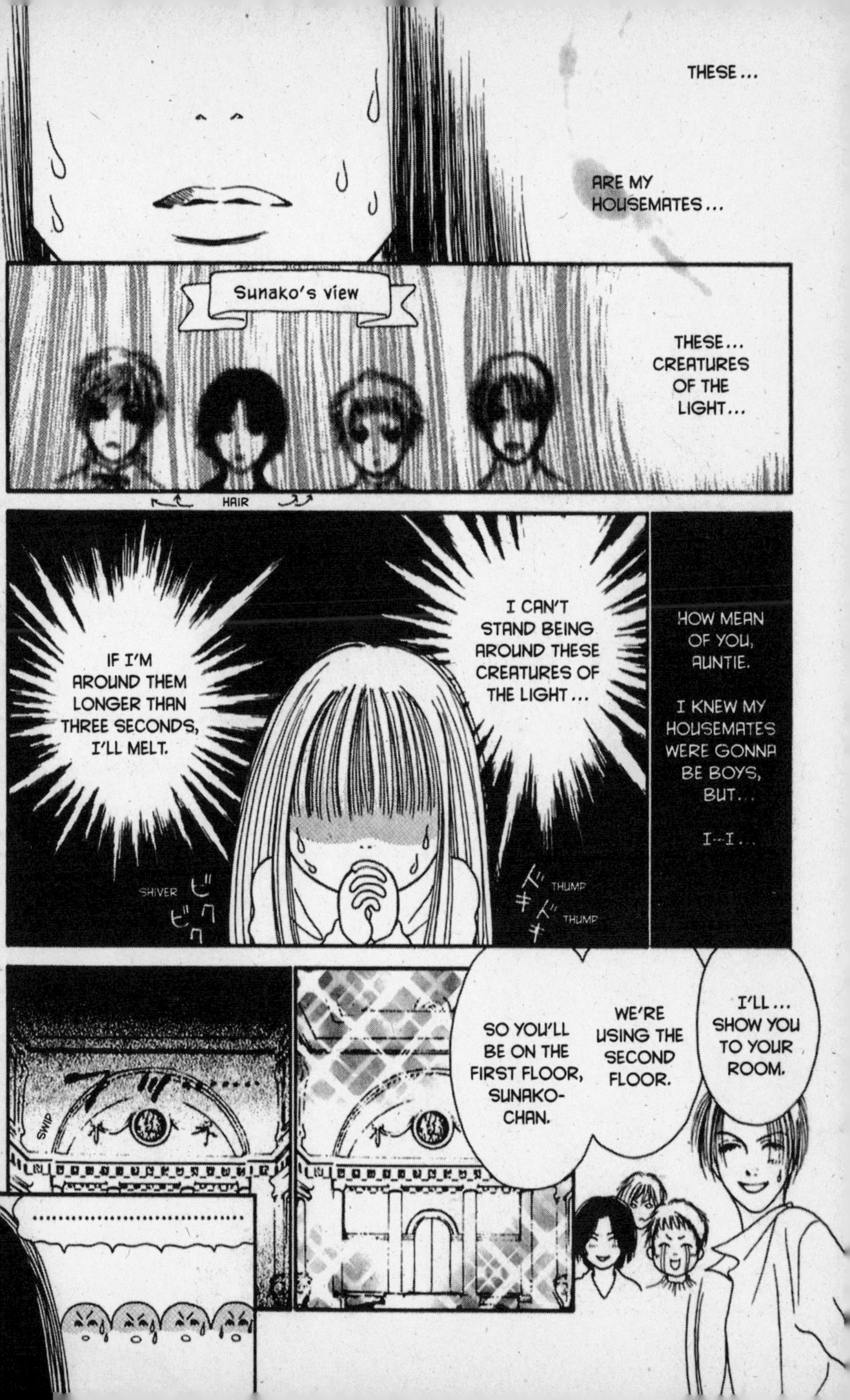
THESE...
ARE MY HOUSEMATES...
Sunako's view
THESE... CREATURES OF THE LIGHT...
HAIR
HOW MEAN OF YOU, AUNTIE.
I KNEW MY HOUSEMATES WERE GONNA BE BOYS, BUT...
I--I...
I CAN'T STAND BEING AROUND THESE CREATURES OF THE LIGHT...
THUMP
THUMP
IF I'M AROUND THEM LONGER THAN THREE SECONDS, I'LL MELT.
SHIVER
I'LL... SHOW YOU TO YOUR ROOM.
WE'RE USING THE SECOND FLOOR.
SO YOU'LL BE ON THE FIRST FLOOR, SUNAKO-CHAN.
SWIP
......
....

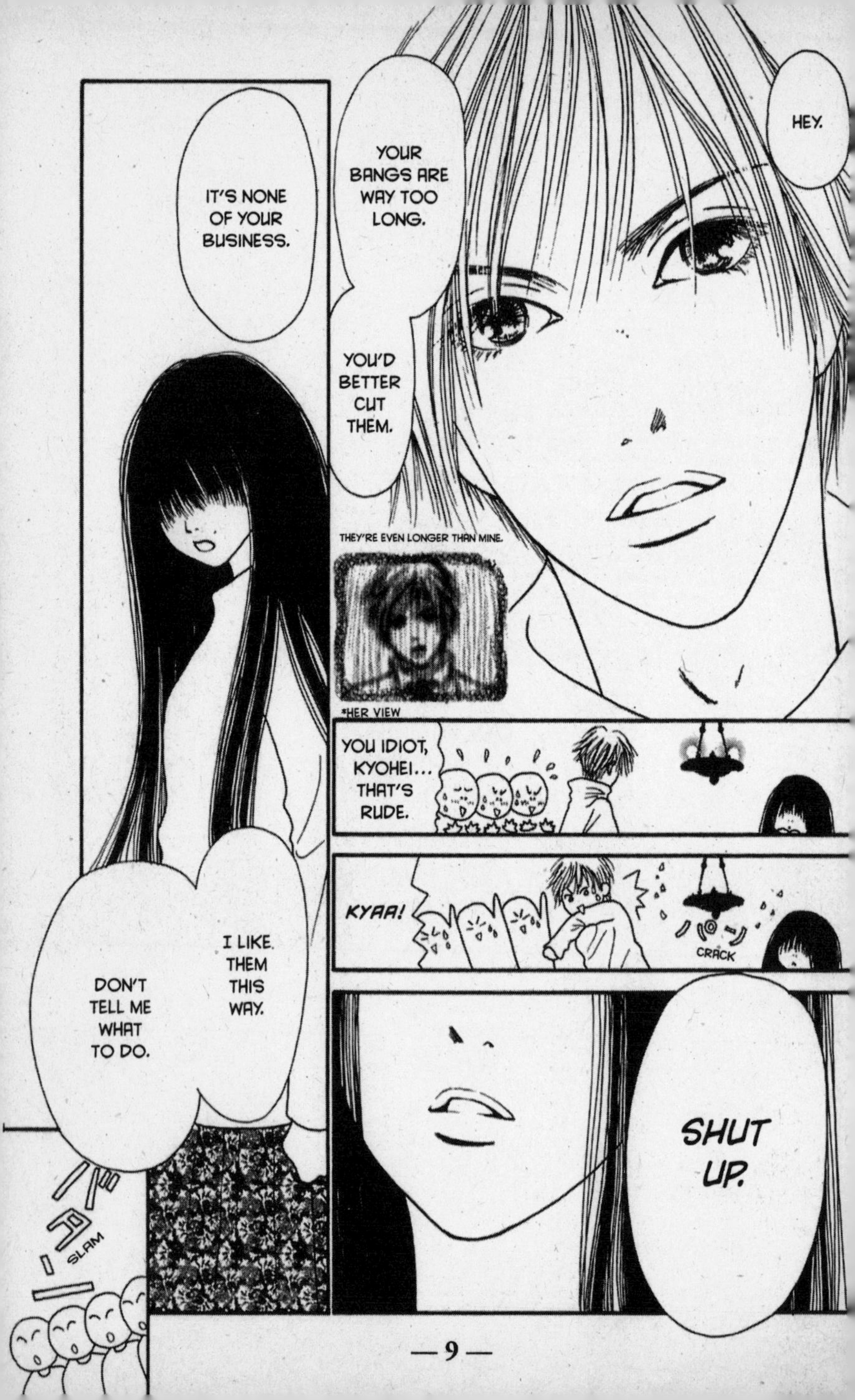
HEY.
YOUR BANGS ARE WAY TOO LONG.
YOU'D BETTER CUT THEM.
THEY'RE EVEN LONGER THAN MINE.
*HER VIEW
YOU IDIOT, KYOHEI... THAT'S RUDE.
KYAA!
CRACK
SHUT UP.
IT'S NONE OF YOUR BUSINESS.
I LIKE THEM THIS WAY.
DON'T TELL ME WHAT TO DO.
SLAM

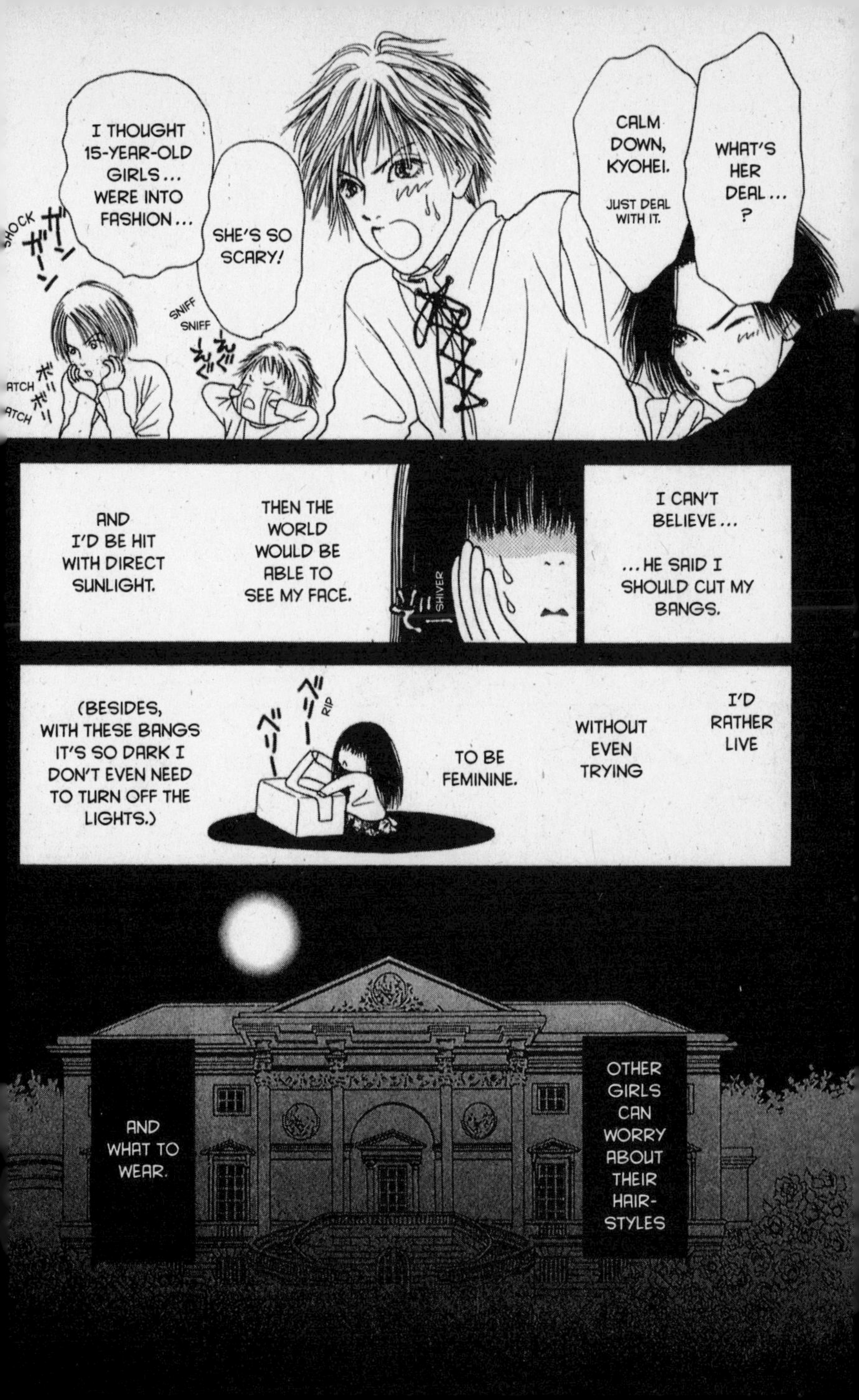
WHAT'S HER DEAL...?
CALM DOWN, KYOHEI.
JUST DEAL WITH IT.
SHE'S SO SCARY!
SNIFF SNIFF
I THOUGHT 15-YEAR-OLD GIRLS... WERE INTO FASHION...
SHOCK
I CAN'T BELIEVE...
...HE SAID I SHOULD CUT MY BANGS.
SHIVER
THEN THE WORLD WOULD BE ABLE TO SEE MY FACE.
AND I'D BE HIT WITH DIRECT SUNLIGHT.
I'D RATHER LIVE
WITHOUT EVEN TRYING
TO BE FEMININE.
RIP
(BESIDES, WITH THESE BANGS IT'S SO DARK I DON'T EVEN NEED TO TURN OFF THE LIGHTS.)
OTHER GIRLS CAN WORRY ABOUT THEIR HAIR-STYLES
AND WHAT TO WEAR.

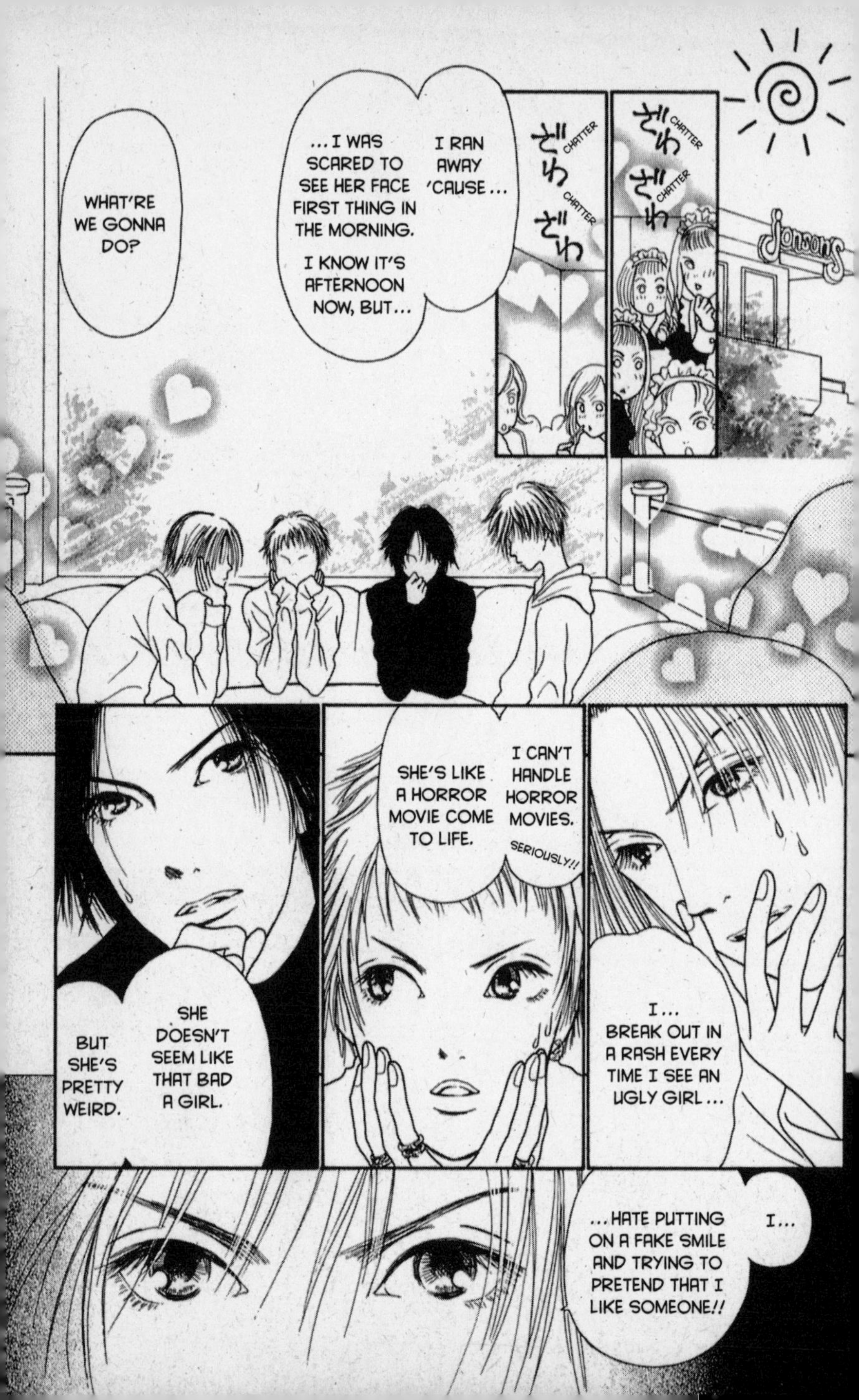
ざわ CHATTER
ざわ CHATTER
ざわ CHATTER
ざわ CHATTER
I RAN AWAY 'CAUSE…
…I WAS SCARED TO SEE HER FACE FIRST THING IN THE MORNING.
I KNOW IT'S AFTERNOON NOW, BUT…
WHAT'RE WE GONNA DO?
I… BREAK OUT IN A RASH EVERY TIME I SEE AN UGLY GIRL…
I CAN'T HANDLE HORROR MOVIES.
SHE'S LIKE A HORROR MOVIE COME TO LIFE.
SERIOUSLY!!
SHE DOESN'T SEEM LIKE THAT BAD A GIRL.
BUT SHE'S PRETTY WEIRD.
I…
…HATE PUTTING ON A FAKE SMILE AND TRYING TO PRETEND THAT I LIKE SOMEONE!!

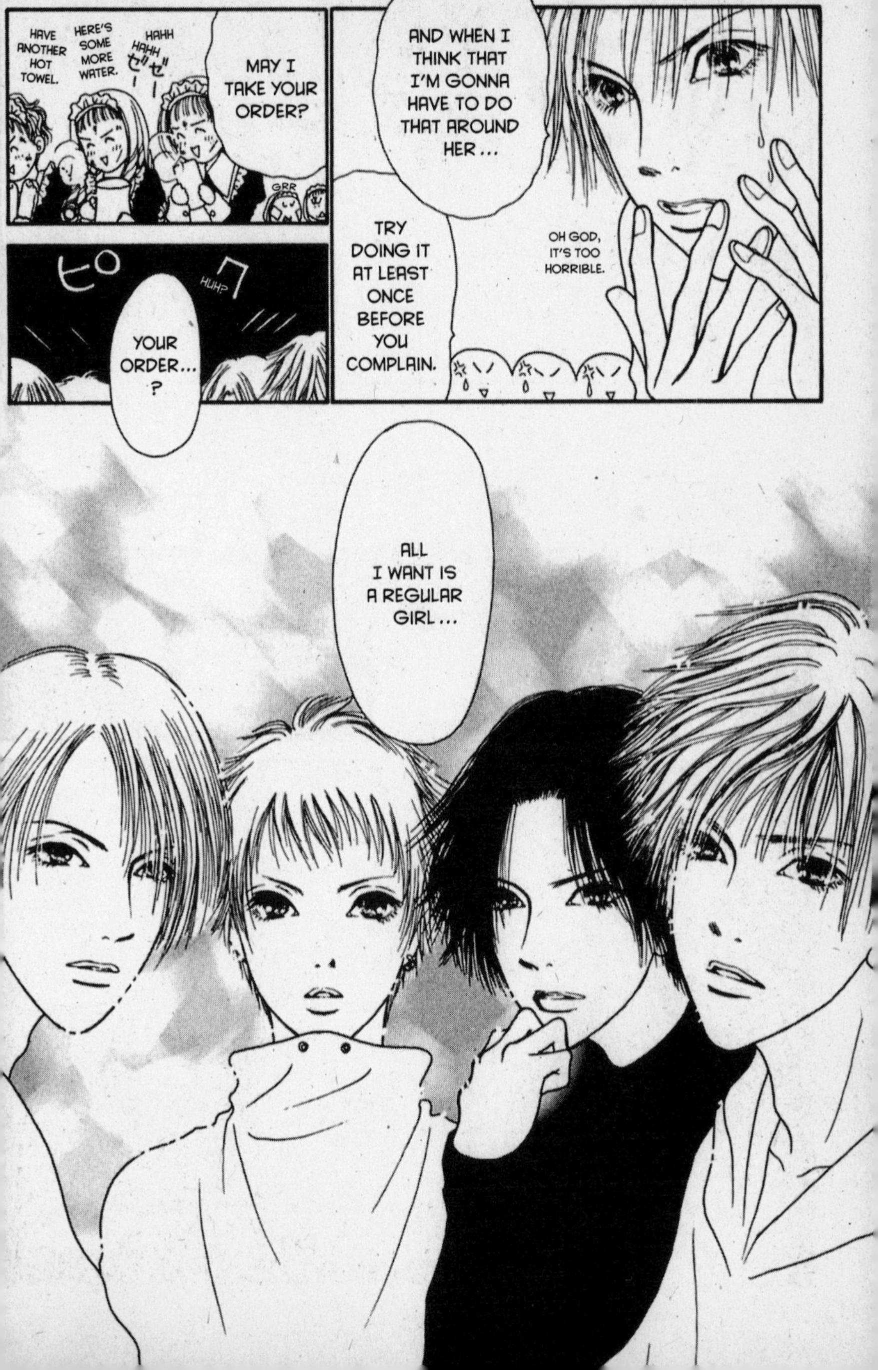
AND WHEN I THINK THAT I'M GONNA HAVE TO DO THAT AROUND HER...
OH GOD, IT'S TOO HORRIBLE.
TRY DOING IT AT LEAST ONCE BEFORE YOU COMPLAIN.
MAY I TAKE YOUR ORDER?
HAHH HAHH ゼィゼィ
HERE'S SOME MORE WATER.
HAVE ANOTHER HOT TOWEL.
GRR
ピク
HUH?
YOUR ORDER... ?
ALL I WANT IS A REGULAR GIRL...

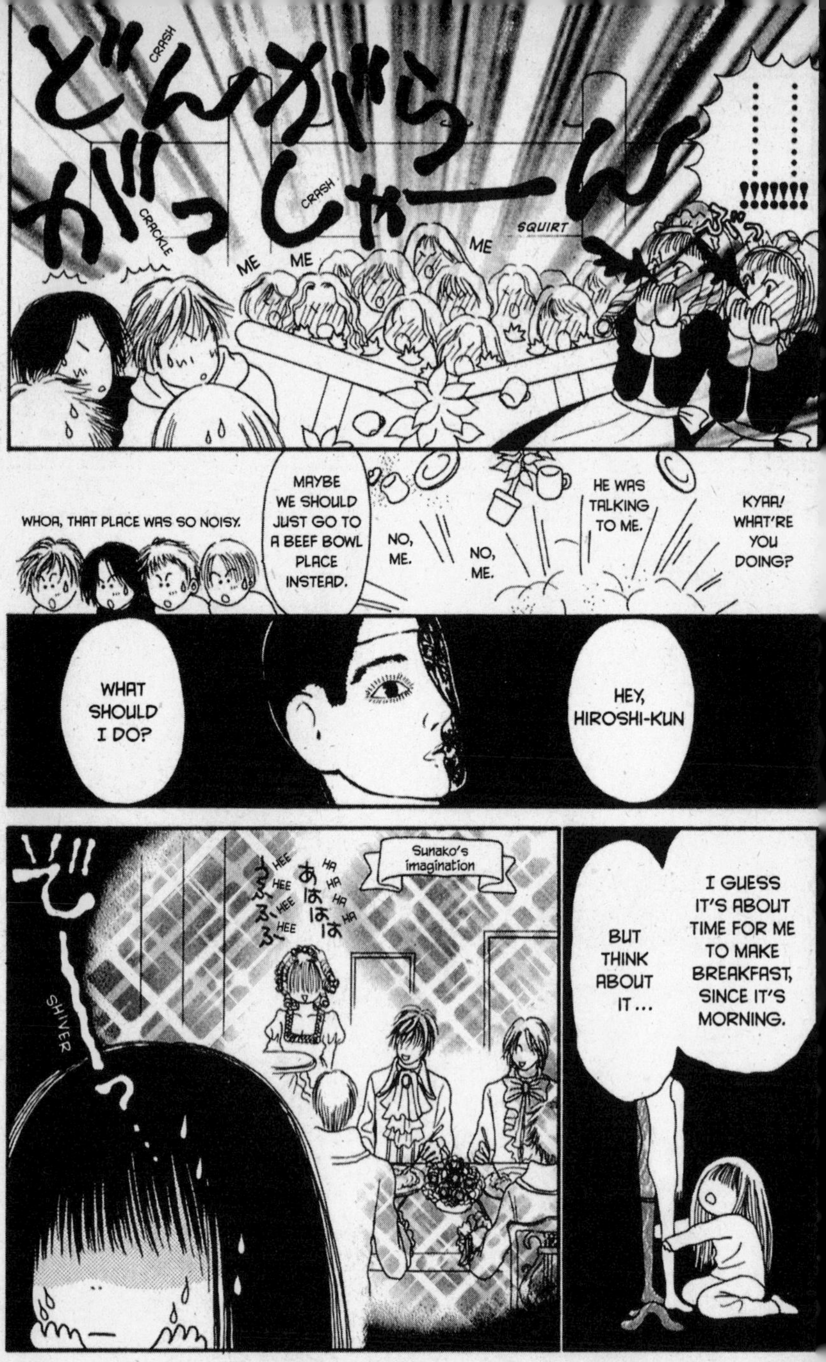
……!!!!!!!
どんがらがっしゃーん
CRASH
CRASH
CRACKLE
SQUIRT
ME
ME
ME
KYAA! WHAT'RE YOU DOING?
HE WAS TALKING TO ME.
NO, ME.
NO, ME.
MAYBE WE SHOULD JUST GO TO A BEEF BOWL PLACE INSTEAD.
WHOA, THAT PLACE WAS SO NOISY.
HEY, HIROSHI-KUN
WHAT SHOULD I DO?
I GUESS IT'S ABOUT TIME FOR ME TO MAKE BREAKFAST, SINCE IT'S MORNING.
BUT THINK ABOUT IT…
Sunako's imagination
あははは
HA HA HA HA
うふふふ
HEE HEE HEE HEE
SHIVER

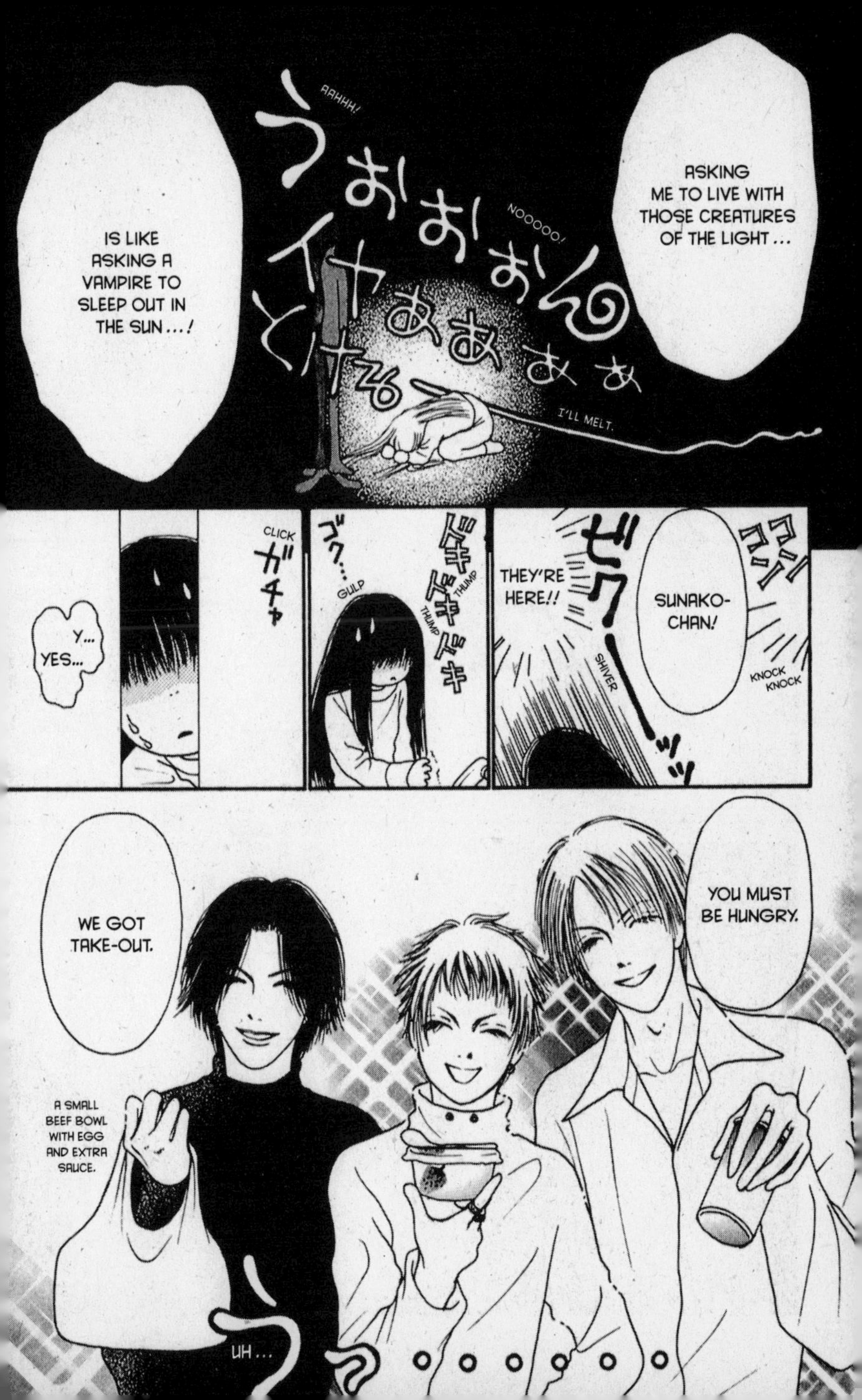
ASKING ME TO LIVE WITH THOSE CREATURES OF THE LIGHT...
AAHHH!
NOOOOO!
I'LL MELT.
IS LIKE ASKING A VAMPIRE TO SLEEP OUT IN THE SUN...!
KNOCK KNOCK
SUNAKO-CHAN!
THEY'RE HERE!!
SHIVER
THUMP THUMP
GULP
CLICK
Y... YES...
YOU MUST BE HUNGRY.
WE GOT TAKE-OUT.
A SMALL BEEF BOWL WITH EGG AND EXTRA SAUCE.
UH...

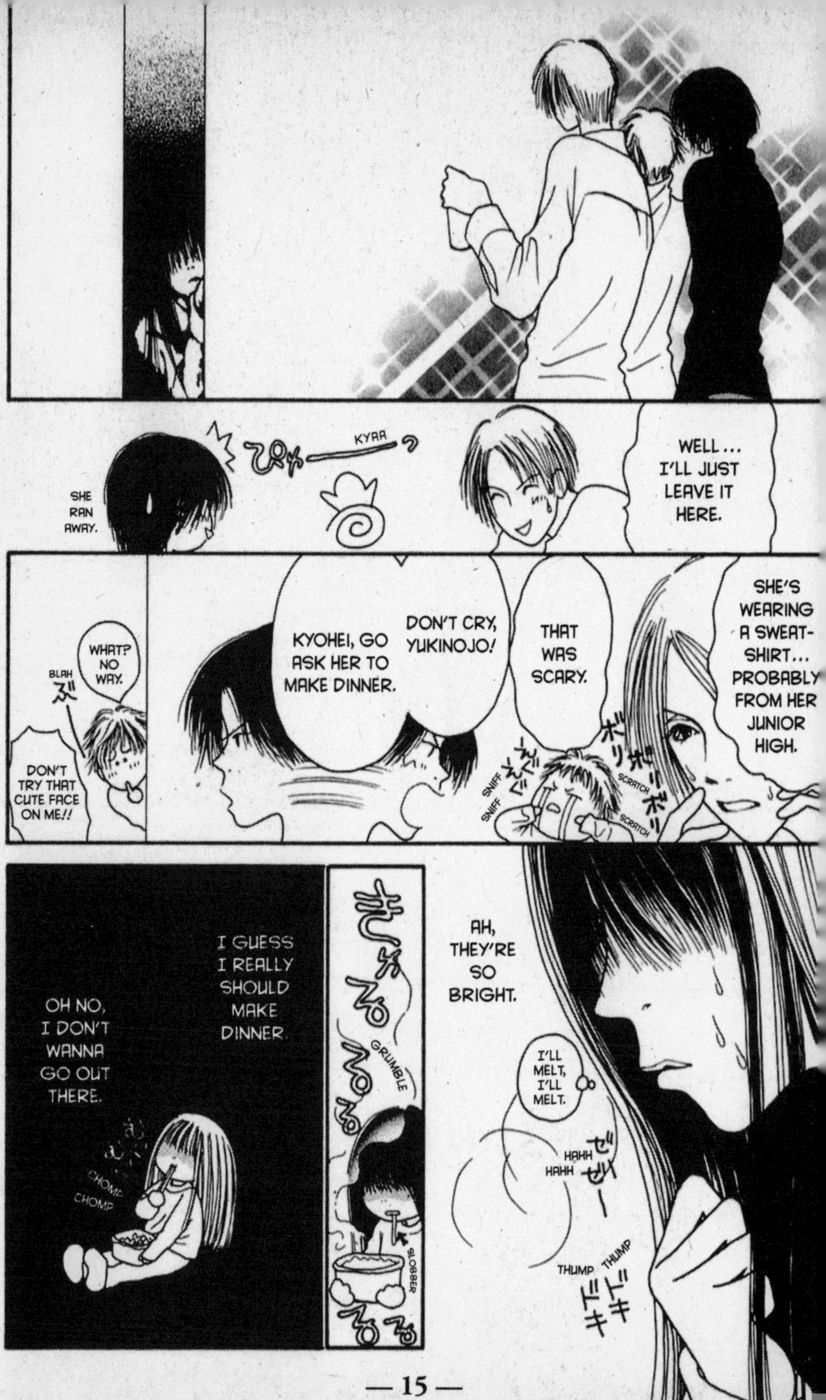
WELL... I'LL JUST LEAVE IT HERE.
KYAA
SHE RAN AWAY.
SHE'S WEARING A SWEAT-SHIRT... PROBABLY FROM HER JUNIOR HIGH.
THAT WAS SCARY.
SNIFF SNIFF
SCRATCH SCRATCH
DON'T CRY, YUKINOJO!
KYOHEI, GO ASK HER TO MAKE DINNER.
WHAT? NO WAY.
BLAH
DON'T TRY THAT CUTE FACE ON ME!!
AH, THEY'RE SO BRIGHT.
I'LL MELT, I'LL MELT.
HAHH HAHH
THUMP THUMP
GRUMBLE
SLOBBER
I GUESS I REALLY SHOULD MAKE DINNER.
OH NO, I DON'T WANNA GO OUT THERE.
CHOMP CHOMP

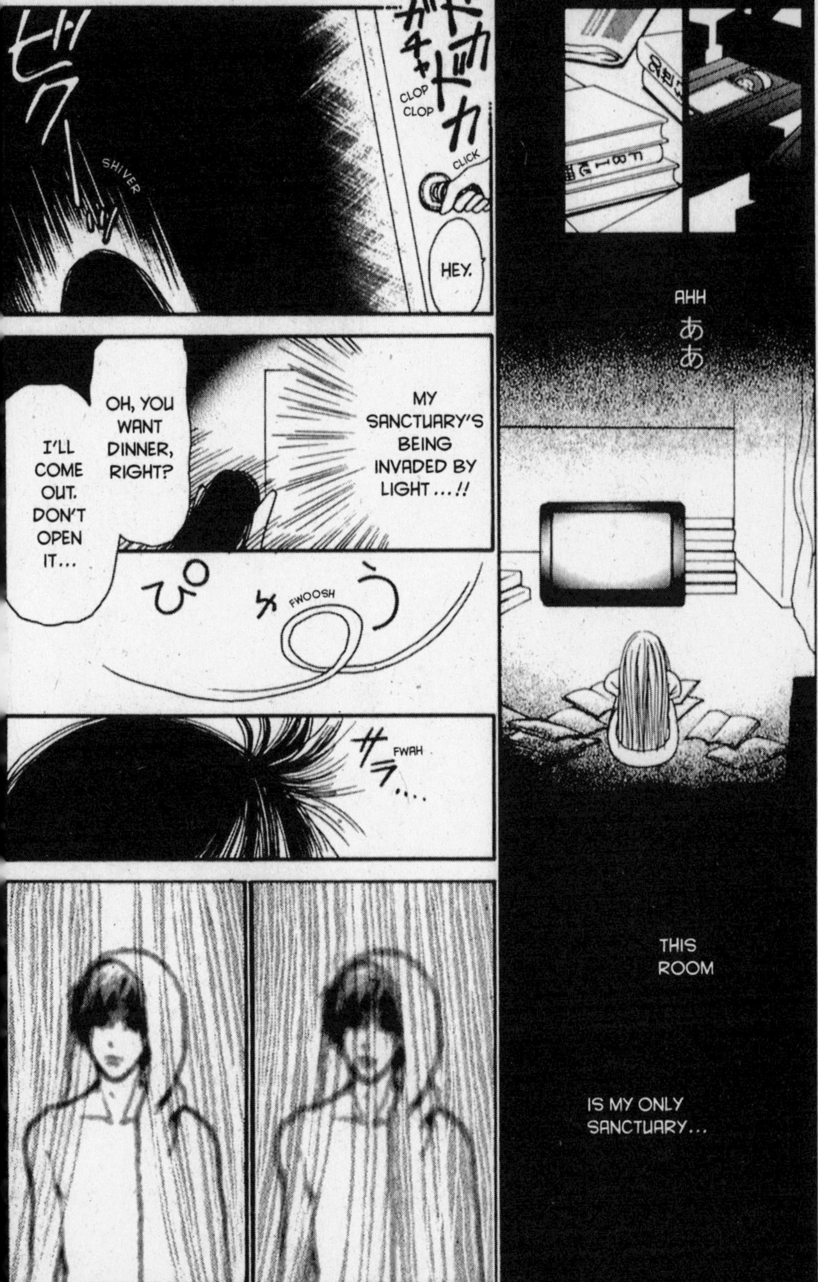
AHH
ああ
THIS ROOM
IS MY ONLY SANCTUARY...
ドカドカ
CLOP CLOP
ガチャ
CLICK
HEY.
ビクー
SHIVER
MY SANCTUARY'S BEING INVADED BY LIGHT...!!
OH, YOU WANT DINNER, RIGHT?
I'LL COME OUT. DON'T OPEN IT...
ぴゅう
FWOOSH
サラ...
FWAH
SUNAKO'S VIEW

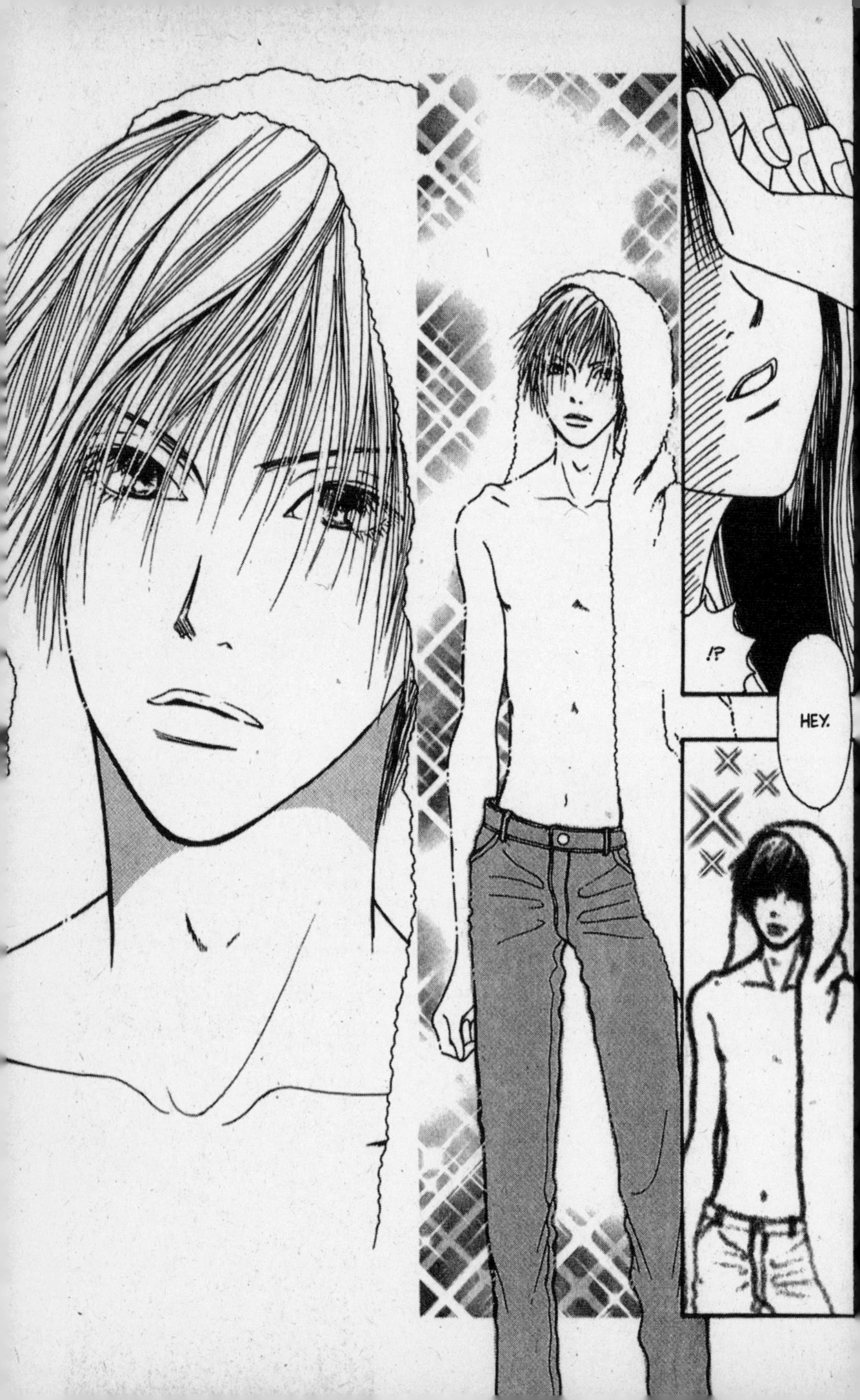
!?
HEY.

AH......
AAAAAAHHHH!
ぶっ
SQUIRT
WHAT HAPPENED?
バババ
WHOOSH
SO KYOHEI FINALLY HIT HER!!
GO AWAY...
DON'T COME IN HERE...
ガクガク
SHIVER
KYOHEI, DID YOU MAKE A MOVE ON HER?
THERE'S NO WAY YOU'D DO THAT, RIGHT?
WHO THE HELL DO YOU THINK YOU ARE... SCREAMING AND SHOUTING...
... "GO AWAY" ...
RUMBLE
RIGHT IN MY FACE...?

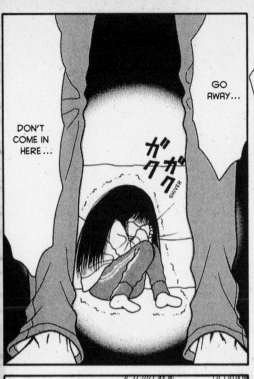

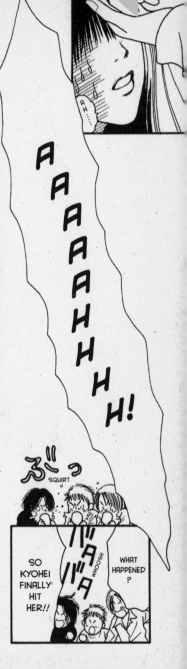

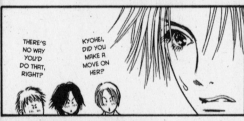

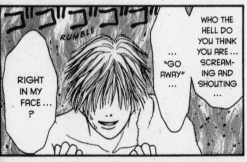

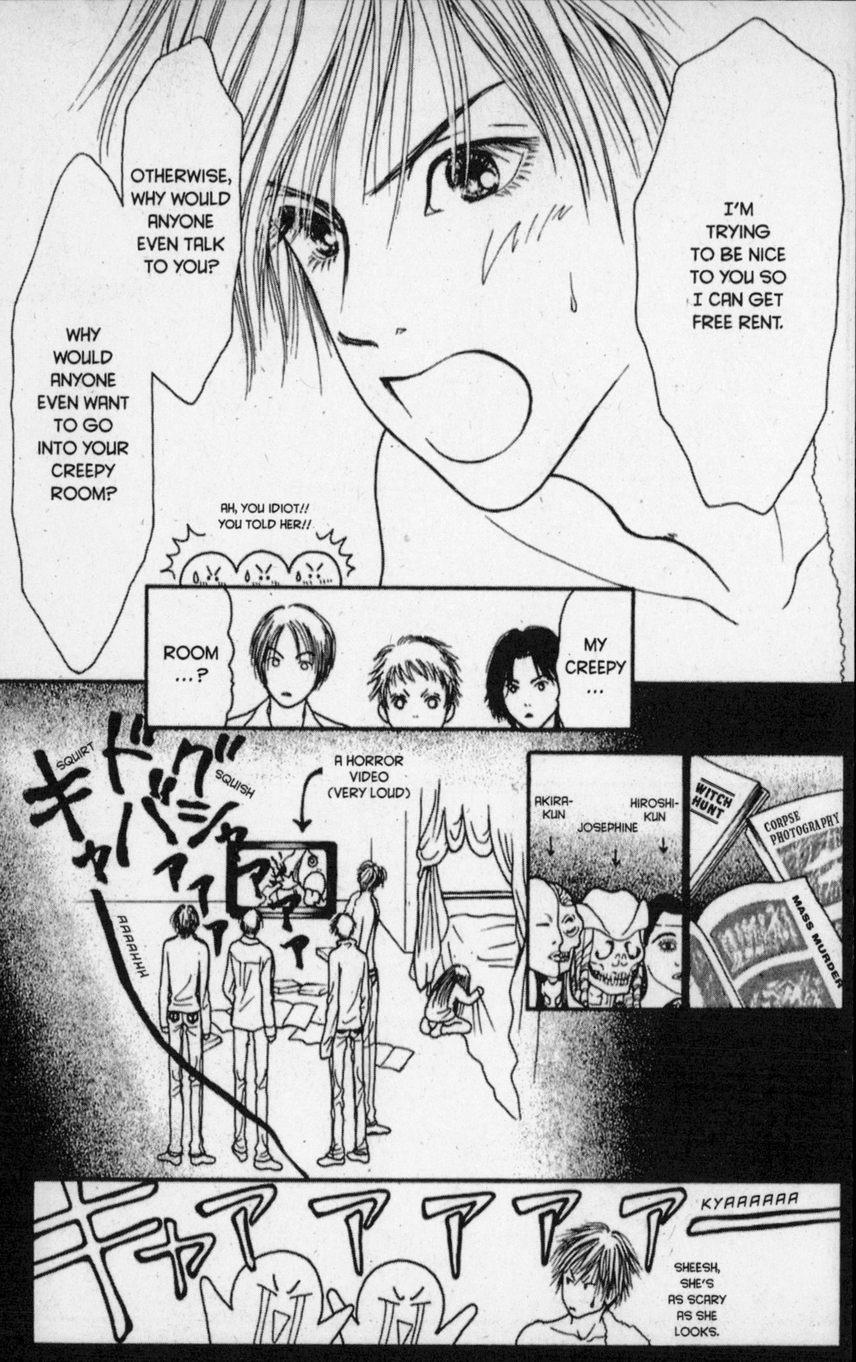
I'M TRYING TO BE NICE TO YOU SO I CAN GET FREE RENT.
OTHERWISE, WHY WOULD ANYONE EVEN TALK TO YOU?
WHY WOULD ANYONE EVEN WANT TO GO INTO YOUR CREEPY ROOM?
AH, YOU IDIOT!! YOU TOLD HER!!
MY CREEPY ...
ROOM ...?
WITCH HUNT
CORPSE PHOTOGRAPHY
MASS MURDER
HIROSHI-KUN
JOSEPHINE
AKIRA-KUN
A HORROR VIDEO (VERY LOUD)
SQUISH
SQUIRT
AAAAHHH
KYAAAAAAA
SHEESH, SHE'S AS SCARY AS SHE LOOKS.

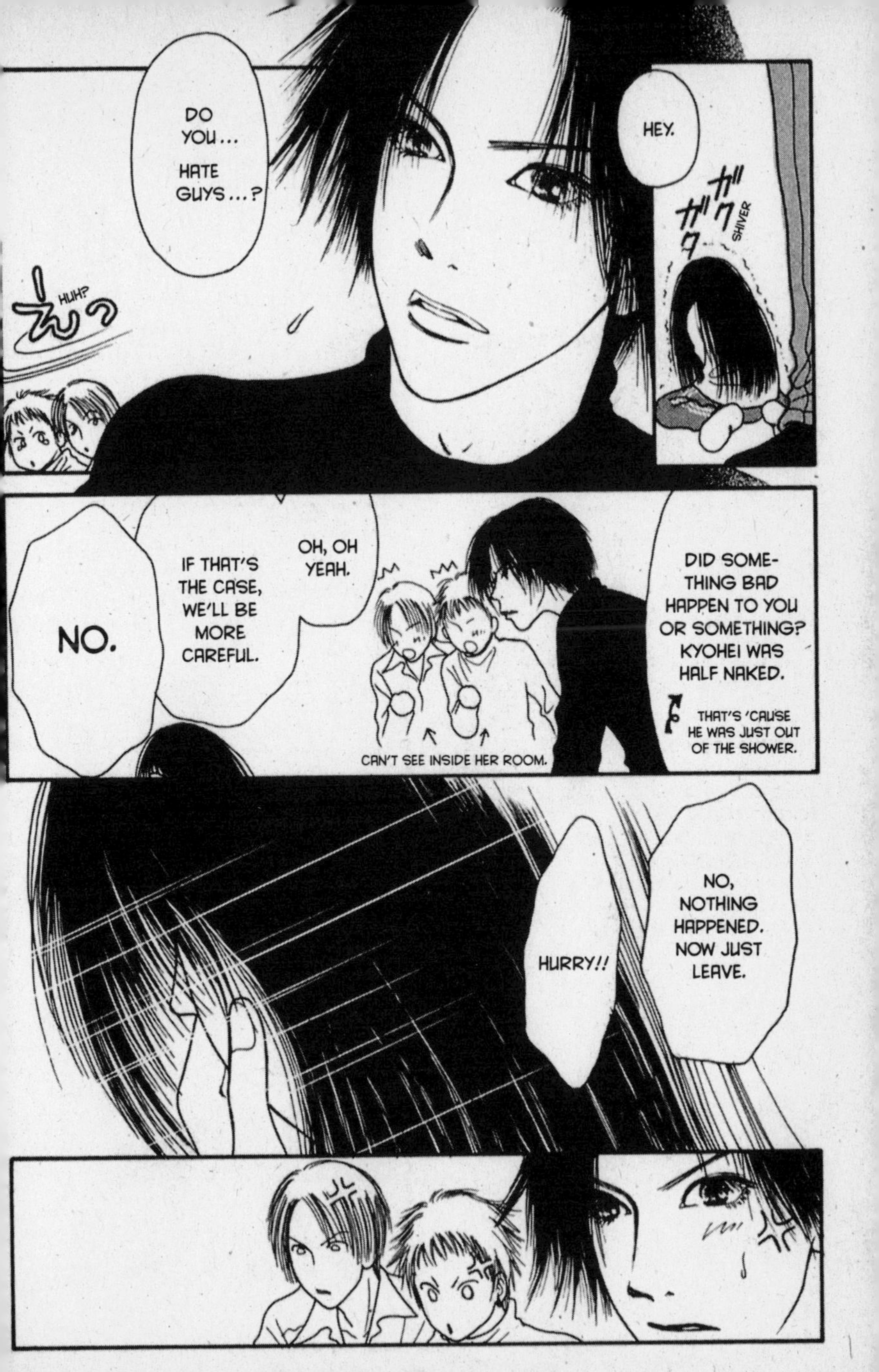
HEY.
ガクガク
SHIVER
DO YOU... HATE GUYS...?
えっ
HUH?
DID SOME-THING BAD HAPPEN TO YOU OR SOMETHING? KYOHEI WAS HALF NAKED.
THAT'S 'CAUSE HE WAS JUST OUT OF THE SHOWER.
OH, OH YEAH.
IF THAT'S THE CASE, WE'LL BE MORE CAREFUL.
CAN'T SEE INSIDE HER ROOM.
NO.
NO, NOTHING HAPPENED. NOW JUST LEAVE.
HURRY!!

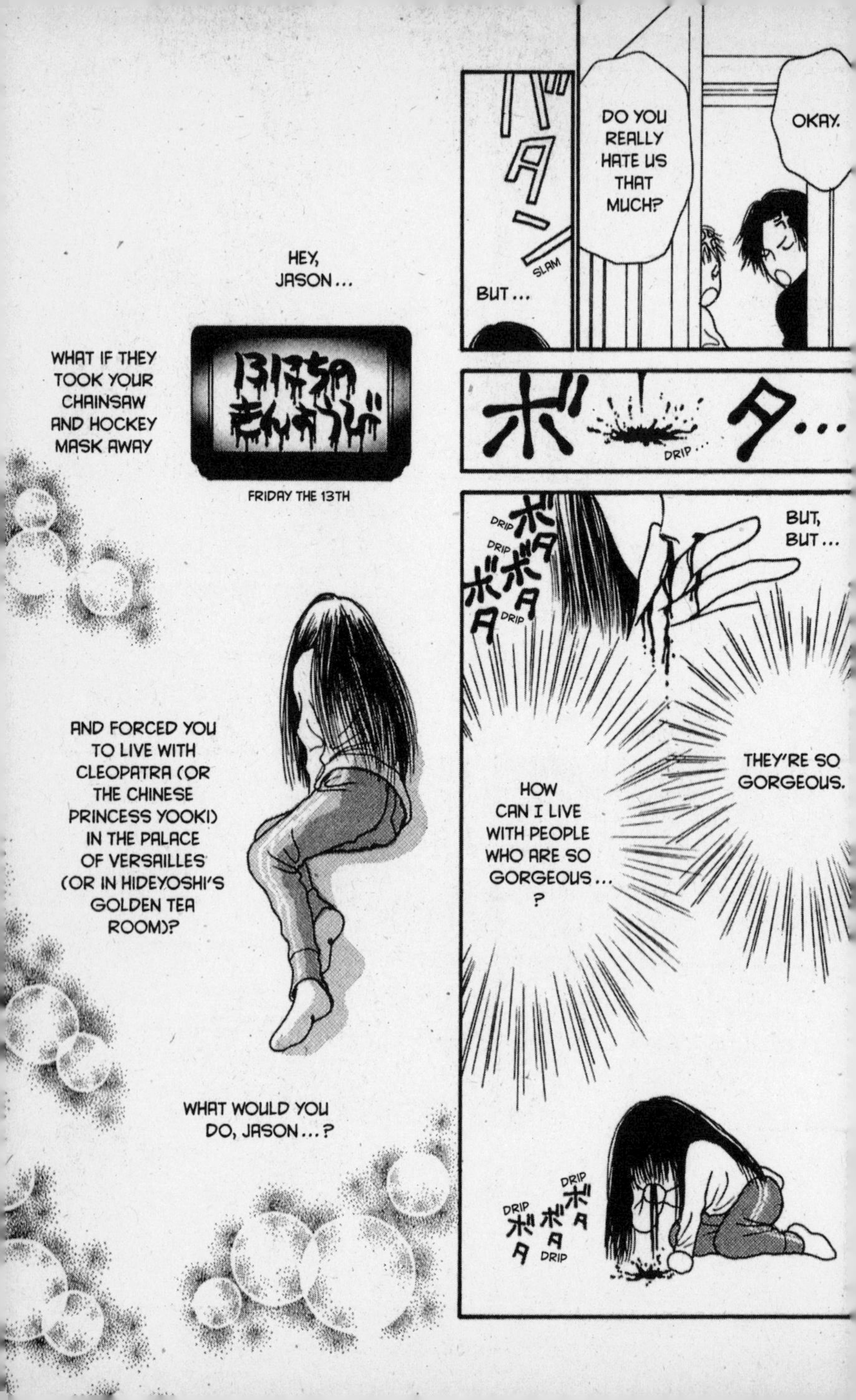
OKAY.
DO YOU REALLY HATE US THAT MUCH?
バタン
SLAM
BUT...
ボタ...
DRIP...
BUT, BUT...
ボタ ボタ ボタ
DRIP DRIP DRIP
THEY'RE SO GORGEOUS.
HOW CAN I LIVE WITH PEOPLE WHO ARE SO GORGEOUS...?
ボタ ボタ ボタ
DRIP DRIP DRIP
HEY, JASON...
WHAT IF THEY TOOK YOUR CHAINSAW AND HOCKEY MASK AWAY
FRIDAY THE 13TH
AND FORCED YOU TO LIVE WITH CLEOPATRA (OR THE CHINESE PRINCESS YOOKI) IN THE PALACE OF VERSAILLES (OR IN HIDEYOSHI'S GOLDEN TEA ROOM)?
WHAT WOULD YOU DO, JASON...?

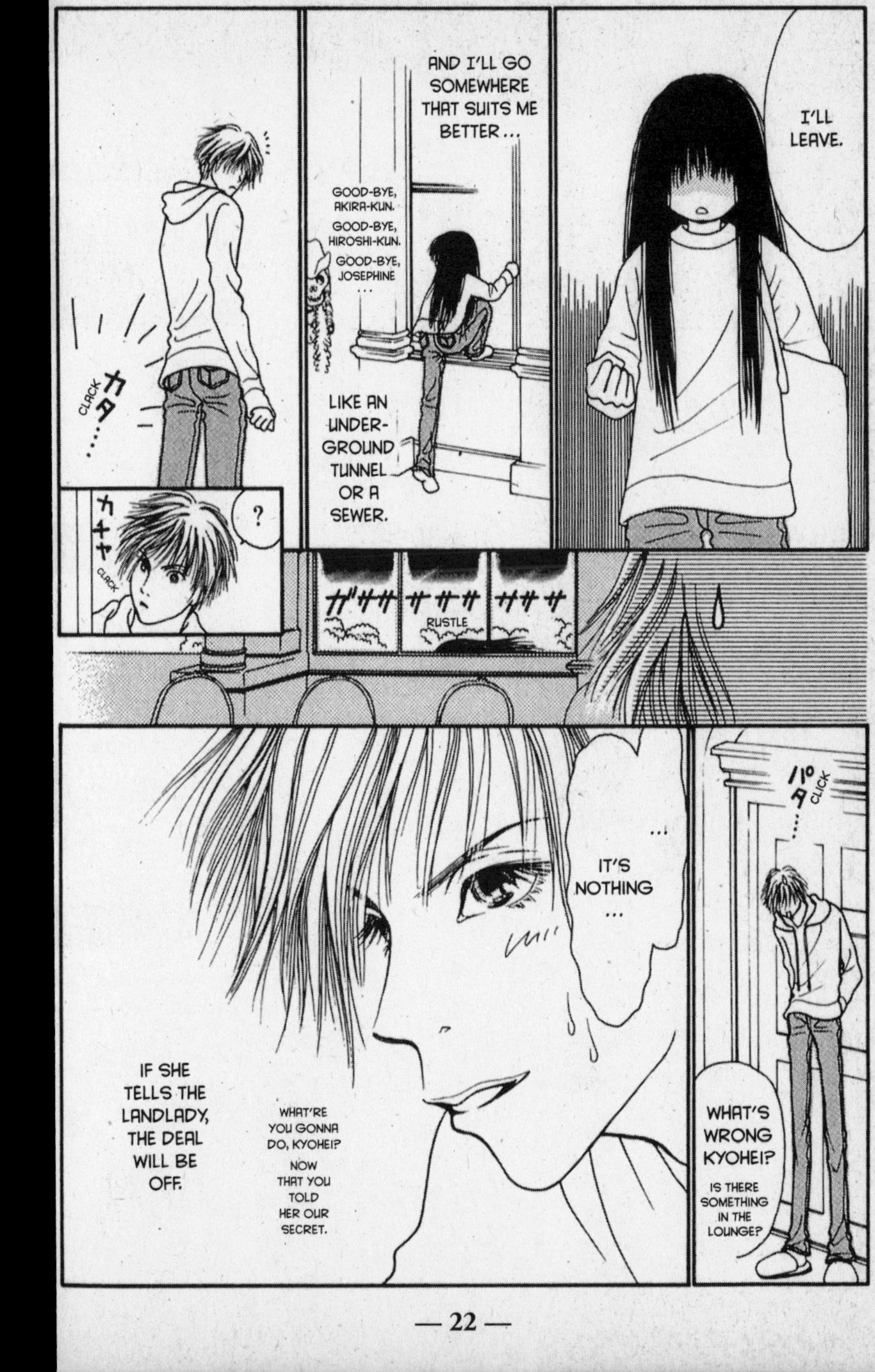
I'LL LEAVE.
AND I'LL GO SOMEWHERE THAT SUITS ME BETTER...
GOOD-BYE, AKIRA-KUN.
GOOD-BYE, HIROSHI-KUN.
GOOD-BYE, JOSEPHINE ...
LIKE AN UNDER-GROUND TUNNEL OR A SEWER.
カタ...
CLACK
カチャ
CLACK
?
ガササ ササ ササ
RUSTLE
パタ...
CLACK
WHAT'S WRONG KYOHEI?
IS THERE SOMETHING IN THE LOUNGE?
...
IT'S NOTHING ...
WHAT'RE YOU GONNA DO, KYOHEI?
NOW THAT YOU TOLD HER OUR SECRET.
IF SHE TELLS THE LANDLADY, THE DEAL WILL BE OFF.

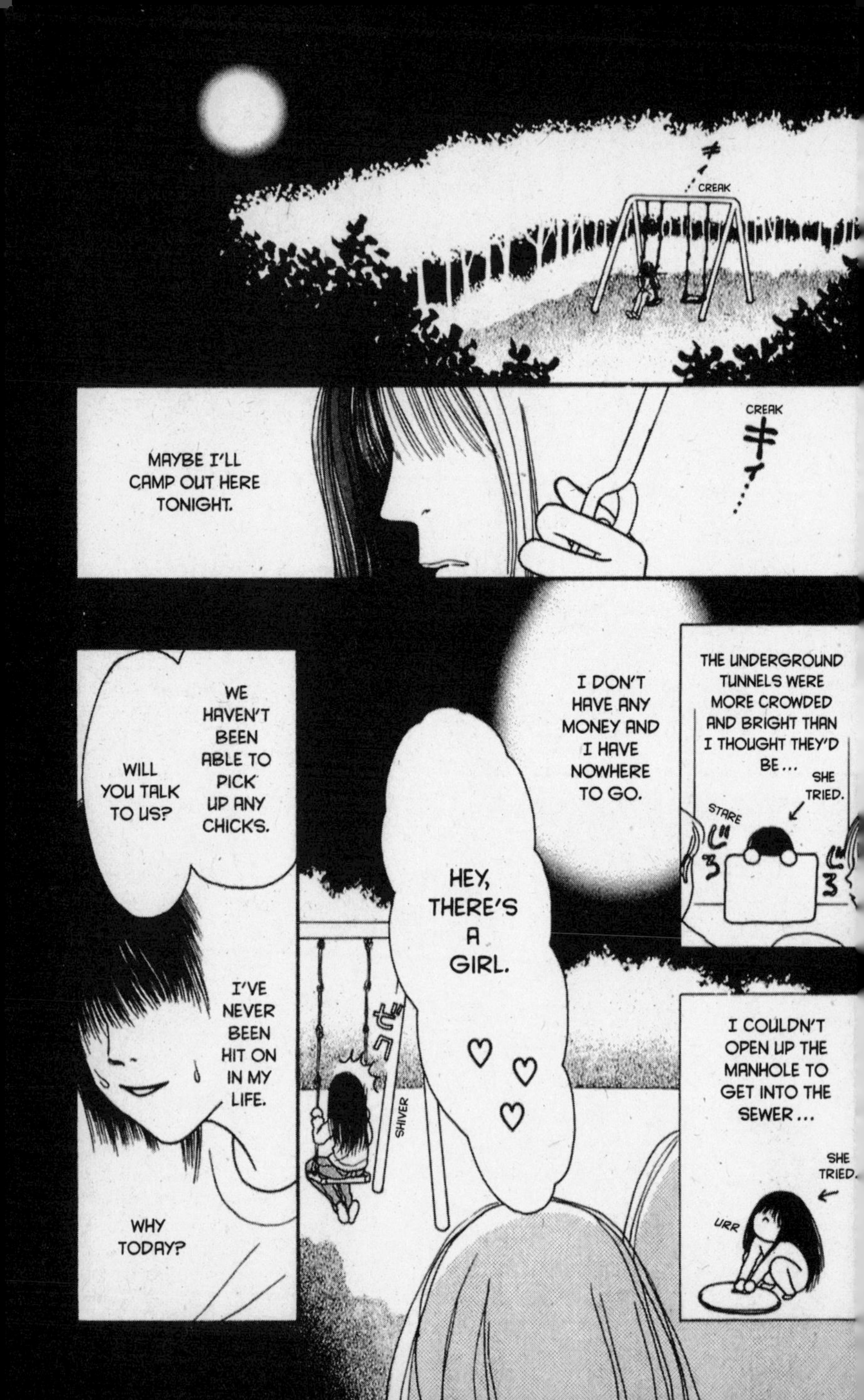
CREAK
CREAK
MAYBE I'LL CAMP OUT HERE TONIGHT.
THE UNDERGROUND TUNNELS WERE MORE CROWDED AND BRIGHT THAN I THOUGHT THEY'D BE...
SHE TRIED.
STARE
I COULDN'T OPEN UP THE MANHOLE TO GET INTO THE SEWER...
SHE TRIED.
URR
I DON'T HAVE ANY MONEY AND I HAVE NOWHERE TO GO.
HEY, THERE'S A GIRL.
SHIVER
WE HAVEN'T BEEN ABLE TO PICK UP ANY CHICKS.
WILL YOU TALK TO US?
I'VE NEVER BEEN HIT ON IN MY LIFE.
WHY TODAY?

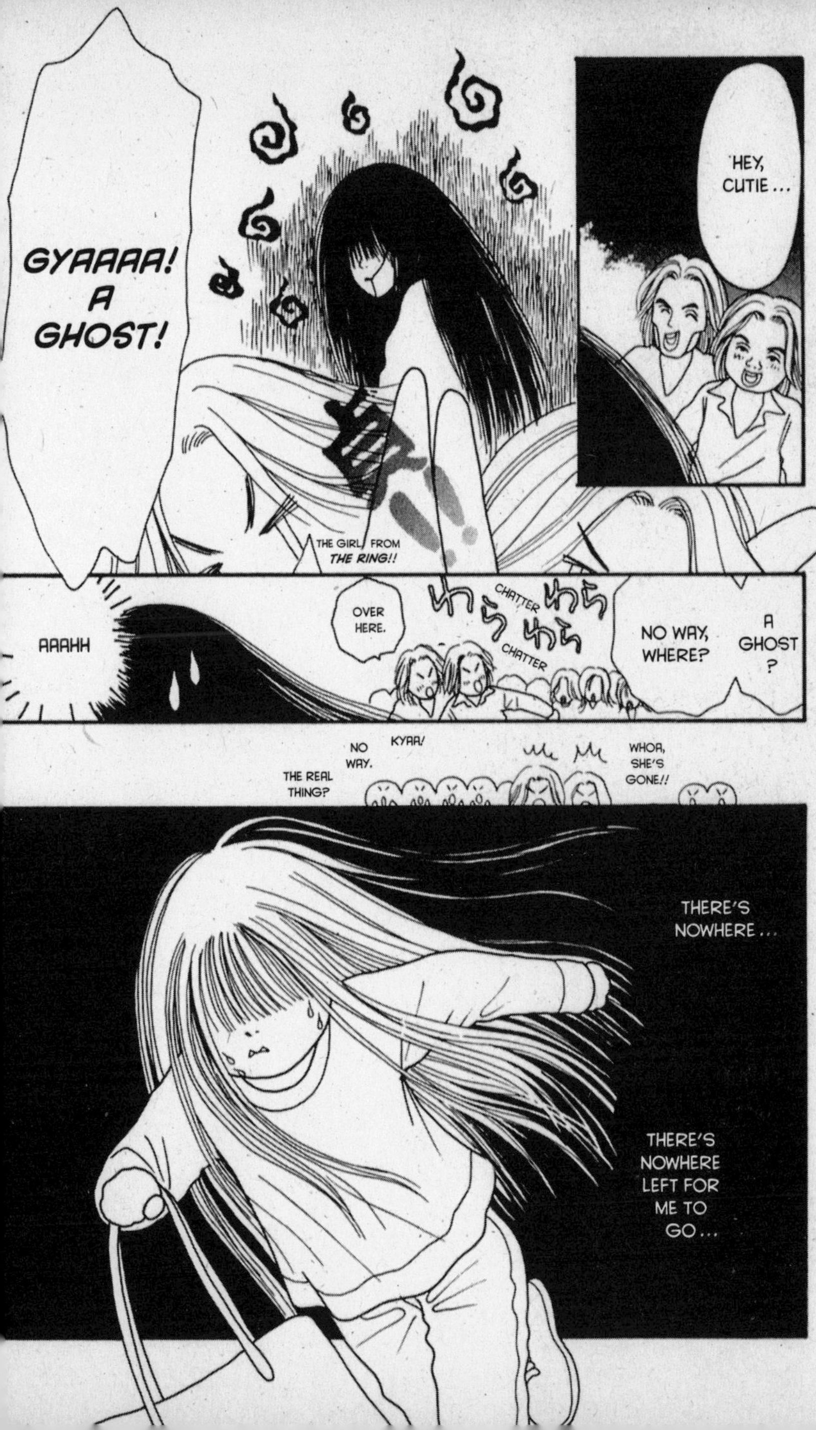
HEY, CUTIE…
GYAAAA! A GHOST!
THE GIRL FROM THE RING!!
A GHOST?
NO WAY, WHERE?
CHATTER
CHATTER
OVER HERE.
AAAHH
WHOA, SHE'S GONE!!
KYAA!
NO WAY.
THE REAL THING?
THERE'S NOWHERE…
THERE'S NOWHERE LEFT FOR ME TO GO…

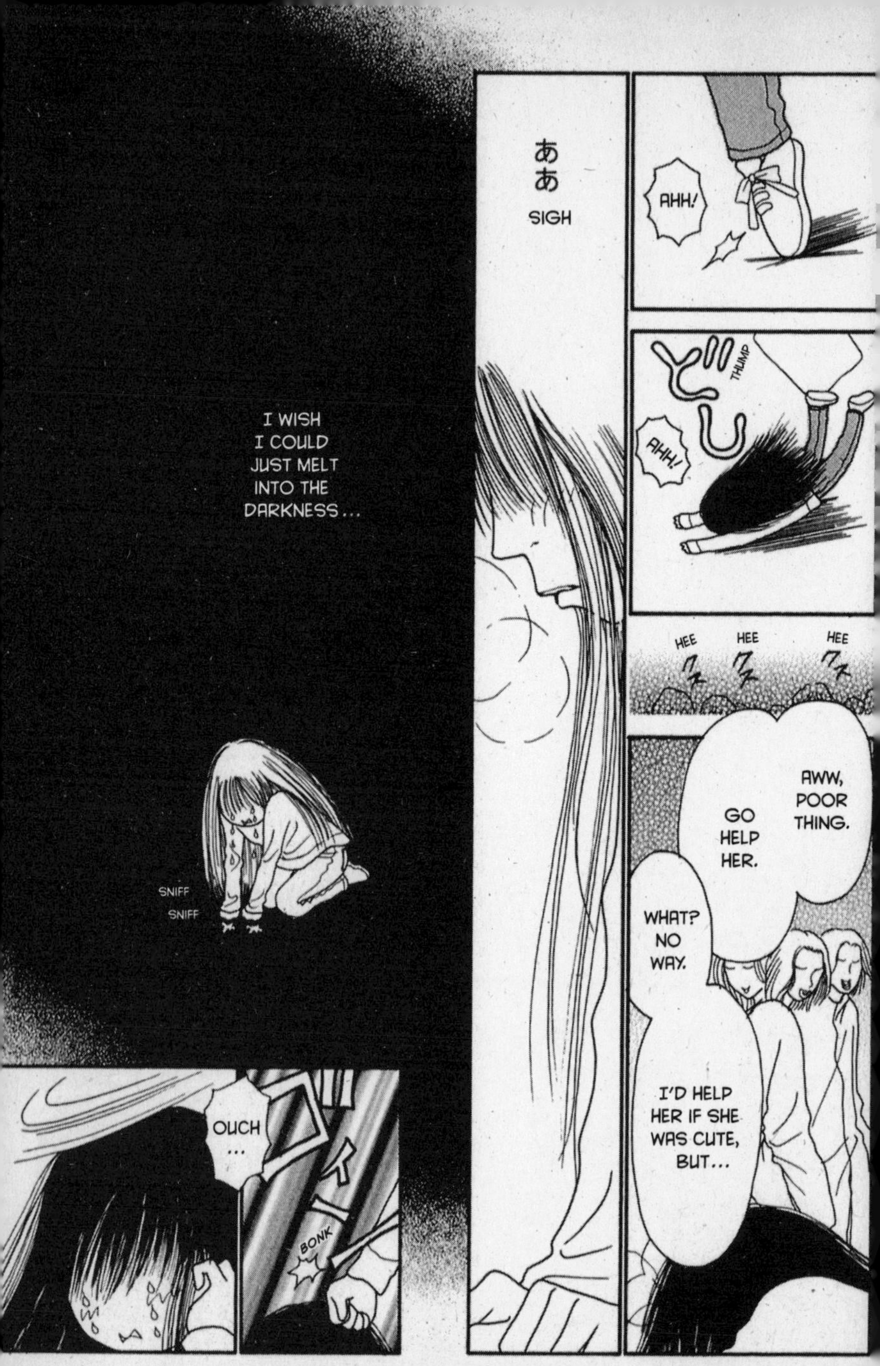
AHH!
AHH!
THUMP
HEE
HEE
HEE
AWW, POOR THING.
GO HELP HER.
WHAT? NO WAY.
I'D HELP HER IF SHE WAS CUTE, BUT...
ああ
SIGH
I WISH I COULD JUST MELT INTO THE DARKNESS...
SNIFF
SNIFF
BONK
OUCH ...

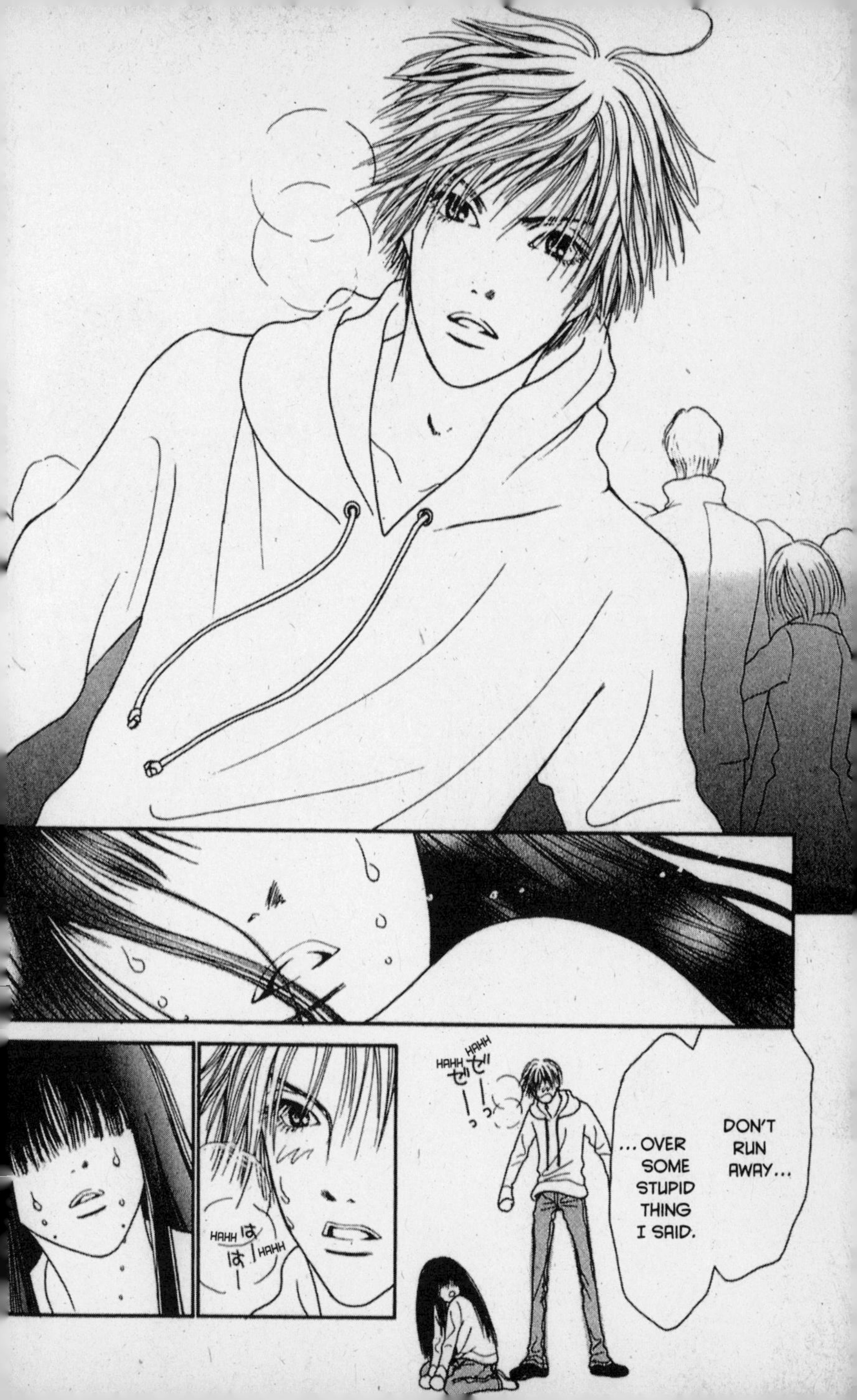

HAHH ぜー
HAHH ぜーっ
DON'T RUN AWAY...
...OVER SOME STUPID THING I SAID.
HAHH はー
HAHH はー

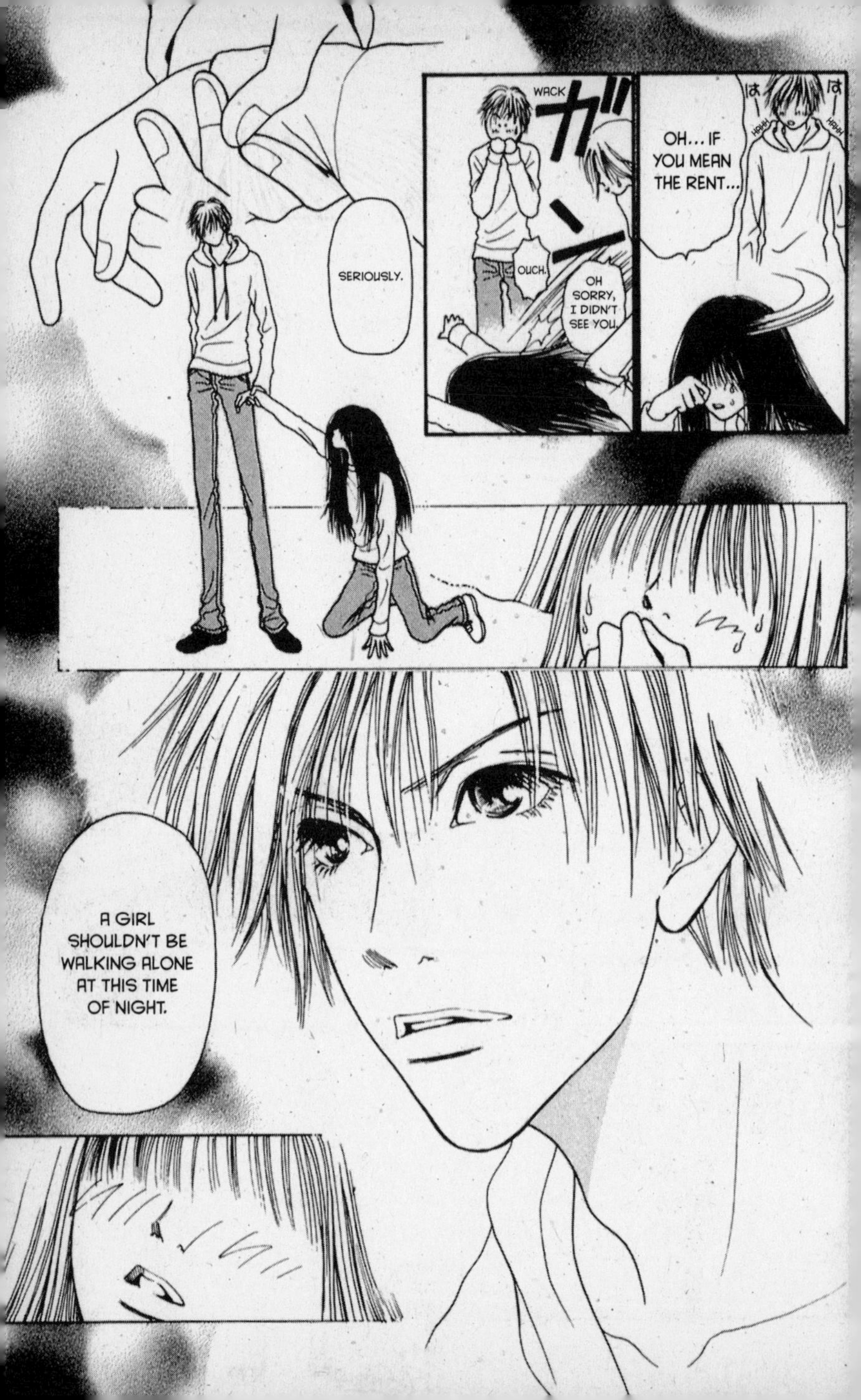
HAHH
HAHH
OH... IF YOU MEAN THE RENT...
WACK
OUCH.
OH SORRY, I DIDN'T SEE YOU.
SERIOUSLY.
A GIRL SHOULDN'T BE WALKING ALONE AT THIS TIME OF NIGHT.

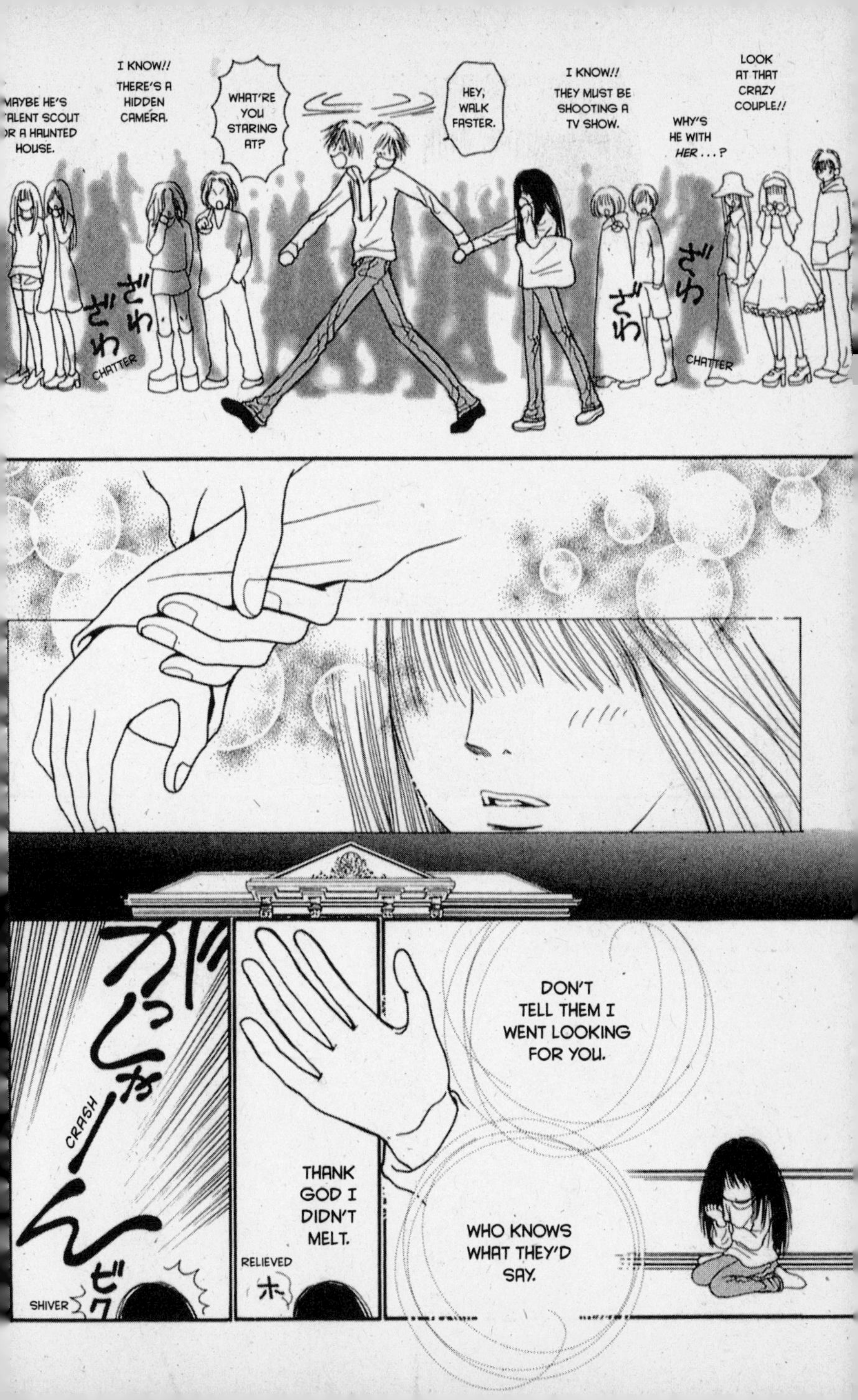
LOOK AT THAT CRAZY COUPLE!!
WHY'S HE WITH *HER*...?
ざわ ざわ
CHATTER
I KNOW!! THEY MUST BE SHOOTING A TV SHOW.
HEY, WALK FASTER.
WHAT'RE YOU STARING AT?
I KNOW!! THERE'S A HIDDEN CAMERA.
MAYBE HE'S ALENT SCOUT R A HAUNTED HOUSE.
ざわ ざわ
CHATTER
DON'T TELL THEM I WENT LOOKING FOR YOU.
WHO KNOWS WHAT THEY'D SAY.
THANK GOD I DIDN'T MELT.
ホ
RELIEVED
ガっしゃーん
CRASH
ビク
SHIVER

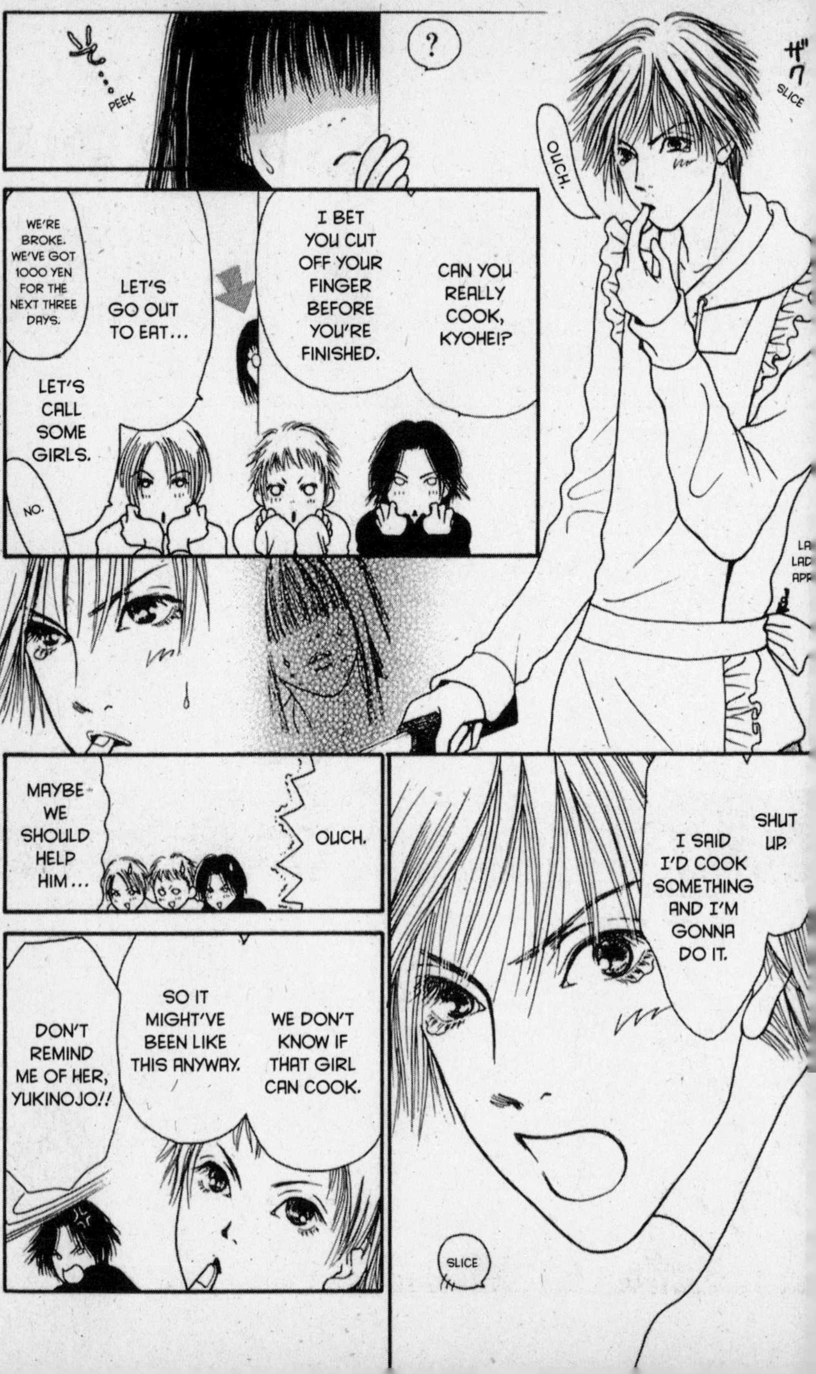
ザク
SLICE
OUCH.
?
PEEK
CAN YOU REALLY COOK, KYOHEI?
I BET YOU CUT OFF YOUR FINGER BEFORE YOU'RE FINISHED.
LET'S GO OUT TO EAT...
WE'RE BROKE. WE'VE GOT 1000 YEN FOR THE NEXT THREE DAYS.
LET'S CALL SOME GIRLS.
NO.
SHUT UP.
I SAID I'D COOK SOMETHING AND I'M GONNA DO IT.
SLICE
OUCH.
MAYBE WE SHOULD HELP HIM...
WE DON'T KNOW IF THAT GIRL CAN COOK.
SO IT MIGHT'VE BEEN LIKE THIS ANYWAY.
DON'T REMIND ME OF HER, YUKINOJO!!
NOTE: 1000 yen is approximately $10

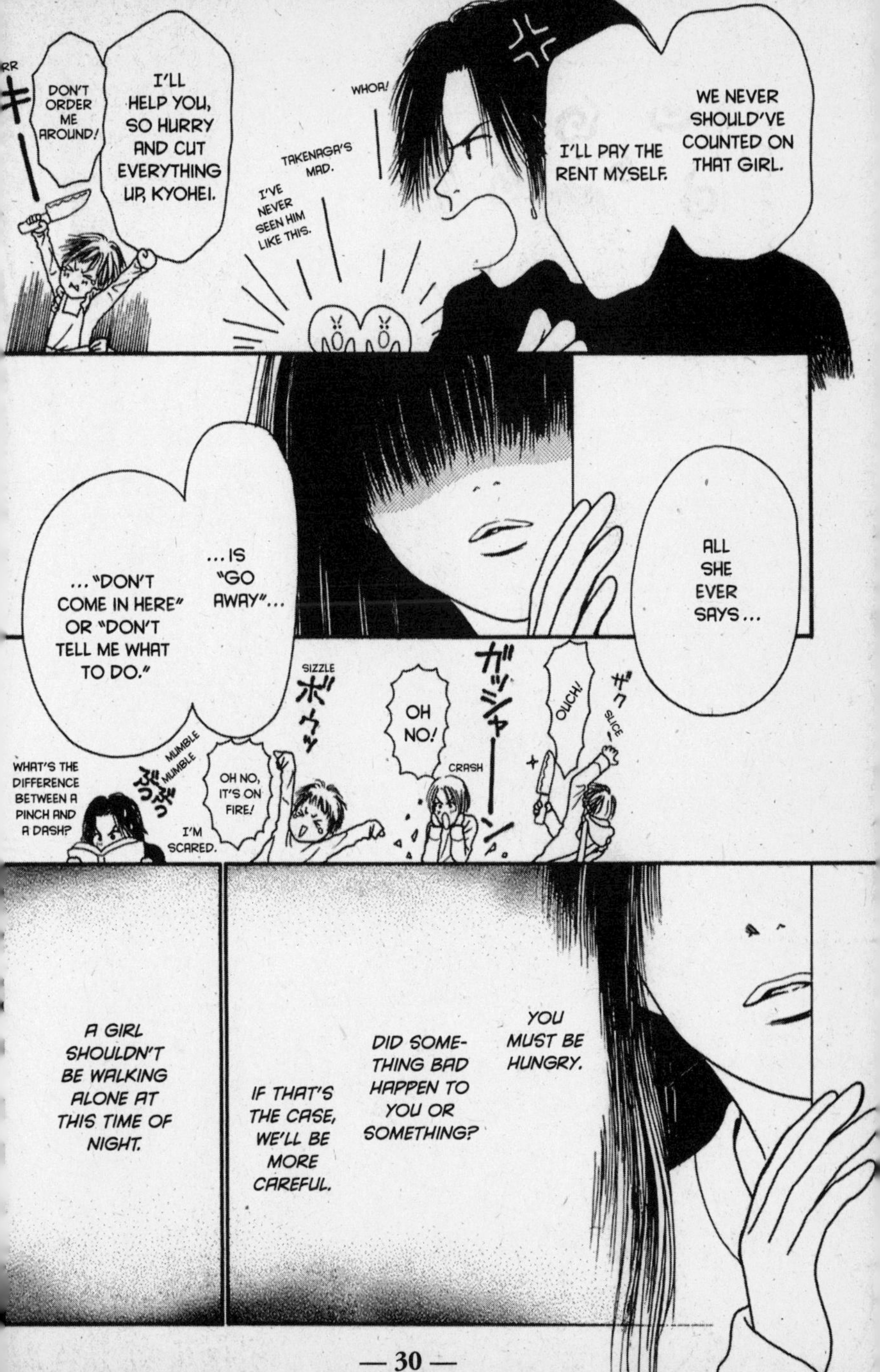
WE NEVER SHOULD'VE COUNTED ON THAT GIRL.
I'LL PAY THE RENT MYSELF.
WHOA!
TAKENAGA'S MAD.
I'VE NEVER SEEN HIM LIKE THIS.
I'LL HELP YOU, SO HURRY AND CUT EVERYTHING UP, KYOHEI.
DON'T ORDER ME AROUND!
キー
RR
ALL SHE EVER SAYS...
...IS "GO AWAY"...
..."DON'T COME IN HERE" OR "DON'T TELL ME WHAT TO DO."
ギク
SLICE
OUCH!
ガッシャーン
CRASH
OH NO!
ボウッ
SIZZLE
OH NO, IT'S ON FIRE!
ぶつぶつ
MUMBLE MUMBLE
I'M SCARED.
WHAT'S THE DIFFERENCE BETWEEN A PINCH AND A DASH?
YOU MUST BE HUNGRY.
DID SOMETHING BAD HAPPEN TO YOU OR SOMETHING?
IF THAT'S THE CASE, WE'LL BE MORE CAREFUL.
A GIRL SHOULDN'T BE WALKING ALONE AT THIS TIME OF NIGHT.

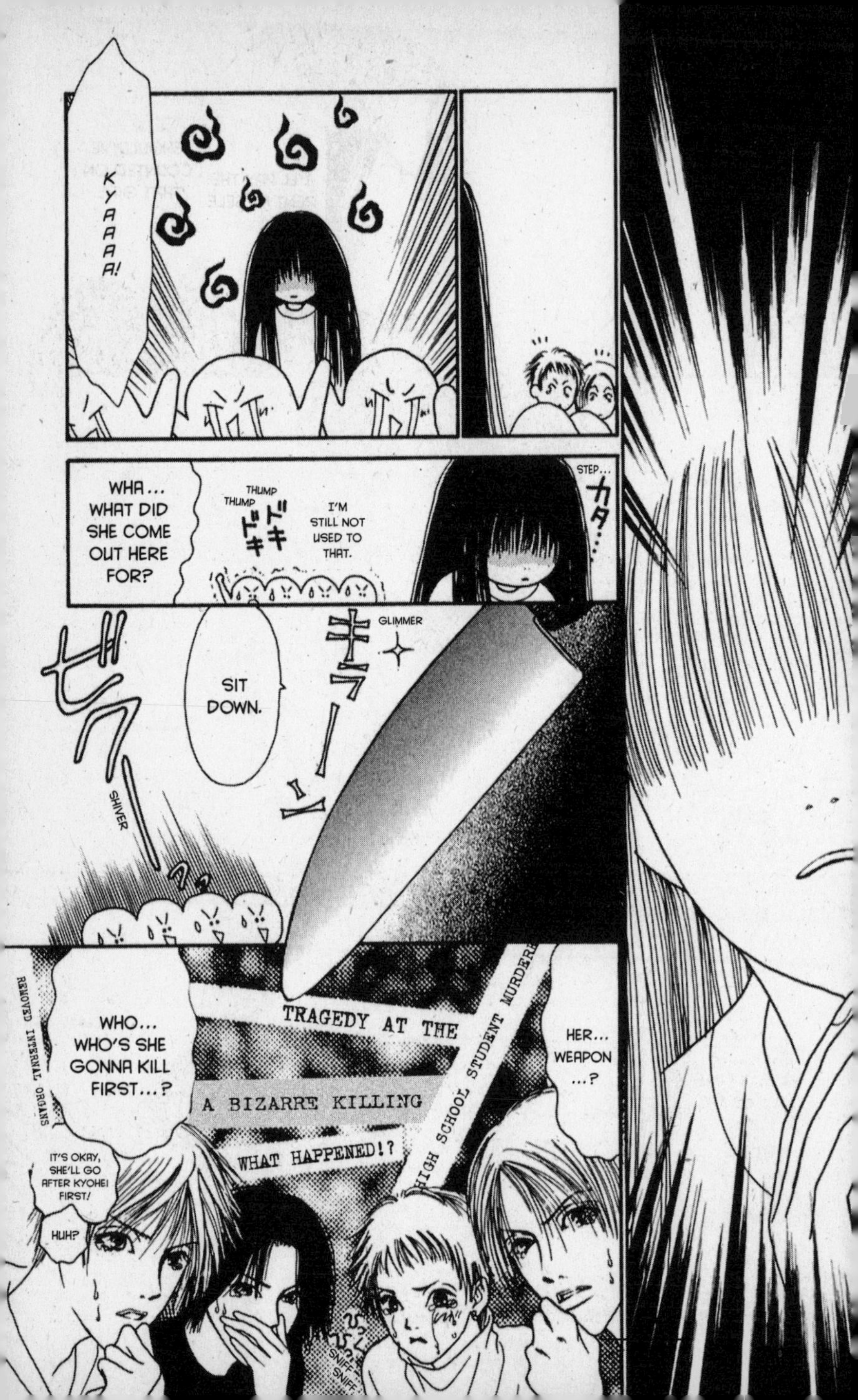
KYAAAA!
STEP...
カタ...
I'M STILL NOT USED TO THAT.
THUMP THUMP
ドキドキ
WHA... WHAT DID SHE COME OUT HERE FOR?
GLIMMER
キラーン
SIT DOWN.
SHIVER
HER... WEAPON ...?
HIGH SCHOOL STUDENT MURDER
TRAGEDY AT THE
A BIZARRE KILLING
WHAT HAPPENED!?
WHO... WHO'S SHE GONNA KILL FIRST...?
REMOVED INTERNAL ORGANS
IT'S OKAY, SHE'LL GO AFTER KYOHEI FIRST!
HUH?
SNIFF SNIFF

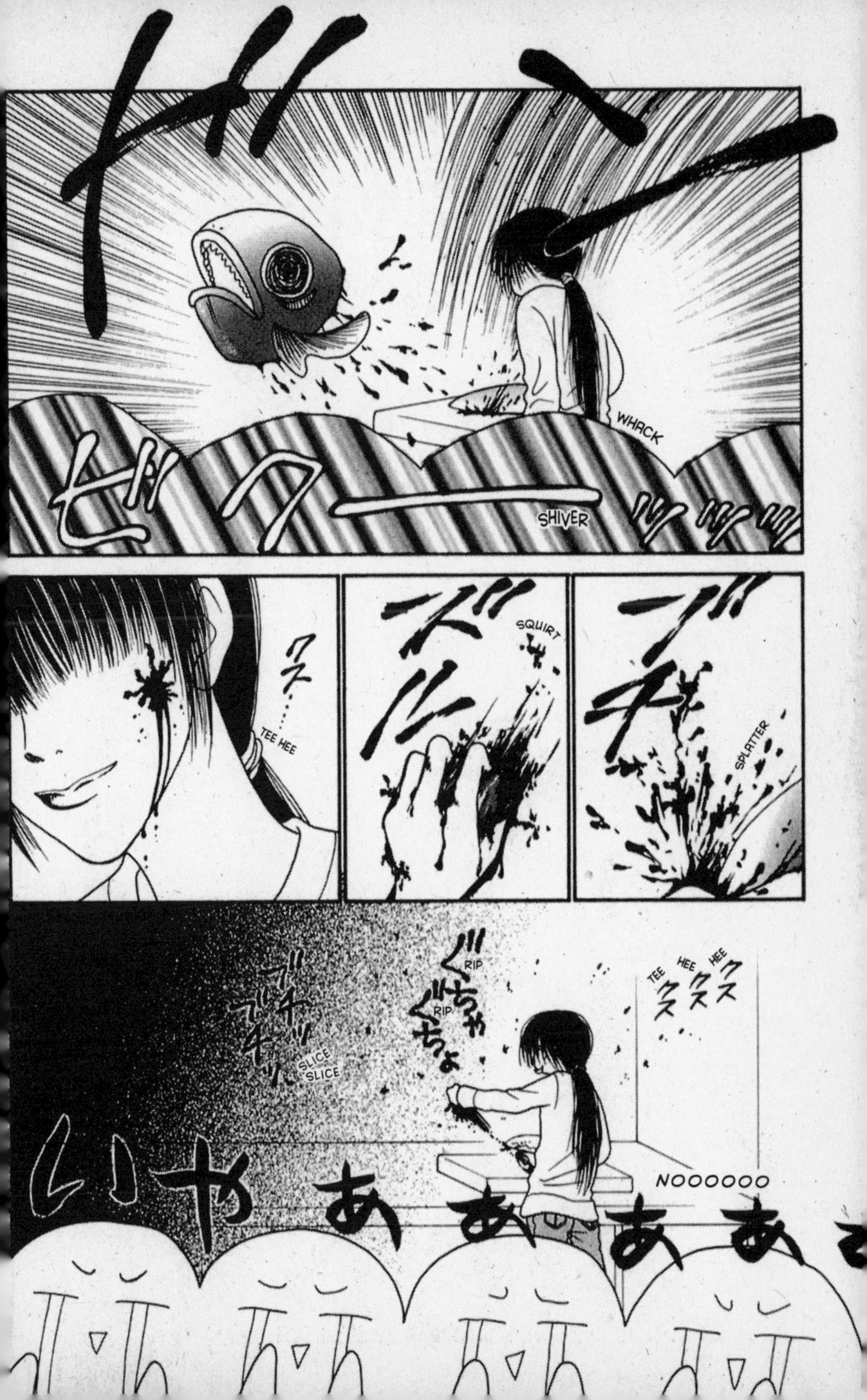
WHACK
SHIVER
SPLATTER
SQUIRT
TEE HEE
TEE HEE HEE
RIP
RIP
SLICE
SLICE
NOOOOOO

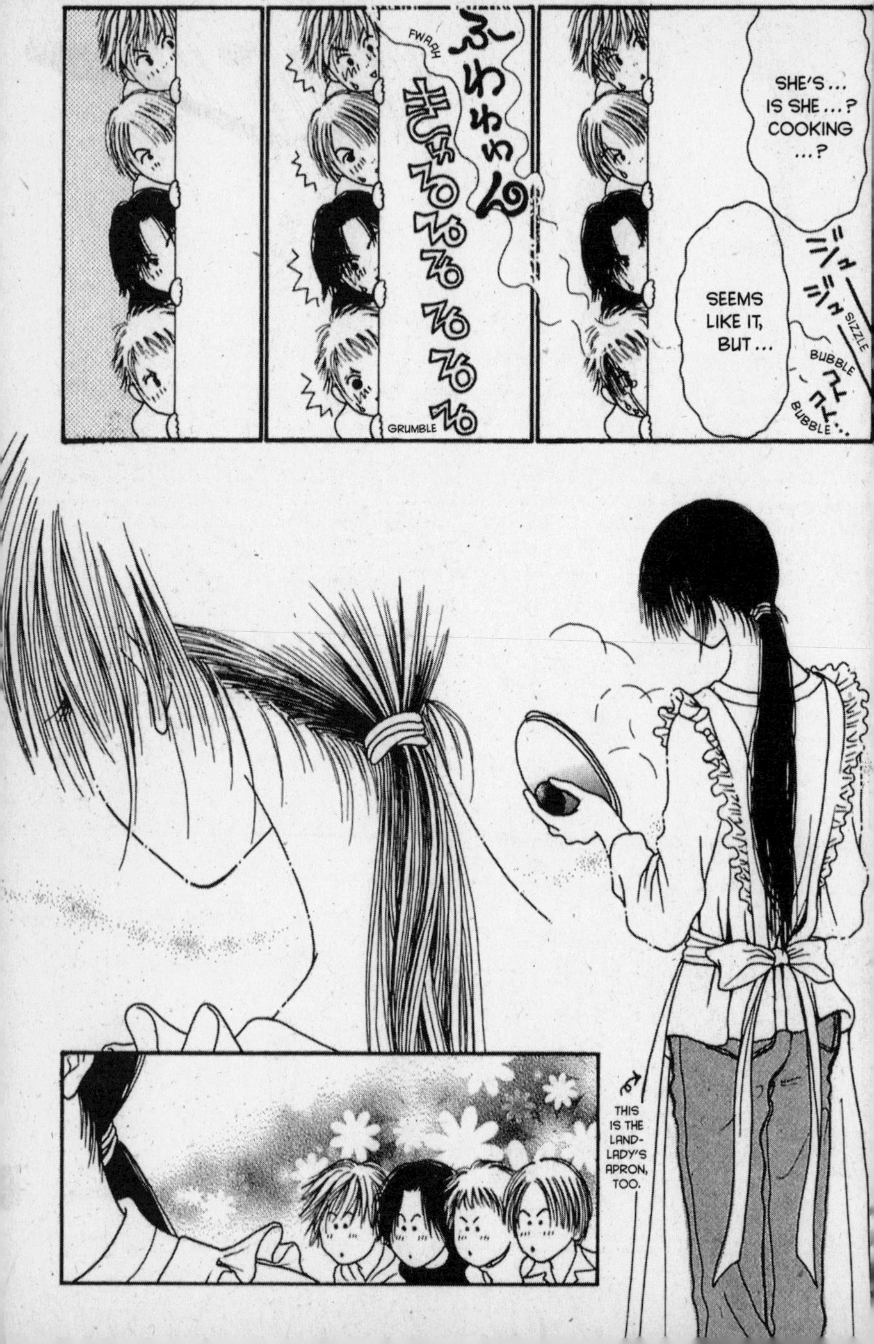
SHE'S... IS SHE...? COOKING...?
SEEMS LIKE IT, BUT...
ジュジュ
SIZZLE
コトコト
BUBBLE BUBBLE...
FWAAH
GRUMBLE
THIS IS THE LANDLADY'S APRON, TOO.

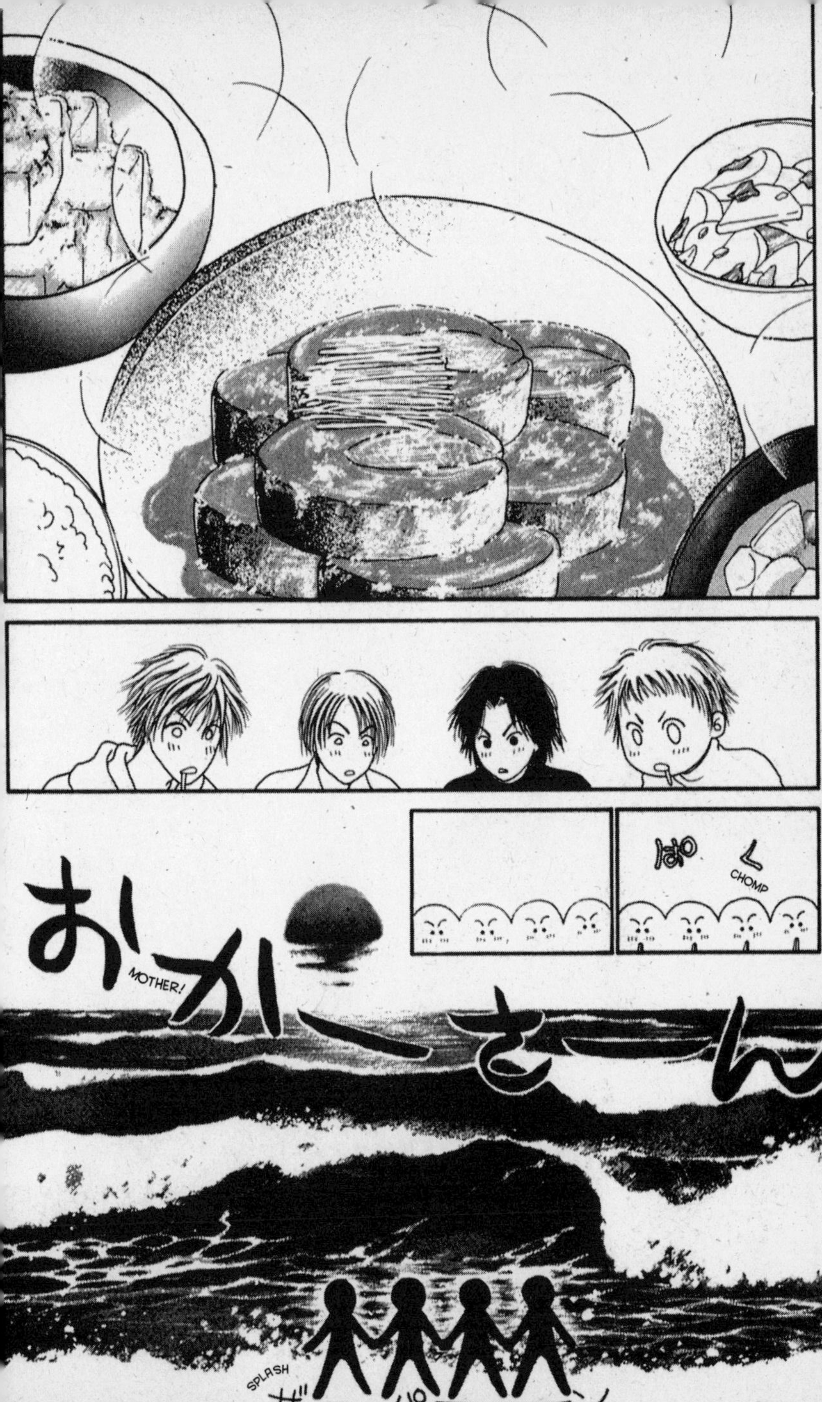
ぱく
CHOMP
おかーさーん
MOTHER!
ザッパー
SPLASH

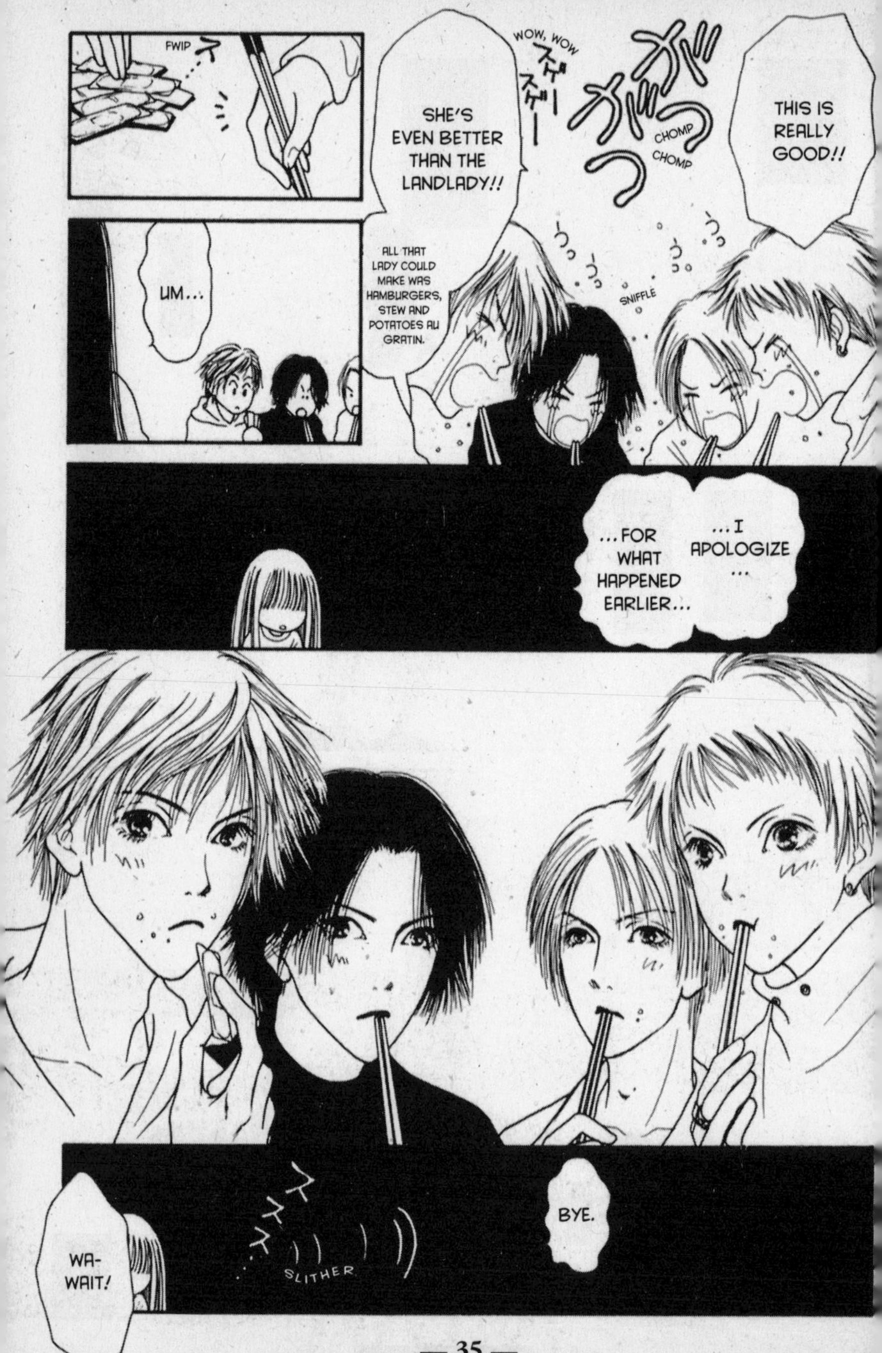
THIS IS REALLY GOOD!!
CHOMP CHOMP
WOW, WOW
SHE'S EVEN BETTER THAN THE LANDLADY!!
SNIFFLE
ALL THAT LADY COULD MAKE WAS HAMBURGERS, STEW AND POTATOES AU GRATIN.
FWIP
UM...
...I APOLOGIZE...
...FOR WHAT HAPPENED EARLIER...
BYE.
SLITHER
WA-WAIT!

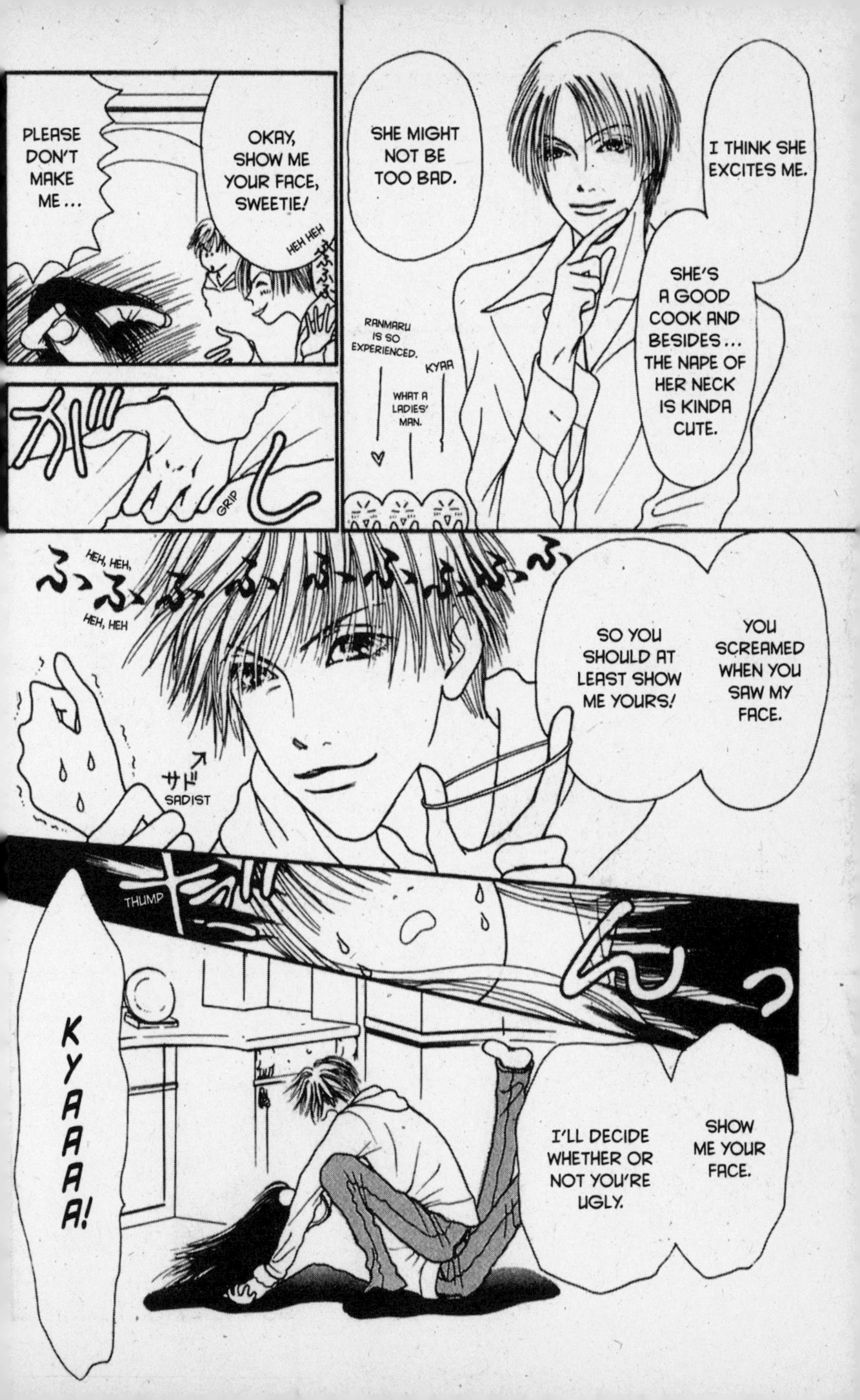
I THINK SHE EXCITES ME.
SHE'S A GOOD COOK AND BESIDES... THE NAPE OF HER NECK IS KINDA CUTE.
SHE MIGHT NOT BE TOO BAD.
KYAA
RANMARU IS SO EXPERIENCED.
WHAT A LADIES' MAN.
OKAY, SHOW ME YOUR FACE, SWEETIE!
HEH HEH
PLEASE DON'T MAKE ME...
GRIP
YOU SCREAMED WHEN YOU SAW MY FACE.
SO YOU SHOULD AT LEAST SHOW ME YOURS!
HEH, HEH,
HEH, HEH
SADIST
THUMP
SHOW ME YOUR FACE.
I'LL DECIDE WHETHER OR NOT YOU'RE UGLY.
KYAAAAAA!

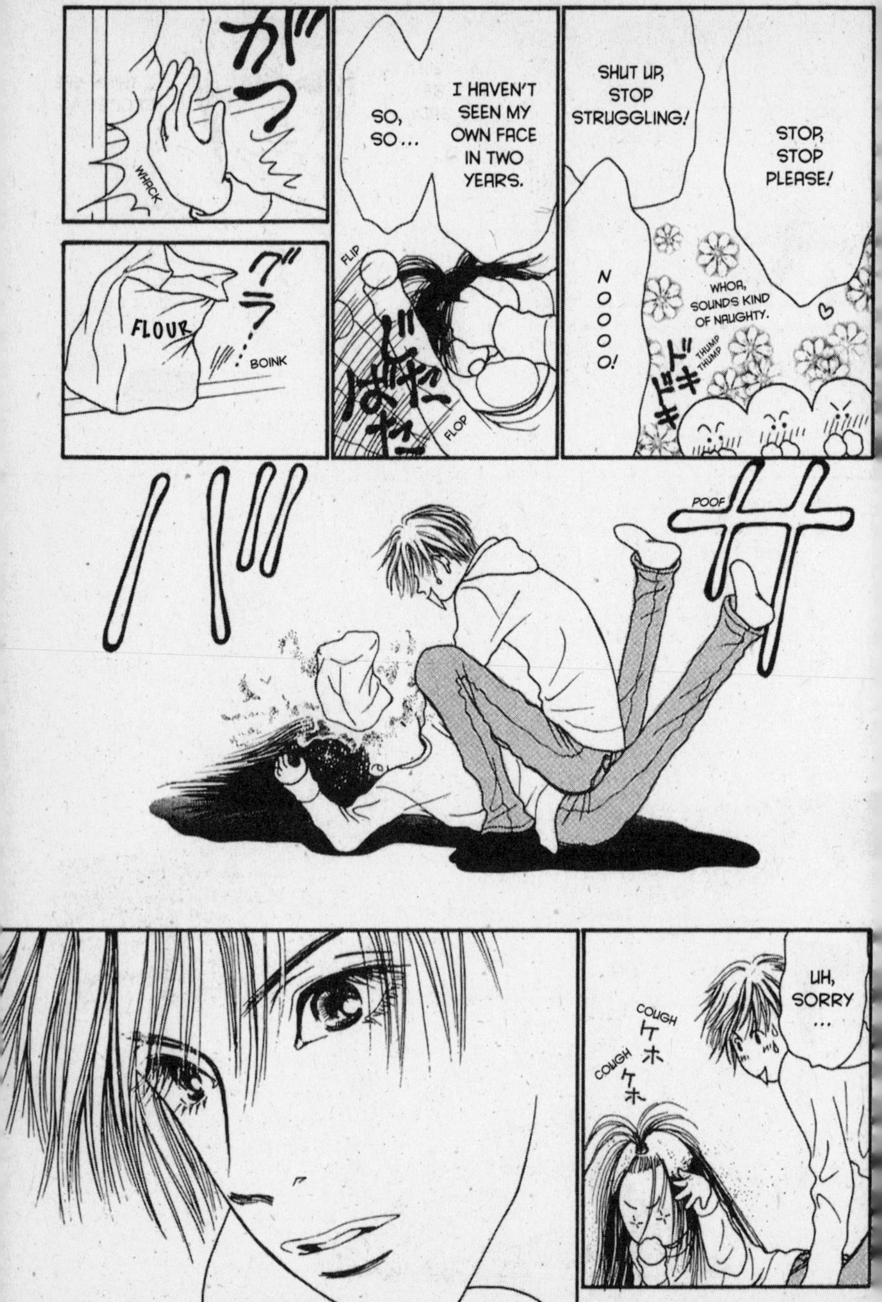
STOP, STOP PLEASE!
SHUT UP, STOP STRUGGLING!
NOOOOO!
WHOA, SOUNDS KIND OF NAUGHTY.
THUMP THUMP
I HAVEN'T SEEN MY OWN FACE IN TWO YEARS.
SO, SO...
FLIP
FLOP
WHACK
FLOUR
BOINK
POOF
UH, SORRY ...
COUGH
COUGH

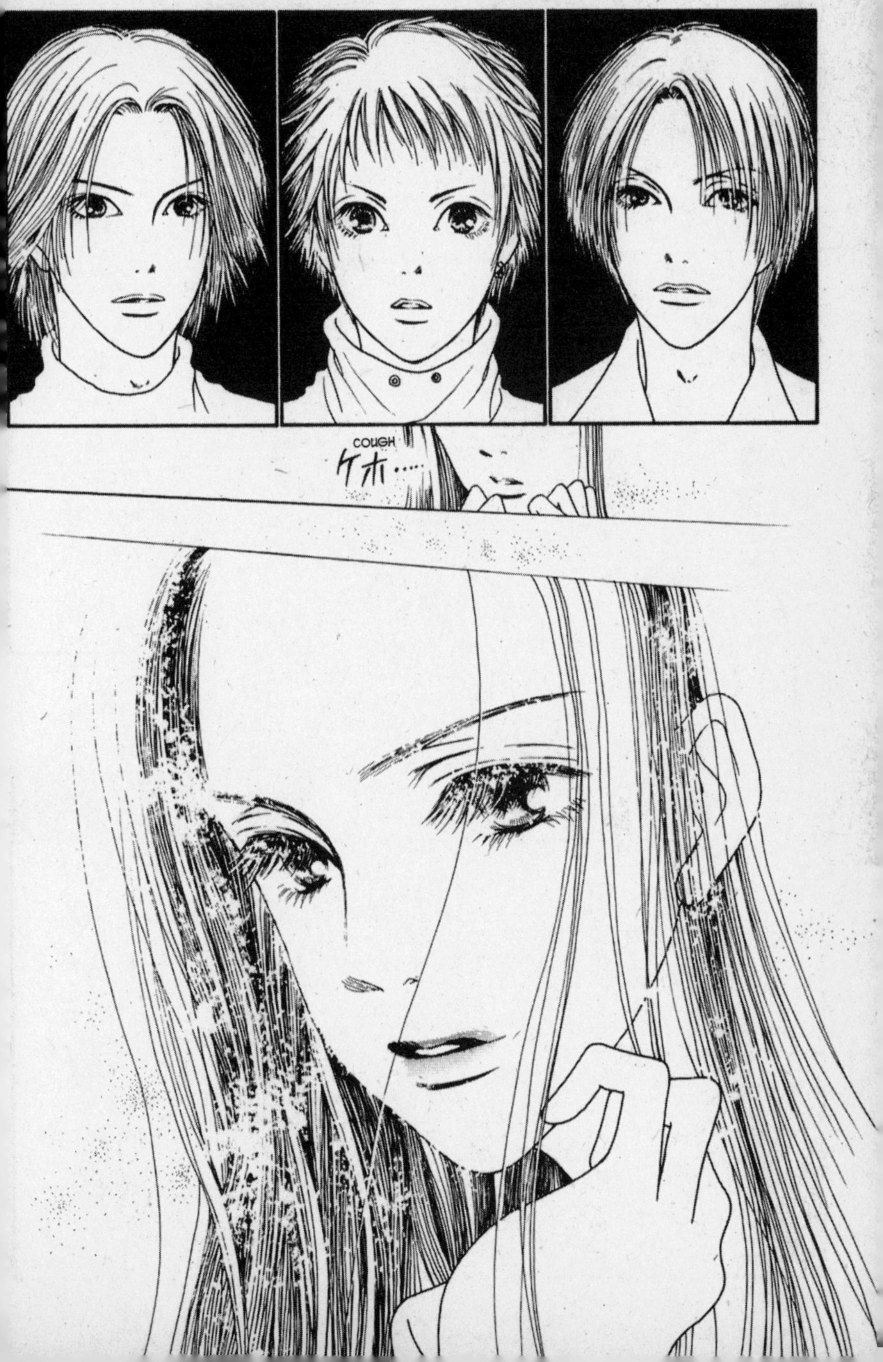
COUGH
ケホ.....

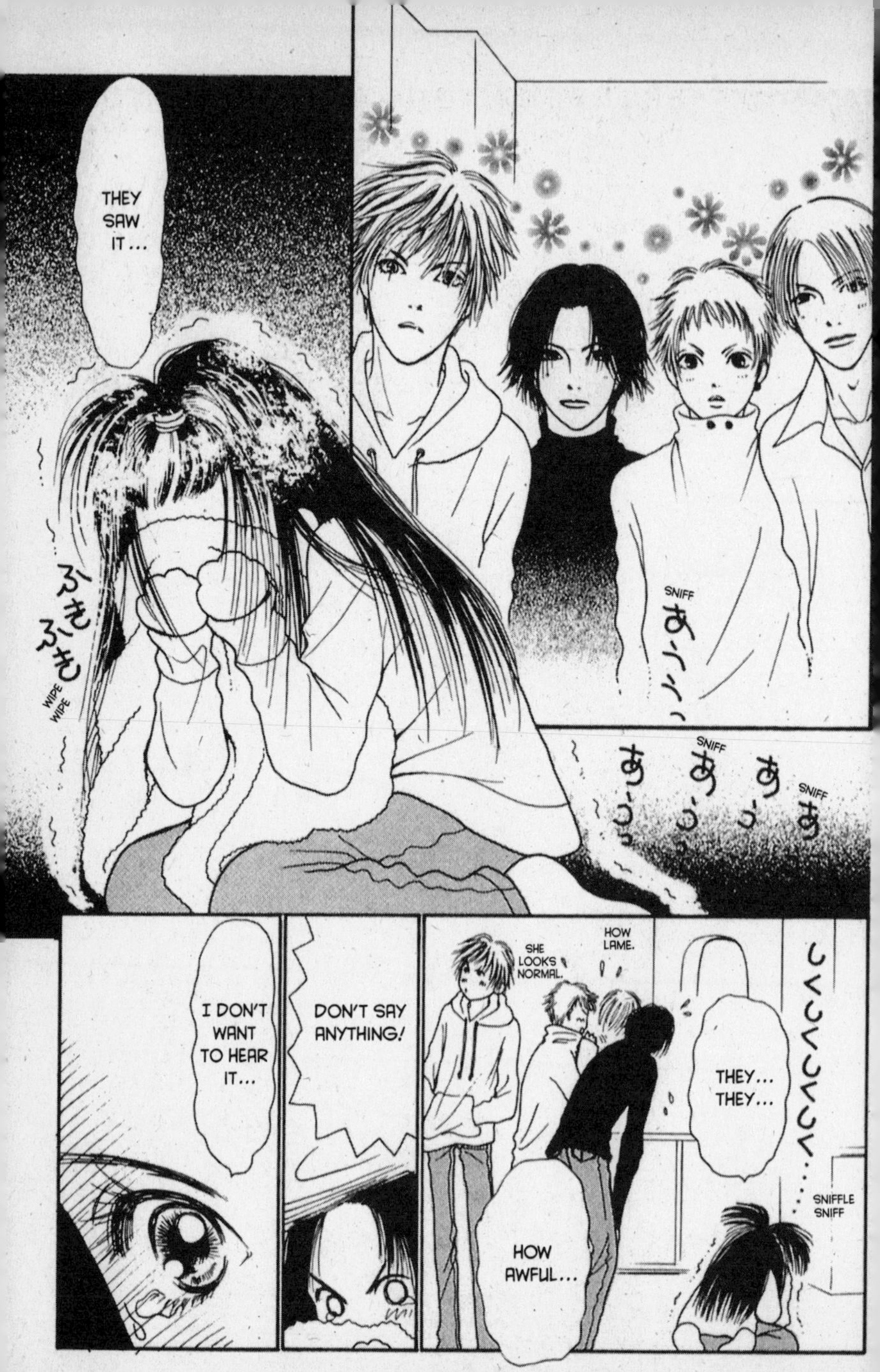
SNIFF
あううう、
SNIFF
あうう
SNIFF
あうう
あうう
THEY SAW IT...
ふきふき
WIPE WIPE
HOW LAME.
SHE LOOKS NORMAL.
THEY... THEY...
しくしくしくしく...
SNIFFLE SNIFF
HOW AWFUL...
DON'T SAY ANYTHING!
I DON'T WANT TO HEAR IT...

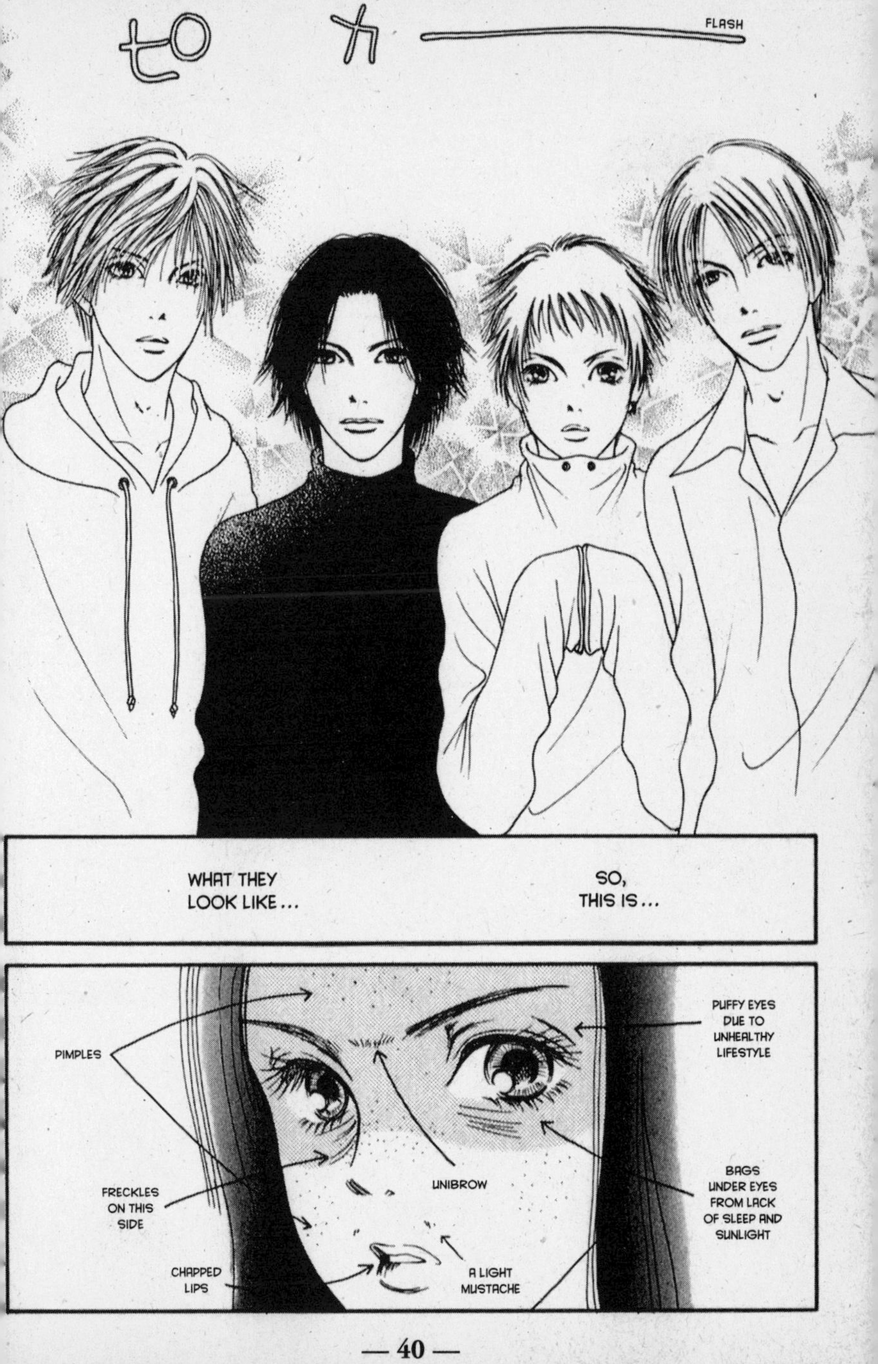
ピカー
FLASH
SO, THIS IS...
WHAT THEY LOOK LIKE...
PUFFY EYES DUE TO UNHEALTHY LIFESTYLE
PIMPLES
UNIBROW
BAGS UNDER EYES FROM LACK OF SLEEP AND SUNLIGHT
FRECKLES ON THIS SIDE
A LIGHT MUSTACHE
CHAPPED LIPS

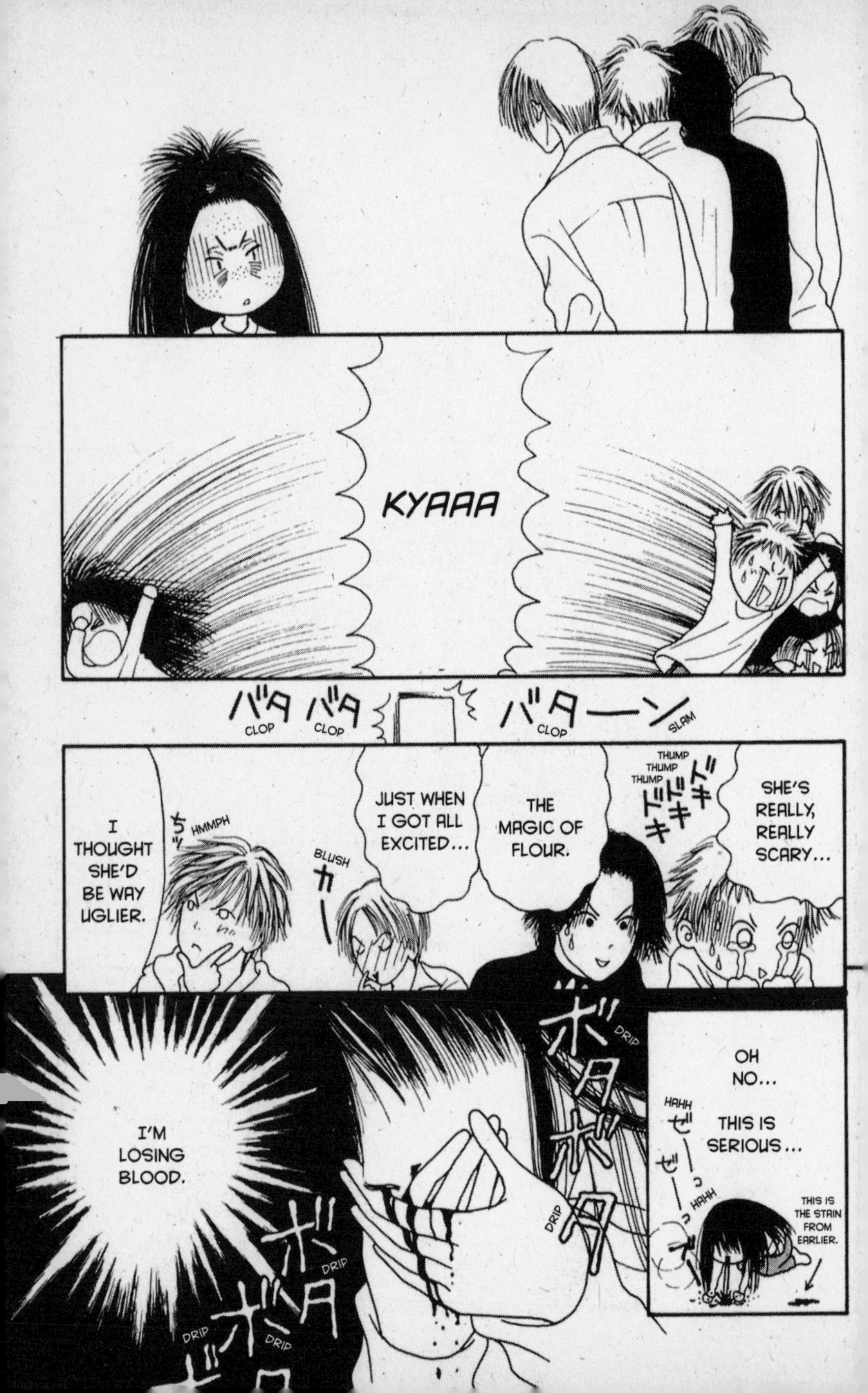
KYAAA
SLAM
バターン
CLOP
バタ
CLOP
バタ
CLOP
SHE'S REALLY, REALLY SCARY...
ドキドキ
THUMP THUMP THUMP
THE MAGIC OF FLOUR.
JUST WHEN I GOT ALL EXCITED...
カー
BLUSH
HMMPH
I THOUGHT SHE'D BE WAY UGLIER.
OH NO...
THIS IS SERIOUS...
HAHH
HAHH
THIS IS THE STAIN FROM EARLIER.
DRIP
DRIP
I'M LOSING BLOOD.
DRIP
DRIP
DRIP

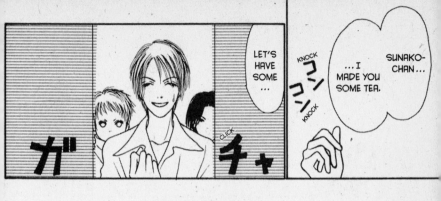

LET'S HAVE SOME ...

...I MADE YOU SOME TEA.

SUNAKO-CHAN...

KNOCK コン コン KNOCK

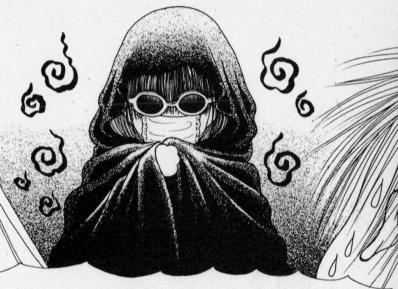

AAAAAHH

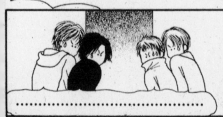

ズルズルズルズル
DRAG

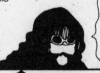

IF I'M IN A BRIGHT PLACE FOR MORE THAN THREE SECONDS I'LL MELT...

A BLACK SHEET. (SHE USES IT AS A CURTAIN.)

— 42 —

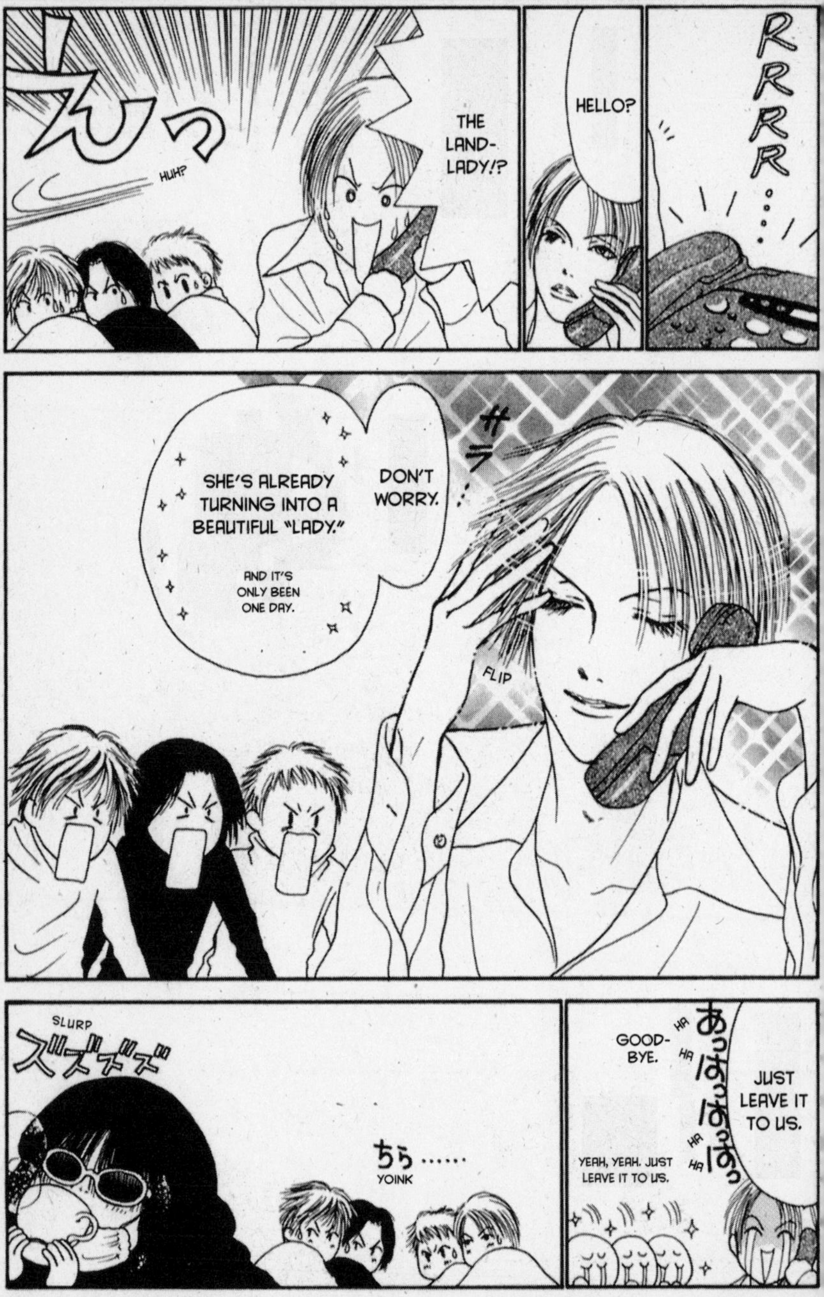
RRRR....
HELLO?
THE LAND-LADY!?
えひっ!
HUH?
DON'T WORRY.
SHE'S ALREADY TURNING INTO A BEAUTIFUL "LADY."
AND IT'S ONLY BEEN ONE DAY.
サラ
FLIP
JUST LEAVE IT TO US.
あっはっはっはっ
HA HA HA HA
GOOD-BYE.
YEAH, YEAH. JUST LEAVE IT TO US.
SLURP
ズズズズ
ちら……
YOINK

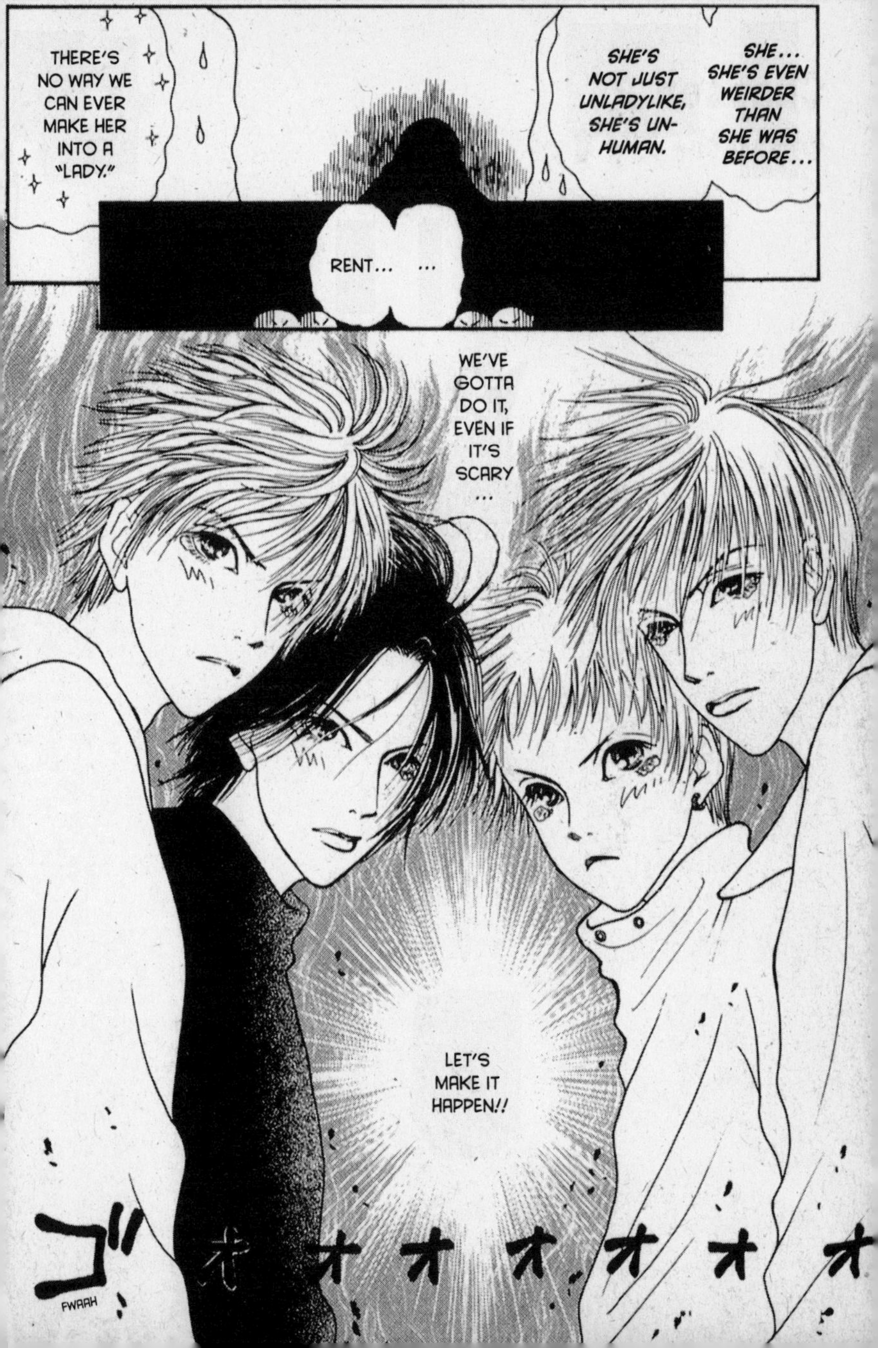
SHE... SHE'S EVEN WEIRDER THAN SHE WAS BEFORE...
SHE'S NOT JUST UNLADYLIKE, SHE'S UN-HUMAN.
THERE'S NO WAY WE CAN EVER MAKE HER INTO A "LADY."
RENT... ...
WE'VE GOTTA DO IT, EVEN IF IT'S SCARY...
LET'S MAKE IT HAPPEN!!
ゴオオオオオオオ
FWAAH

Chapter 2
Behind the Iron Curtain!

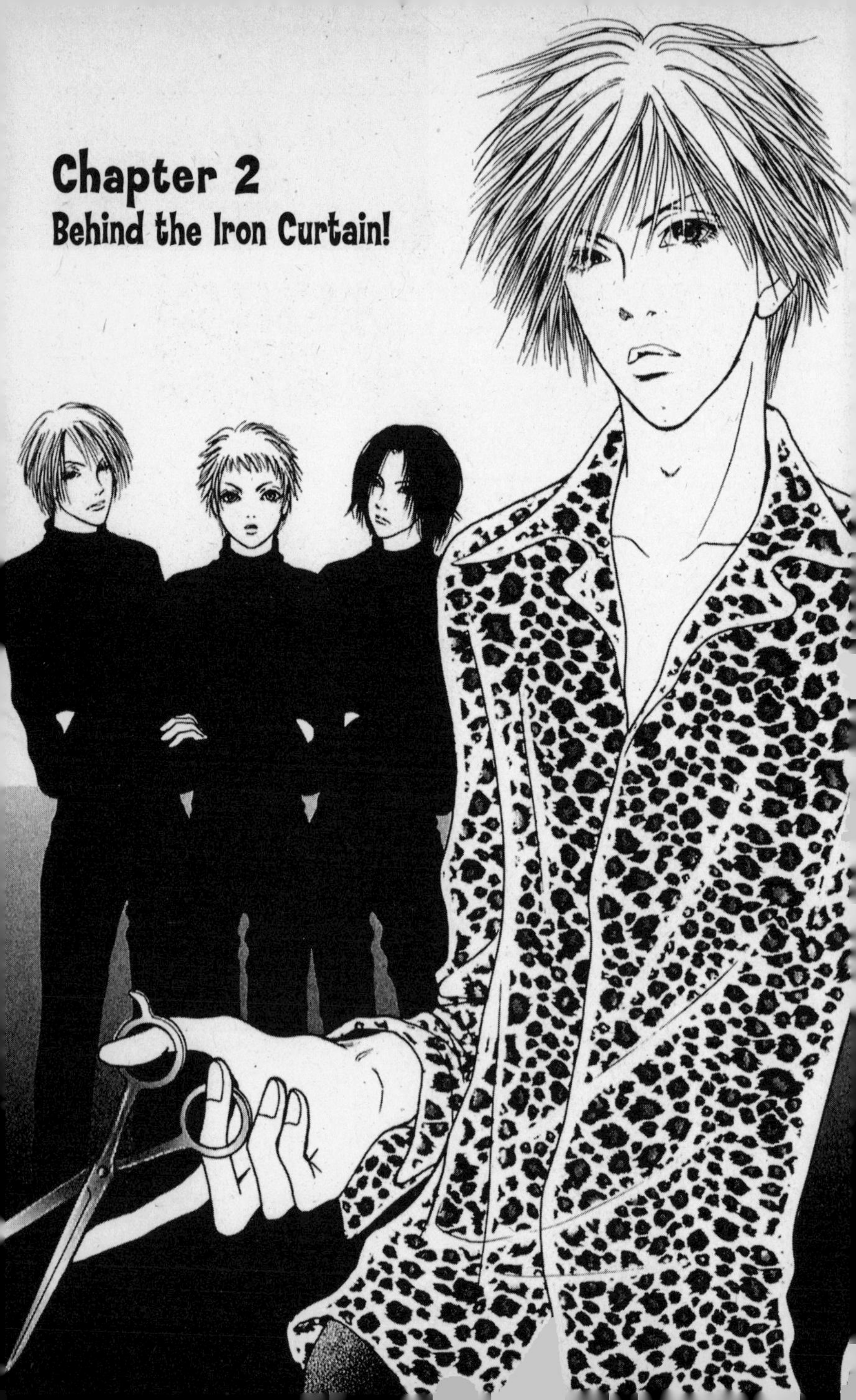

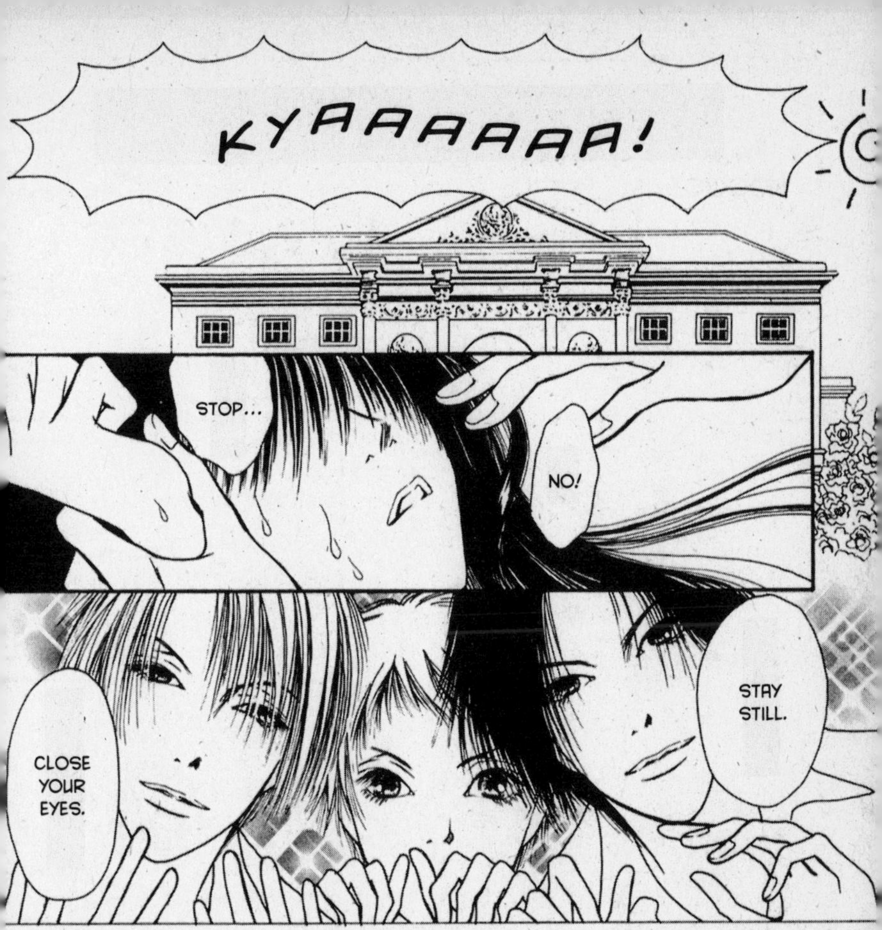
KYAAAAAAA!
NO!
STOP...
STAY STILL.
CLOSE YOUR EYES.

KYOHEI TAKANO

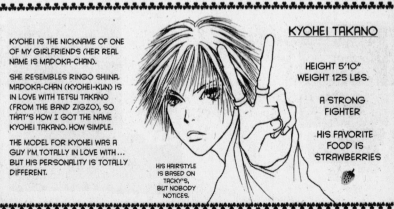

KYOHEI IS THE NICKNAME OF ONE OF MY GIRLFRIENDS (HER REAL NAME IS MADOKA-CHAN).

SHE RESEMBLES RINGO SHIINA. MADOKA-CHAN (KYOHEI-KUN) IS IN LOVE WITH TETSU TAKANO (FROM THE BAND ZIGZO), SO THAT'S HOW I GOT THE NAME KYOHEI TAKANO. HOW SIMPLE.

THE MODEL FOR KYOHEI WAS A GUY I'M TOTALLY IN LOVE WITH ... BUT HIS PERSONALITY IS TOTALLY DIFFERENT.

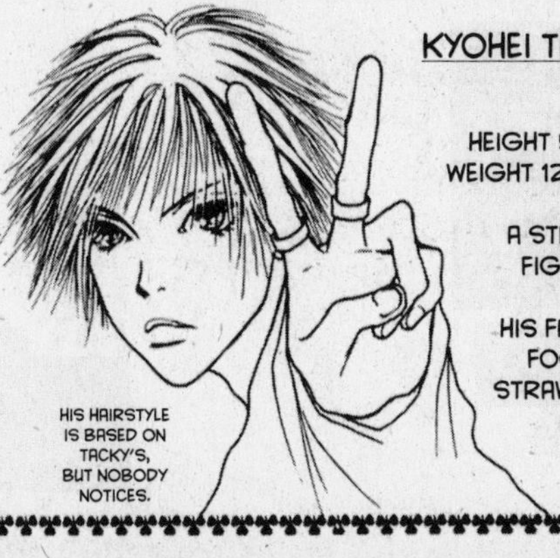
HIS HAIRSTYLE IS BASED ON TACKY'S, BUT NOBODY NOTICES.

HEIGHT 5'10"
WEIGHT 125 LBS.

A STRONG FIGHTER

HIS FAVORITE FOOD IS STRAWBERRIES

NOTE: TACKY IS PROBABLY A JAPANESE SINGER.

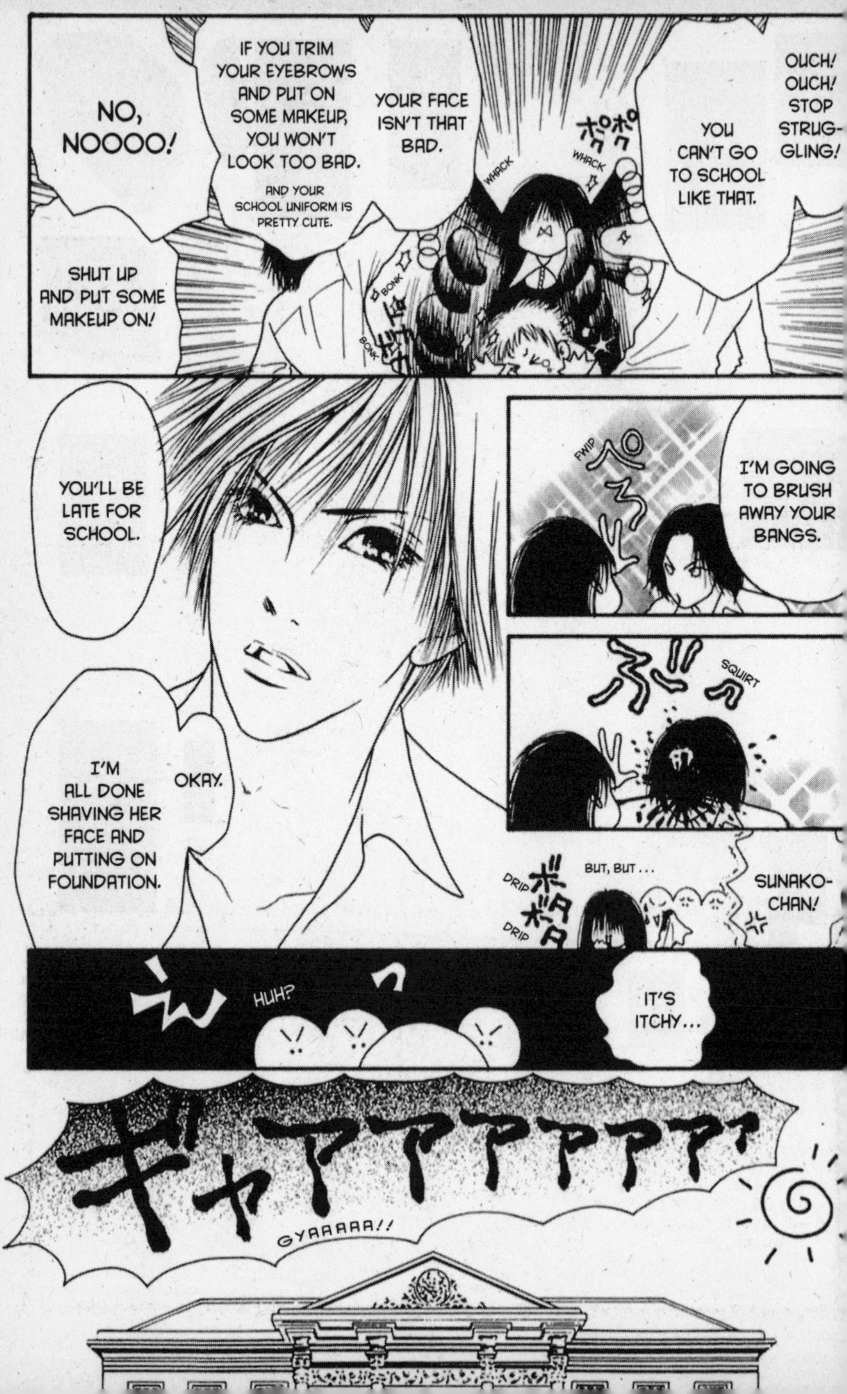
OUCH! OUCH! STOP STRUG-GLING!
YOU CAN'T GO TO SCHOOL LIKE THAT.
WHACK
WHACK
YOUR FACE ISN'T THAT BAD.
IF YOU TRIM YOUR EYEBROWS AND PUT ON SOME MAKEUP, YOU WON'T LOOK TOO BAD.
AND YOUR SCHOOL UNIFORM IS PRETTY CUTE.
NO, NOOOO!
BONK
BONK
SHUT UP AND PUT SOME MAKEUP ON!
I'M GOING TO BRUSH AWAY YOUR BANGS.
FWIP
SQUIRT
SUNAKO-CHAN!
BUT, BUT . . .
DRIP
DRIP
YOU'LL BE LATE FOR SCHOOL.
OKAY.
I'M ALL DONE SHAVING HER FACE AND PUTTING ON FOUNDATION.
IT'S ITCHY...
HUH?
GYAAAAA!!

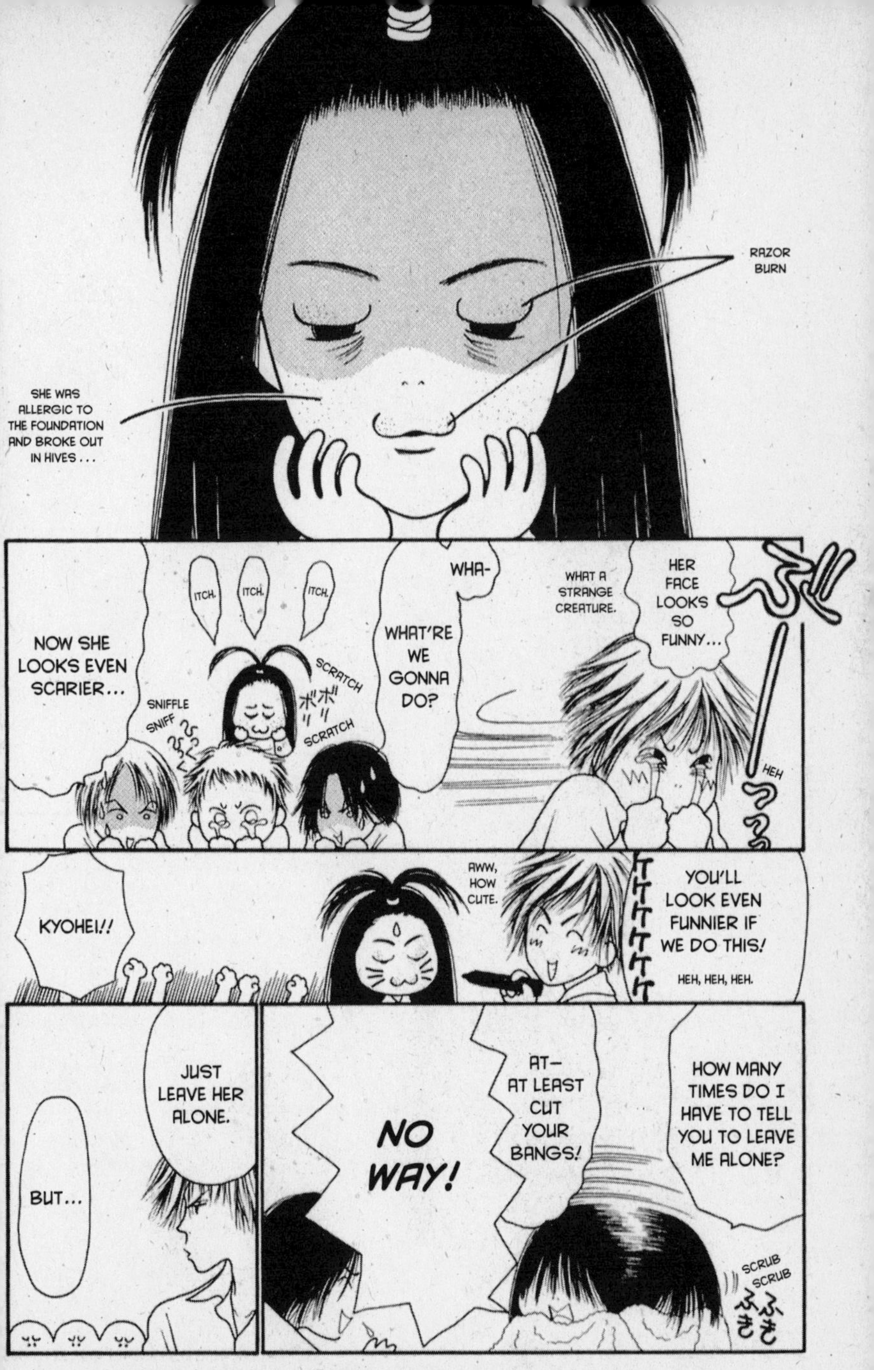

RAZOR BURN
SHE WAS ALLERGIC TO THE FOUNDATION AND BROKE OUT IN HIVES . . .
HER FACE LOOKS SO FUNNY...
WHAT A STRANGE CREATURE.
HEH
WHA-
WHAT'RE WE GONNA DO?
ITCH.
ITCH.
ITCH.
SCRATCH
SCRATCH
SNIFFLE
SNIFF
NOW SHE LOOKS EVEN SCARIER...
YOU'LL LOOK EVEN FUNNIER IF WE DO THIS!
HEH, HEH, HEH.
AWW, HOW CUTE.
KYOHEI!!
HOW MANY TIMES DO I HAVE TO TELL YOU TO LEAVE ME ALONE?
SCRUB
SCRUB
AT— AT LEAST CUT YOUR BANGS!
NO WAY!
JUST LEAVE HER ALONE.
BUT...

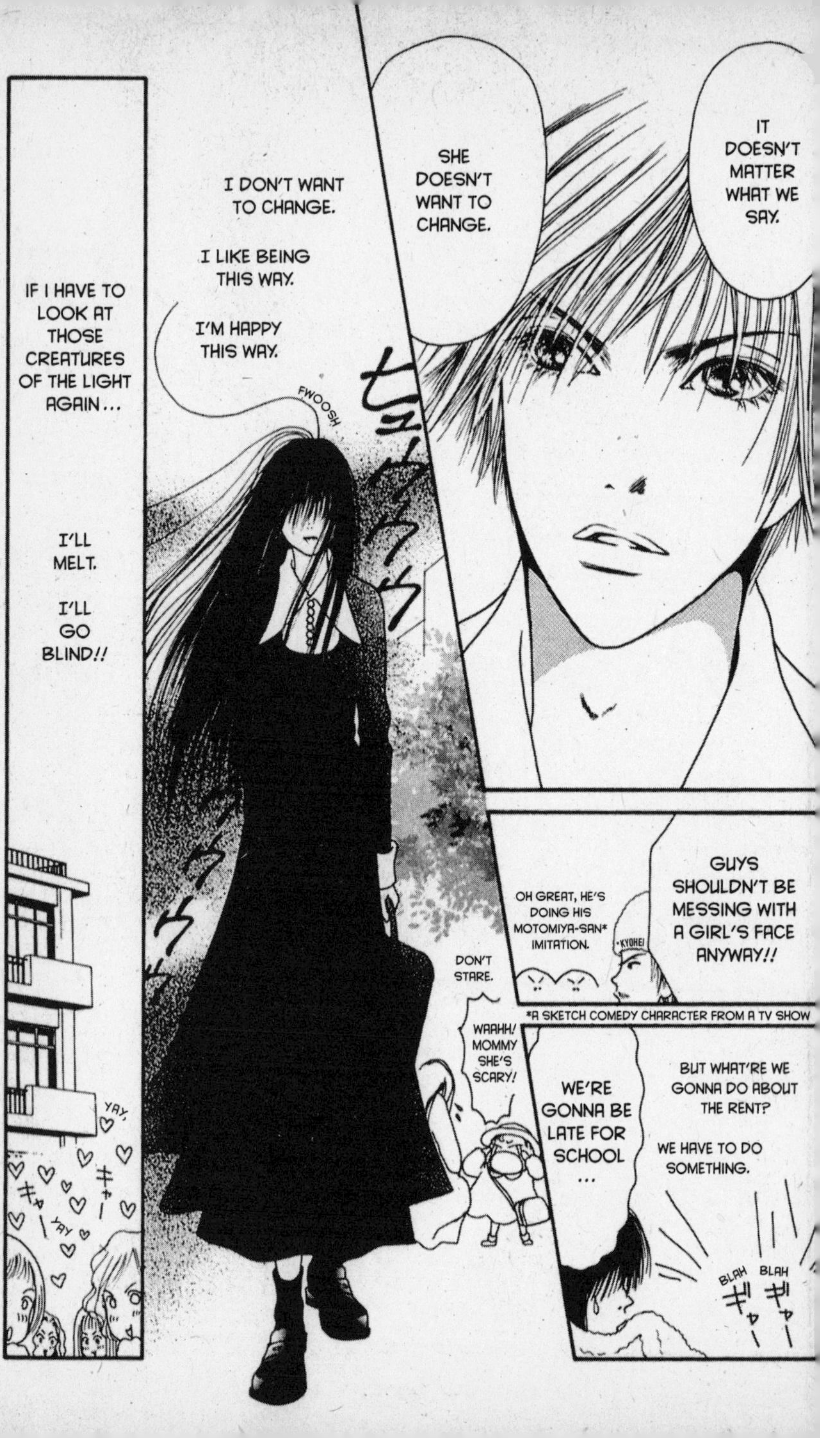
IT DOESN'T MATTER WHAT WE SAY.
SHE DOESN'T WANT TO CHANGE.
GUYS SHOULDN'T BE MESSING WITH A GIRL'S FACE ANYWAY!!
OH GREAT, HE'S DOING HIS MOTOMIYA-SAN* IMITATION.
KYOHEI
*A SKETCH COMEDY CHARACTER FROM A TV SHOW
BUT WHAT'RE WE GONNA DO ABOUT THE RENT?
WE HAVE TO DO SOMETHING.
WE'RE GONNA BE LATE FOR SCHOOL ...
BLAH BLAH
I DON'T WANT TO CHANGE.
I LIKE BEING THIS WAY.
I'M HAPPY THIS WAY.
FWOOSH
DON'T STARE.
WAAHH! MOMMY SHE'S SCARY!
IF I HAVE TO LOOK AT THOSE CREATURES OF THE LIGHT AGAIN...
I'LL MELT.
I'LL GO BLIND!!
YAY,
YAY

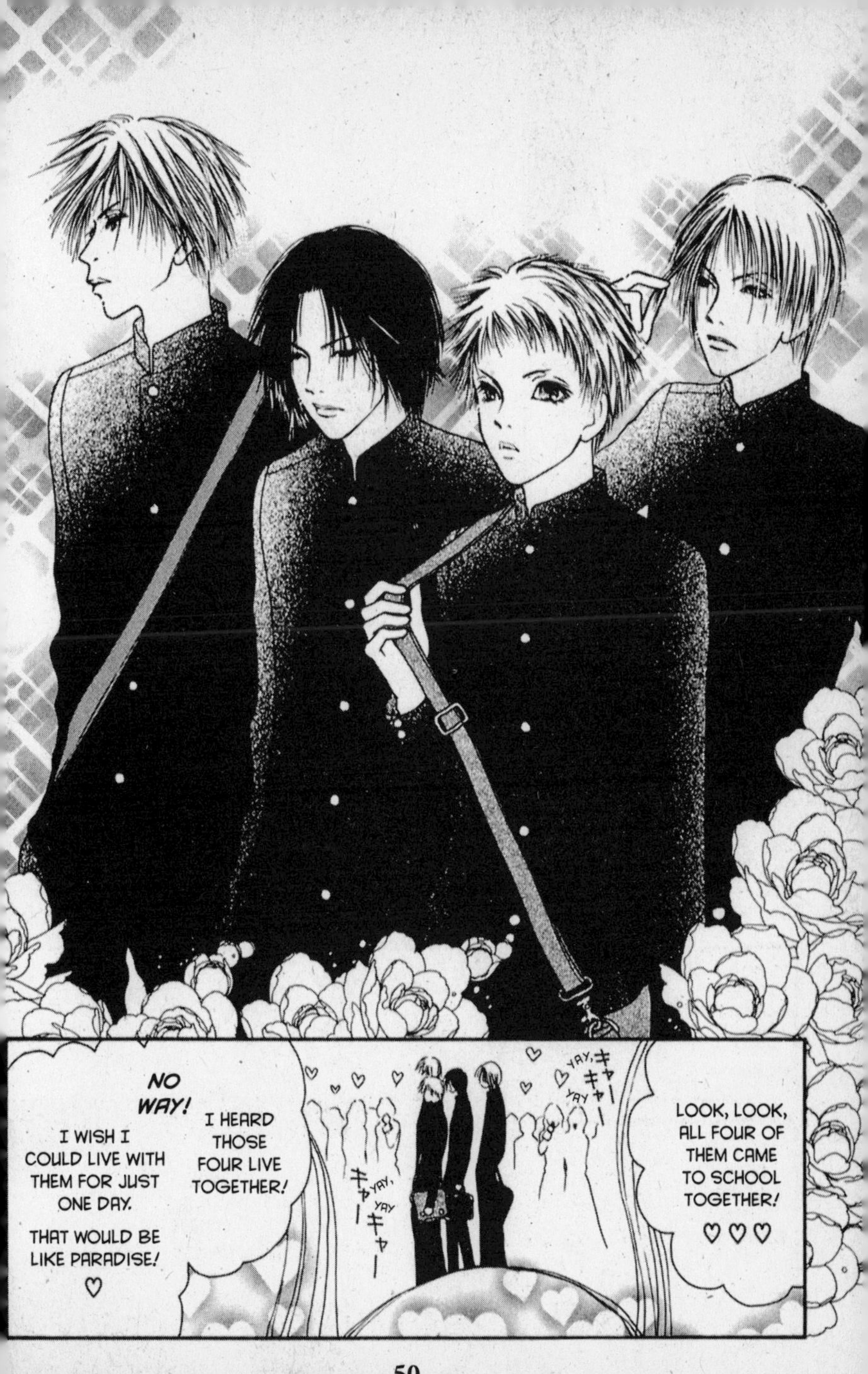
LOOK, LOOK, ALL FOUR OF THEM CAME TO SCHOOL TOGETHER! ♡♡♡
YAY, キャー YAY キャー
YAY, キャー YAY キャー
I HEARD THOSE FOUR LIVE TOGETHER!
NO WAY!
I WISH I COULD LIVE WITH THEM FOR JUST ONE DAY.
THAT WOULD BE LIKE PARADISE! ♡

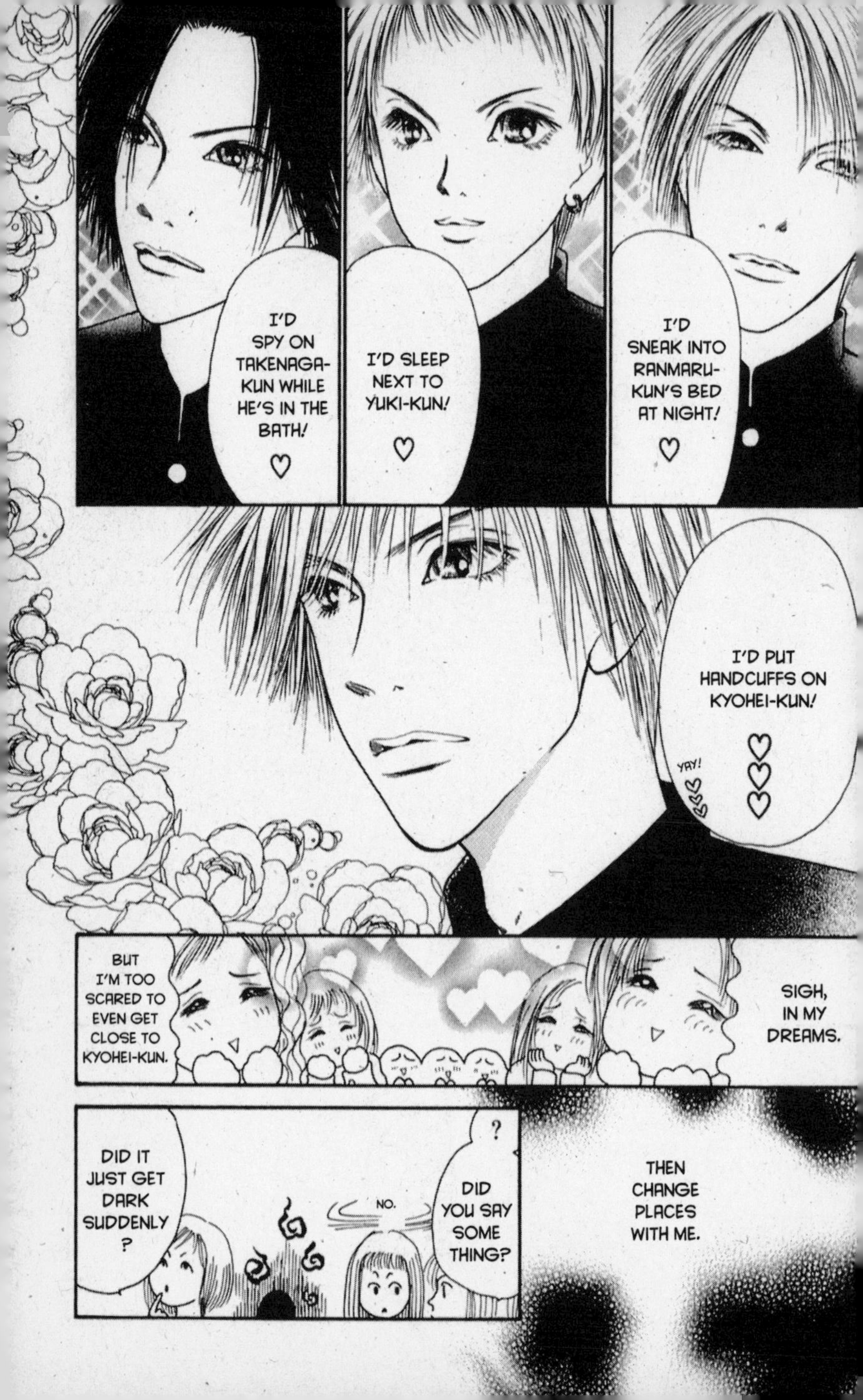
I'D SNEAK INTO RANMARU-KUN'S BED AT NIGHT! ♡
I'D SLEEP NEXT TO YUKI-KUN! ♡
I'D SPY ON TAKENAGA-KUN WHILE HE'S IN THE BATH! ♡
I'D PUT HANDCUFFS ON KYOHEI-KUN! ♡♡♡
YAY! ♡♡♡
SIGH, IN MY DREAMS.
BUT I'M TOO SCARED TO EVEN GET CLOSE TO KYOHEI-KUN.
THEN CHANGE PLACES WITH ME.
? DID YOU SAY SOME THING?
NO.
DID IT JUST GET DARK SUDDENLY?

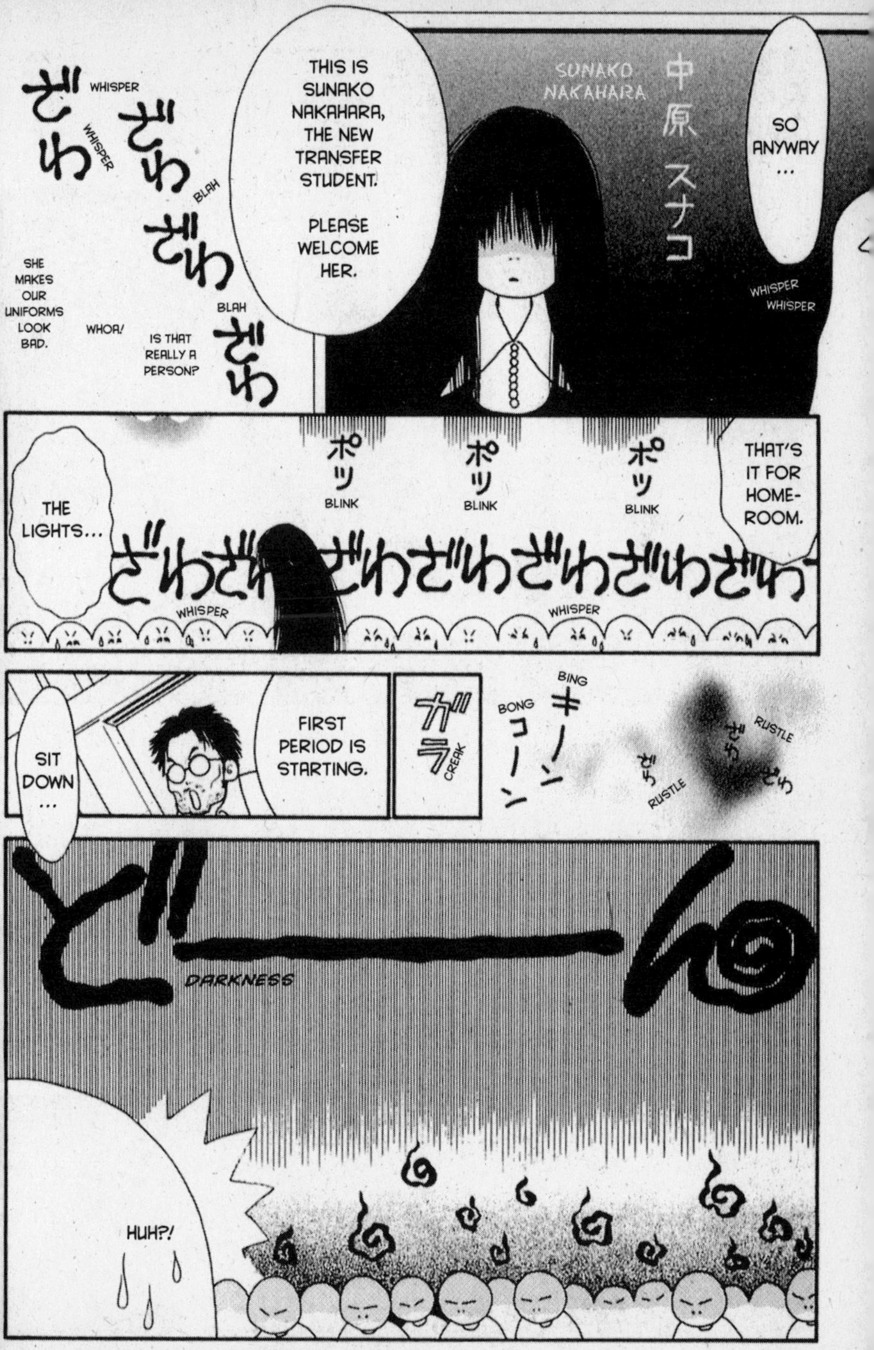
SO ANYWAY...
中原スナコ
SUNAKO NAKAHARA
WHISPER WHISPER
THIS IS SUNAKO NAKAHARA, THE NEW TRANSFER STUDENT.
PLEASE WELCOME HER.
ざわ BLAH
IS THAT REALLY A PERSON?
ざわ BLAH
ざわ WHISPER
ざわ WHISPER
WHOA!
SHE MAKES OUR UNIFORMS LOOK BAD.
THAT'S IT FOR HOMEROOM.
ポツ BLINK
ポツ BLINK
ポツ BLINK
ざわざわざわざわざわざわざわ
WHISPER
WHISPER
THE LIGHTS...
キーンコーン
BING
BONG
ざわ RUSTLE
ざわ RUSTLE
ガラ
CREAK
FIRST PERIOD IS STARTING.
SIT DOWN...
どーーん
DARKNESS
HUH?!

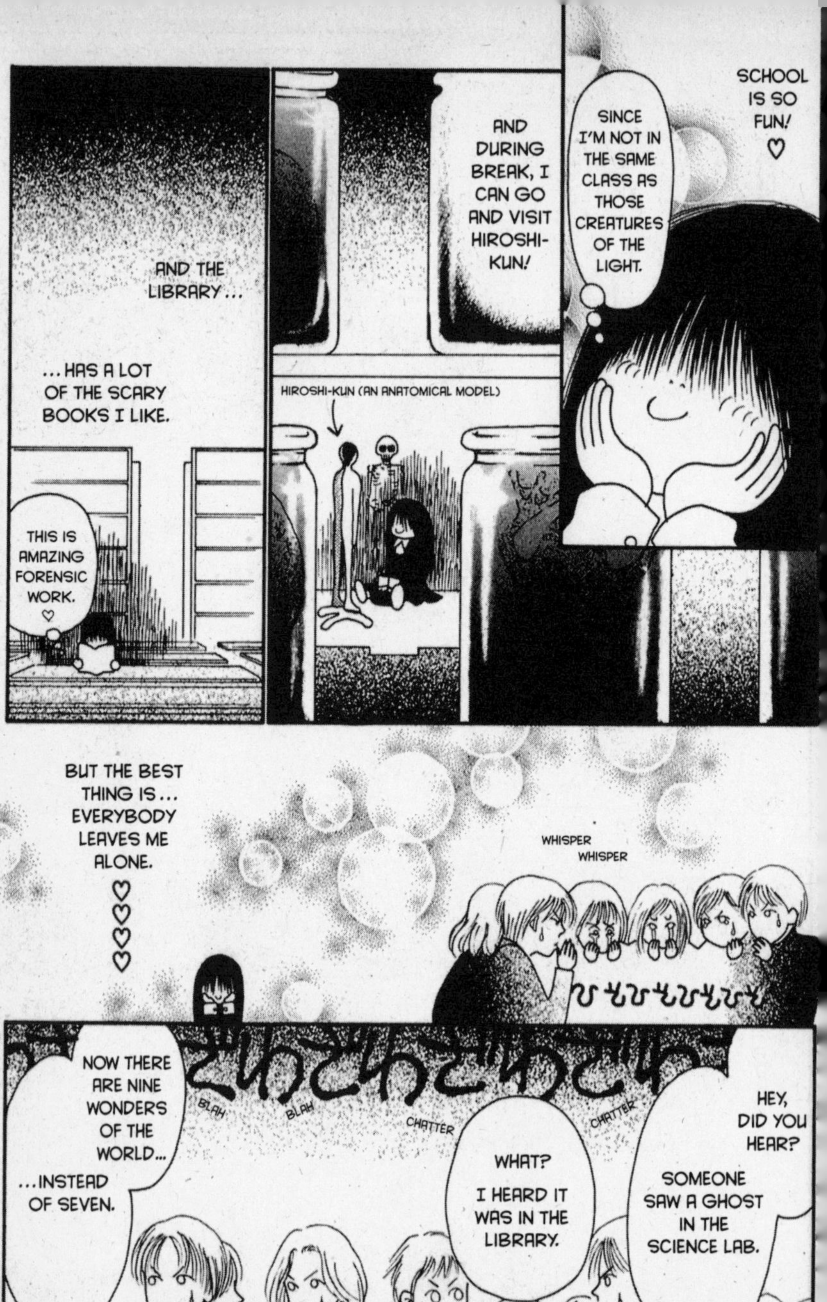
SCHOOL IS SO FUN! ♡
SINCE I'M NOT IN THE SAME CLASS AS THOSE CREATURES OF THE LIGHT.
AND DURING BREAK, I CAN GO AND VISIT HIROSHI-KUN!
HIROSHI-KUN (AN ANATOMICAL MODEL)
AND THE LIBRARY...
...HAS A LOT OF THE SCARY BOOKS I LIKE.
THIS IS AMAZING FORENSIC WORK. ♡
BUT THE BEST THING IS... EVERYBODY LEAVES ME ALONE. ♡♡♡♡
WHISPER WHISPER
ひそひそひそひそ
HEY, DID YOU HEAR?
SOMEONE SAW A GHOST IN THE SCIENCE LAB.
WHAT? I HEARD IT WAS IN THE LIBRARY.
ざわざわざわざわ
CHATTER
CHATTER
BLAH
BLAH
NOW THERE ARE NINE WONDERS OF THE WORLD...
...INSTEAD OF SEVEN.

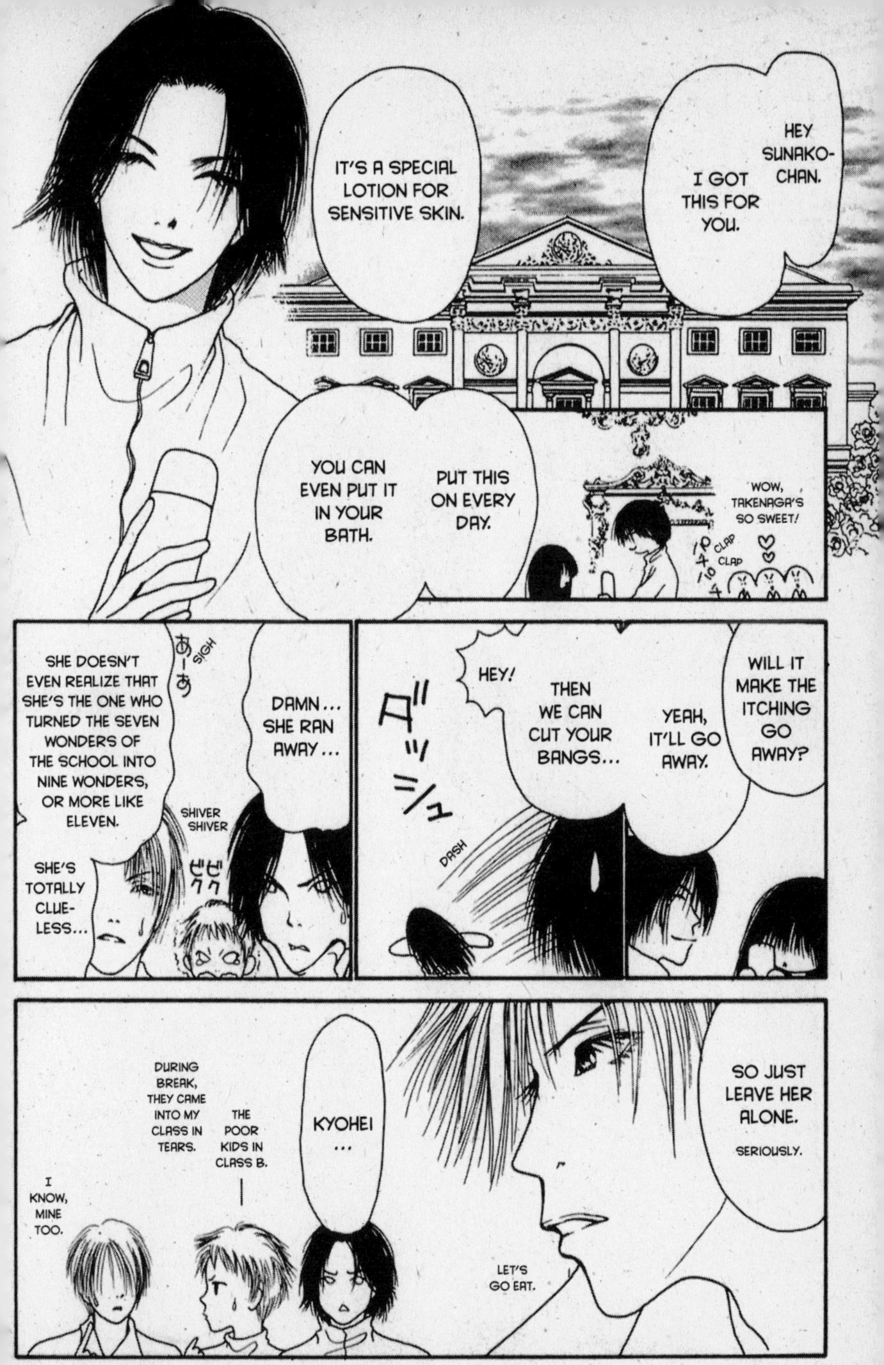
HEY SUNAKO-CHAN.
I GOT THIS FOR YOU.
IT'S A SPECIAL LOTION FOR SENSITIVE SKIN.
PUT THIS ON EVERY DAY.
YOU CAN EVEN PUT IT IN YOUR BATH.
WOW, TAKENAGA'S SO SWEET!
CLAP
CLAP
WILL IT MAKE THE ITCHING GO AWAY?
YEAH, IT'LL GO AWAY.
THEN WE CAN CUT YOUR BANGS...
HEY!
DASH
DAMN... SHE RAN AWAY...
SIGH
SHE DOESN'T EVEN REALIZE THAT SHE'S THE ONE WHO TURNED THE SEVEN WONDERS OF THE SCHOOL INTO NINE WONDERS, OR MORE LIKE ELEVEN.
SHIVER SHIVER
SHE'S TOTALLY CLUE-LESS...
SO JUST LEAVE HER ALONE.
SERIOUSLY.
LET'S GO EAT.
KYOHEI ...
THE POOR KIDS IN CLASS B.
DURING BREAK, THEY CAME INTO MY CLASS IN TEARS.
I KNOW, MINE TOO.

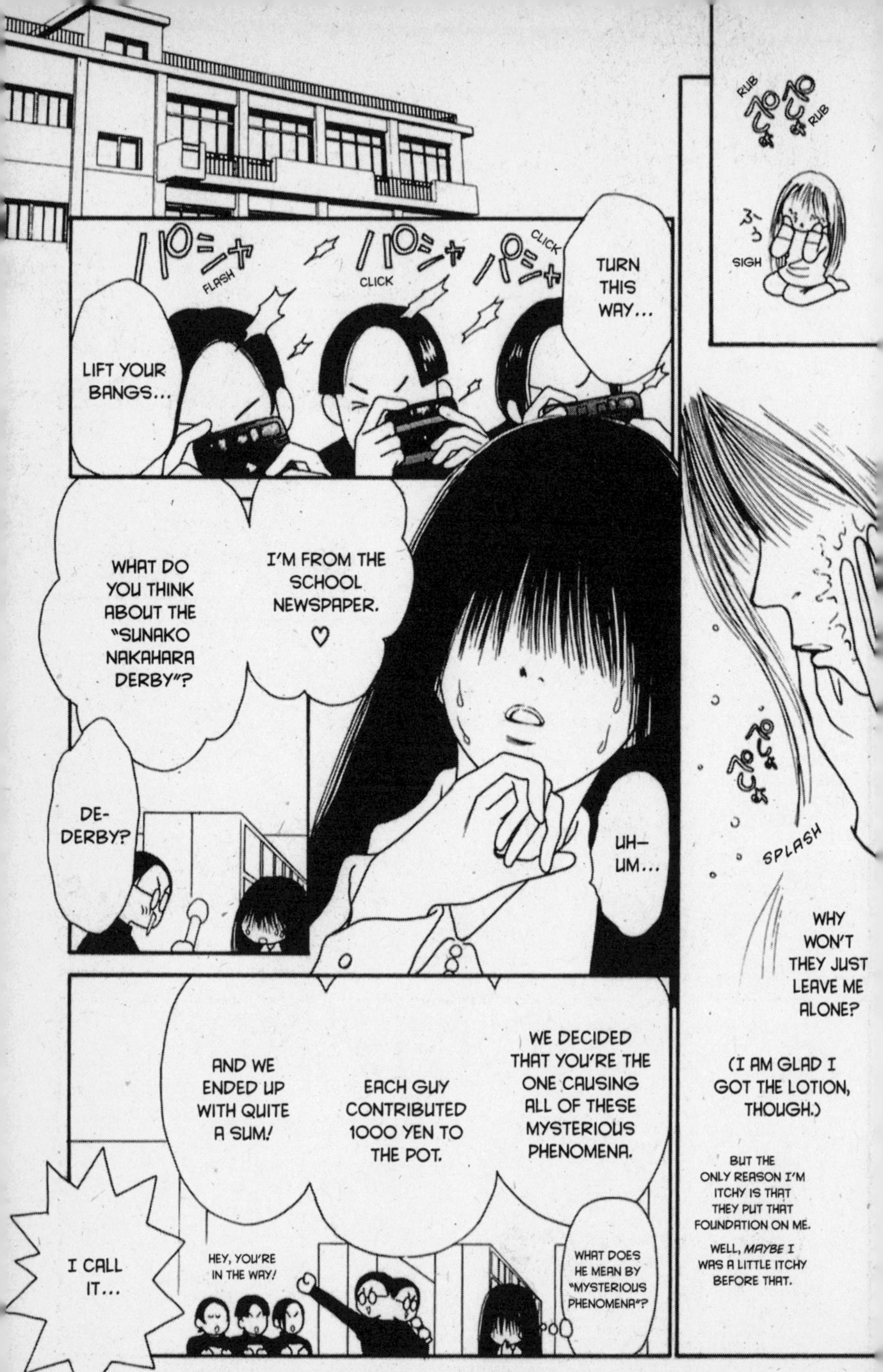
RUB RUB
SIGH
SPLASH
WHY WON'T THEY JUST LEAVE ME ALONE?
(I AM GLAD I GOT THE LOTION, THOUGH.)
BUT THE ONLY REASON I'M ITCHY IS THAT THEY PUT THAT FOUNDATION ON ME.
WELL, *MAYBE* I WAS A LITTLE ITCHY BEFORE THAT.
CLICK
CLICK
FLASH
TURN THIS WAY...
LIFT YOUR BANGS...
UH— UM...
I'M FROM THE SCHOOL NEWSPAPER. ♡
WHAT DO YOU THINK ABOUT THE "SUNAKO NAKAHARA DERBY"?
DE- DERBY?
WE DECIDED THAT YOU'RE THE ONE CAUSING ALL OF THESE MYSTERIOUS PHENOMENA.
EACH GUY CONTRIBUTED 1000 YEN TO THE POT.
AND WE ENDED UP WITH QUITE A SUM!
WHAT DOES HE MEAN BY "MYSTERIOUS PHENOMENA"?
HEY, YOU'RE IN THE WAY!
I CALL IT...

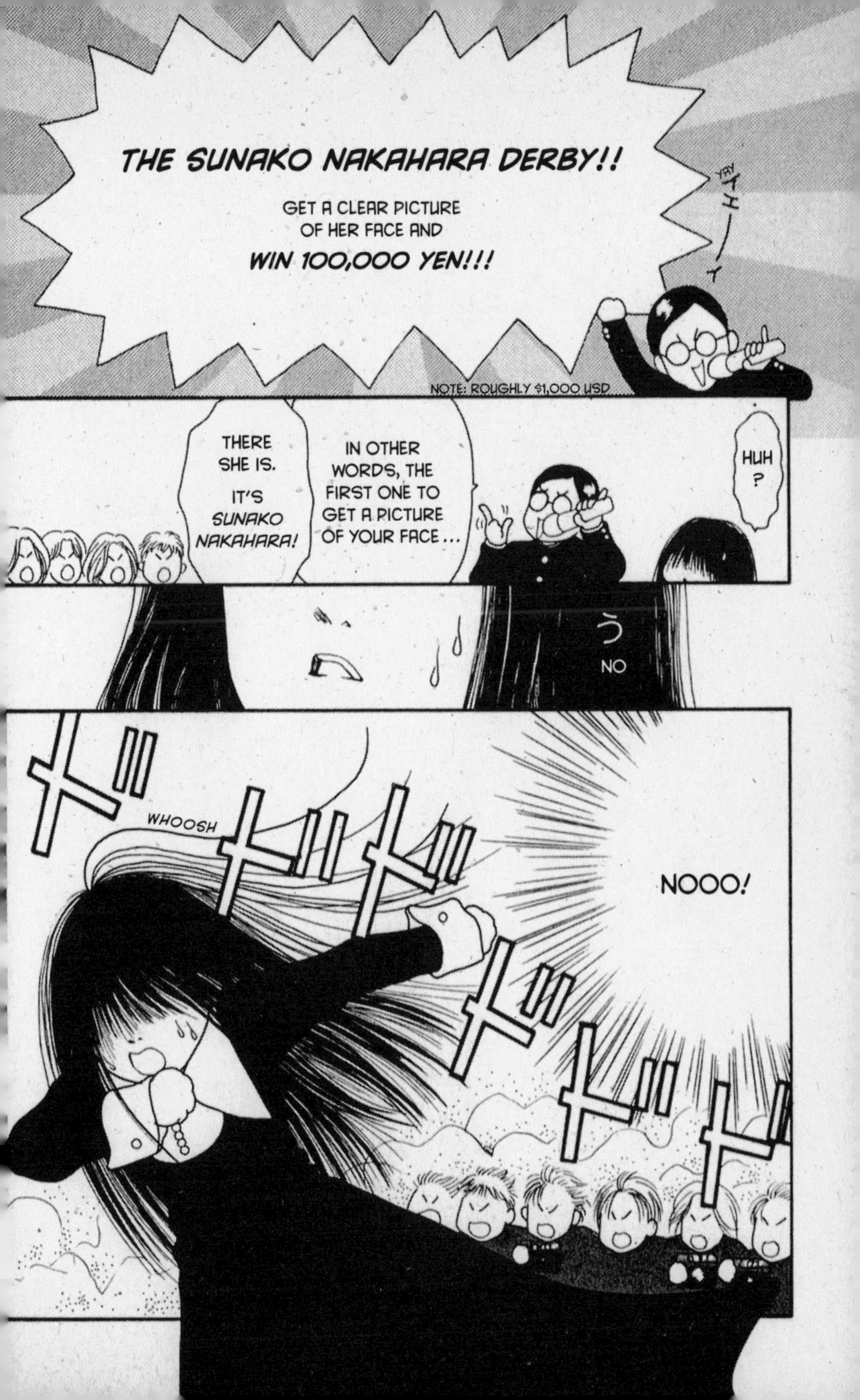
THE SUNAKO NAKAHARA DERBY!!
GET A CLEAR PICTURE OF HER FACE AND
WIN 100,000 YEN!!!
YAY
NOTE: ROUGHLY $1,000 USD
HUH?
IN OTHER WORDS, THE FIRST ONE TO GET A PICTURE OF YOUR FACE...
THERE SHE IS.
IT'S SUNAKO NAKAHARA!
う
NO
NOOO!
WHOOSH

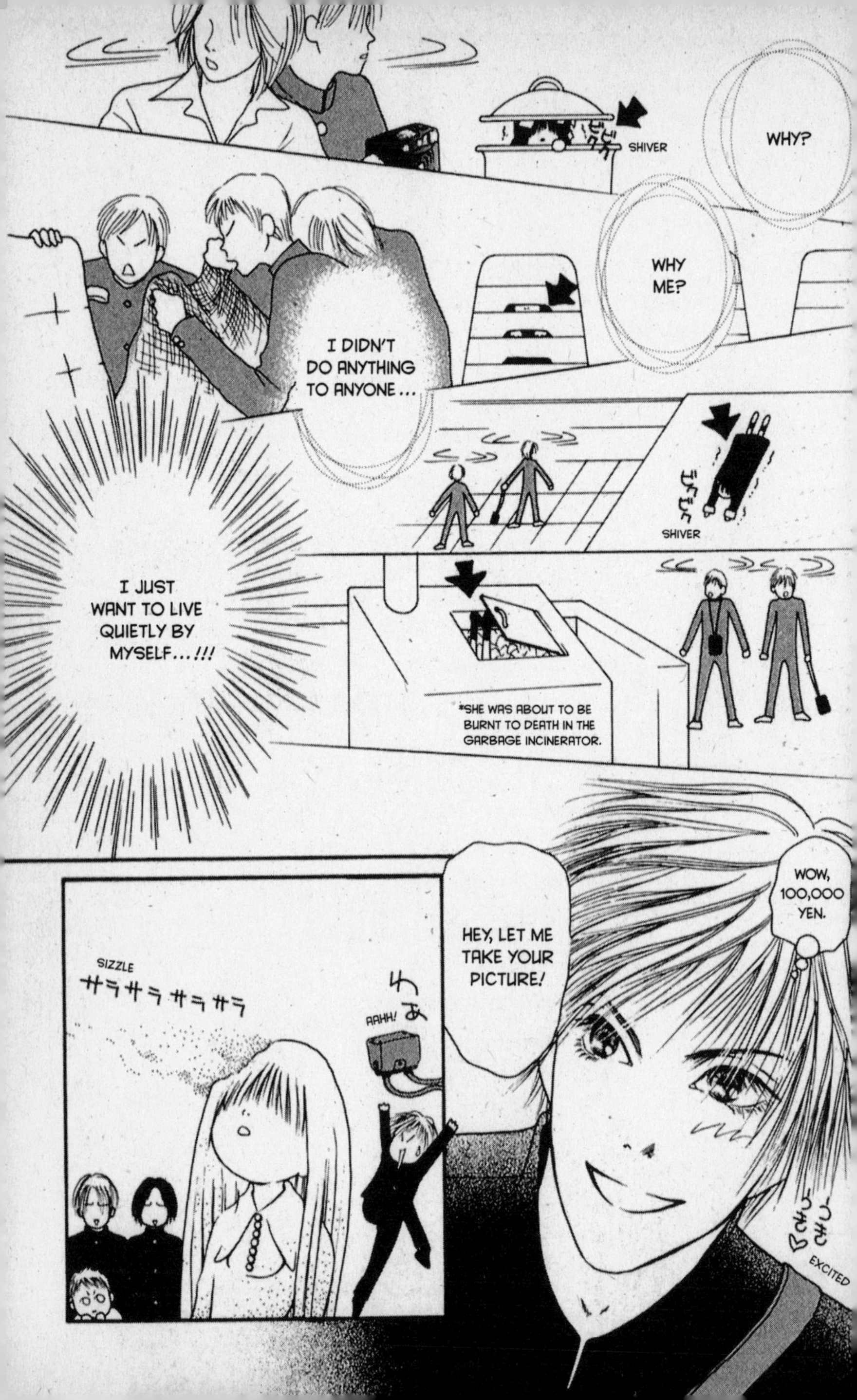
SHIVER
WHY?
WHY ME?
I DIDN'T DO ANYTHING TO ANYONE...
SHIVER
*SHE WAS ABOUT TO BE BURNT TO DEATH IN THE GARBAGE INCINERATOR.
I JUST WANT TO LIVE QUIETLY BY MYSELF...!!!
WOW, 100,000 YEN.
HEY, LET ME TAKE YOUR PICTURE!
EXCITED
SIZZLE
サラサラサラサラ
AAHH!

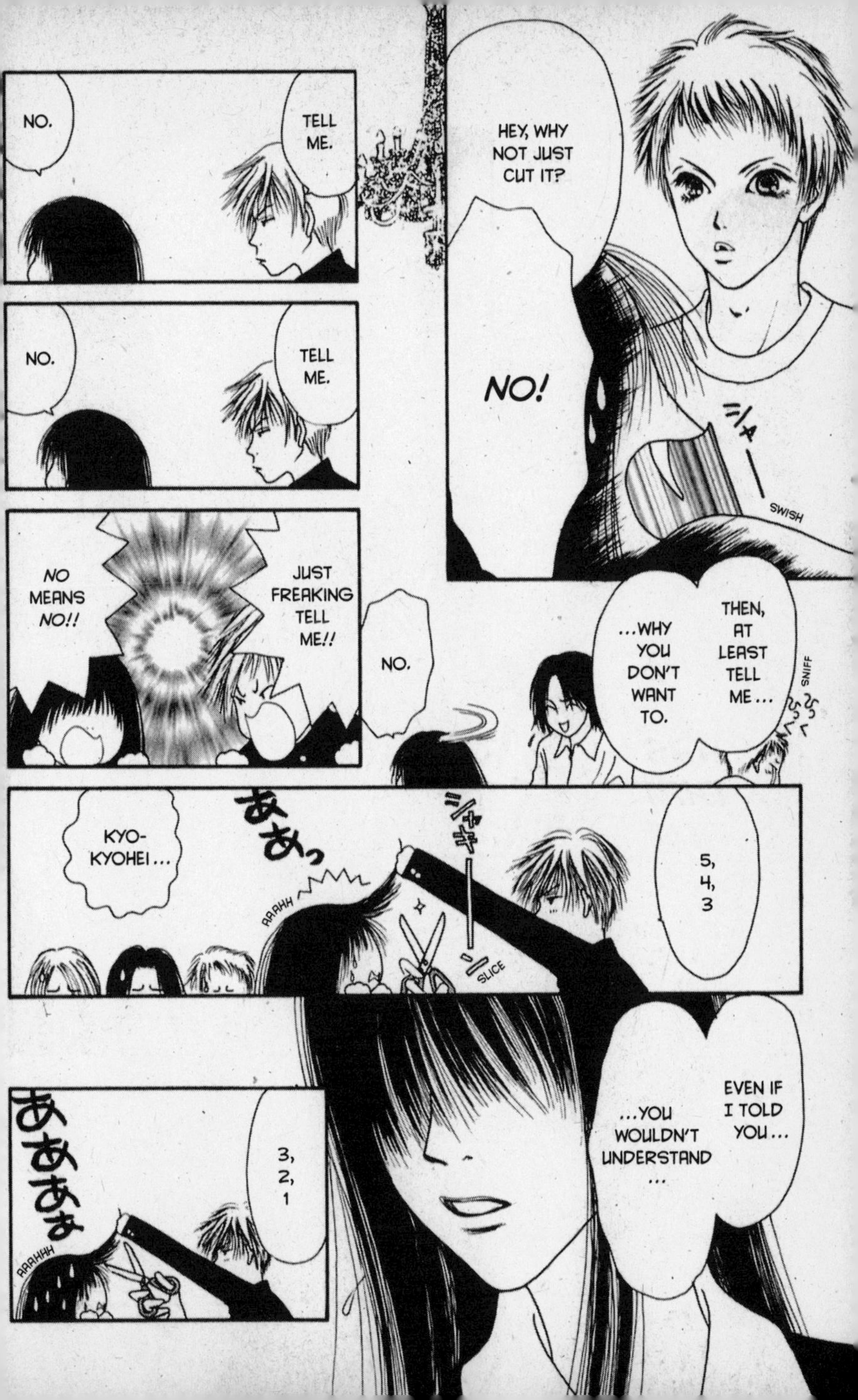

HEY, WHY NOT JUST CUT IT?
NO!
SWISH
TELL ME.
NO.
TELL ME.
NO.
JUST FREAKING TELL ME!!
NO MEANS NO!!
THEN, AT LEAST TELL ME...
...WHY YOU DON'T WANT TO.
SNIFF
NO.
5, 4, 3
SLICE
AAAHH
KYO-KYOHEI...
EVEN IF I TOLD YOU...
...YOU WOULDN'T UNDERSTAND...
3, 2, 1
AAAHHH

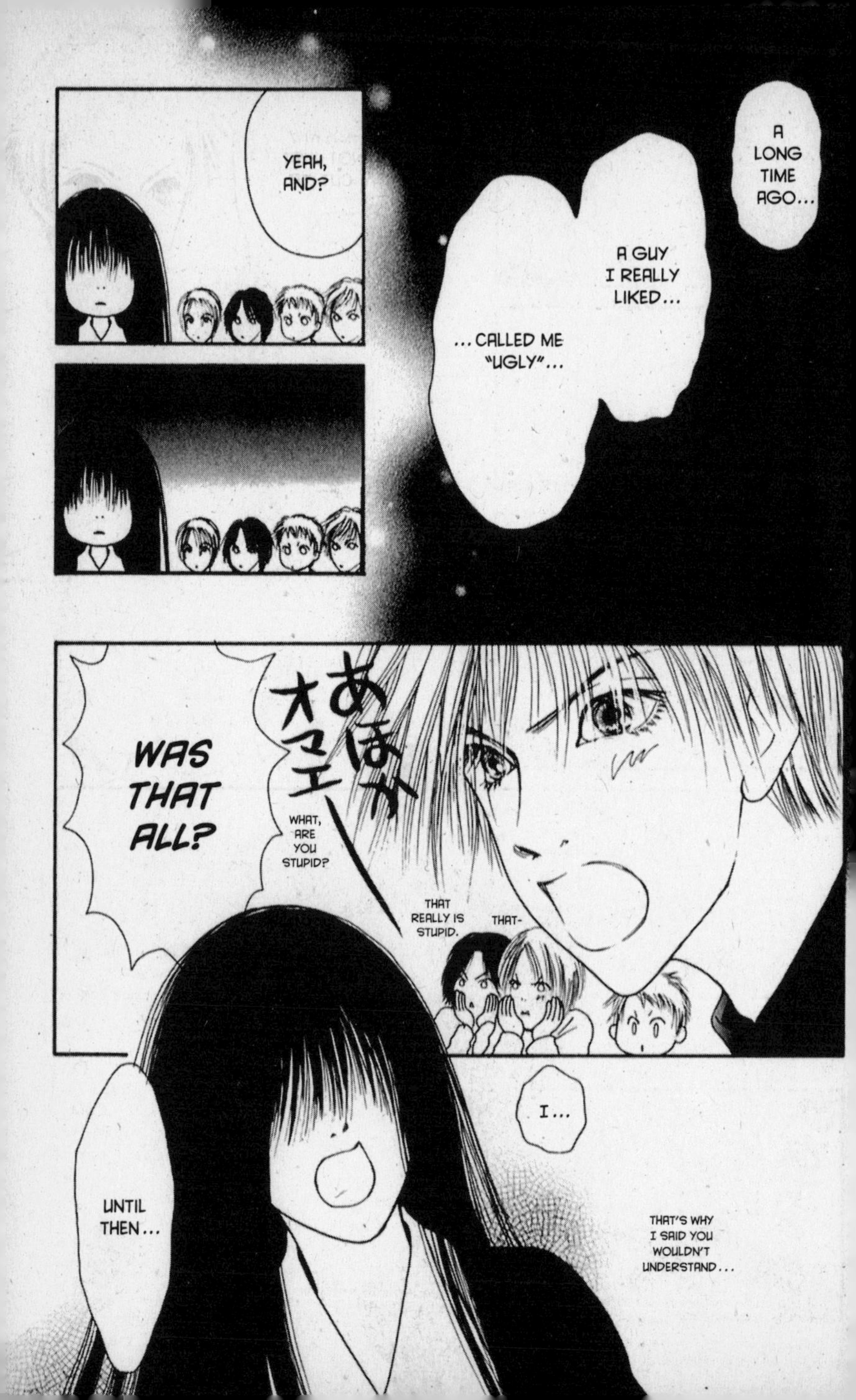
A LONG TIME AGO...
A GUY I REALLY LIKED...
...CALLED ME "UGLY"...
YEAH, AND?
あほか オマエ
WAS THAT ALL?
WHAT, ARE YOU STUPID?
THAT-
THAT REALLY IS STUPID.
I...
THAT'S WHY I SAID YOU WOULDN'T UNDERSTAND...
UNTIL THEN...

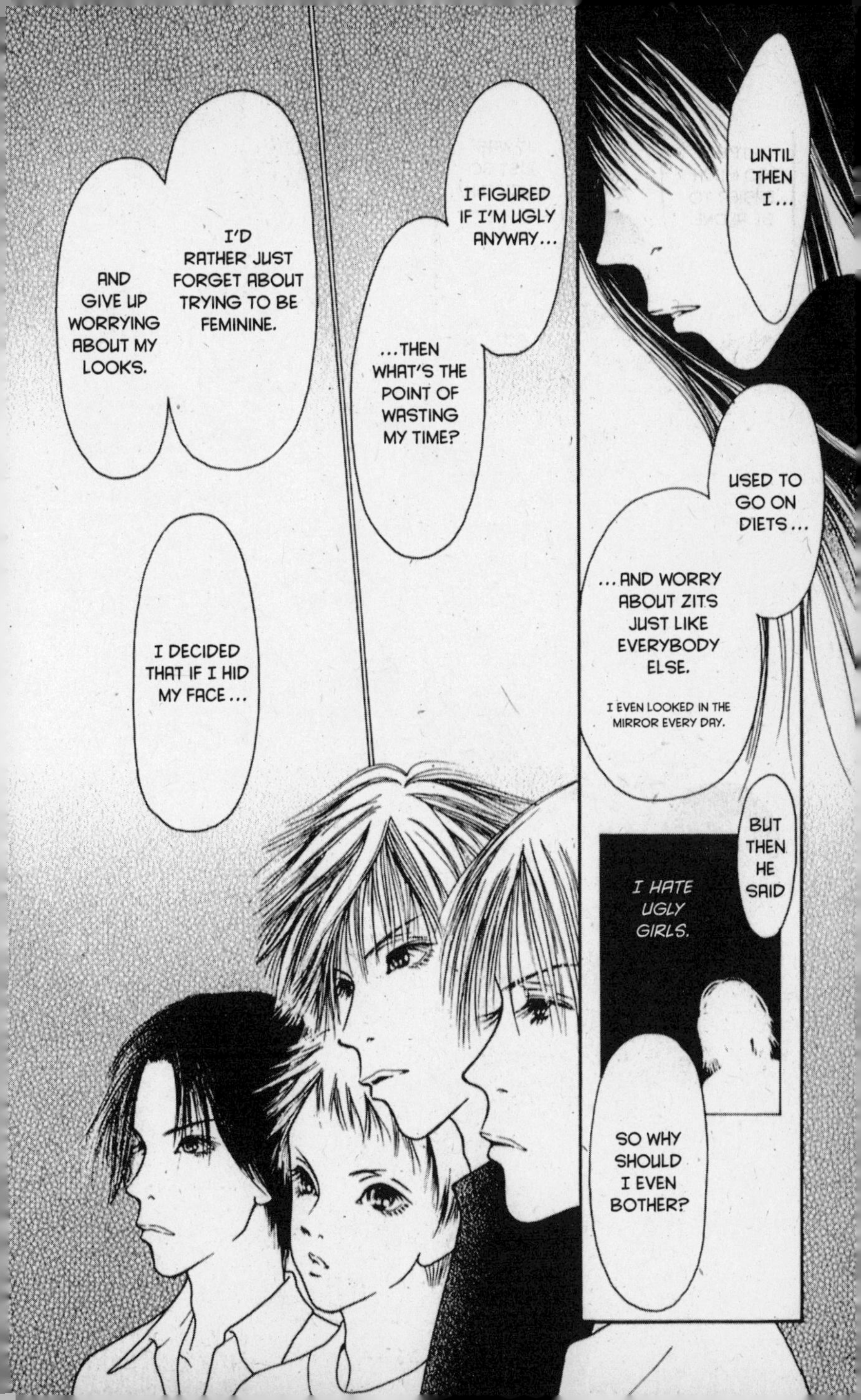
UNTIL THEN I...
USED TO GO ON DIETS...
...AND WORRY ABOUT ZITS JUST LIKE EVERYBODY ELSE.
I EVEN LOOKED IN THE MIRROR EVERY DAY.
BUT THEN HE SAID
I HATE UGLY GIRLS.
SO WHY SHOULD I EVEN BOTHER?
I FIGURED IF I'M UGLY ANYWAY...
...THEN WHAT'S THE POINT OF WASTING MY TIME?
I'D RATHER JUST FORGET ABOUT TRYING TO BE FEMININE.
AND GIVE UP WORRYING ABOUT MY LOOKS.
I DECIDED THAT IF I HID MY FACE...

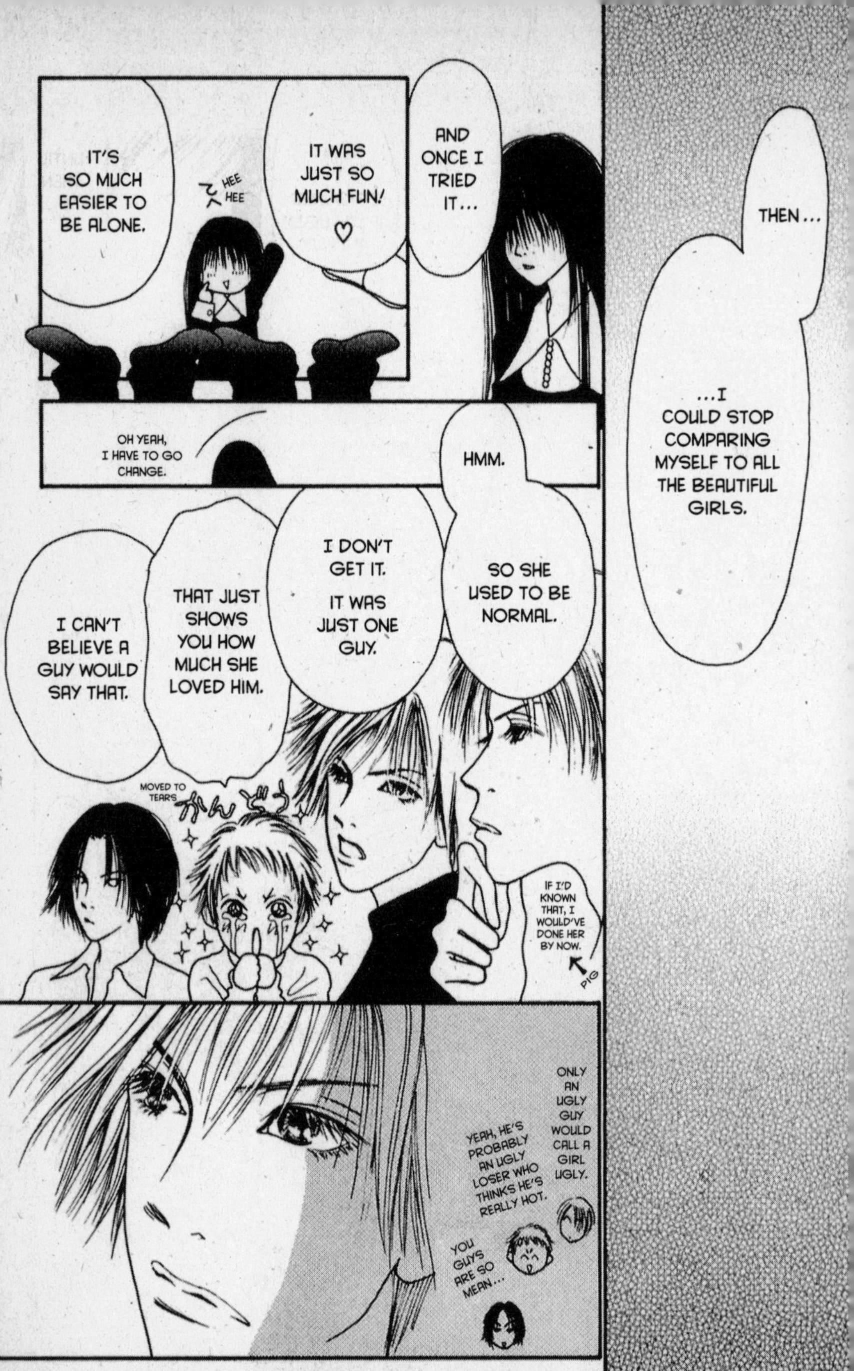
THEN...
...I COULD STOP COMPARING MYSELF TO ALL THE BEAUTIFUL GIRLS.
AND ONCE I TRIED IT...
IT WAS JUST SO MUCH FUN! ♡
HEE HEE
IT'S SO MUCH EASIER TO BE ALONE.
HMM.
OH YEAH, I HAVE TO GO CHANGE.
SO SHE USED TO BE NORMAL.
I DON'T GET IT.
IT WAS JUST ONE GUY.
THAT JUST SHOWS YOU HOW MUCH SHE LOVED HIM.
I CAN'T BELIEVE A GUY WOULD SAY THAT.
MOVED TO TEARS
IF I'D KNOWN THAT, I WOULD'VE DONE HER BY NOW.
PIG
ONLY AN UGLY GUY WOULD CALL A GIRL UGLY.
YEAH, HE'S PROBABLY AN UGLY LOSER WHO THINKS HE'S REALLY HOT.
YOU GUYS ARE SO MEAN...

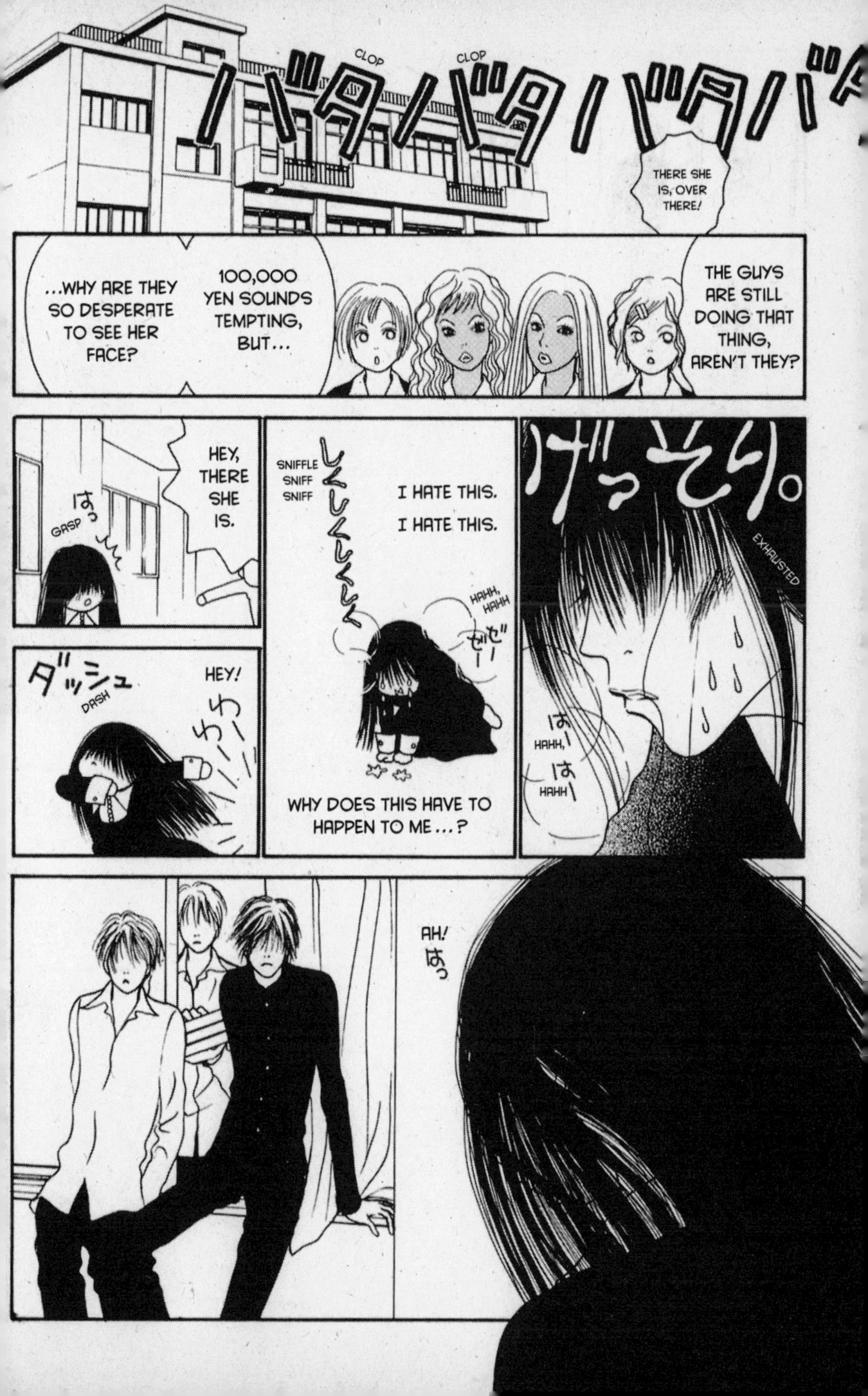
バタバタバタバ
CLOP CLOP
THERE SHE IS, OVER THERE!
THE GUYS ARE STILL DOING THAT THING, AREN'T THEY?
100,000 YEN SOUNDS TEMPTING, BUT...
...WHY ARE THEY SO DESPERATE TO SEE HER FACE?
げっそり。
EXHAUSTED
はぁ HAHH, はぁ HAHH
しくしくしくしく
SNIFFLE SNIFF SNIFF
I HATE THIS.
I HATE THIS.
HAHH, HAHH
ぜぇぜぇ
WHY DOES THIS HAVE TO HAPPEN TO ME...?
HEY, THERE SHE IS.
はっ
GASP
HEY!
ダッシュ
DASH
わわ
AH!
はっ

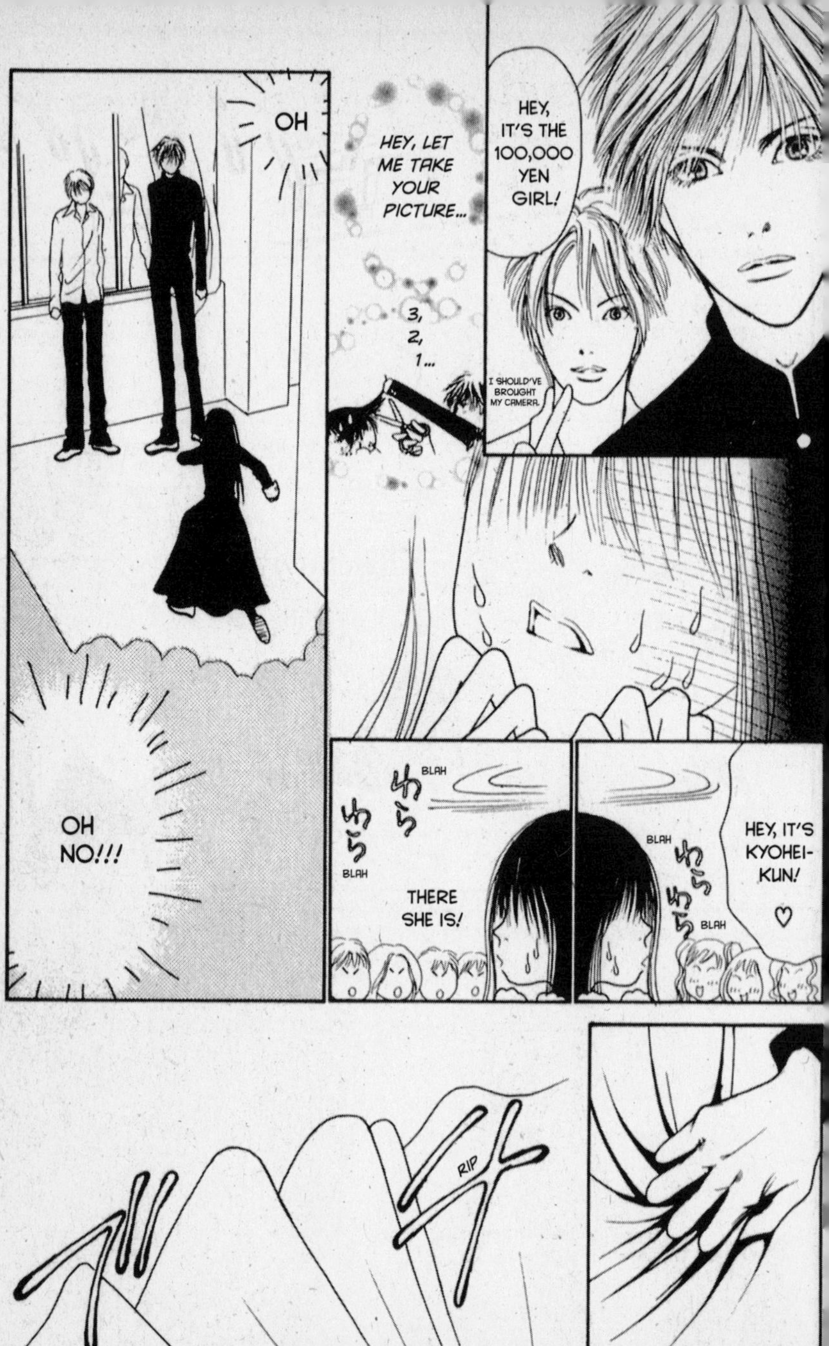
HEY, IT'S THE 100,000 YEN GIRL!
I SHOULD'VE BROUGHT MY CAMERA.
HEY, LET ME TAKE YOUR PICTURE...
3, 2, 1...
HEY, IT'S KYOHEI-KUN! ♡
わらわら
BLAH BLAH
わらわら
BLAH BLAH
THERE SHE IS!
OH
OH NO!!!
RIP

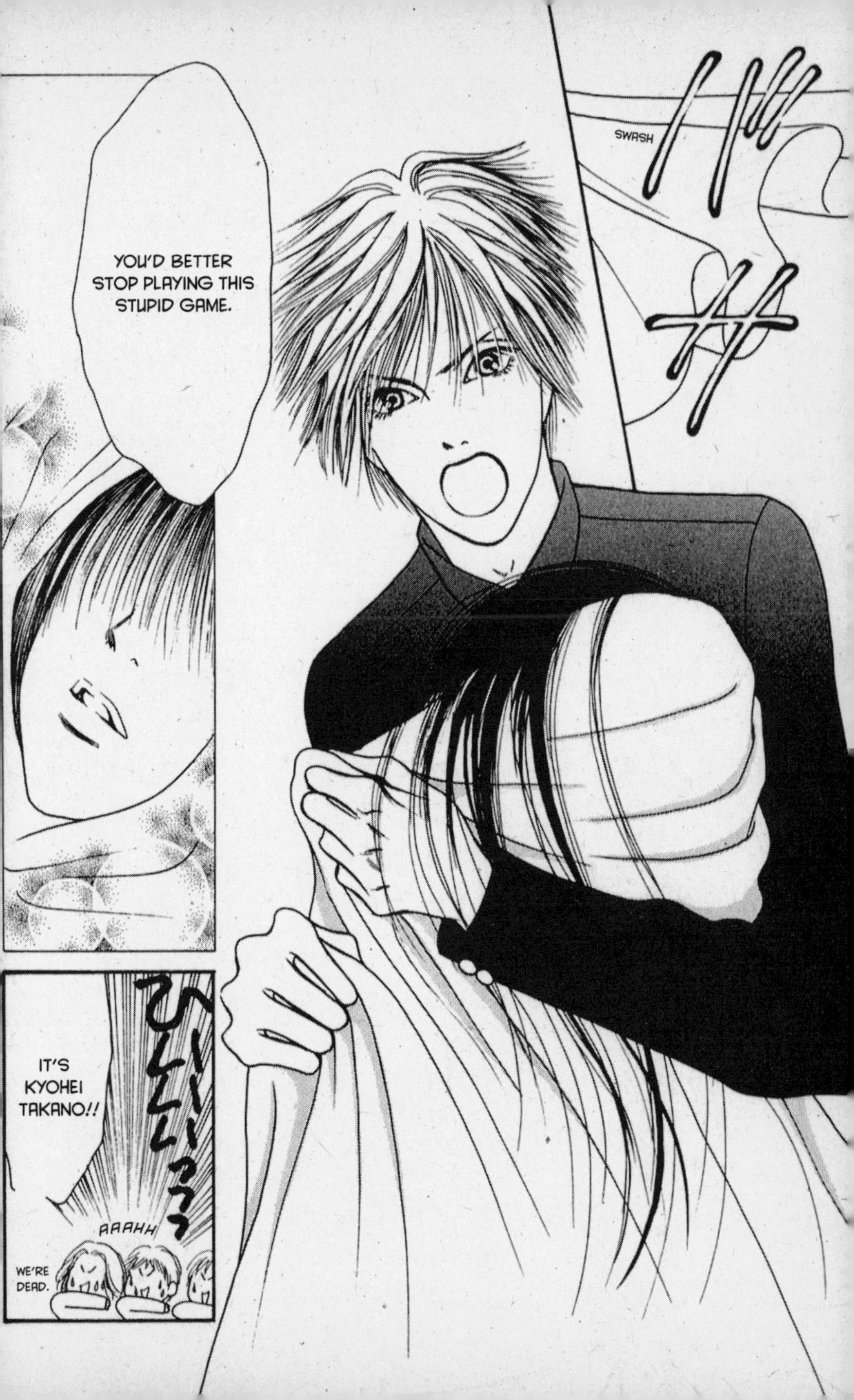
SWASH
YOU'D BETTER STOP PLAYING THIS STUPID GAME.
IT'S KYOHEI TAKANO!!
AAAHH
WE'RE DEAD.

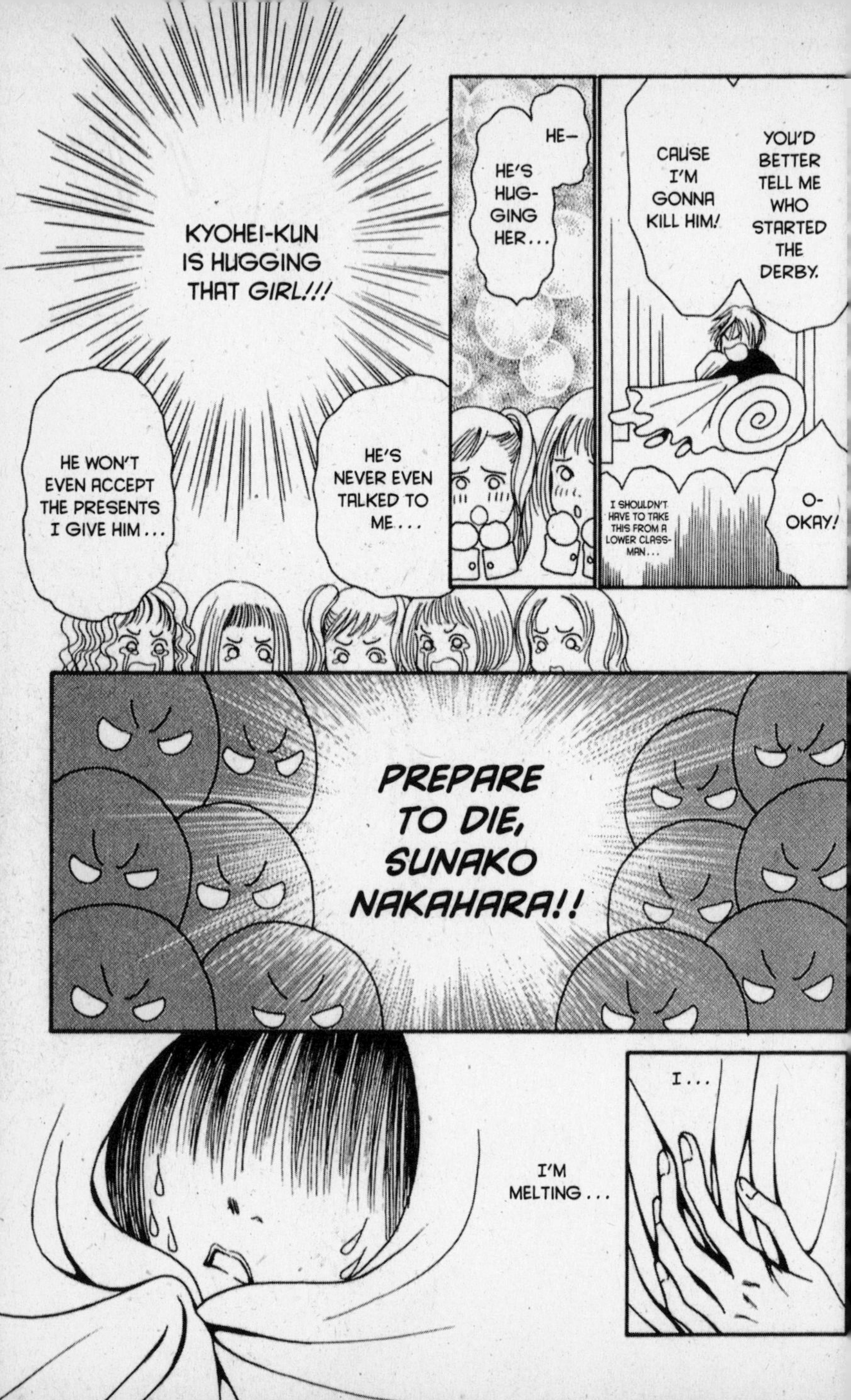
YOU'D BETTER TELL ME WHO STARTED THE DERBY.
CAUSE I'M GONNA KILL HIM!
O-OKAY!
I SHOULDN'T HAVE TO TAKE THIS FROM A LOWER CLASS-MAN...
HE—
HE'S HUG-GING HER...
KYOHEI-KUN IS HUGGING THAT GIRL!!!
HE'S NEVER EVEN TALKED TO ME...
HE WON'T EVEN ACCEPT THE PRESENTS I GIVE HIM...
PREPARE TO DIE, SUNAKO NAKAHARA!!
I...
I'M MELTING...

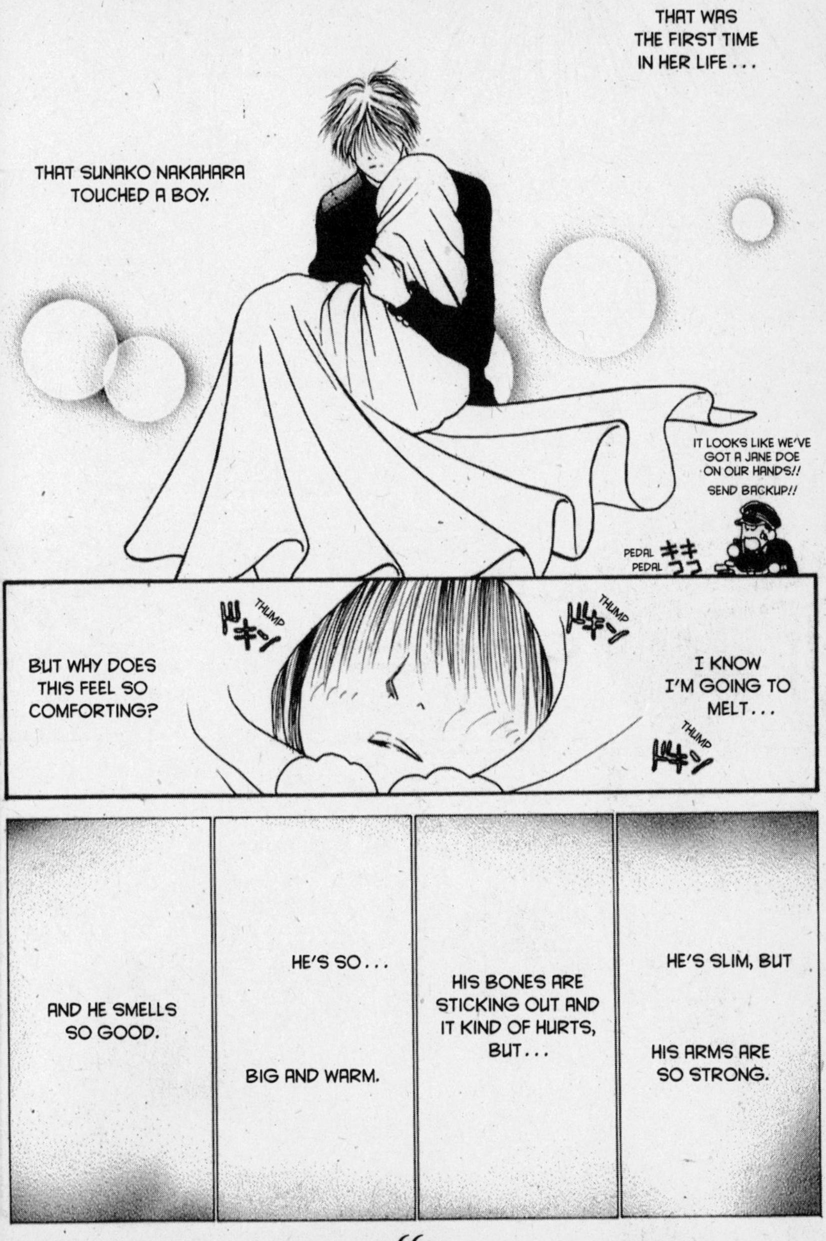
THAT WAS THE FIRST TIME IN HER LIFE . . .
THAT SUNAKO NAKAHARA TOUCHED A BOY.
IT LOOKS LIKE WE'VE GOT A JANE DOE ON OUR HANDS!!
SEND BACKUP!!
PEDAL PEDAL
THUMP
I KNOW I'M GOING TO MELT . . .
THUMP
THUMP
BUT WHY DOES THIS FEEL SO COMFORTING?
HE'S SLIM, BUT
HIS ARMS ARE SO STRONG.
HIS BONES ARE STICKING OUT AND IT KIND OF HURTS, BUT . . .
HE'S SO . . .
BIG AND WARM.
AND HE SMELLS SO GOOD.

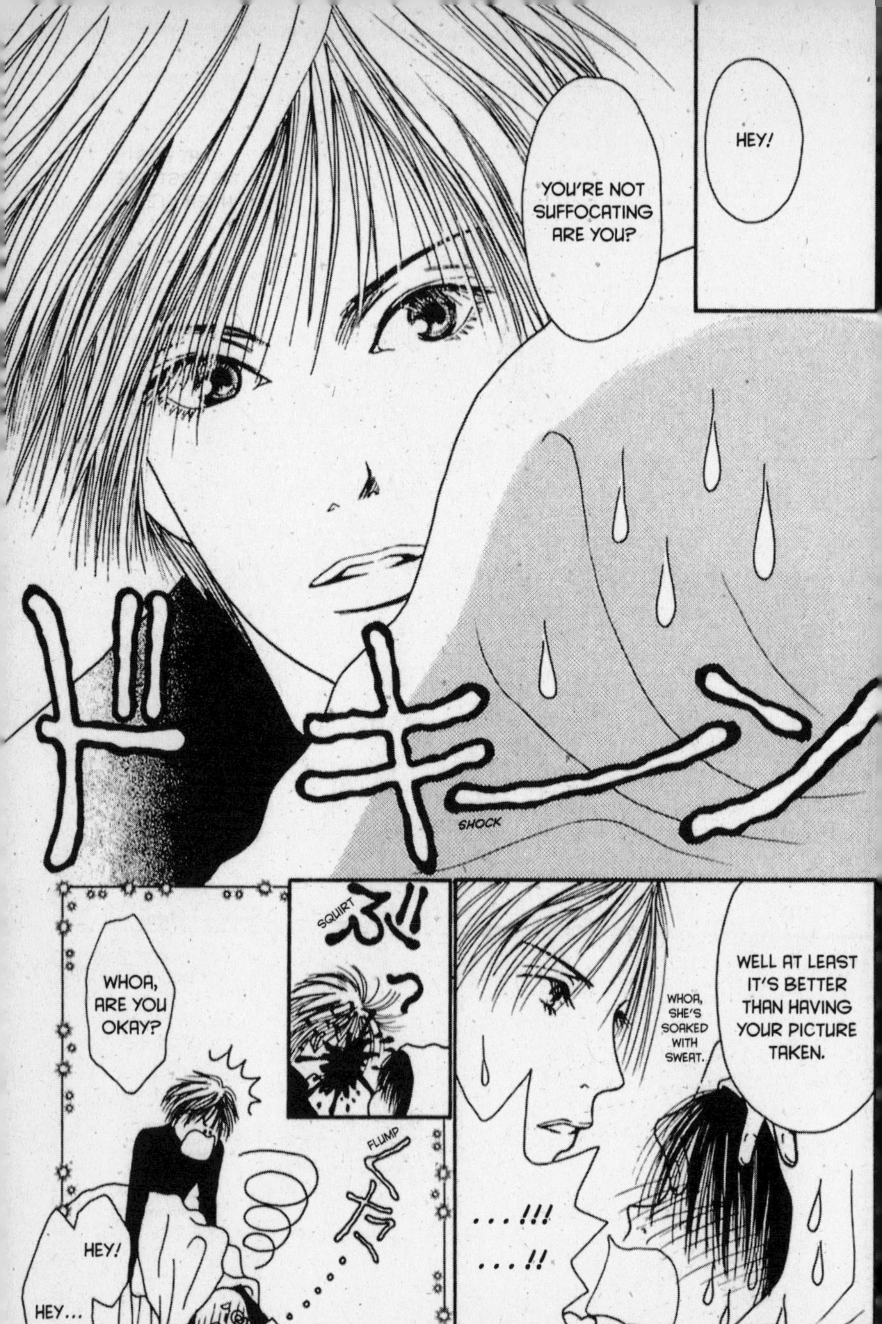
HEY!
YOU'RE NOT SUFFOCATING ARE YOU?
SHOCK
WELL AT LEAST IT'S BETTER THAN HAVING YOUR PICTURE TAKEN.
WHOA, SHE'S SOAKED WITH SWEAT.
...!!!
...!!
SQUIRT
WHOA, ARE YOU OKAY?
FLUMP
HEY!
HEY... !

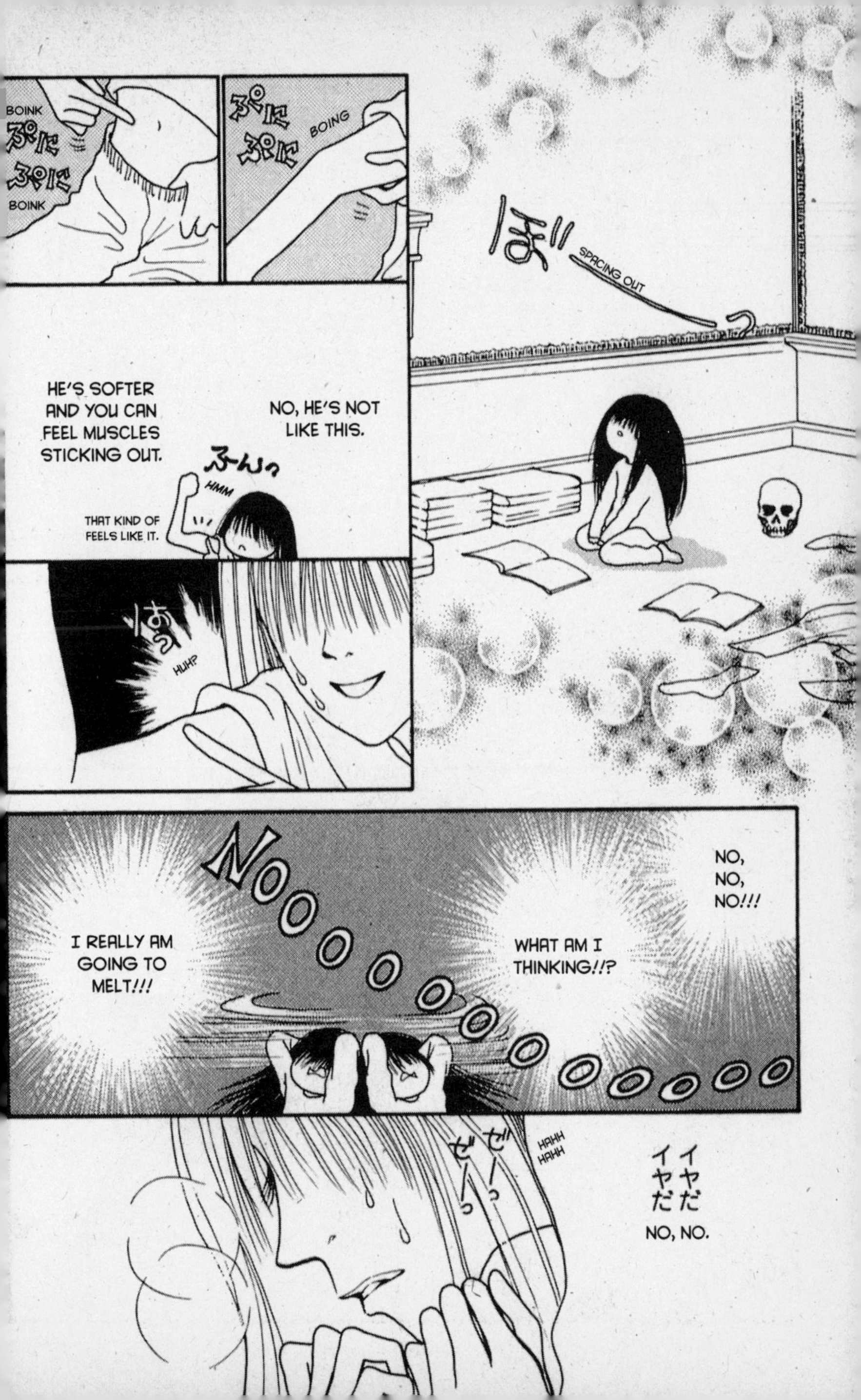
SPACING OUT
ぷに
ぷに
BOING
BOINK
ぷに
ぷに
BOINK
NO, HE'S NOT LIKE THIS.
HE'S SOFTER AND YOU CAN FEEL MUSCLES STICKING OUT.
ふんっ
HMM
THAT KIND OF FEELS LIKE IT.
HUH?
NO, NO, NO!!!
WHAT AM I THINKING!!?
NOOOOOOOOOOOOOOOO
I REALLY AM GOING TO MELT!!!
イヤだ イヤだ
NO, NO.
ぜーっ ぜーっ
HAHH HAHH

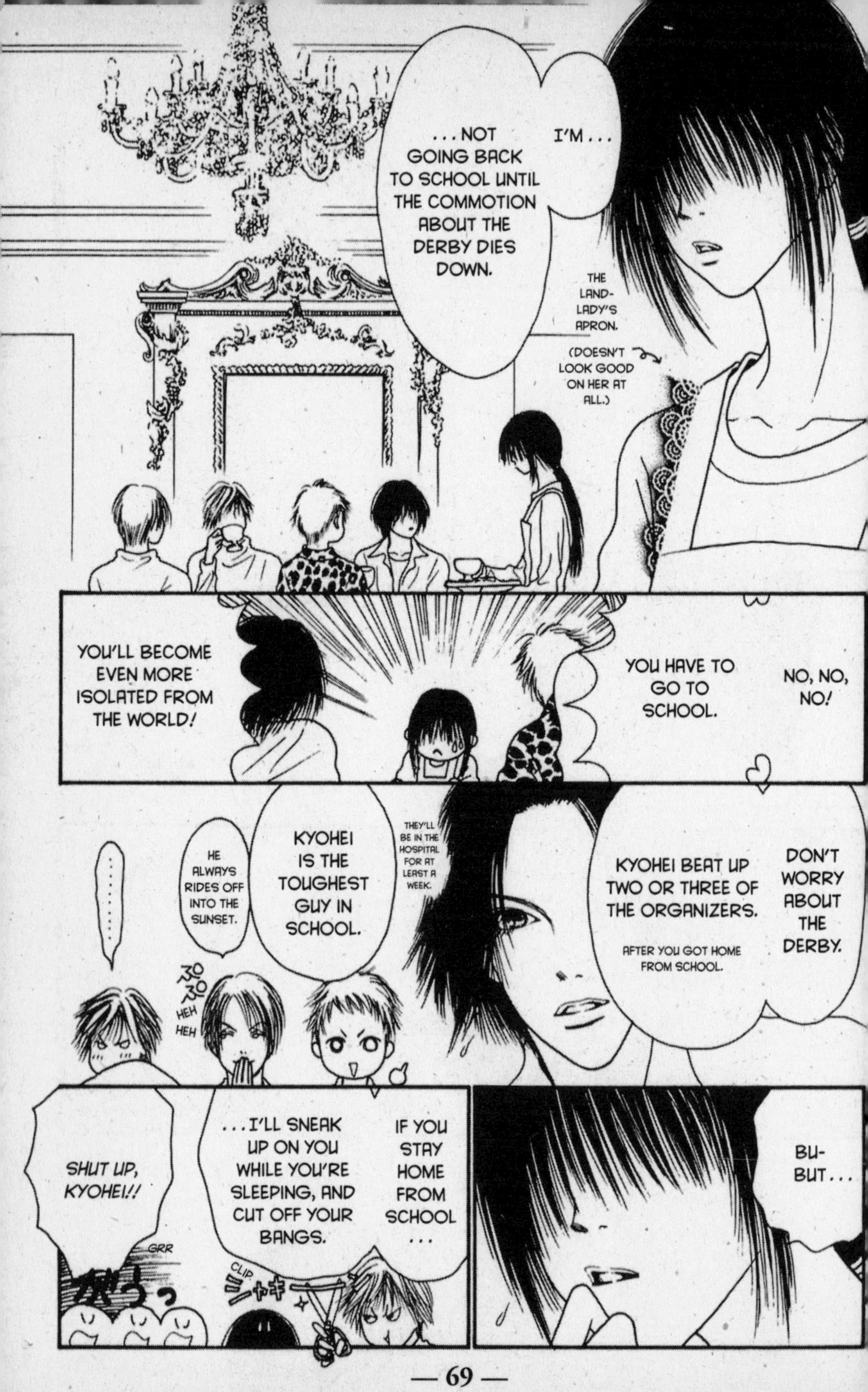
I'M . . .
. . . NOT GOING BACK TO SCHOOL UNTIL THE COMMOTION ABOUT THE DERBY DIES DOWN.
THE LAND-LADY'S APRON.
(DOESN'T LOOK GOOD ON HER AT ALL.)
NO, NO, NO!
YOU HAVE TO GO TO SCHOOL.
YOU'LL BECOME EVEN MORE ISOLATED FROM THE WORLD!
DON'T WORRY ABOUT THE DERBY.
KYOHEI BEAT UP TWO OR THREE OF THE ORGANIZERS.
AFTER YOU GOT HOME FROM SCHOOL.
THEY'LL BE IN THE HOSPITAL FOR AT LEAST A WEEK.
KYOHEI IS THE TOUGHEST GUY IN SCHOOL.
HE ALWAYS RIDES OFF INTO THE SUNSET.
HEH HEH
. . . .
BU-BUT . . .
IF YOU STAY HOME FROM SCHOOL . . .
. . . I'LL SNEAK UP ON YOU WHILE YOU'RE SLEEPING, AND CUT OFF YOUR BANGS.
CLIP
SHUT UP, KYOHEI!!
GRR

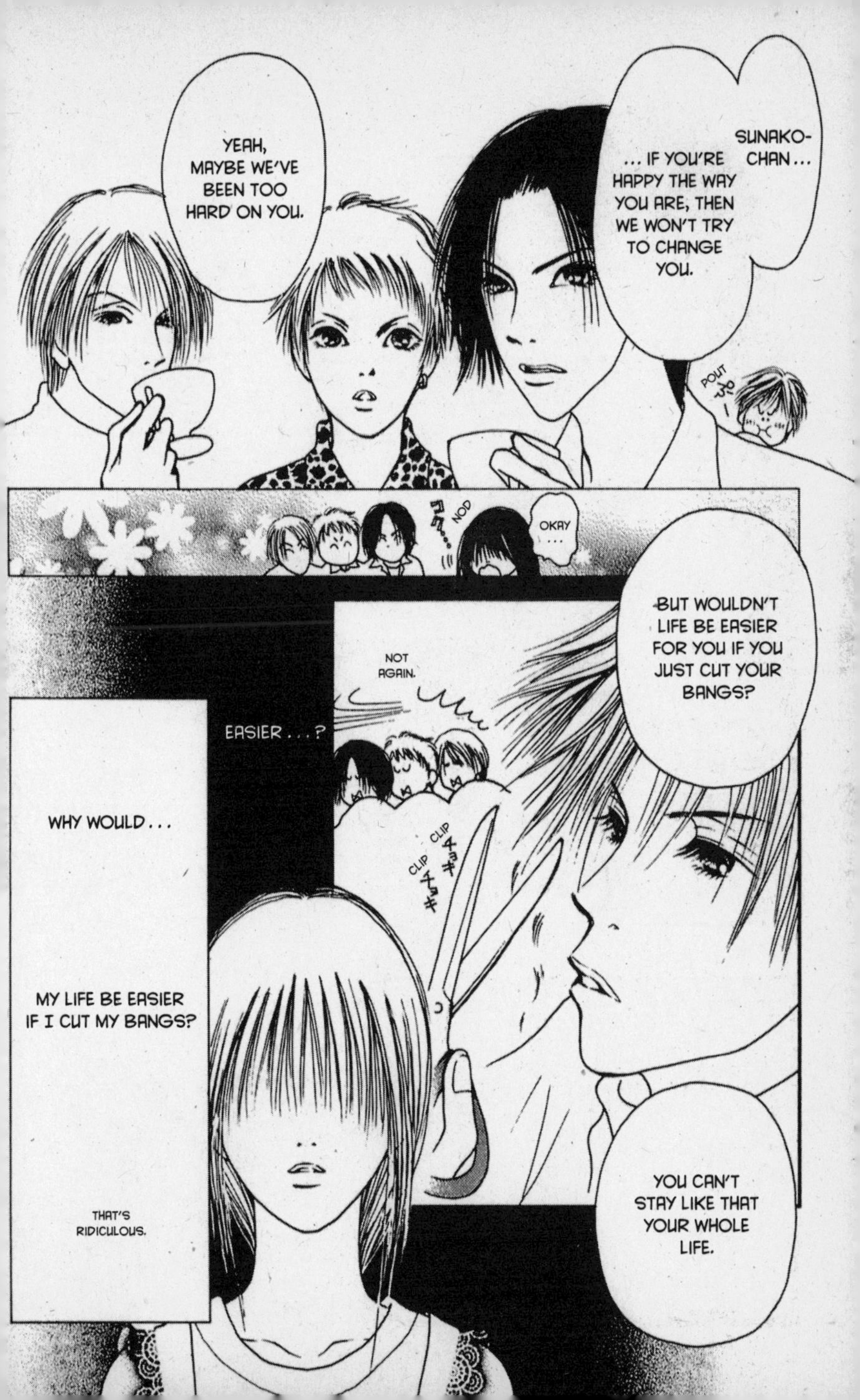
SUNAKO-CHAN . . .
. . . IF YOU'RE HAPPY THE WAY YOU ARE, THEN WE WON'T TRY TO CHANGE YOU.
POUT
YEAH, MAYBE WE'VE BEEN TOO HARD ON YOU.
OKAY . . .
NOD
BUT WOULDN'T LIFE BE EASIER FOR YOU IF YOU JUST CUT YOUR BANGS?
NOT AGAIN.
CLIP CLIP
YOU CAN'T STAY LIKE THAT YOUR WHOLE LIFE.
EASIER . . . ?
WHY WOULD . . .
MY LIFE BE EASIER IF I CUT MY BANGS?
THAT'S RIDICULOUS.

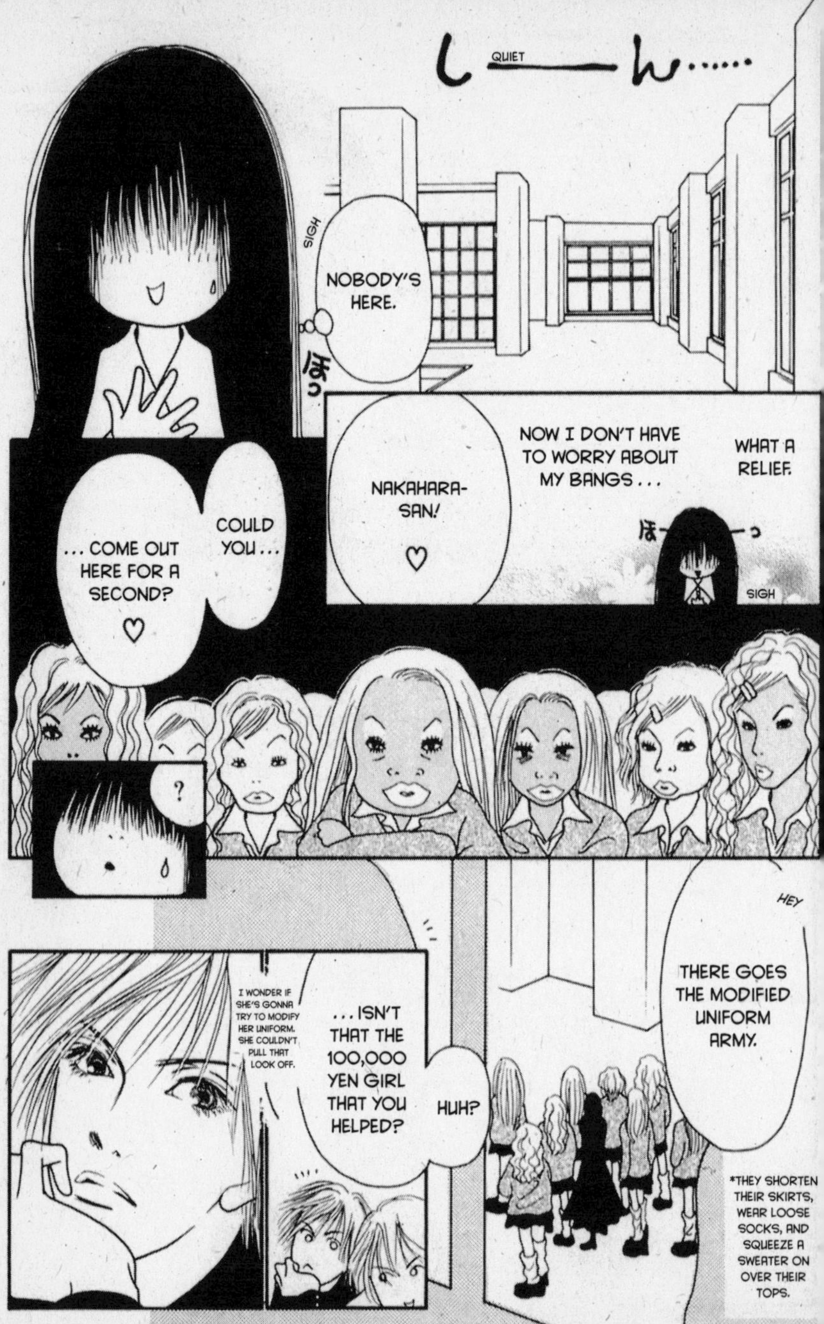

し——ん……
QUIET
SIGH
NOBODY'S HERE.
ほっ
WHAT A RELIEF.
NOW I DON'T HAVE TO WORRY ABOUT MY BANGS . . .
ほ——っ
SIGH
NAKAHARA-SAN! ♡
COULD YOU . . .
. . . COME OUT HERE FOR A SECOND? ♡
?
HEY
THERE GOES THE MODIFIED UNIFORM ARMY.
*THEY SHORTEN THEIR SKIRTS, WEAR LOOSE SOCKS, AND SQUEEZE A SWEATER ON OVER THEIR TOPS.
HUH?
. . . ISN'T THAT THE 100,000 YEN GIRL THAT YOU HELPED?
I WONDER IF SHE'S GONNA TRY TO MODIFY HER UNIFORM. SHE COULDN'T PULL THAT LOOK OFF.

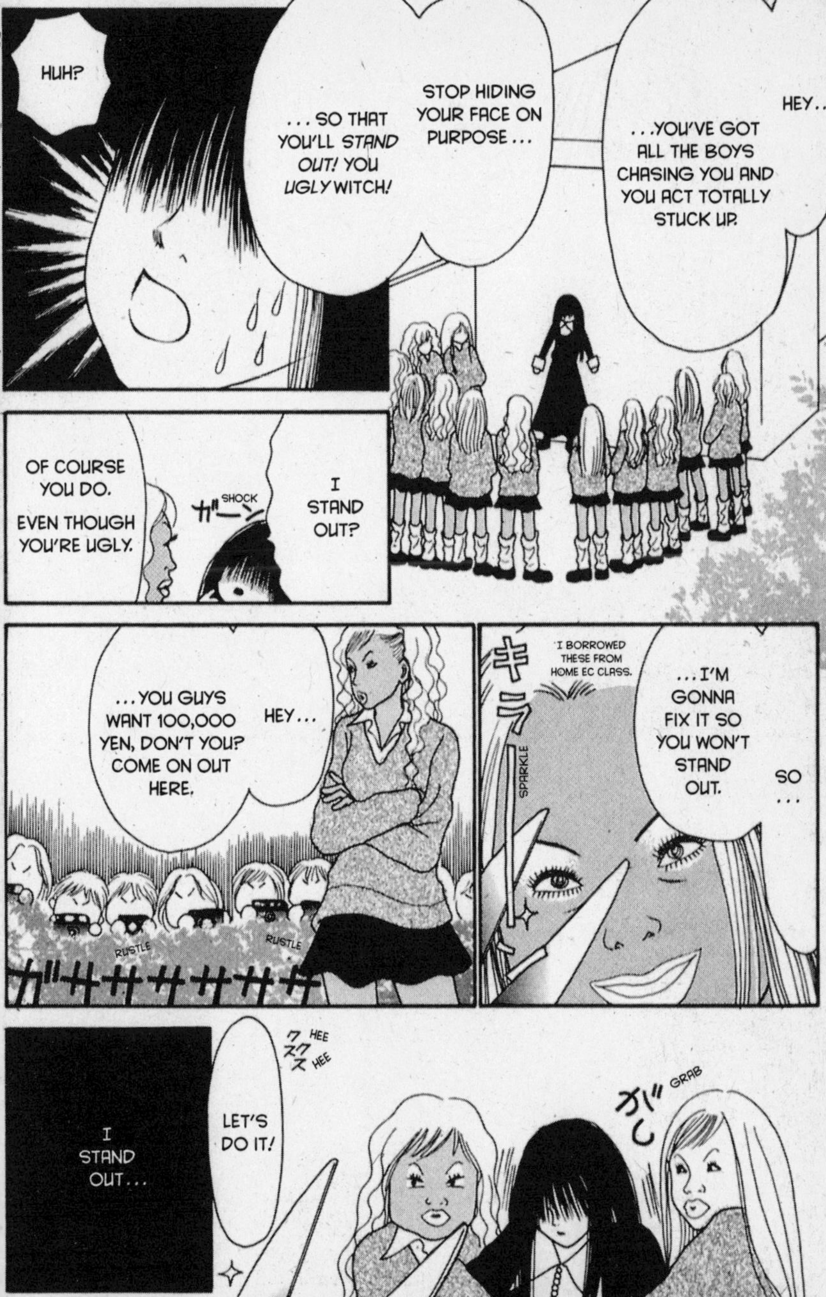
HEY...
...YOU'VE GOT ALL THE BOYS CHASING YOU AND YOU ACT TOTALLY STUCK UP.
STOP HIDING YOUR FACE ON PURPOSE...
...SO THAT YOU'LL *STAND OUT!* YOU *UGLY* WITCH!
HUH?
I STAND OUT?
SHOCK
OF COURSE YOU DO.
EVEN THOUGH YOU'RE UGLY.
SO...
...I'M GONNA FIX IT SO YOU WON'T STAND OUT.
I BORROWED THESE FROM HOME EC CLASS.
SPARKLE
HEY...
...YOU GUYS WANT 100,000 YEN, DON'T YOU? COME ON OUT HERE.
RUSTLE
RUSTLE
GRAB
HEE HEE
LET'S DO IT!
I STAND OUT...

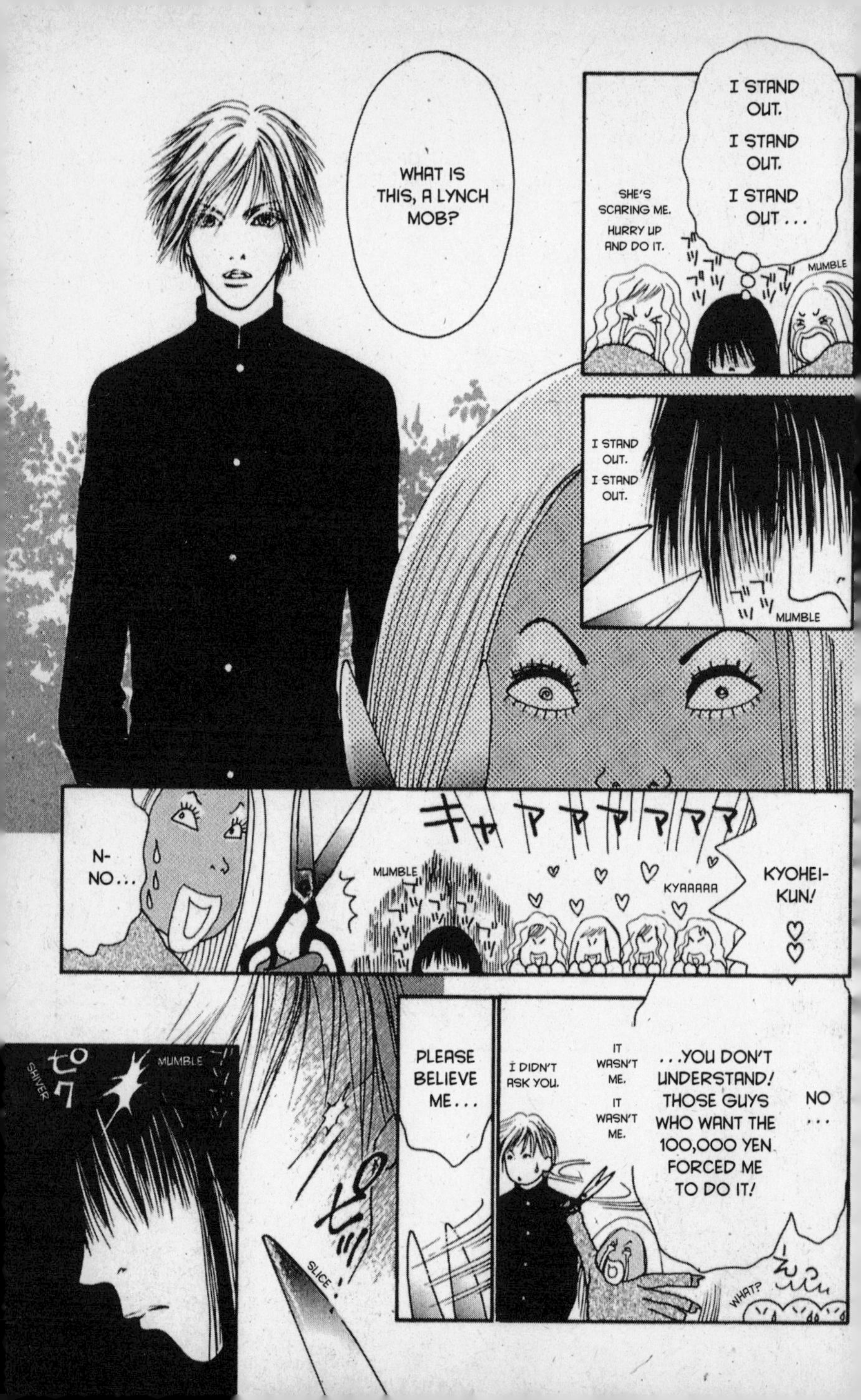

I STAND OUT. I STAND OUT. I STAND OUT . . .
SHE'S SCARING ME. HURRY UP AND DO IT.
MUMBLE
I STAND OUT. I STAND OUT.
MUMBLE
WHAT IS THIS, A LYNCH MOB?
KYOHEI-KUN!
KYAAAAA
キャアアアアアア
MUMBLE
N-NO . . .
NO . . .
. . . YOU DON'T UNDERSTAND! THOSE GUYS WHO WANT THE 100,000 YEN FORCED ME TO DO IT!
IT WASN'T ME. IT WASN'T ME.
WHAT?
I DIDN'T ASK YOU.
PLEASE BELIEVE ME . . .
SLICE!
MUMBLE
SHIVER
ピク

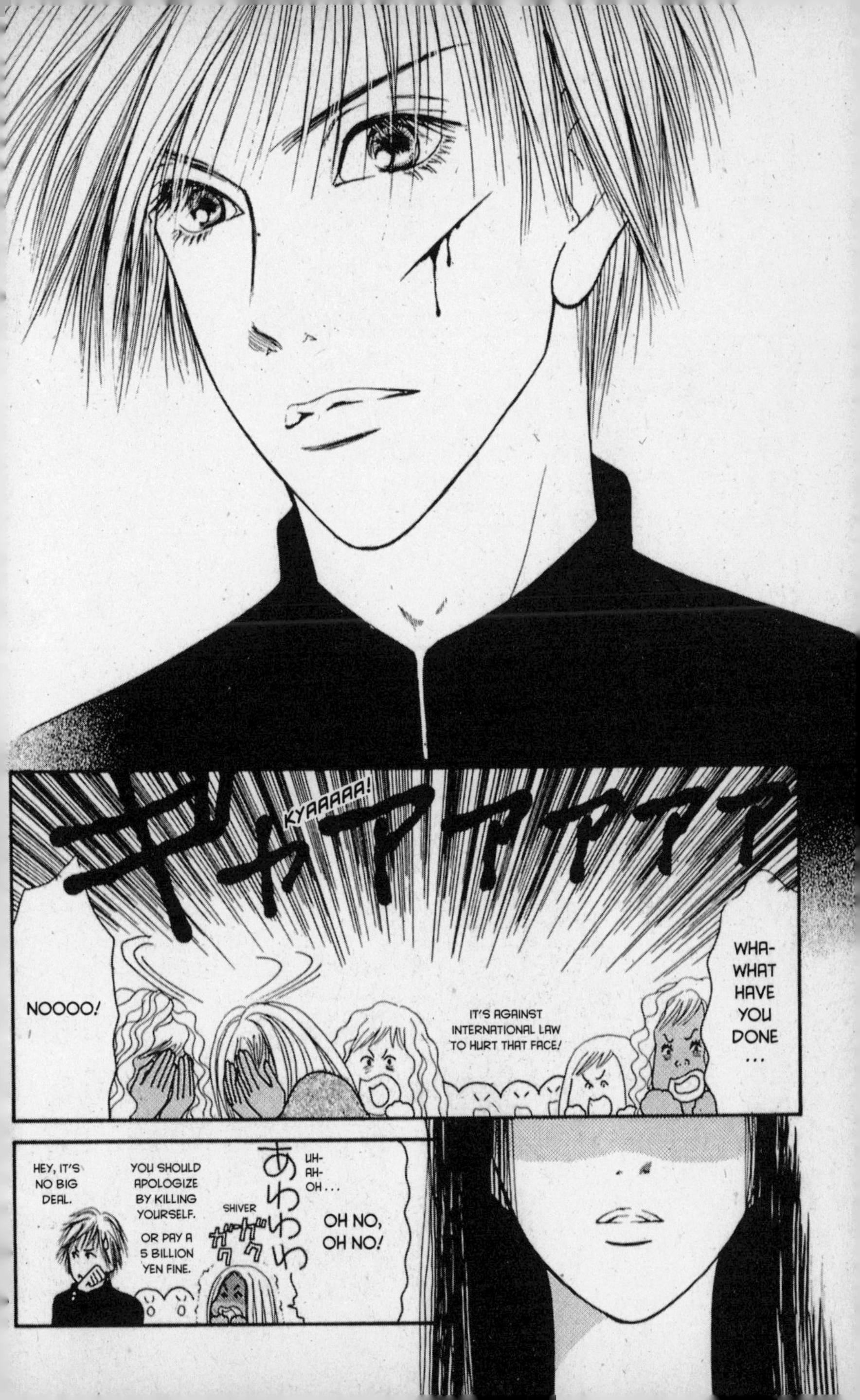
KYAAAAA!
WHA-WHAT HAVE YOU DONE...
IT'S AGAINST INTERNATIONAL LAW TO HURT THAT FACE!
NOOOO!
OH NO, OH NO!
UH-AH-OH...
あわわわ
SHIVER
YOU SHOULD APOLOGIZE BY KILLING YOURSELF.
OR PAY A 5 BILLION YEN FINE.
HEY, IT'S NO BIG DEAL.

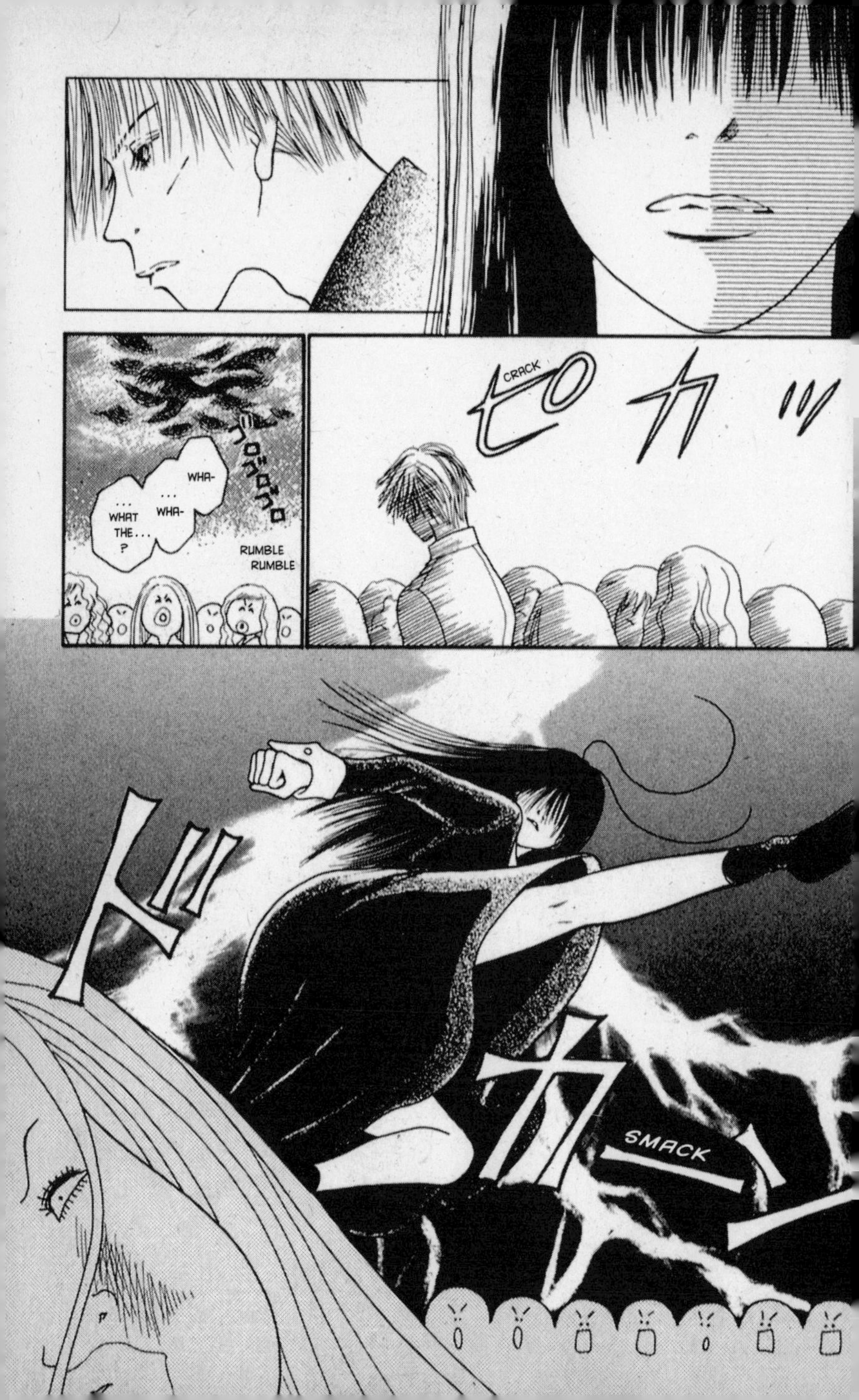
CRACK
RUMBLE RUMBLE
WHA-
... WHA-
... WHAT THE... ?
SMACK

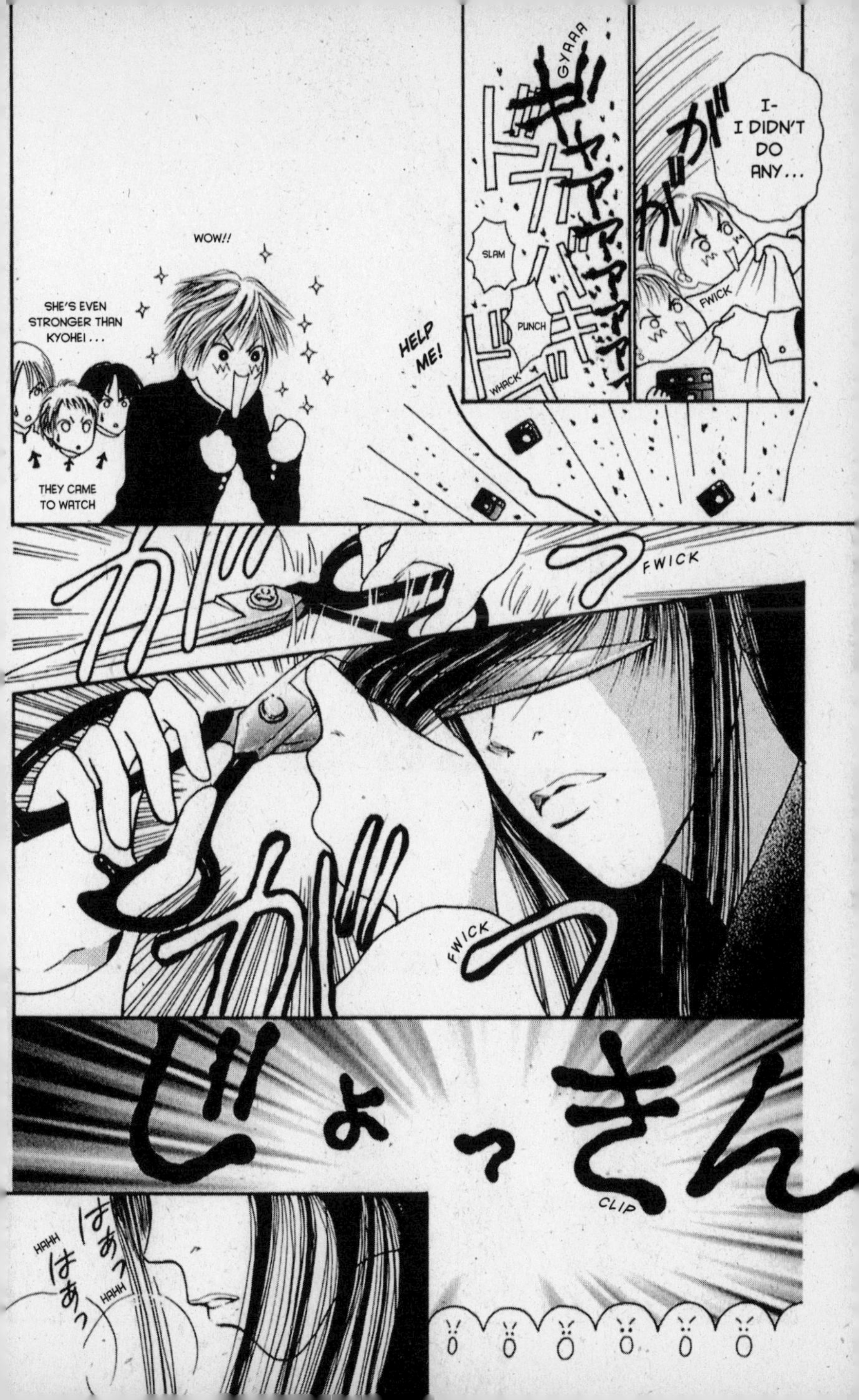
I- I DIDN'T DO ANY...
FWICK
GYAAA
SLAM
PUNCH
WHACK
HELP ME!
WOW!!
SHE'S EVEN STRONGER THAN KYOHEI...
THEY CAME TO WATCH
FWICK
FWICK
CLIP
HAHH
HAHH

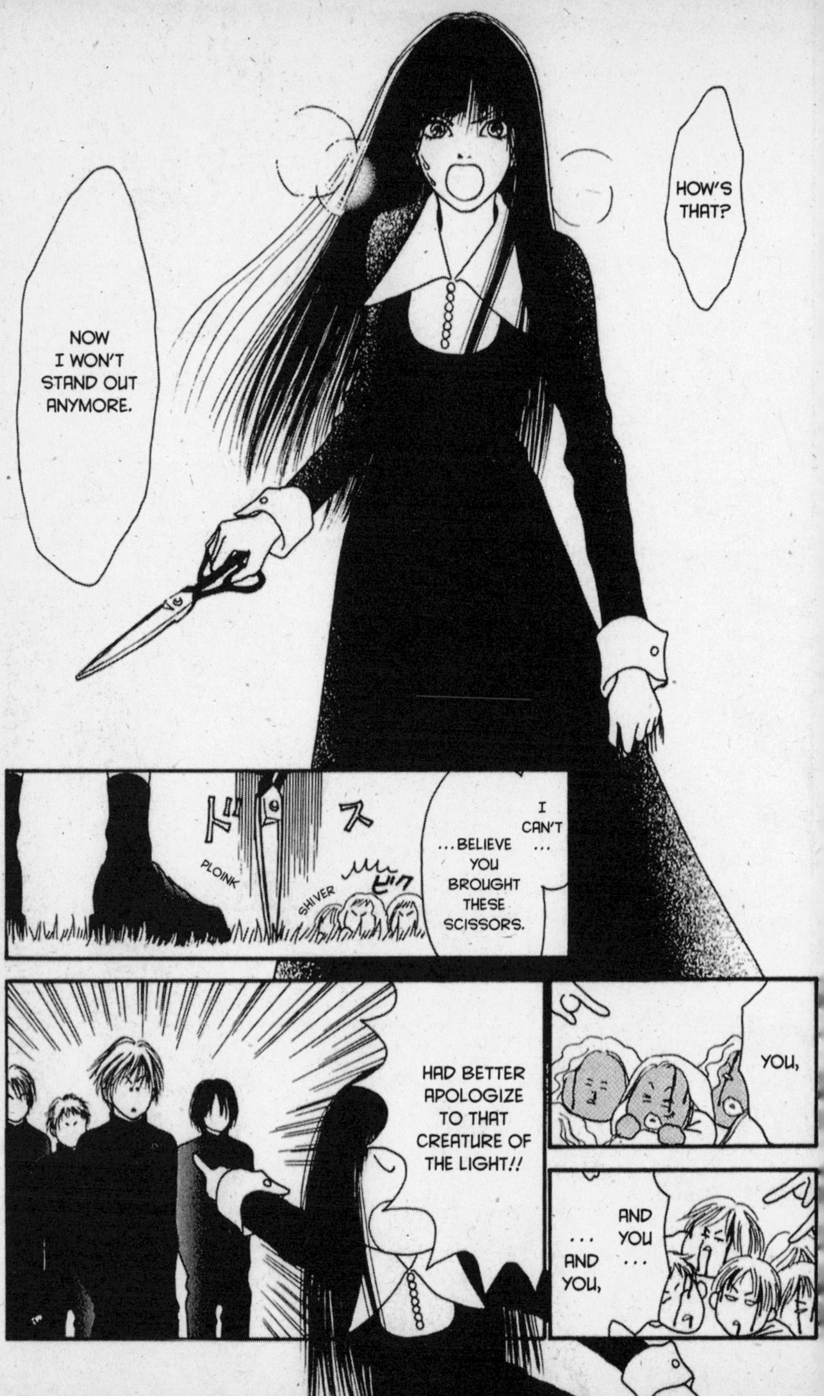
HOW'S THAT?
NOW I WON'T STAND OUT ANYMORE.
I CAN'T ...
...BELIEVE YOU BROUGHT THESE SCISSORS.
ドス
PLOINK
ビク
SHIVER
YOU,
AND YOU ...
... AND YOU,
HAD BETTER APOLOGIZE TO THAT CREATURE OF THE LIGHT!!

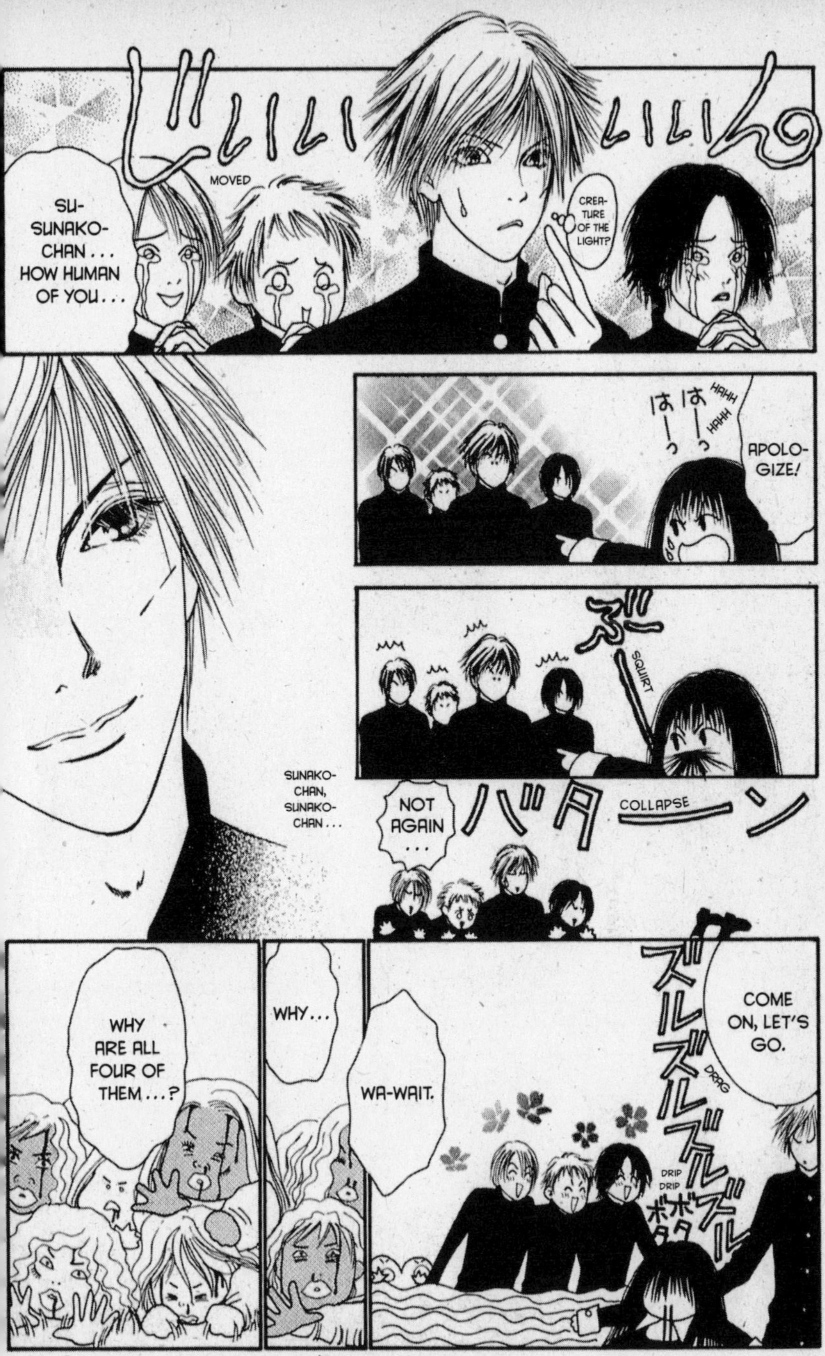

じいいいいいいいん
CREA-TURE OF THE LIGHT?
MOVED
SU-SUNAKO-CHAN . . . HOW HUMAN OF YOU . . .
APOLOGIZE!
はーっ はーっ
HAHH HAHH
ぷー
SQUIRT
バタ――ン
COLLAPSE
NOT AGAIN . . .
SUNAKO-CHAN, SUNAKO-CHAN . . .
COME ON, LET'S GO.
ズルズルズル
DRAG
ボタボタ
DRIP DRIP
WHY . . .
WA-WAIT.
WHY ARE ALL FOUR OF THEM . . . ?

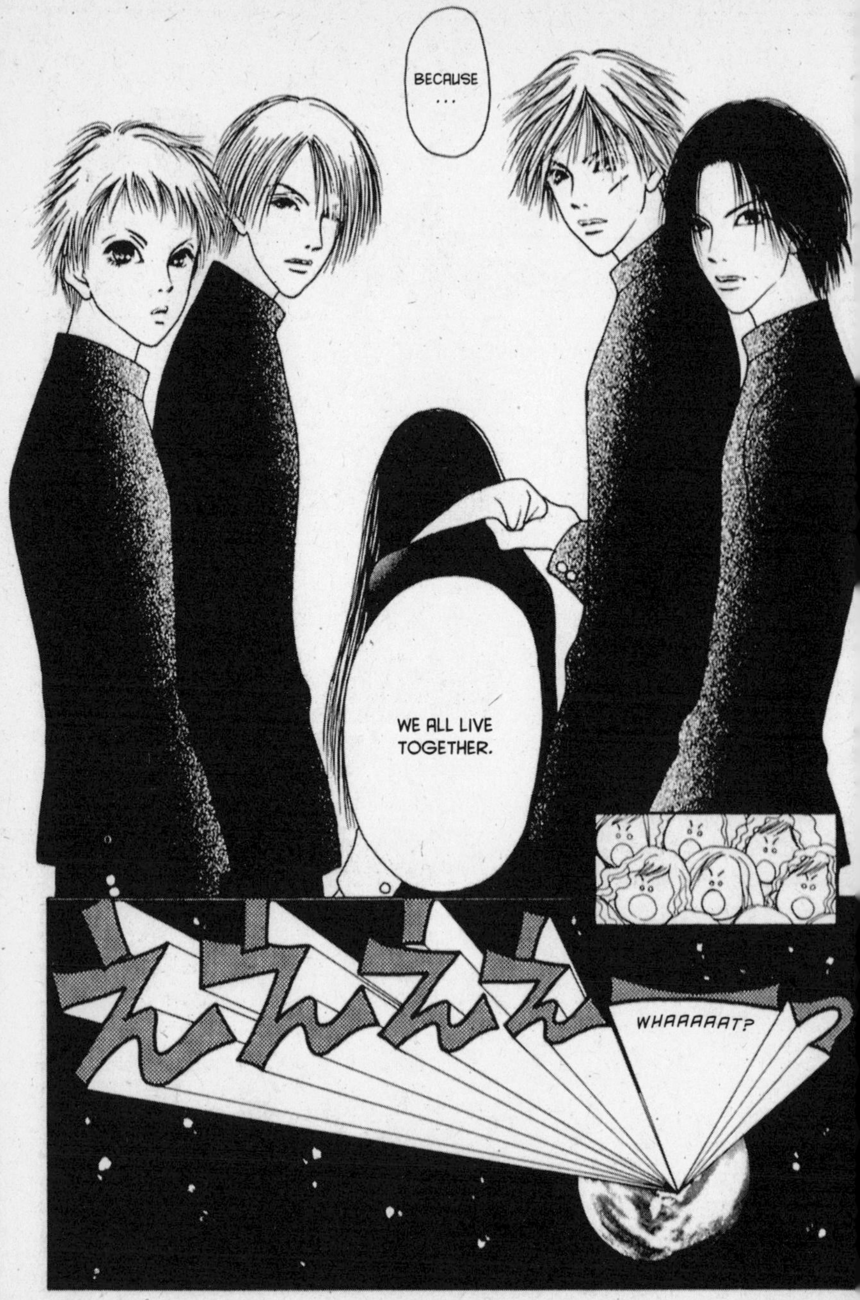
BECAUSE . . .
WE ALL LIVE TOGETHER.
WHAAAAAAT?

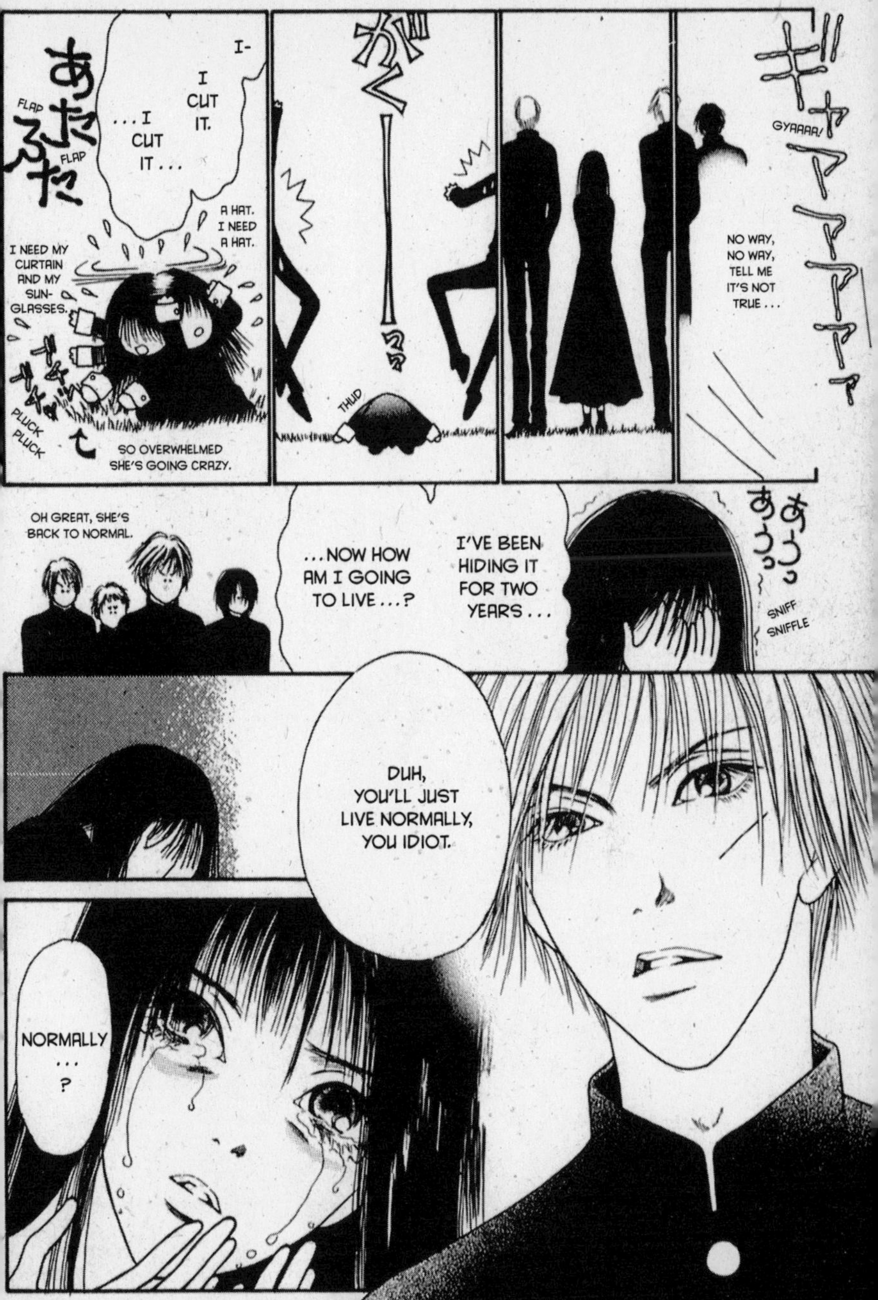
ギャアアアア
GYAAAA!
NO WAY, NO WAY, TELL ME IT'S NOT TRUE . . .
THUD
あたふた
FLAP FLAP
I-
I CUT IT.
. . . I CUT IT . . .
A HAT. I NEED A HAT.
I NEED MY CURTAIN AND MY SUN-GLASSES.
PLUCK PLUCK
SO OVERWHELMED SHE'S GOING CRAZY.
あうっ あうっ
SNIFF SNIFFLE
I'VE BEEN HIDING IT FOR TWO YEARS . . .
. . . NOW HOW AM I GOING TO LIVE . . . ?
OH GREAT, SHE'S BACK TO NORMAL.
DUH, YOU'LL JUST LIVE NORMALLY, YOU IDIOT.
NORMALLY . . . ?

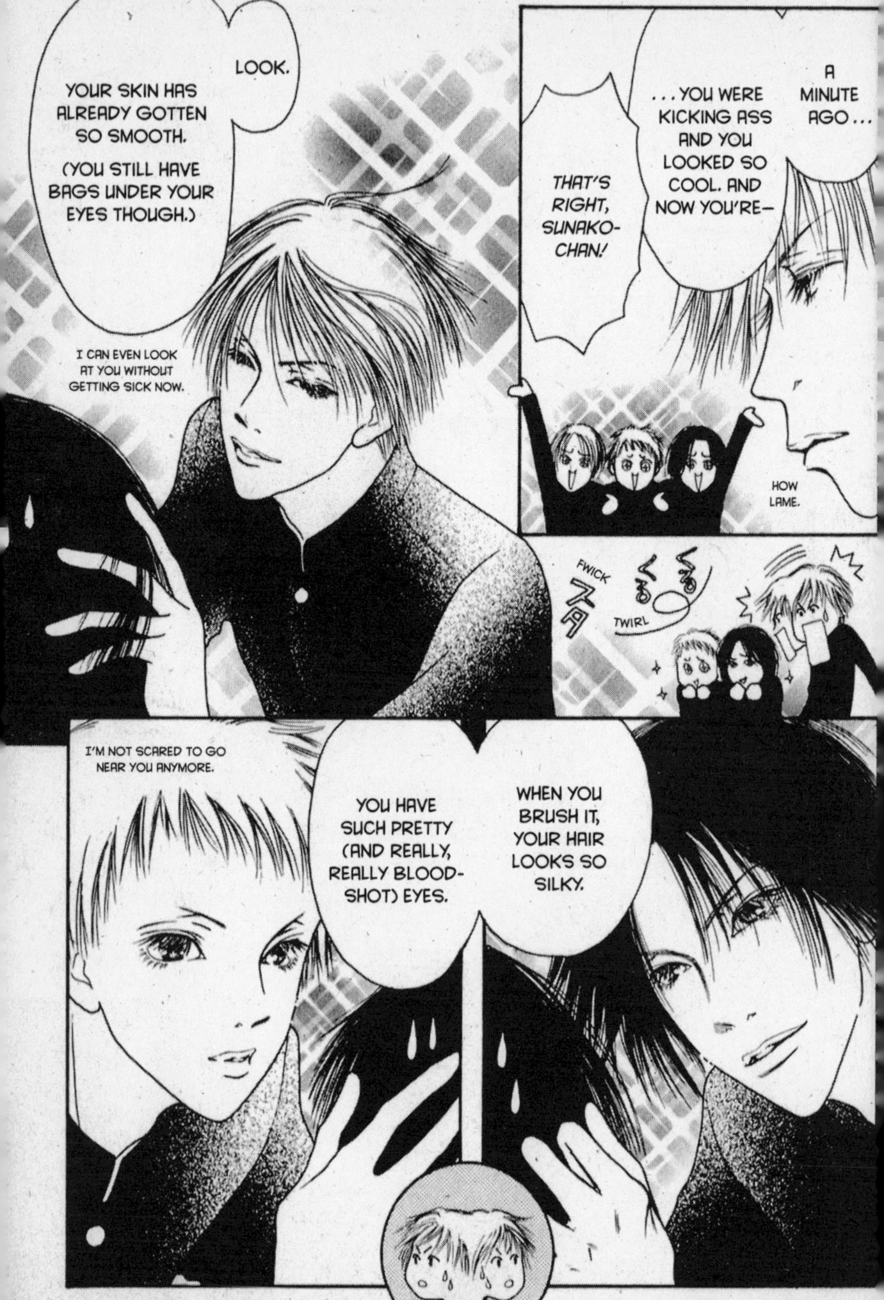
A MINUTE AGO...
...YOU WERE KICKING ASS AND YOU LOOKED SO COOL. AND NOW YOU'RE—
THAT'S RIGHT, SUNAKO-CHAN!
HOW LAME.
FWICK
スタ
くるくる
TWIRL
LOOK.
YOUR SKIN HAS ALREADY GOTTEN SO SMOOTH.
(YOU STILL HAVE BAGS UNDER YOUR EYES THOUGH.)
I CAN EVEN LOOK AT YOU WITHOUT GETTING SICK NOW.
WHEN YOU BRUSH IT, YOUR HAIR LOOKS SO SILKY.
YOU HAVE SUCH PRETTY (AND REALLY, REALLY BLOOD-SHOT) EYES.
I'M NOT SCARED TO GO NEAR YOU ANYMORE.

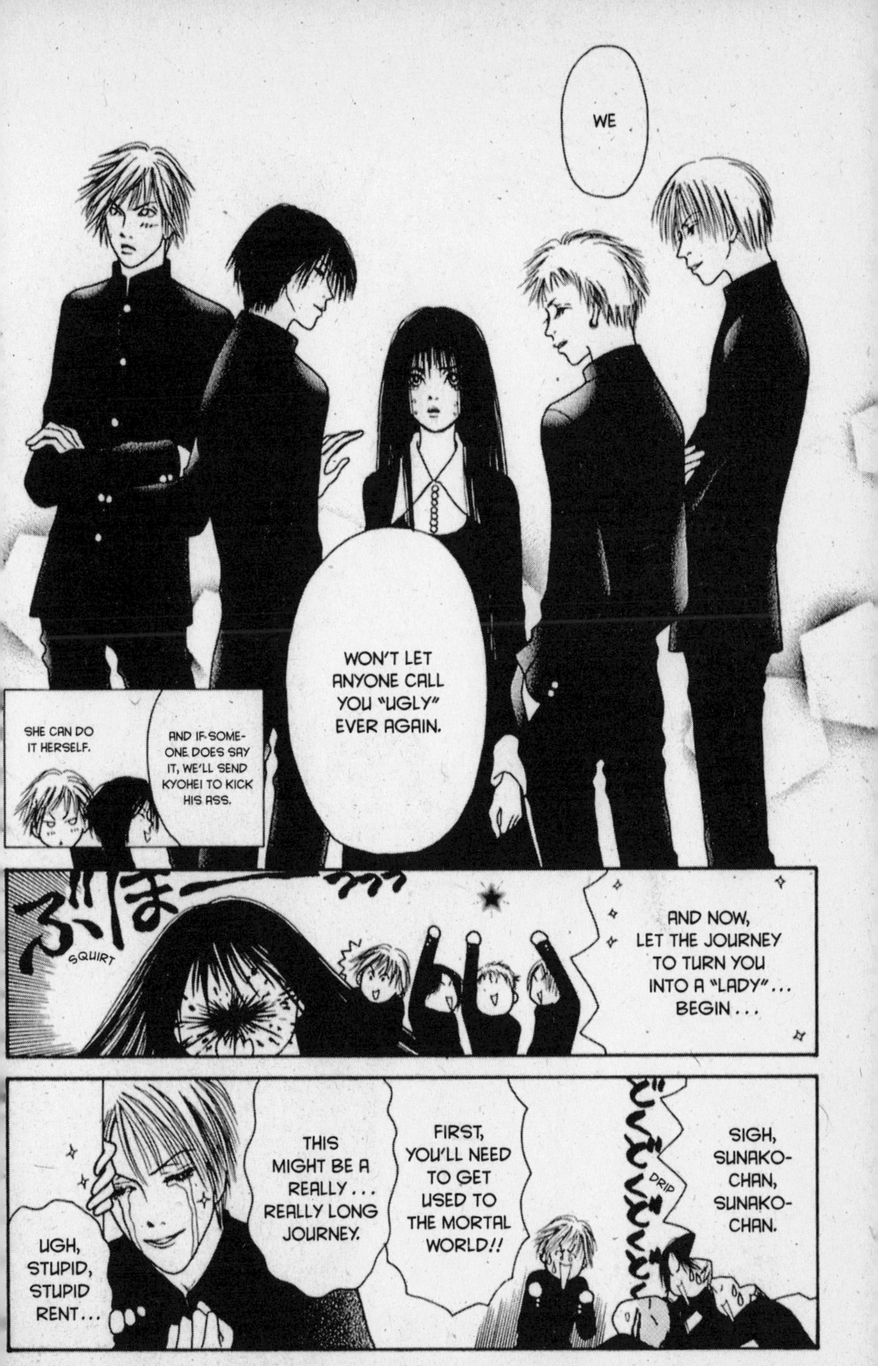
WE
WON'T LET ANYONE CALL YOU "UGLY" EVER AGAIN.
AND IF SOME-ONE DOES SAY IT, WE'LL SEND KYOHEI TO KICK HIS ASS.
SHE CAN DO IT HERSELF.
AND NOW, LET THE JOURNEY TO TURN YOU INTO A "LADY"... BEGIN...
SQUIRT
SIGH, SUNAKO-CHAN, SUNAKO-CHAN.
DRIP
FIRST, YOU'LL NEED TO GET USED TO THE MORTAL WORLD!!
THIS MIGHT BE A REALLY... REALLY LONG JOURNEY.
UGH, STUPID, STUPID RENT...

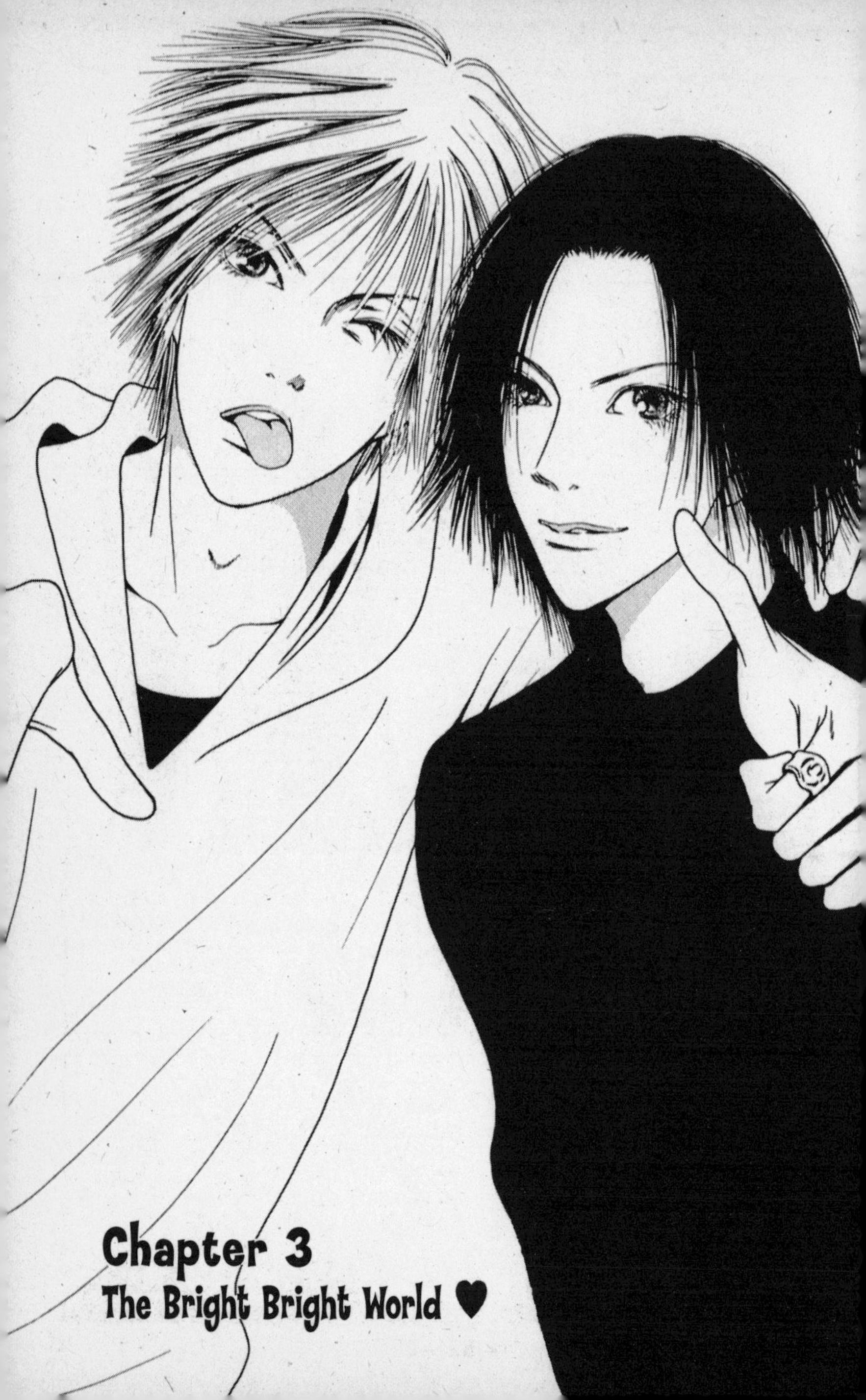

Chapter 3

The Bright Bright World ♥

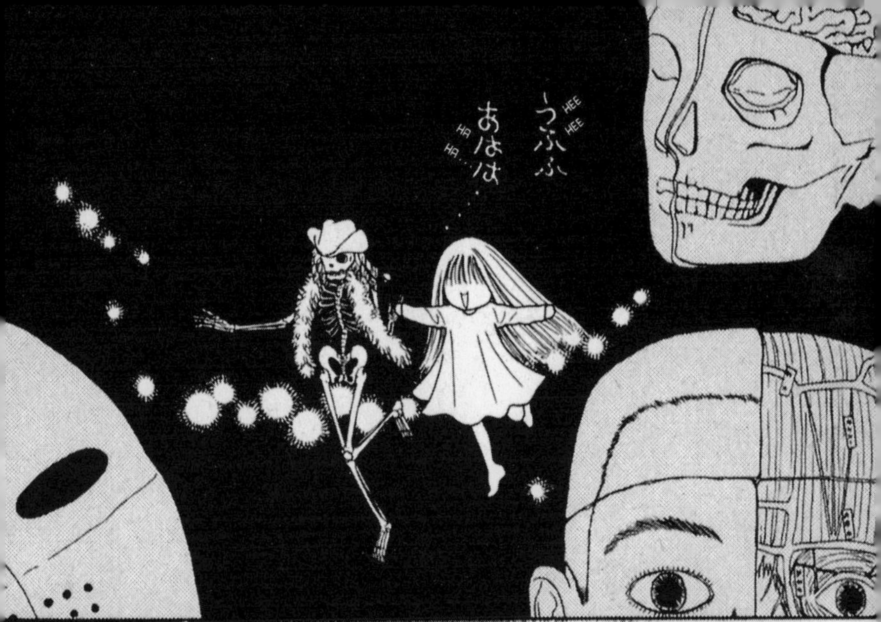
うふふ
HEE HEE
あはは
HA HA...

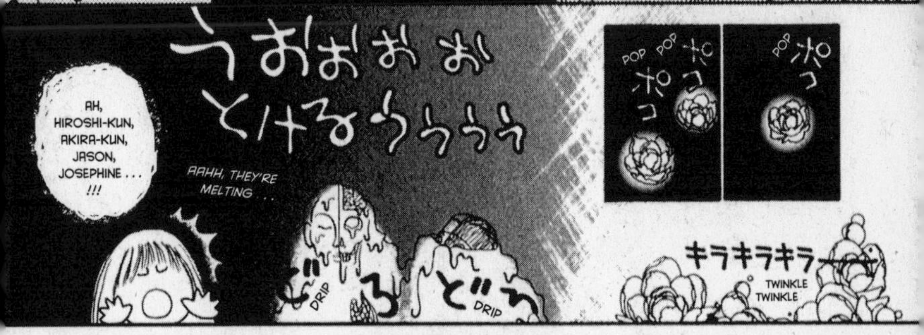
ポコポコ
POP POP
ポコ
POP
うおぉおおお
とけるううう
AH, HIROSHI-KUN, AKIRA-KUN, JASON, JOSEPHINE . . . !!!
AAHH, THEY'RE MELTING . . .
どろ
DRIP
どろ
DRIP
キラキラキラ
TWINKLE TWINKLE

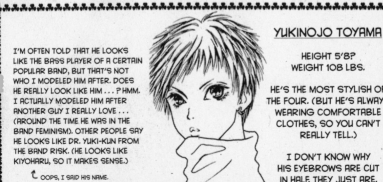

YUKINOJO TOYAMA

HEIGHT 5'8?
WEIGHT 108 LBS.

HE'S THE MOST STYLISH OF THE FOUR. (BUT HE'S ALWAYS WEARING COMFORTABLE CLOTHES, SO YOU CAN'T REALLY TELL.)

I DON'T KNOW WHY HIS EYEBROWS ARE CUT IN HALF. THEY JUST ARE.

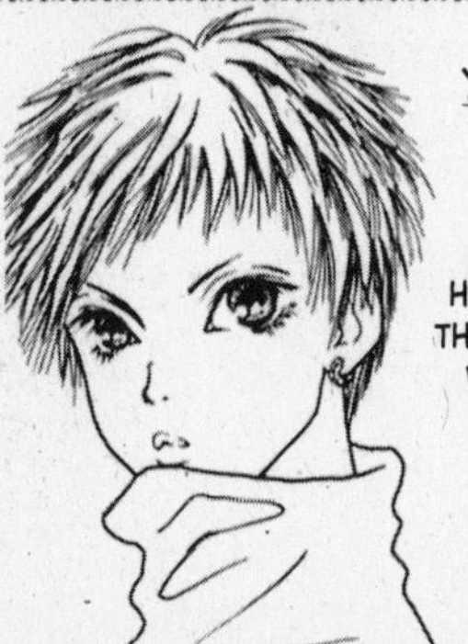

I'M OFTEN TOLD THAT HE LOOKS LIKE THE BASS PLAYER OF A CERTAIN POPULAR BAND, BUT THAT'S NOT WHO I MODELED HIM AFTER. DOES HE REALLY LOOK LIKE HIM . . . ? HMM. I ACTUALLY MODELED HIM AFTER ANOTHER GUY I REALLY LOVE . . . (AROUND THE TIME HE WAS IN THE BAND FEMINISM). OTHER PEOPLE SAY HE LOOKS LIKE DR. YUKI-KUN FROM THE BAND RISK. (HE LOOKS LIKE KIYOHARU, SO IT MAKES SENSE.)

↑ OOPS, I SAID HIS NAME.

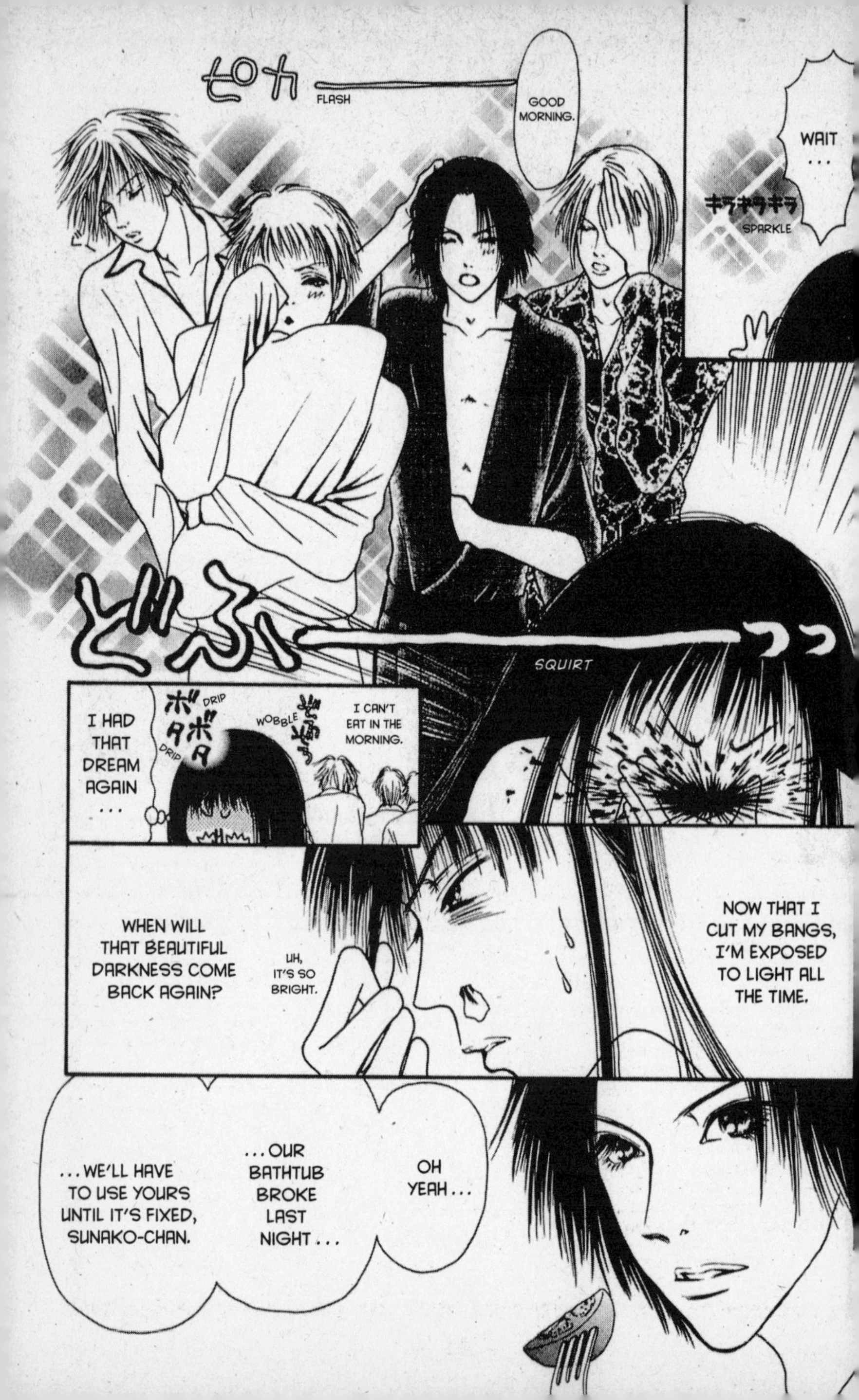
WAIT . . .
キラキラキラ
SPARKLE
ピカ
FLASH
GOOD MORNING.
SQUIRT
I CAN'T EAT IN THE MORNING.
WOBBLE
DRIP
DRIP
I HAD THAT DREAM AGAIN . . .
NOW THAT I CUT MY BANGS, I'M EXPOSED TO LIGHT ALL THE TIME.
UH, IT'S SO BRIGHT.
WHEN WILL THAT BEAUTIFUL DARKNESS COME BACK AGAIN?
OH YEAH . . .
. . . OUR BATHTUB BROKE LAST NIGHT . . .
. . . WE'LL HAVE TO USE YOURS UNTIL IT'S FIXED, SUNAKO-CHAN.

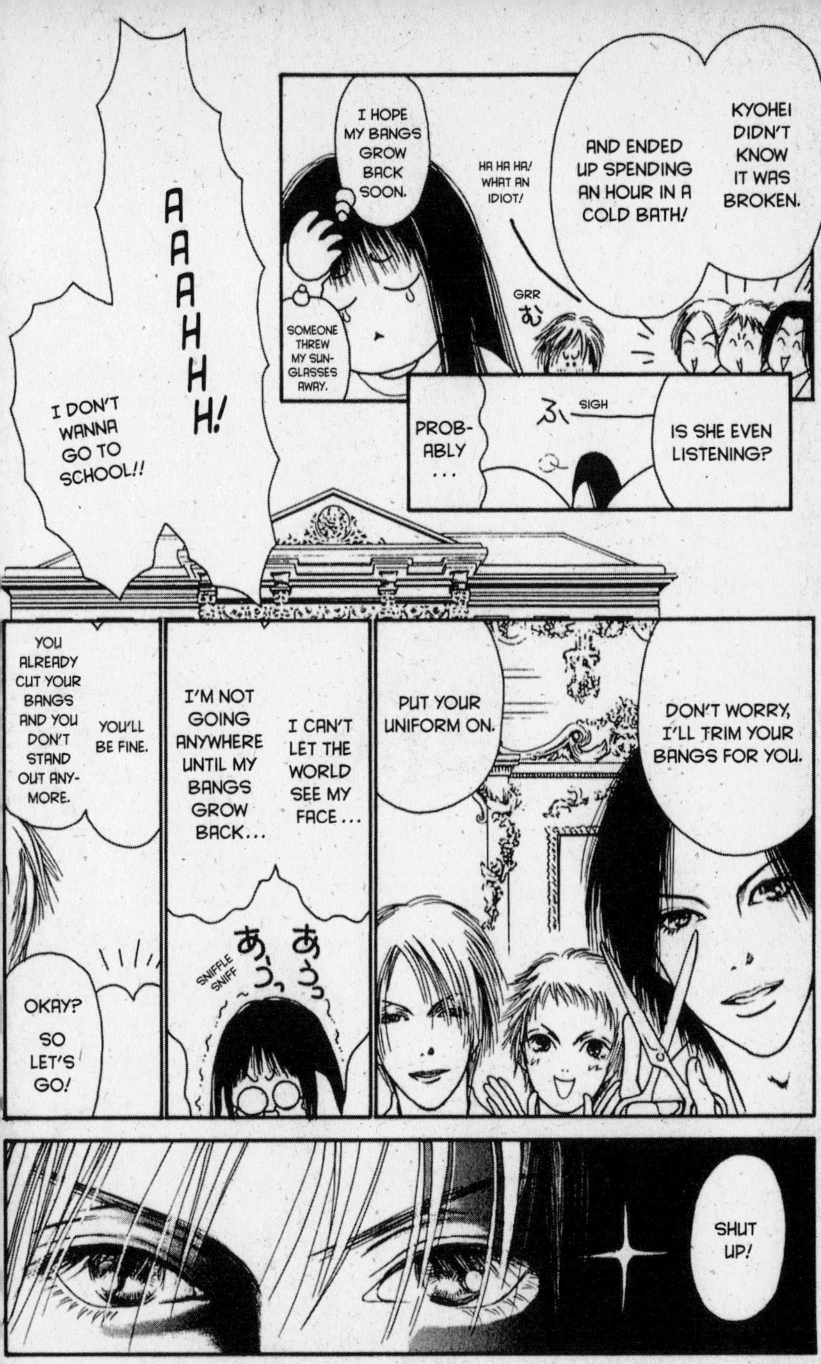
KYOHEI DIDN'T KNOW IT WAS BROKEN.
AND ENDED UP SPENDING AN HOUR IN A COLD BATH!
HA HA HA! WHAT AN IDIOT!
む GRR
I HOPE MY BANGS GROW BACK SOON.
SOMEONE THREW MY SUN-GLASSES AWAY.
IS SHE EVEN LISTENING?
ふ SIGH
PROB-ABLY . . .
AAAHHH!
I DON'T WANNA GO TO SCHOOL!!
DON'T WORRY, I'LL TRIM YOUR BANGS FOR YOU.
PUT YOUR UNIFORM ON.
I CAN'T LET THE WORLD SEE MY FACE . . .
I'M NOT GOING ANYWHERE UNTIL MY BANGS GROW BACK . . .
あうっ あうっ
SNIFFLE SNIFF
YOU'LL BE FINE.
YOU ALREADY CUT YOUR BANGS AND YOU DON'T STAND OUT ANY-MORE.
OKAY?
SO LET'S GO!
SHUT UP!

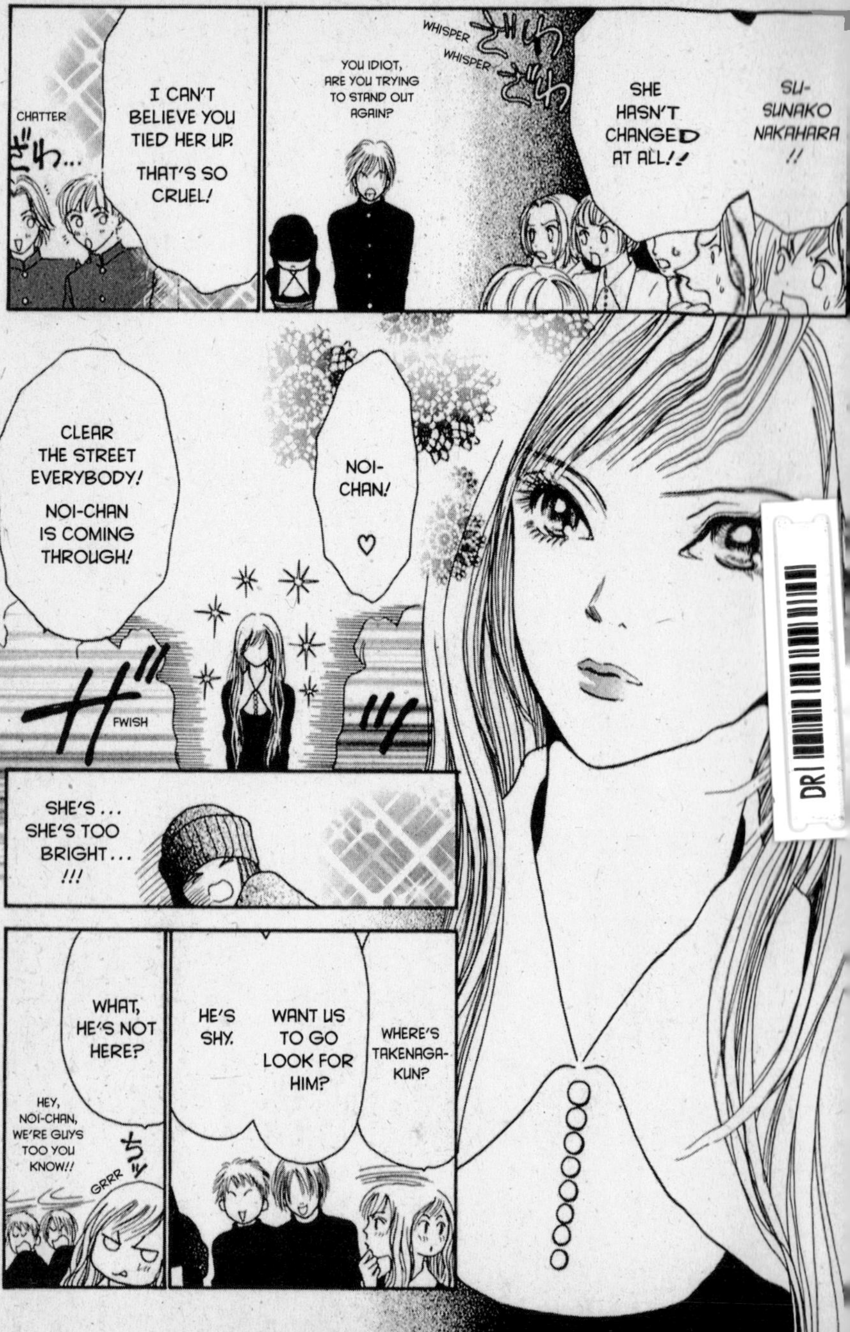
SU-SUNAKO NAKAHARA!!
SHE HASN'T CHANGED AT ALL!!
WHISPER
WHISPER
YOU IDIOT, ARE YOU TRYING TO STAND OUT AGAIN?
I CAN'T BELIEVE YOU TIED HER UP.
THAT'S SO CRUEL!
CHATTER
NOI-CHAN! ♡
CLEAR THE STREET EVERYBODY!
NOI-CHAN IS COMING THROUGH!
FWISH
SHE'S... SHE'S TOO BRIGHT...!!!
WHERE'S TAKENAGA-KUN?
WANT US TO GO LOOK FOR HIM?
HE'S SHY.
WHAT, HE'S NOT HERE?
GRRR
HEY, NOI-CHAN, WE'RE GUYS TOO YOU KNOW!!

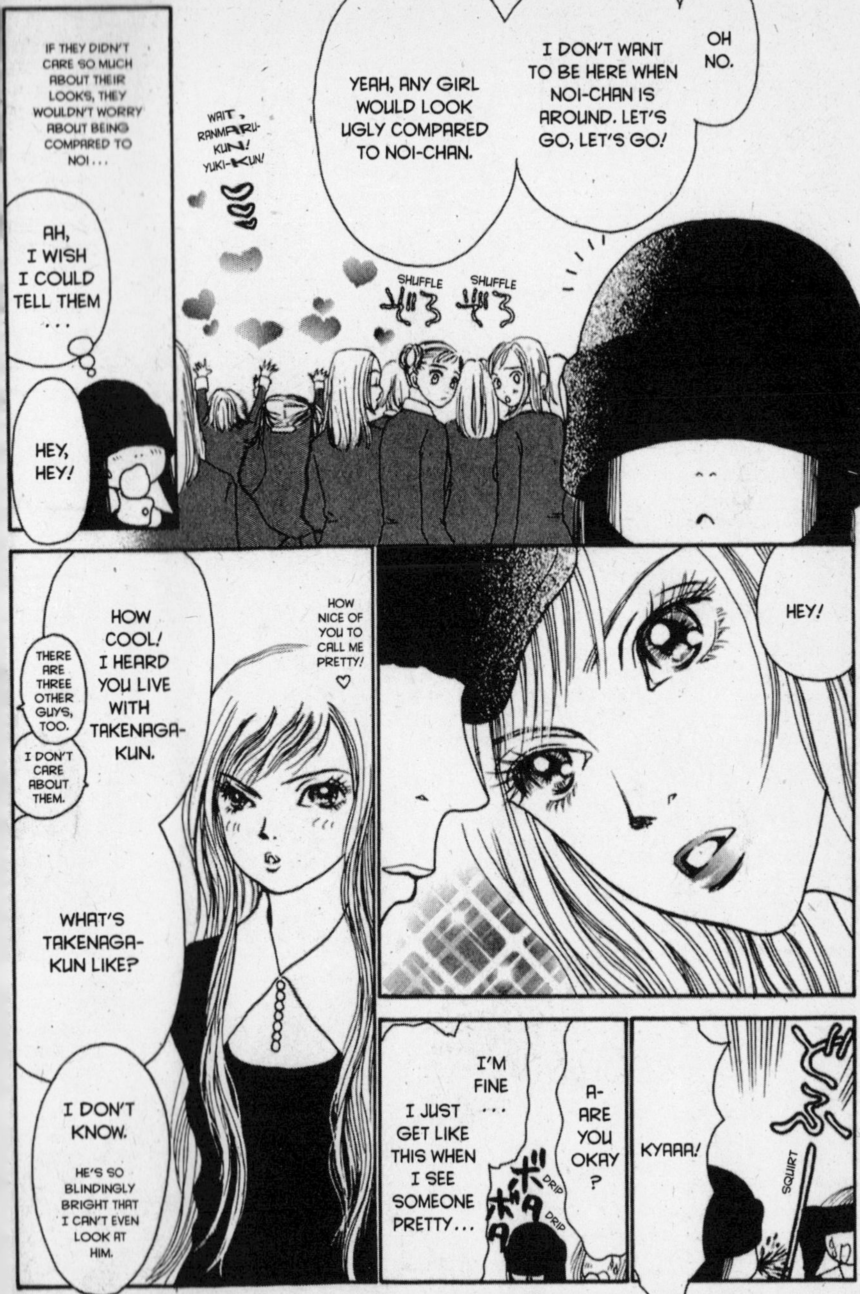
OH NO.
I DON'T WANT TO BE HERE WHEN NOI-CHAN IS AROUND. LET'S GO, LET'S GO!
YEAH, ANY GIRL WOULD LOOK UGLY COMPARED TO NOI-CHAN.
SHUFFLE
SHUFFLE
WAIT, RANMARU-KUN! YUKI-KUN!
IF THEY DIDN'T CARE SO MUCH ABOUT THEIR LOOKS, THEY WOULDN'T WORRY ABOUT BEING COMPARED TO NOI . . .
AH, I WISH I COULD TELL THEM . . .
HEY, HEY!
HEY!
KYAAA!
SQUIRT
A-ARE YOU OKAY?
I'M FINE . . .
I JUST GET LIKE THIS WHEN I SEE SOMEONE PRETTY . . .
DRIP
DRIP
HOW NICE OF YOU TO CALL ME PRETTY! ♡
HOW COOL! I HEARD YOU LIVE WITH TAKENAGA-KUN.
THERE ARE THREE OTHER GUYS, TOO.
I DON'T CARE ABOUT THEM.
WHAT'S TAKENAGA-KUN LIKE?
I DON'T KNOW.
HE'S SO BLINDINGLY BRIGHT THAT I CAN'T EVEN LOOK AT HIM.

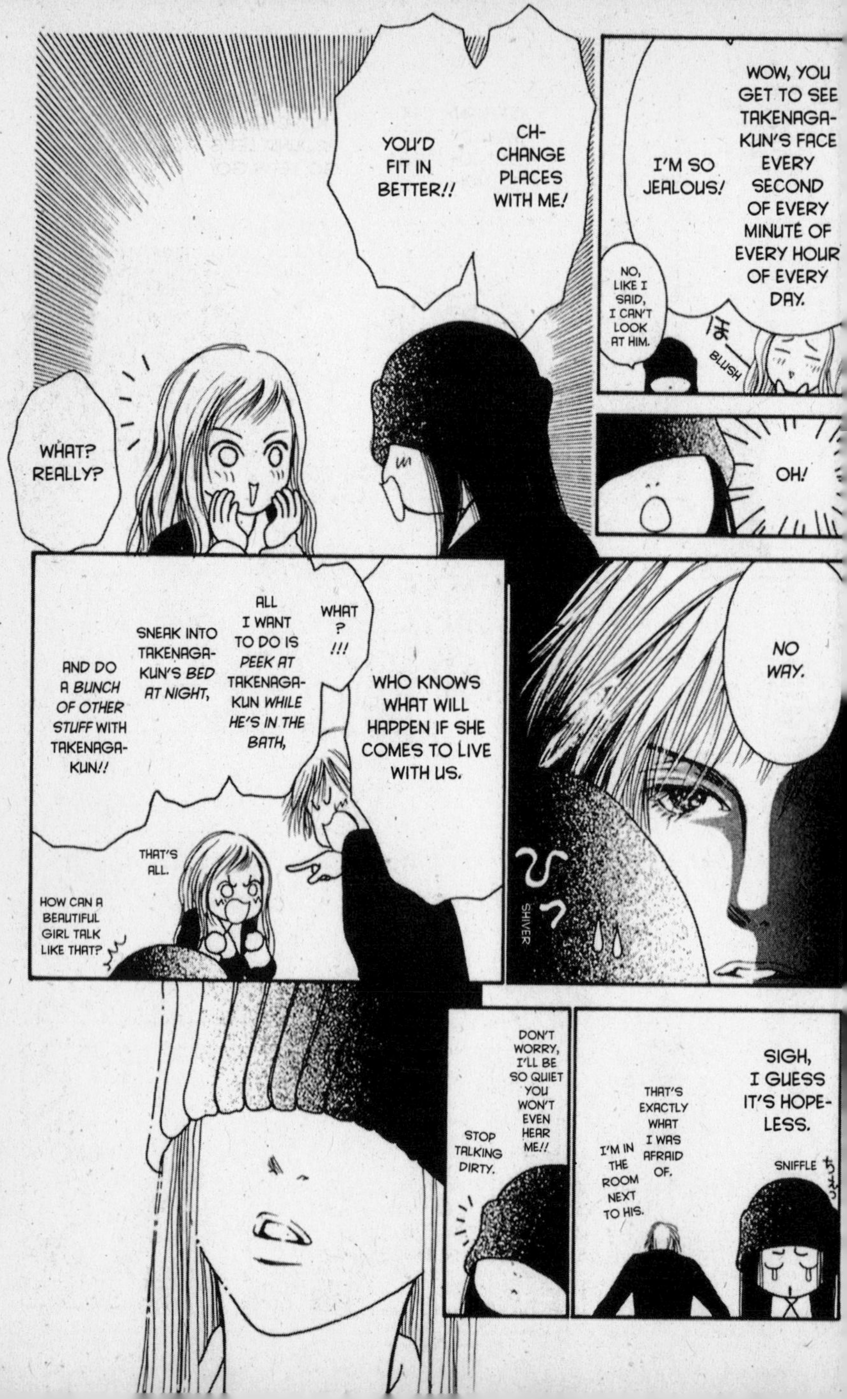

WOW, YOU GET TO SEE TAKENAGA-KUN'S FACE EVERY SECOND OF EVERY MINUTE OF EVERY HOUR OF EVERY DAY.
I'M SO JEALOUS!
NO, LIKE I SAID, I CAN'T LOOK AT HIM.
BLUSH
OH!
CH- CHANGE PLACES WITH ME!
YOU'D FIT IN BETTER!!
WHAT? REALLY?
NO WAY.
SHIVER
WHO KNOWS WHAT WILL HAPPEN IF SHE COMES TO LIVE WITH US.
WHAT?!!!
ALL I WANT TO DO IS PEEK AT TAKENAGA-KUN WHILE HE'S IN THE BATH,
SNEAK INTO TAKENAGA-KUN'S BED AT NIGHT,
AND DO A BUNCH OF OTHER STUFF WITH TAKENAGA-KUN!!
THAT'S ALL.
HOW CAN A BEAUTIFUL GIRL TALK LIKE THAT?
SIGH, I GUESS IT'S HOPE-LESS.
SNIFFLE
THAT'S EXACTLY WHAT I WAS AFRAID OF.
I'M IN THE ROOM NEXT TO HIS.
DON'T WORRY, I'LL BE SO QUIET YOU WON'T EVEN HEAR ME!!
STOP TALKING DIRTY.

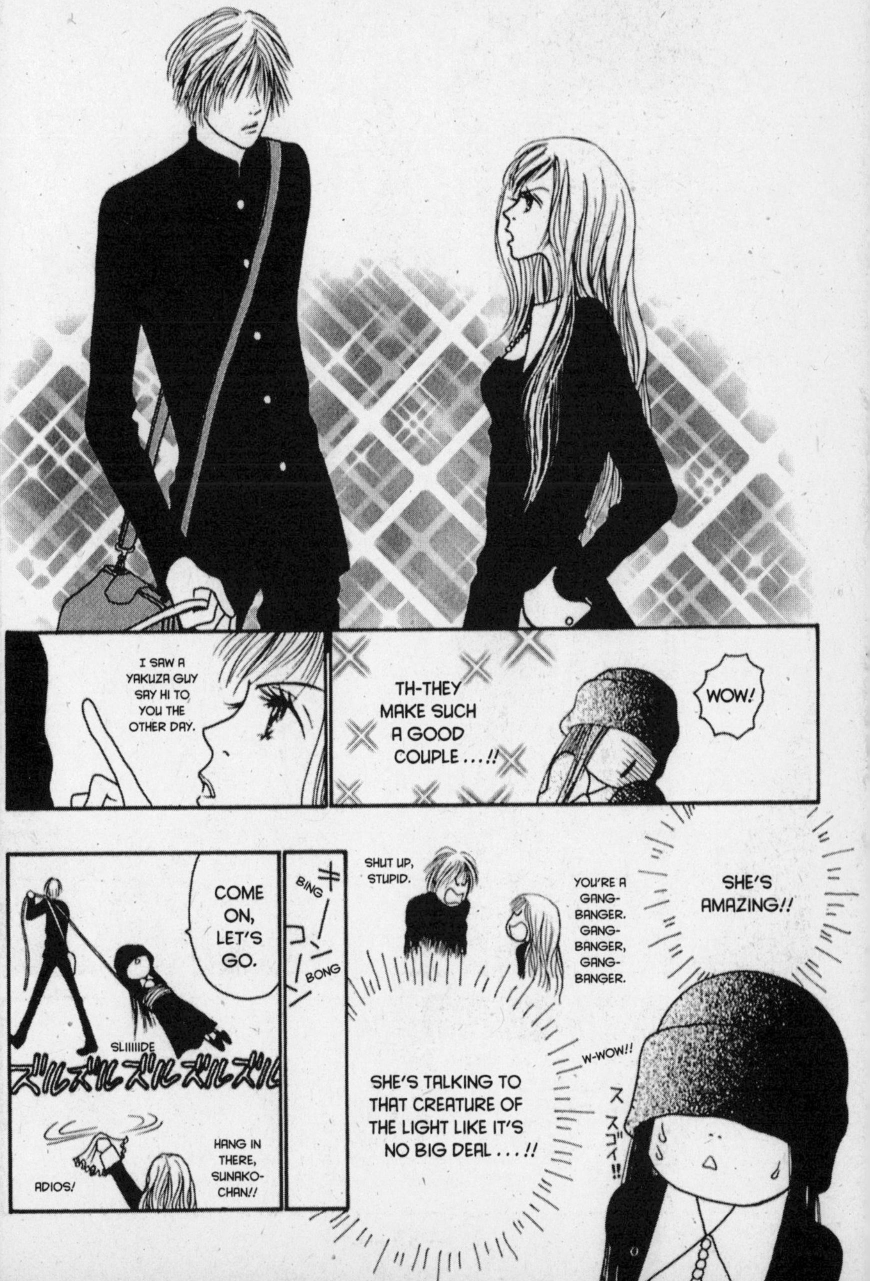
WOW!
TH-THEY MAKE SUCH A GOOD COUPLE . . . !!
I SAW A YAKUZA GUY SAY HI TO YOU THE OTHER DAY.
SHE'S AMAZING!!
YOU'RE A GANG-BANGER. GANG-BANGER, GANG-BANGER.
SHUT UP, STUPID.
W-WOW!!
スゴイ!!
SHE'S TALKING TO THAT CREATURE OF THE LIGHT LIKE IT'S NO BIG DEAL . . . !!
BING
BONG
COME ON, LET'S GO.
SLIIIIIDE
ズルズルズルズルズル
HANG IN THERE, SUNAKO-CHAN!!
ADIOS!

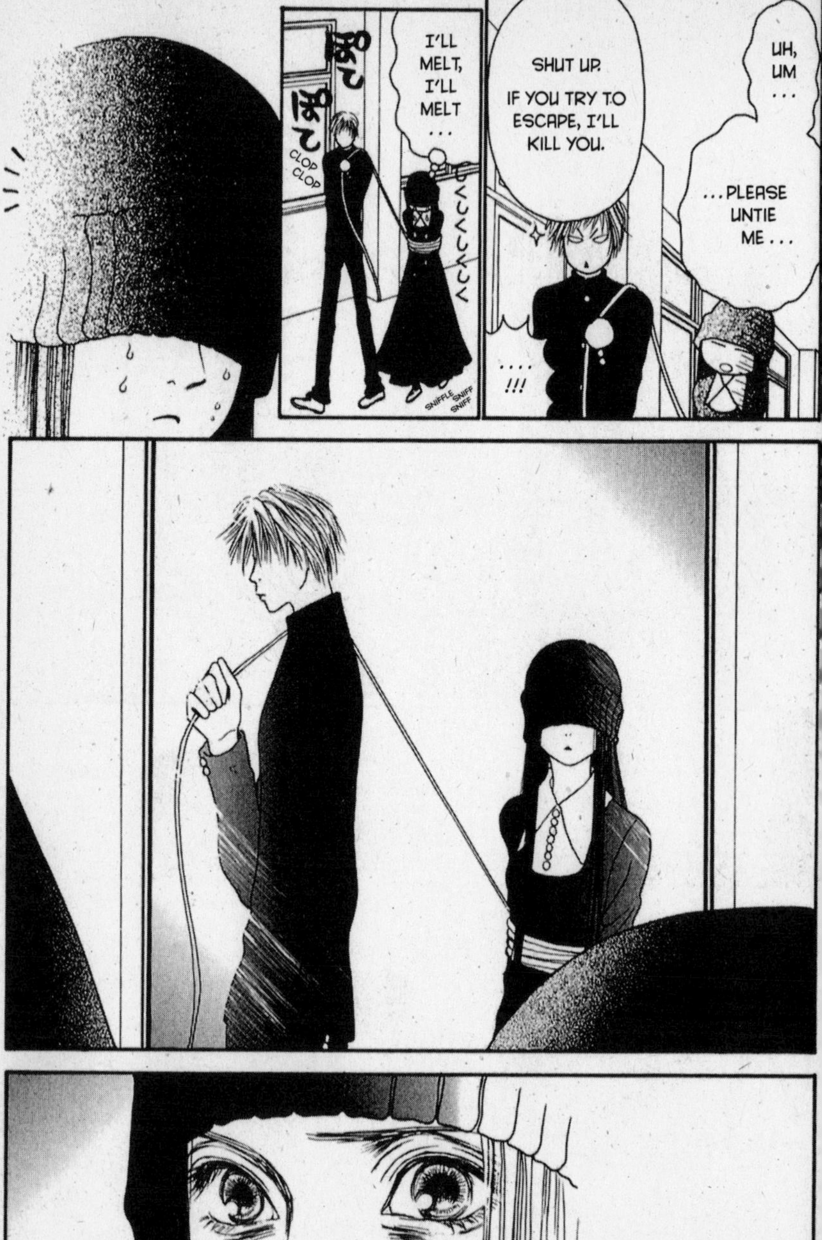
UH, UM . . .
SHUT UP.
IF YOU TRY TO ESCAPE, I'LL KILL YOU.
. . . PLEASE UNTIE ME . . .
. . . .
!!!
I'LL MELT, I'LL MELT . . .
ぽて ぽて
CLOP CLOP
SNIFFLE SNIFF SNIFF

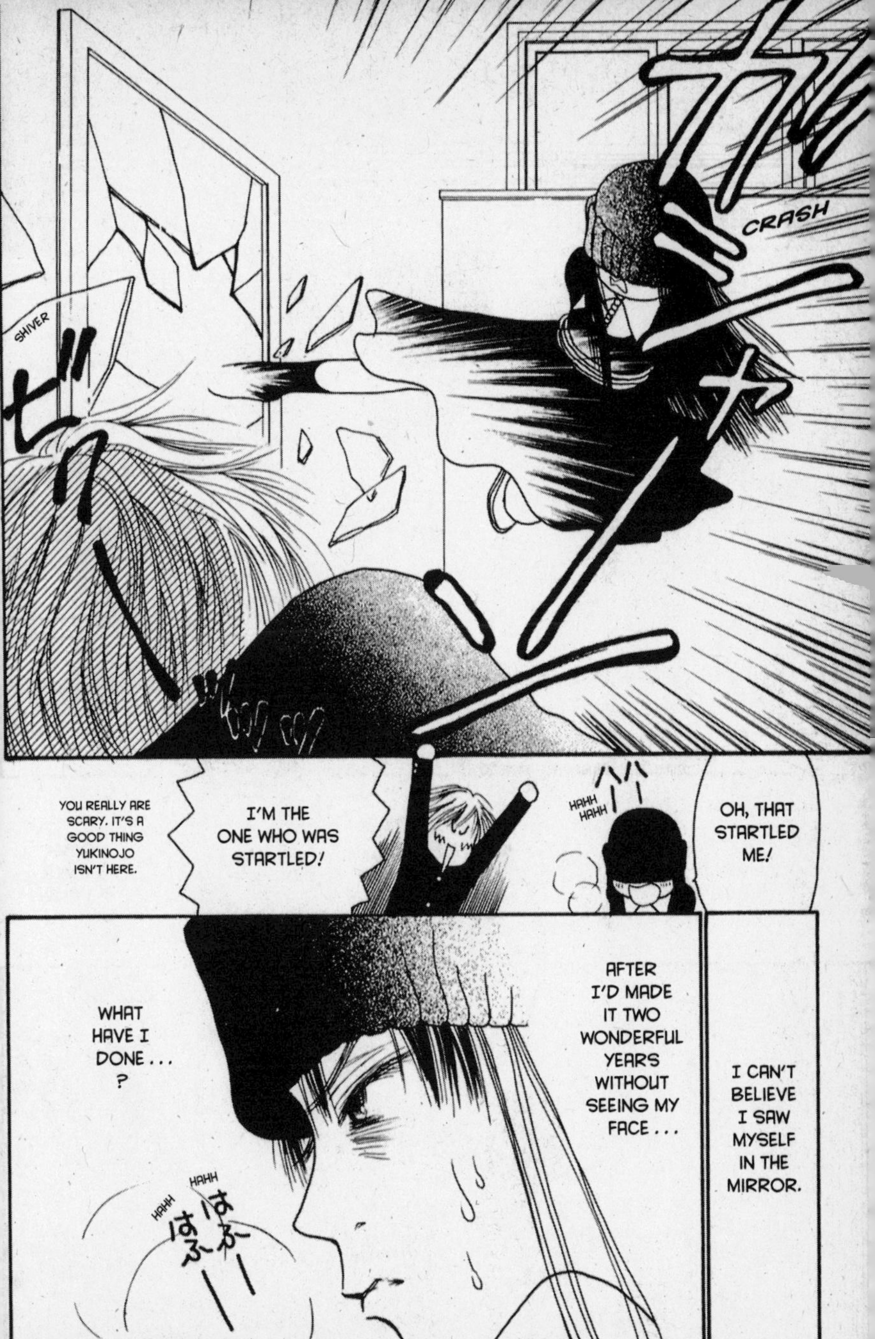
CRASH
SHIVER
HAHH HAHH
OH, THAT STARTLED ME!
I'M THE ONE WHO WAS STARTLED!
YOU REALLY ARE SCARY. IT'S A GOOD THING YUKINOJO ISN'T HERE.
I CAN'T BELIEVE I SAW MYSELF IN THE MIRROR.
AFTER I'D MADE IT TWO WONDERFUL YEARS WITHOUT SEEING MY FACE . . .
WHAT HAVE I DONE . . . ?
HAHH HAHH

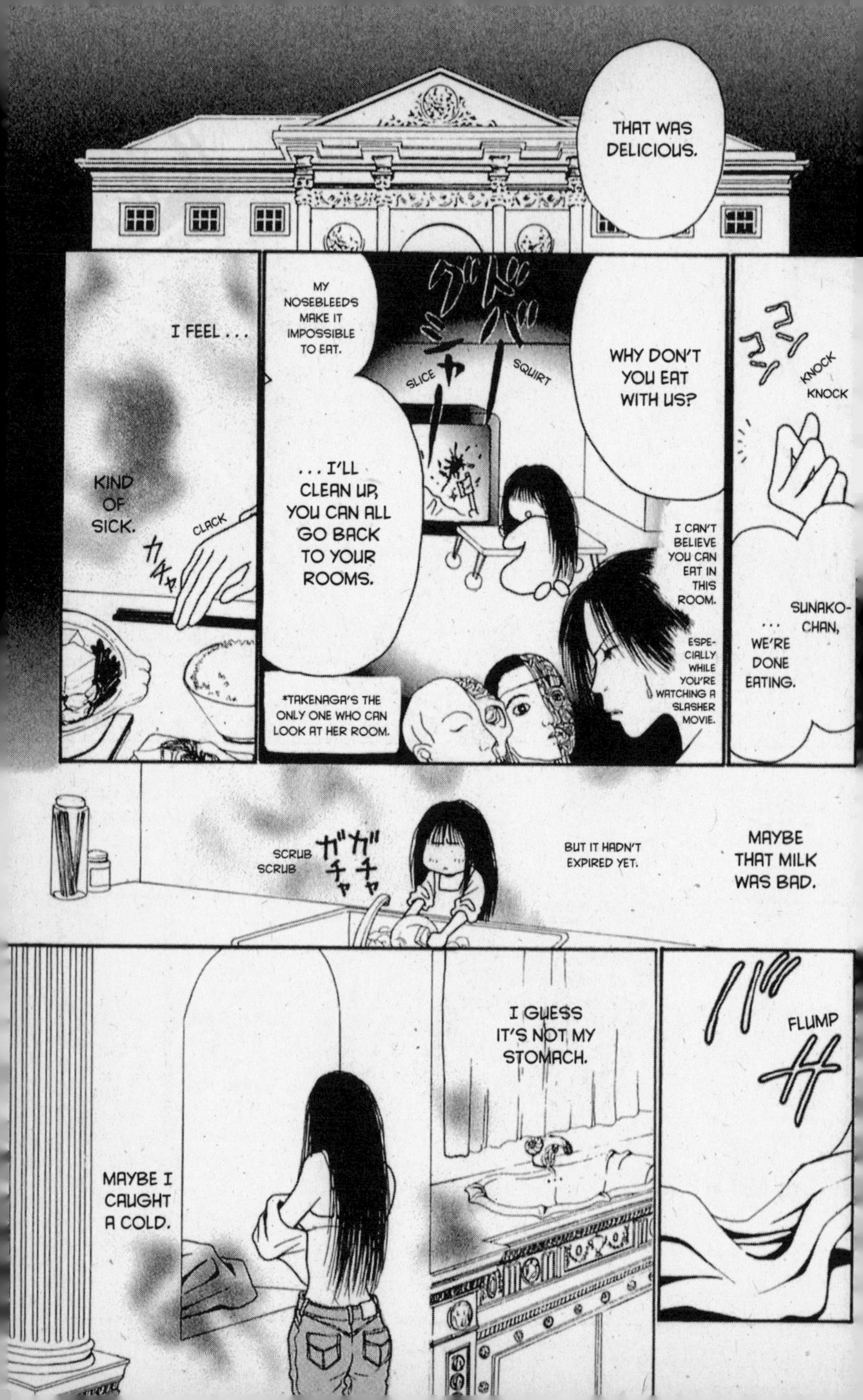
THAT WAS DELICIOUS.
KNOCK KNOCK
SUNAKO-CHAN, . . . WE'RE DONE EATING.
WHY DON'T YOU EAT WITH US?
I CAN'T BELIEVE YOU CAN EAT IN THIS ROOM.
ESPECIALLY WHILE YOU'RE WATCHING A SLASHER MOVIE.
SQUIRT
SLICE
MY NOSEBLEEDS MAKE IT IMPOSSIBLE TO EAT.
. . . I'LL CLEAN UP, YOU CAN ALL GO BACK TO YOUR ROOMS.
*TAKENAGA'S THE ONLY ONE WHO CAN LOOK AT HER ROOM.
I FEEL . . .
KIND OF SICK.
CLACK
MAYBE THAT MILK WAS BAD.
BUT IT HADN'T EXPIRED YET.
SCRUB SCRUB
FLUMP
I GUESS IT'S NOT MY STOMACH.
MAYBE I CAUGHT A COLD.

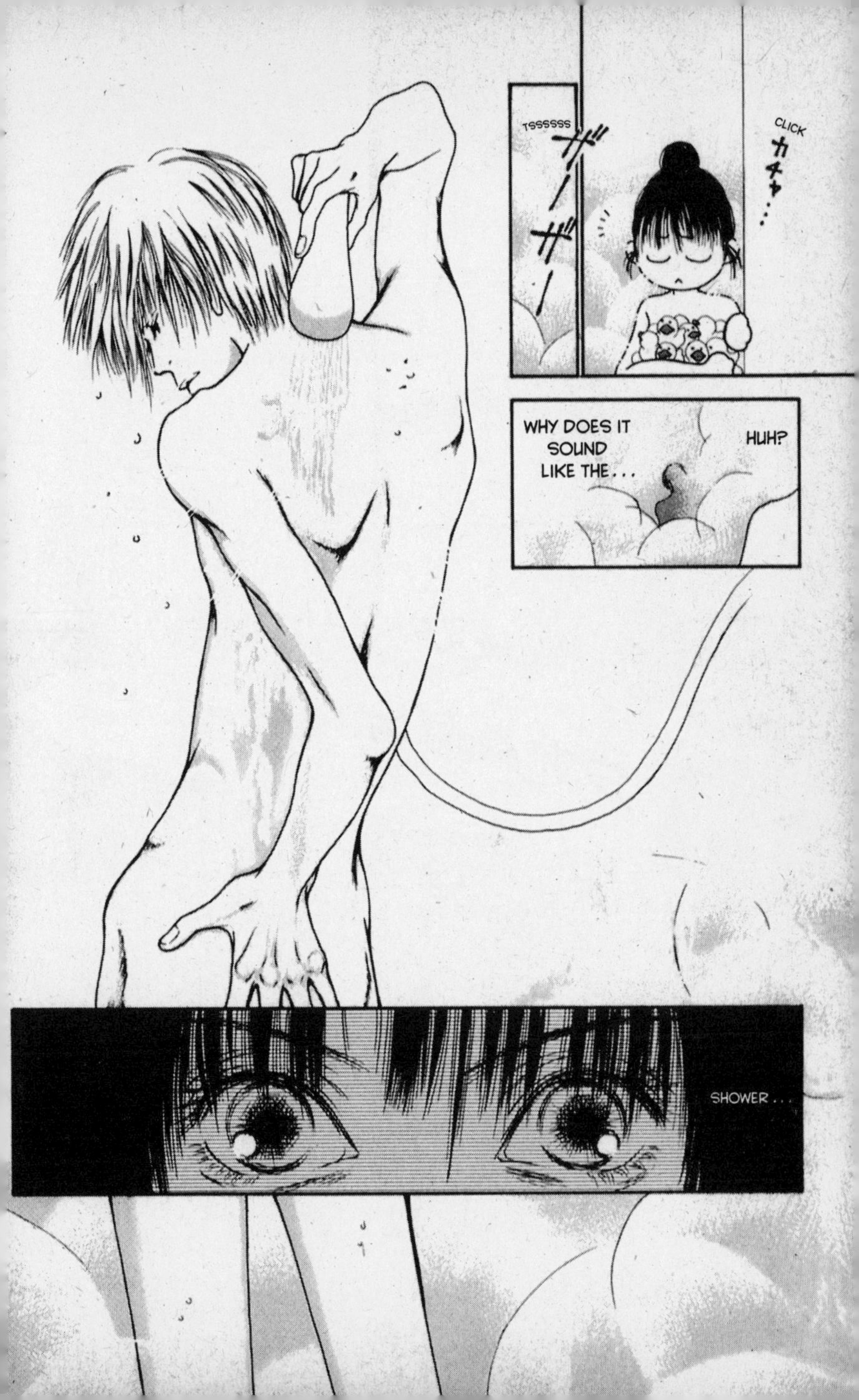

CLICK
カチャ...
TSSSSS
ザーザー
HUH?
WHY DOES IT SOUND LIKE THE...
SHOWER...

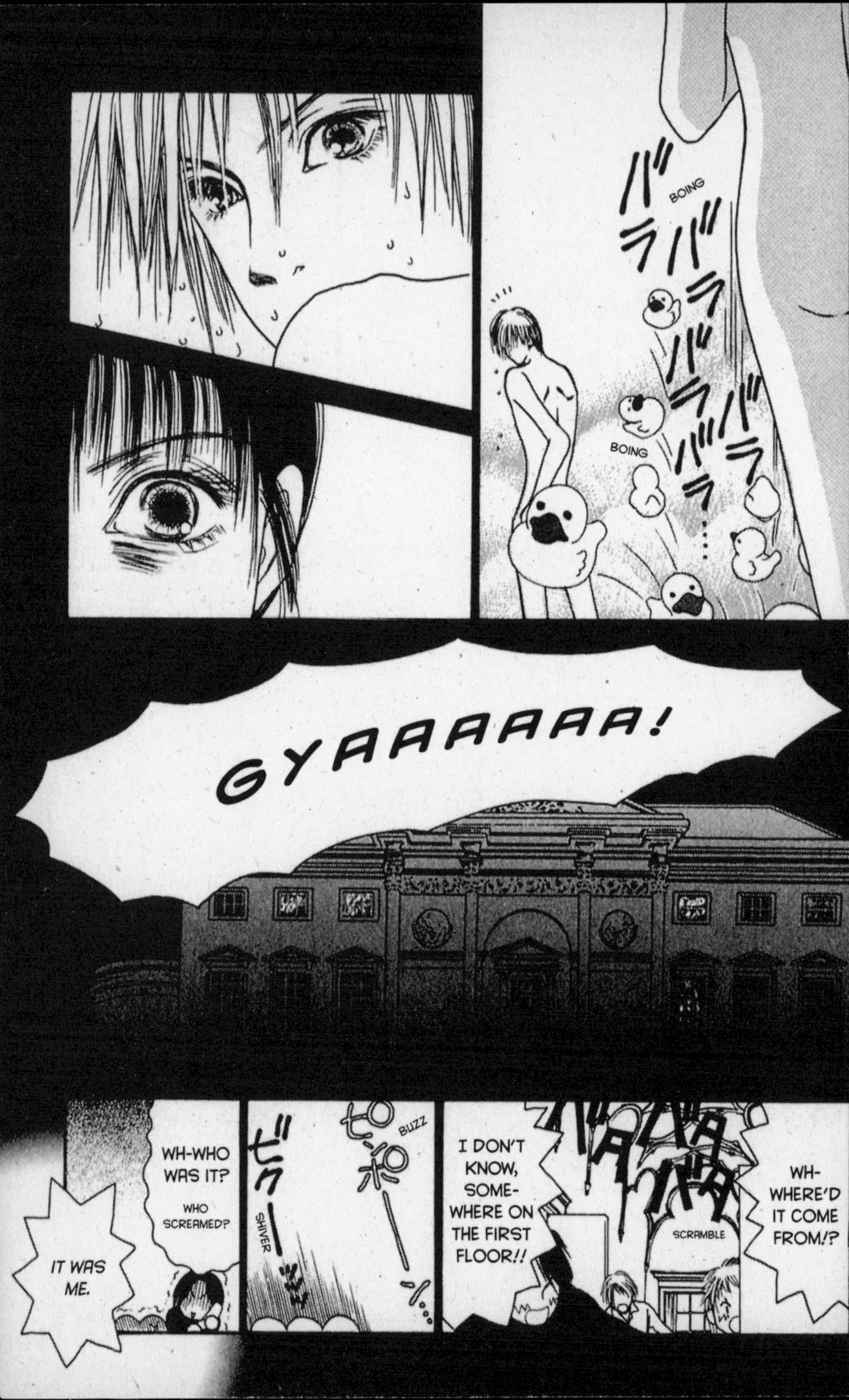
BOING
BOING
GYAAAAAAA!
WH-WHERE'D IT COME FROM!?
SCRAMBLE
I DON'T KNOW, SOME-WHERE ON THE FIRST FLOOR!!
BUZZ
SHIVER
WH-WHO WAS IT?
WHO SCREAMED?
IT WAS ME.

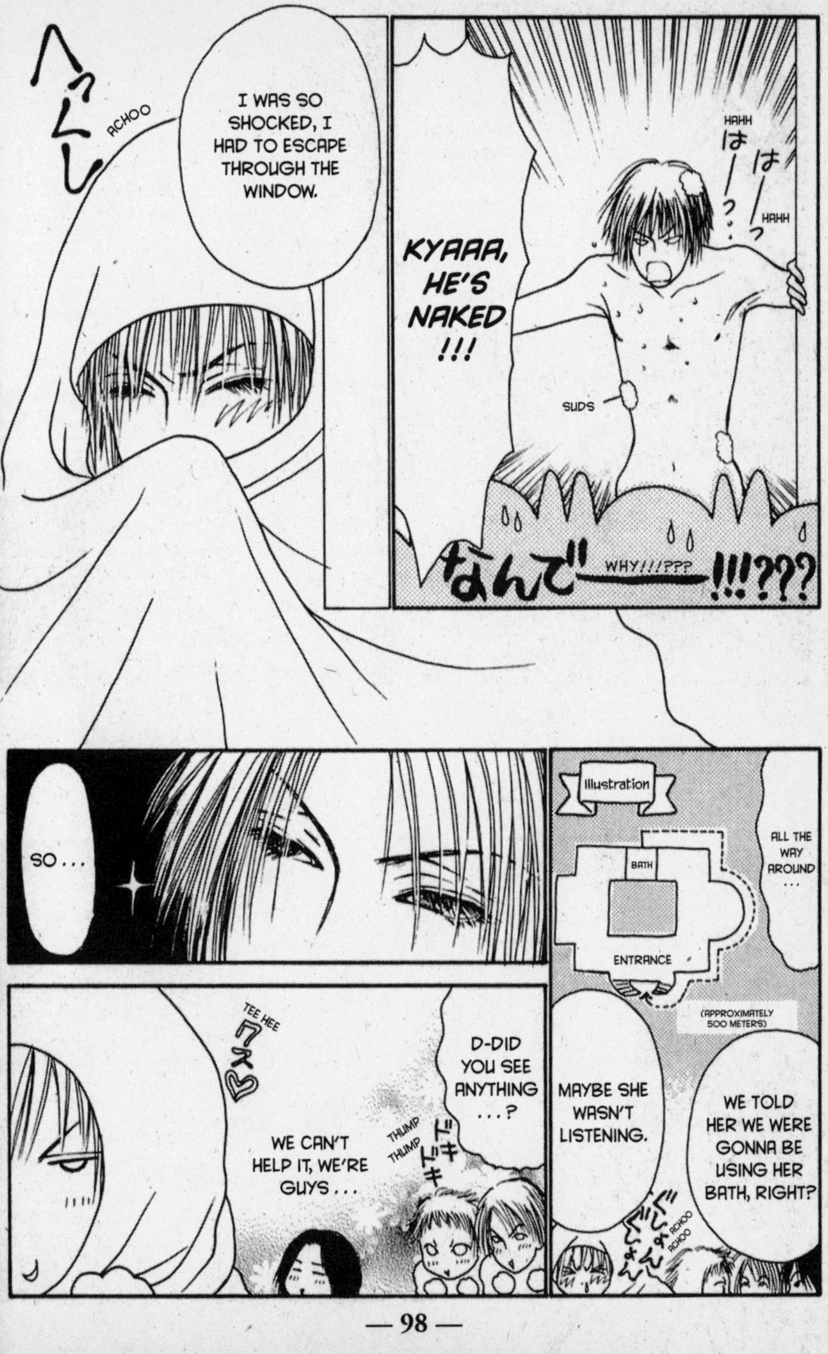
KYAAA, HE'S NAKED !!!
はーっ
HAHH
はーっ
HAHH
SUDS
なんでーー!!!???
WHY!!!???
I WAS SO SHOCKED, I HAD TO ESCAPE THROUGH THE WINDOW.
へっくし
ACHOO
Illustration
BATH
ENTRANCE
ALL THE WAY AROUND ...
(APPROXIMATELY 500 METERS)
WE TOLD HER WE WERE GONNA BE USING HER BATH, RIGHT?
ぐしゅんぐしゅん
ACHOO ACHOO
MAYBE SHE WASN'T LISTENING.
SO ...
D-DID YOU SEE ANYTHING ...?
ドキドキ
THUMP THUMP
WE CAN'T HELP IT, WE'RE GUYS ...
クスッ♡
TEE HEE

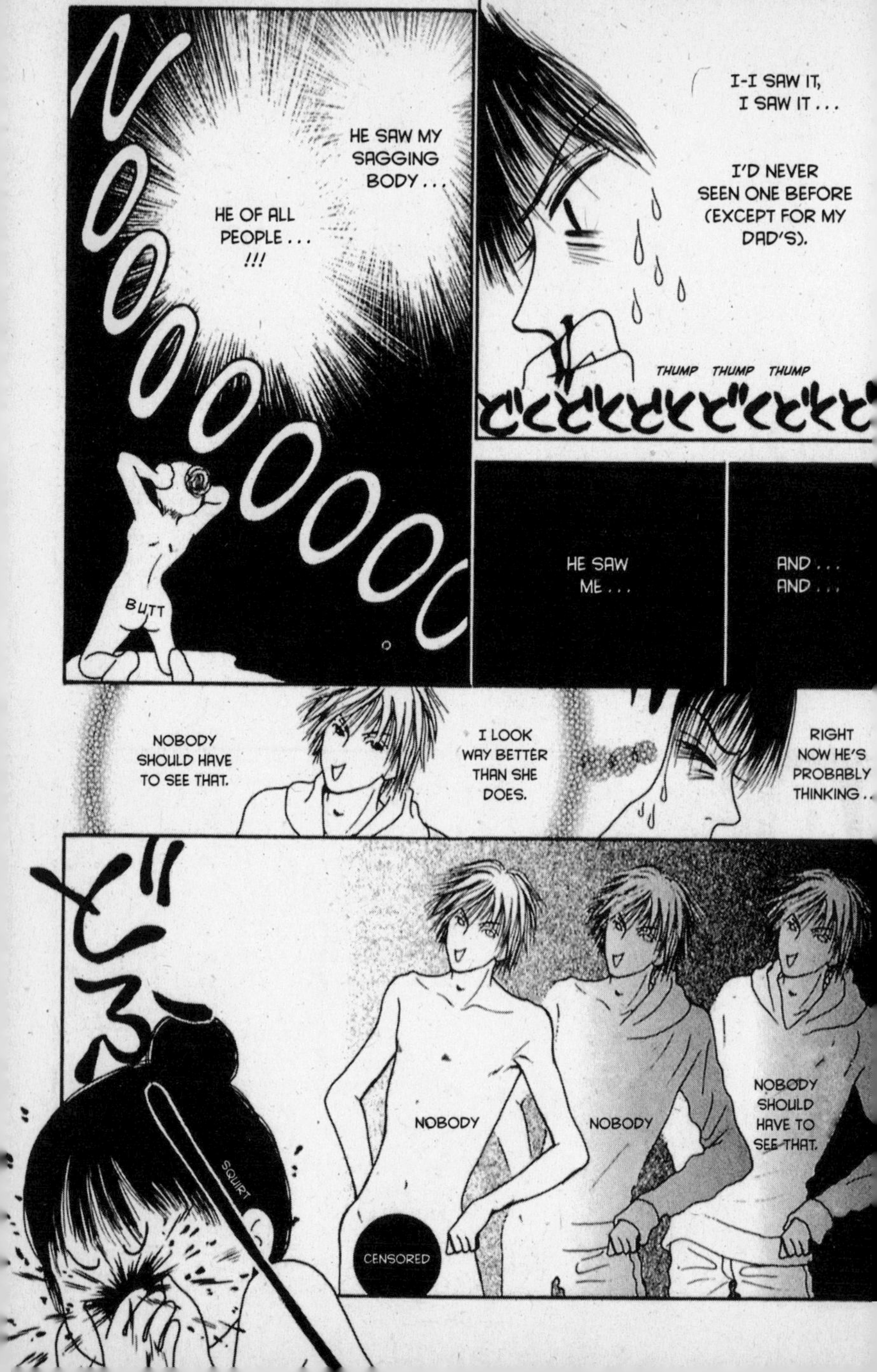

I-I SAW IT, I SAW IT . . .
I'D NEVER SEEN ONE BEFORE (EXCEPT FOR MY DAD'S).
THUMP THUMP THUMP
AND . . . AND . . .
HE SAW ME . . .
HE SAW MY SAGGING BODY . . .
HE OF ALL PEOPLE . . . !!!
NOOOOOOOOOO.
BUTT
RIGHT NOW HE'S PROBABLY THINKING . .
I LOOK WAY BETTER THAN SHE DOES.
NOBODY SHOULD HAVE TO SEE THAT.
NOBODY SHOULD HAVE TO SEE THAT.
NOBODY
NOBODY
CENSORED
SQUIRT

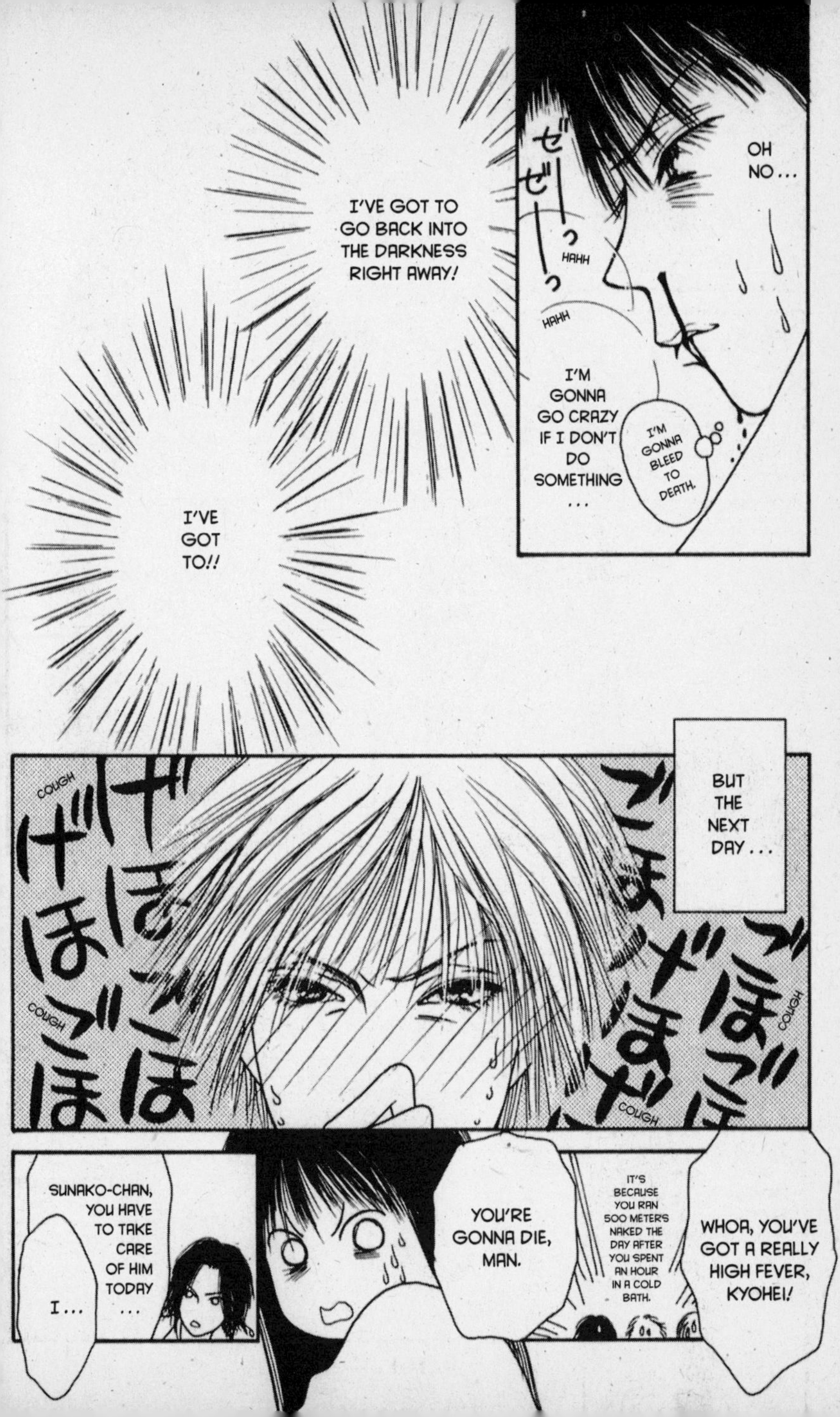
OH NO...
ぜーっ
ぜーっ
HAHH
HAHH
I'M GONNA GO CRAZY IF I DON'T DO SOMETHING...
I'M GONNA BLEED TO DEATH.
I'VE GOT TO GO BACK INTO THE DARKNESS RIGHT AWAY!
I'VE GOT TO!!
BUT THE NEXT DAY...
COUGH
COUGH
COUGH
COUGH
WHOA, YOU'VE GOT A REALLY HIGH FEVER, KYOHEI!
IT'S BECAUSE YOU RAN 500 METERS NAKED THE DAY AFTER YOU SPENT AN HOUR IN A COLD BATH.
YOU'RE GONNA DIE, MAN.
SUNAKO-CHAN, YOU HAVE TO TAKE CARE OF HIM TODAY...
I...

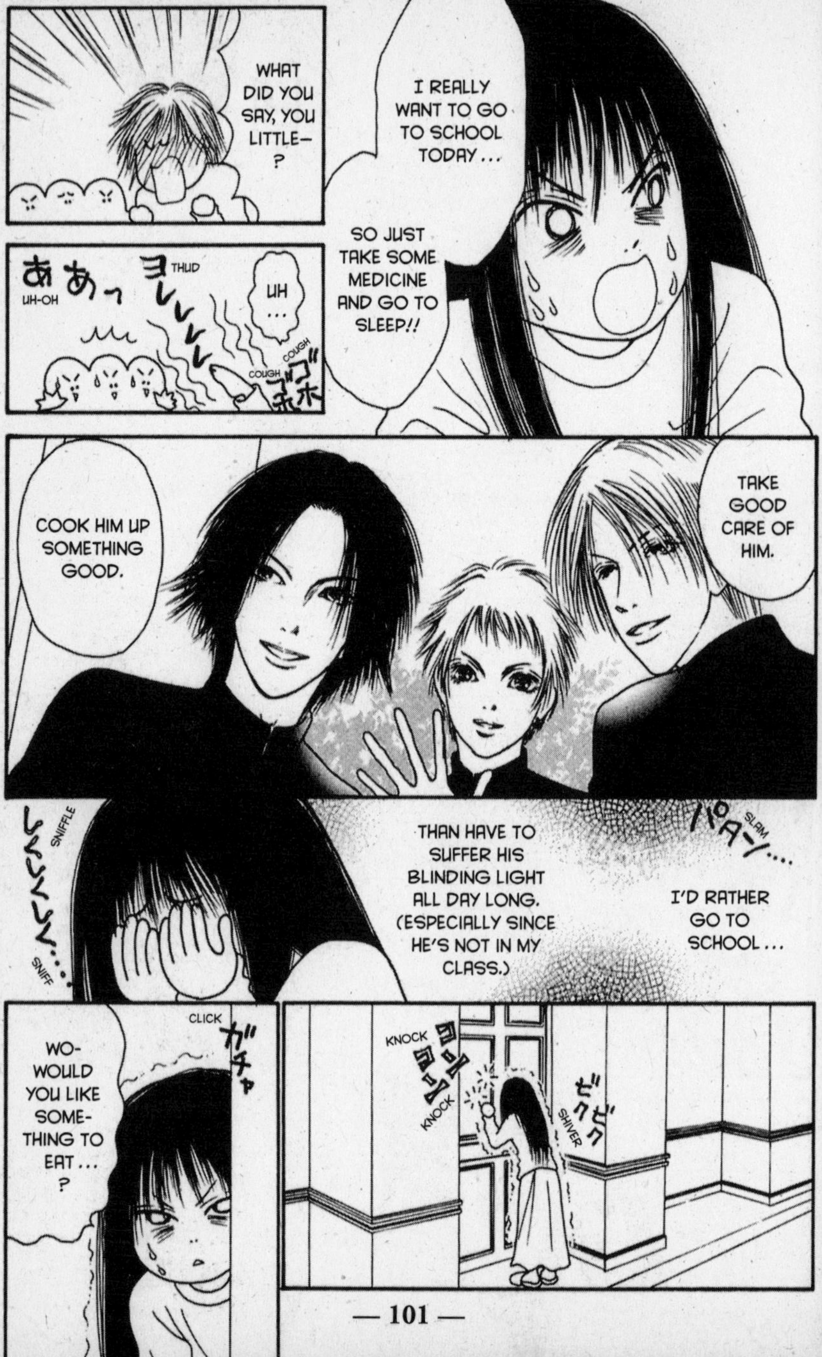

I REALLY WANT TO GO TO SCHOOL TODAY...
SO JUST TAKE SOME MEDICINE AND GO TO SLEEP!!
WHAT DID YOU SAY, YOU LITTLE—?
ヨレレレレ THUD
ああっ UH-OH
UH...
ゴホ COUGH
ゴホ COUGH
TAKE GOOD CARE OF HIM.
COOK HIM UP SOMETHING GOOD.
パターン... SLAM
I'D RATHER GO TO SCHOOL...
THAN HAVE TO SUFFER HIS BLINDING LIGHT ALL DAY LONG. (ESPECIALLY SINCE HE'S NOT IN MY CLASS.)
しくしくしく... SNIFFLE SNIFF
ビクビク SHIVER
コン KNOCK
コン KNOCK
ガチャ CLICK
WO- WOULD YOU LIKE SOME- THING TO EAT...?

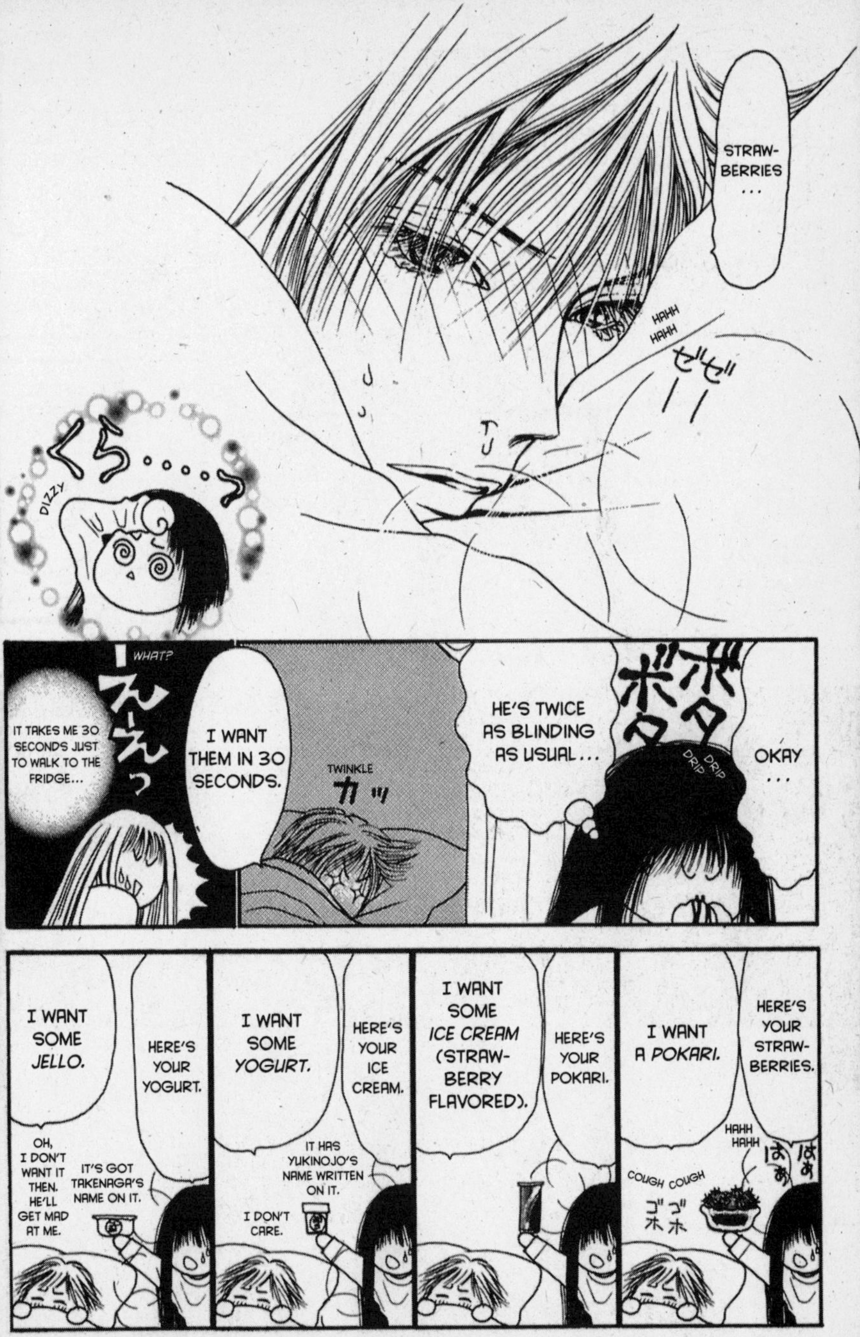
STRAW-BERRIES . . .
HAHH HAHH
くら…っ
DIZZY
OKAY . . .
ボタボタ
DRIP DRIP
HE'S TWICE AS BLINDING AS USUAL . . .
TWINKLE
カッ
I WANT THEM IN 30 SECONDS.
WHAT?
んーんっ
IT TAKES ME 30 SECONDS JUST TO WALK TO THE FRIDGE . . .
HERE'S YOUR STRAW-BERRIES.
I WANT A *POKARI.*
HAHH HAHH
はぁはぁ
COUGH COUGH
ゴホゴホ
HERE'S YOUR POKARI.
I WANT SOME *ICE CREAM* (STRAW-BERRY FLAVORED).
HERE'S YOUR ICE CREAM.
I WANT SOME *YOGURT.*
IT HAS YUKINOJO'S NAME WRITTEN ON IT.
I DON'T CARE.
HERE'S YOUR YOGURT.
I WANT SOME *JELLO.*
IT'S GOT TAKENAGA'S NAME ON IT.
OH, I DON'T WANT IT THEN. HE'LL GET MAD AT ME.

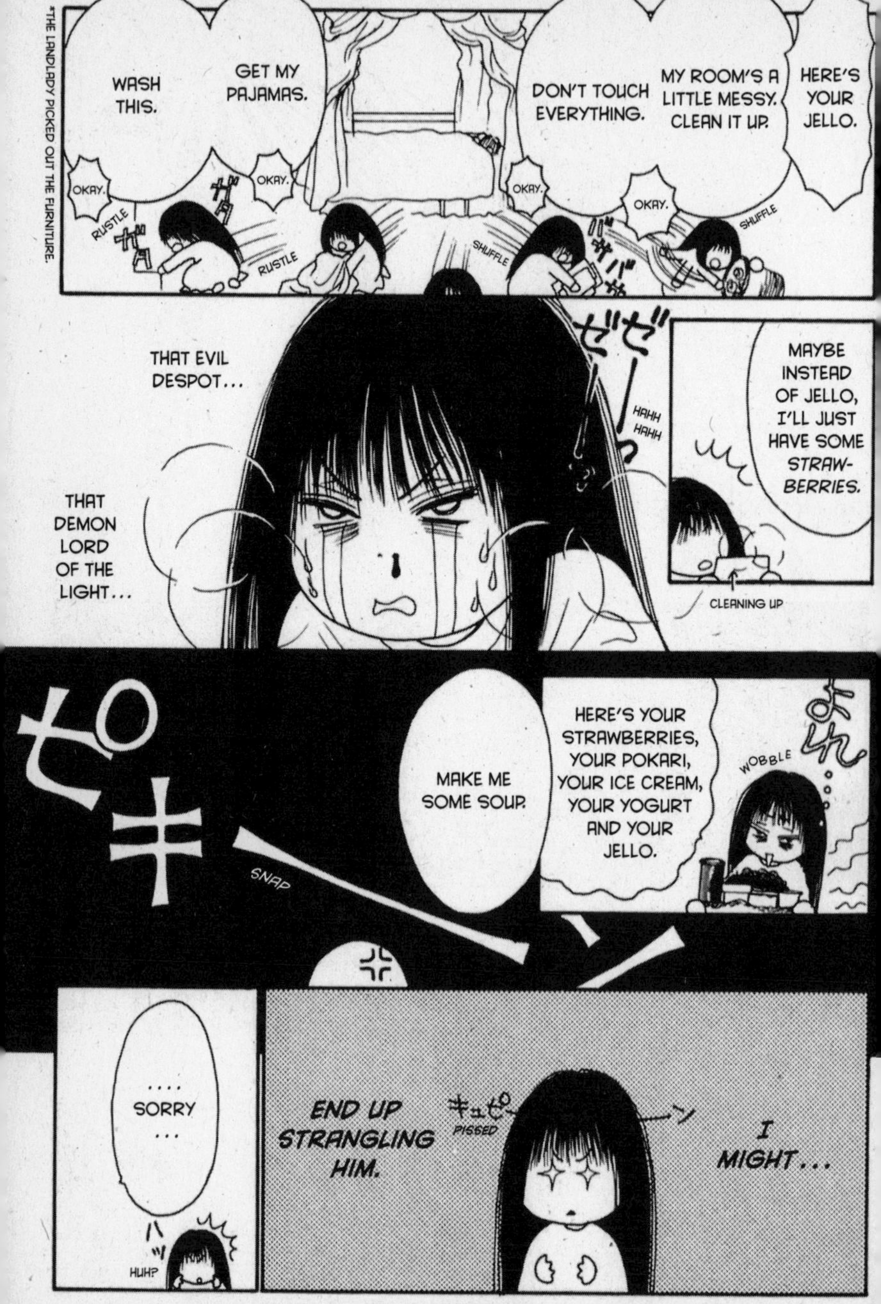
HERE'S YOUR JELLO.
OKAY.
SHUFFLE
MY ROOM'S A LITTLE MESSY. CLEAN IT UP.
DON'T TOUCH EVERYTHING.
OKAY.
SHUFFLE
GET MY PAJAMAS.
OKAY.
RUSTLE
WASH THIS.
OKAY.
RUSTLE
MAYBE INSTEAD OF JELLO, I'LL JUST HAVE SOME STRAWBERRIES.
CLEANING UP
HAHH HAHH
THAT EVIL DESPOT...
THAT DEMON LORD OF THE LIGHT...
WOBBLE
HERE'S YOUR STRAWBERRIES, YOUR POKARI, YOUR ICE CREAM, YOUR YOGURT AND YOUR JELLO.
MAKE ME SOME SOUP.
SNAP
I MIGHT...
PISSED
END UP STRANGLING HIM.
HUH?
....SORRY...

*THE LANDLADY PICKED OUT THE FURNITURE.

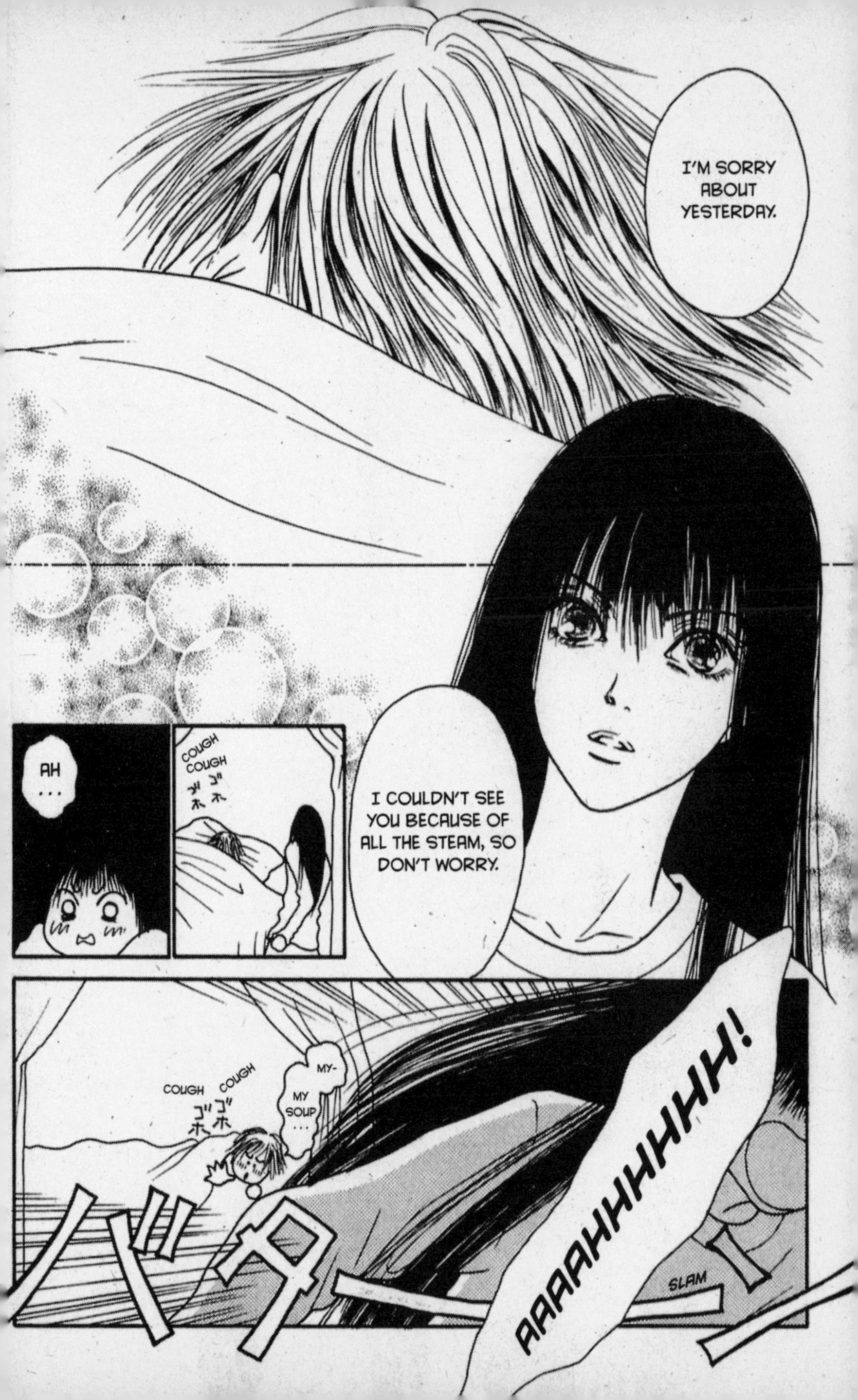
I'M SORRY ABOUT YESTERDAY.
I COULDN'T SEE YOU BECAUSE OF ALL THE STEAM, SO DON'T WORRY.
COUGH COUGH
ゴホ ゴホ
AH ...
AAAAHHHHHHHH!
MY- MY SOUP ...
COUGH COUGH
ゴホ ゴホ
バタ
SLAM

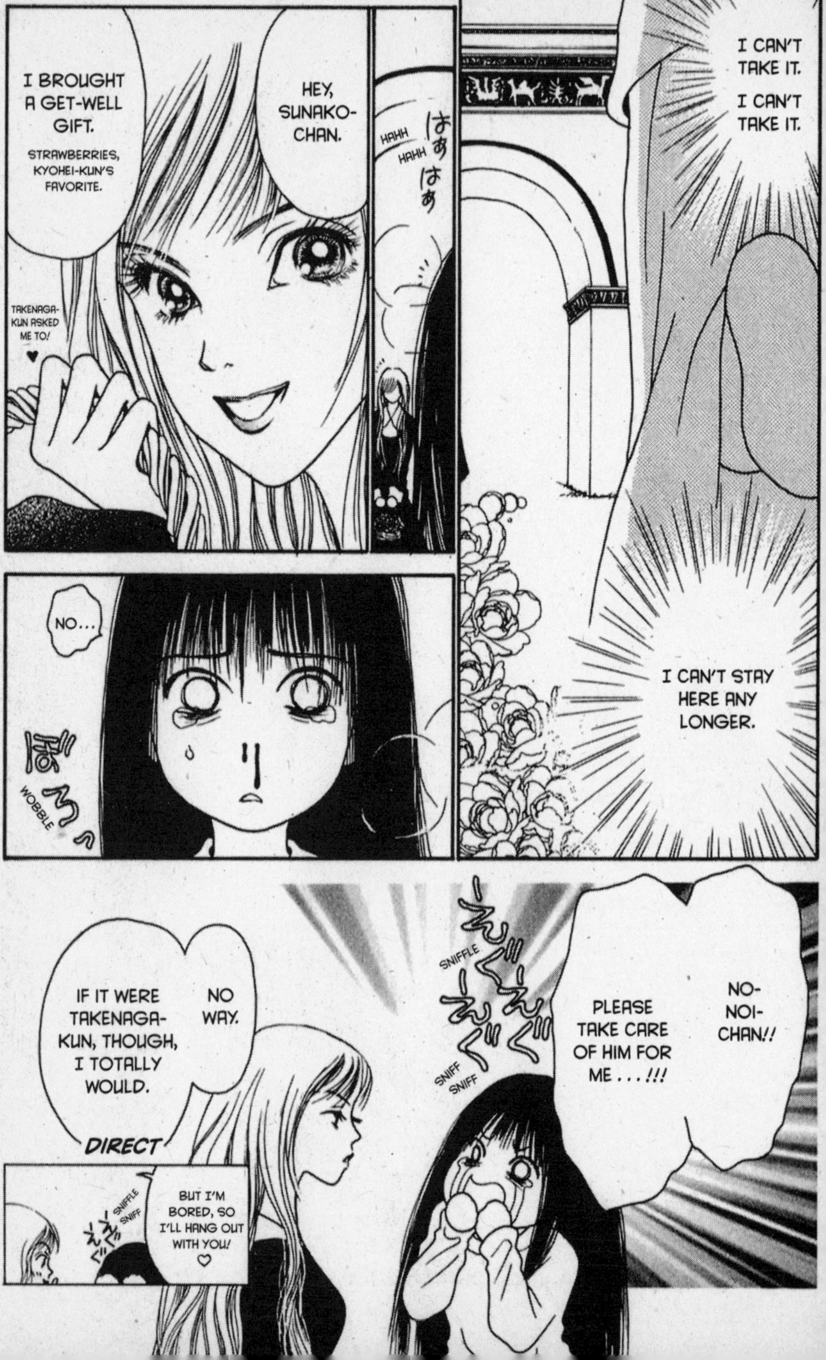
I CAN'T TAKE IT.
I CAN'T TAKE IT.
I CAN'T STAY HERE ANY LONGER.
HAHH HAHH
はあはあ
HEY, SUNAKO-CHAN.
I BROUGHT A GET-WELL GIFT.
STRAWBERRIES, KYOHEI-KUN'S FAVORITE.
TAKENAGA-KUN ASKED ME TO! ♥
NO...
WOBBLE
ぽろっ
NO-NOI-CHAN!!
PLEASE TAKE CARE OF HIM FOR ME...!!!
SNIFFLE
SNIFF SNIFF
えぐえぐ
NO WAY.
IF IT WERE TAKENAGA-KUN, THOUGH, I TOTALLY WOULD.
DIRECT
SNIFFLE SNIFF
BUT I'M BORED, SO I'LL HANG OUT WITH YOU! ♡

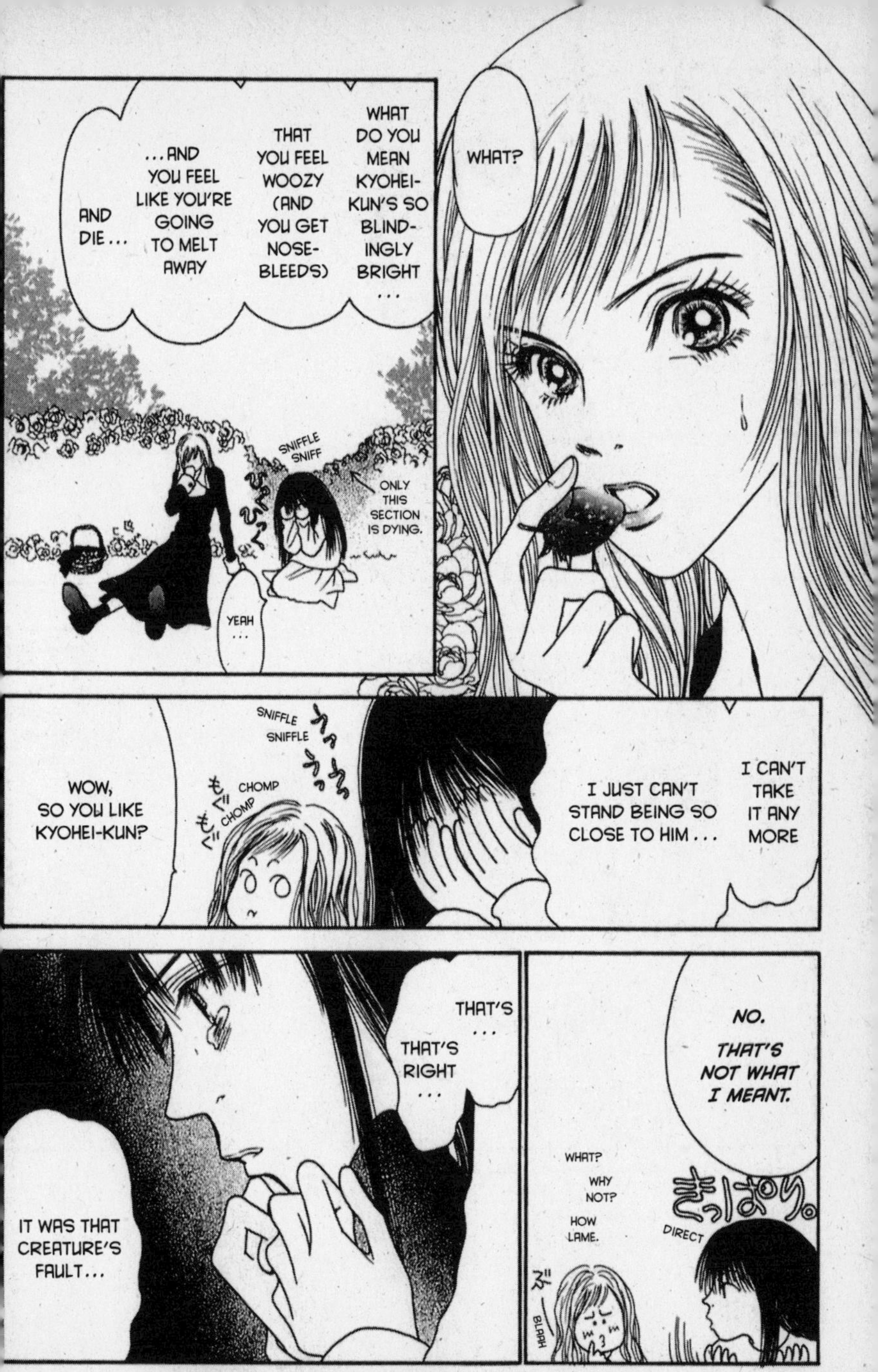
WHAT?
WHAT DO YOU MEAN KYOHEI-KUN'S SO BLINDINGLY BRIGHT . . .
THAT YOU FEEL WOOZY (AND YOU GET NOSEBLEEDS)
. . . AND YOU FEEL LIKE YOU'RE GOING TO MELT AWAY
AND DIE . . .
SNIFFLE SNIFF
ONLY THIS SECTION IS DYING.
YEAH . . .
I CAN'T TAKE IT ANY MORE
I JUST CAN'T STAND BEING SO CLOSE TO HIM . . .
SNIFFLE SNIFFLE
CHOMP CHOMP
WOW, SO YOU LIKE KYOHEI-KUN?
NO. THAT'S NOT WHAT I MEANT.
DIRECT
WHAT? WHY NOT? HOW LAME.
BLAAH
THAT'S . . .
THAT'S RIGHT . . .
IT WAS THAT CREATURE'S FAULT . . .

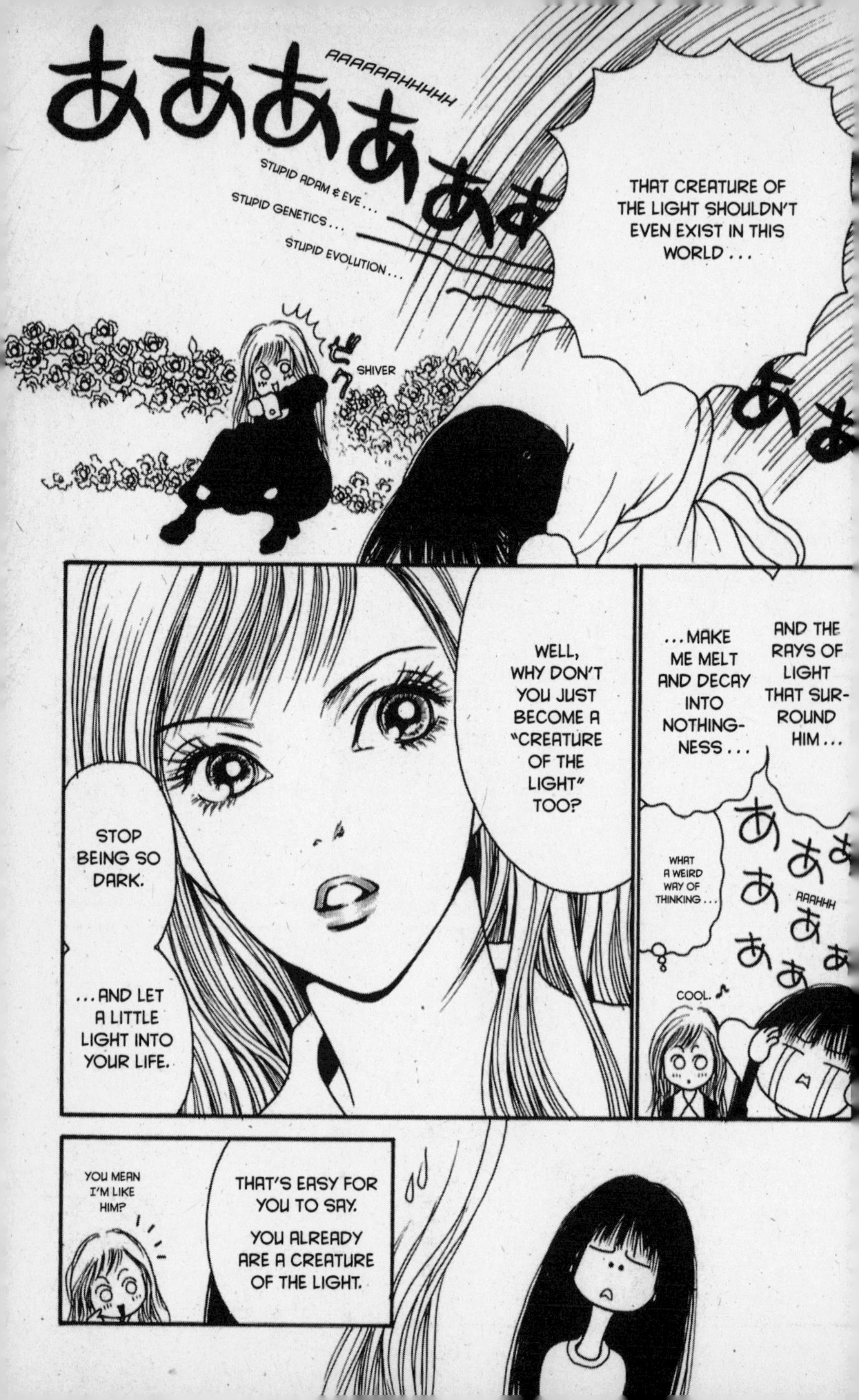

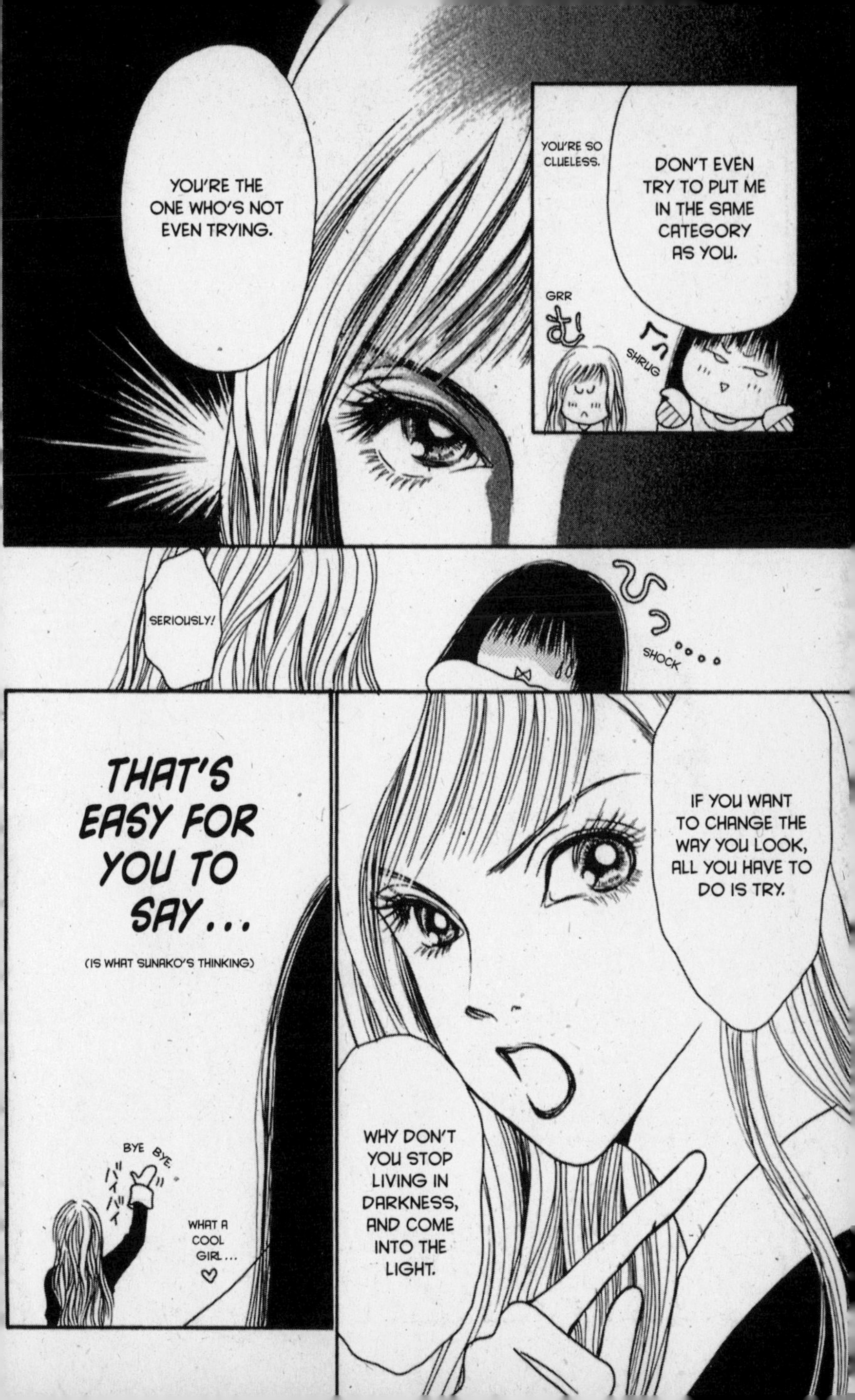
DON'T EVEN TRY TO PUT ME IN THE SAME CATEGORY AS YOU.
YOU'RE SO CLUELESS.
SHRUG
GRR
YOU'RE THE ONE WHO'S NOT EVEN TRYING.
SERIOUSLY!
SHOCK
IF YOU WANT TO CHANGE THE WAY YOU LOOK, ALL YOU HAVE TO DO IS TRY.
WHY DON'T YOU STOP LIVING IN DARKNESS, AND COME INTO THE LIGHT.
THAT'S EASY FOR YOU TO SAY . . .
(IS WHAT SUNAKO'S THINKING)
BYE BYE.
WHAT A COOL GIRL . . . ♥

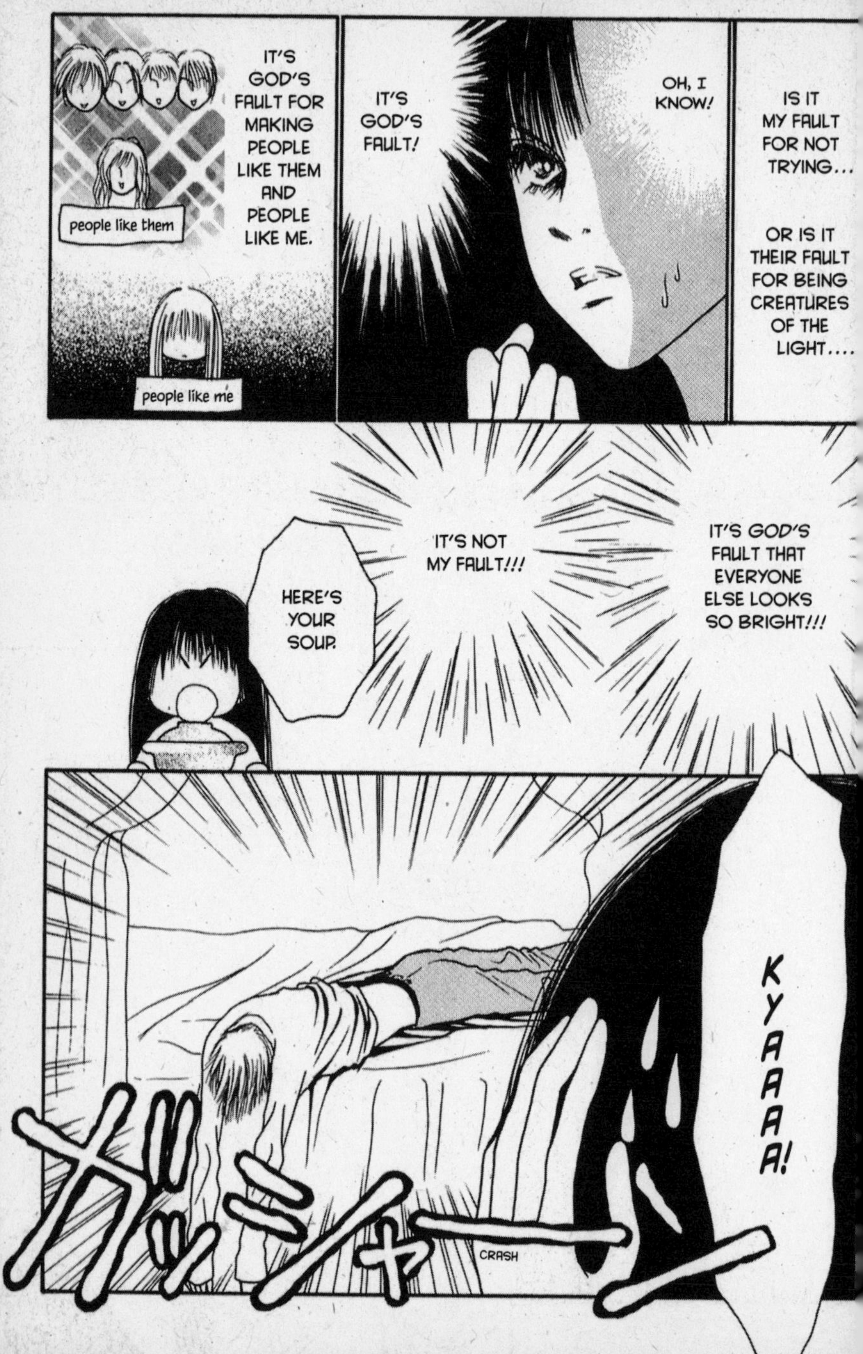
IS IT MY FAULT FOR NOT TRYING...
OR IS IT THEIR FAULT FOR BEING CREATURES OF THE LIGHT....
OH, I KNOW!
IT'S GOD'S FAULT!
IT'S GOD'S FAULT FOR MAKING PEOPLE LIKE THEM AND PEOPLE LIKE ME.
people like them
people like me
IT'S *GOD'S* FAULT THAT EVERYONE ELSE LOOKS SO BRIGHT!!!
IT'S NOT MY FAULT!!!
HERE'S YOUR SOUP.
KYAAAAA!
ガッシャーン
CRASH

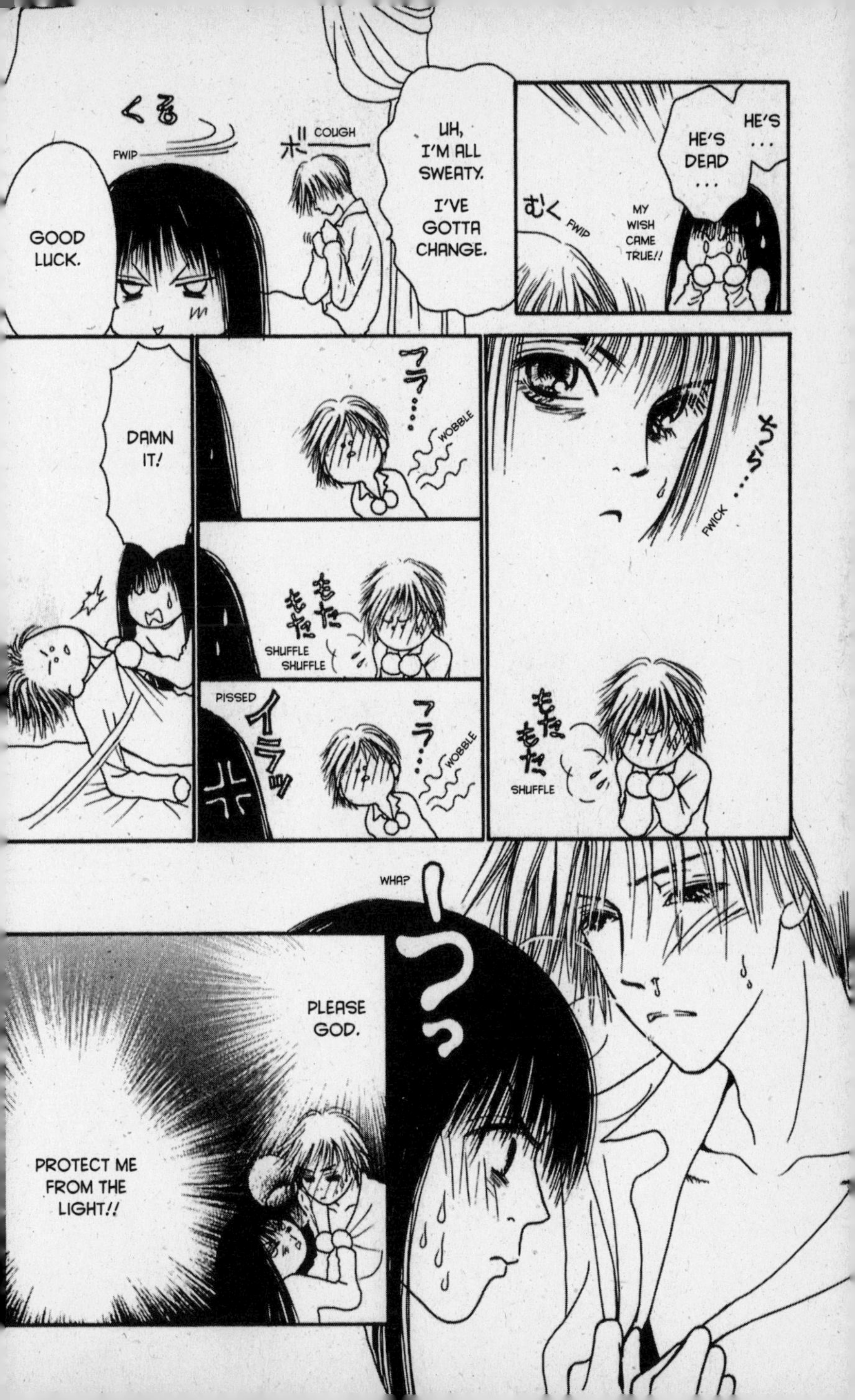
HE'S ...
HE'S DEAD ...
MY WISH CAME TRUE!!
むく
FWIP
UH, I'M ALL SWEATY.
I'VE GOTTA CHANGE.
COUGH
FWIP
GOOD LUCK.
FWICK
SHUFFLE
フラ…
WOBBLE
SHUFFLE SHUFFLE
PISSED
イラッ
フラ…
WOBBLE
DAMN IT!
WHA?
PLEASE GOD.
PROTECT ME FROM THE LIGHT!!

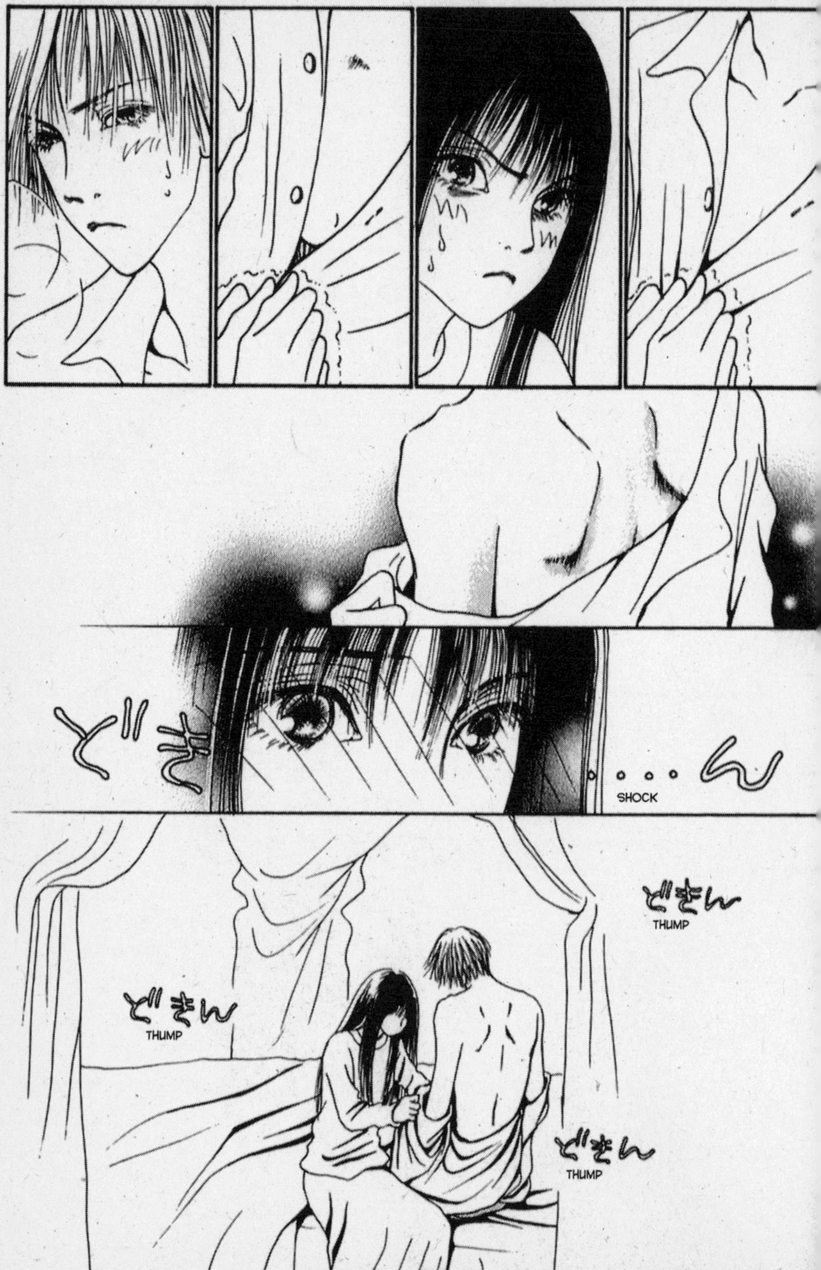
どきん
どきん
どき...ん
SHOCK
どきん
THUMP
どきん
THUMP
どきん
THUMP

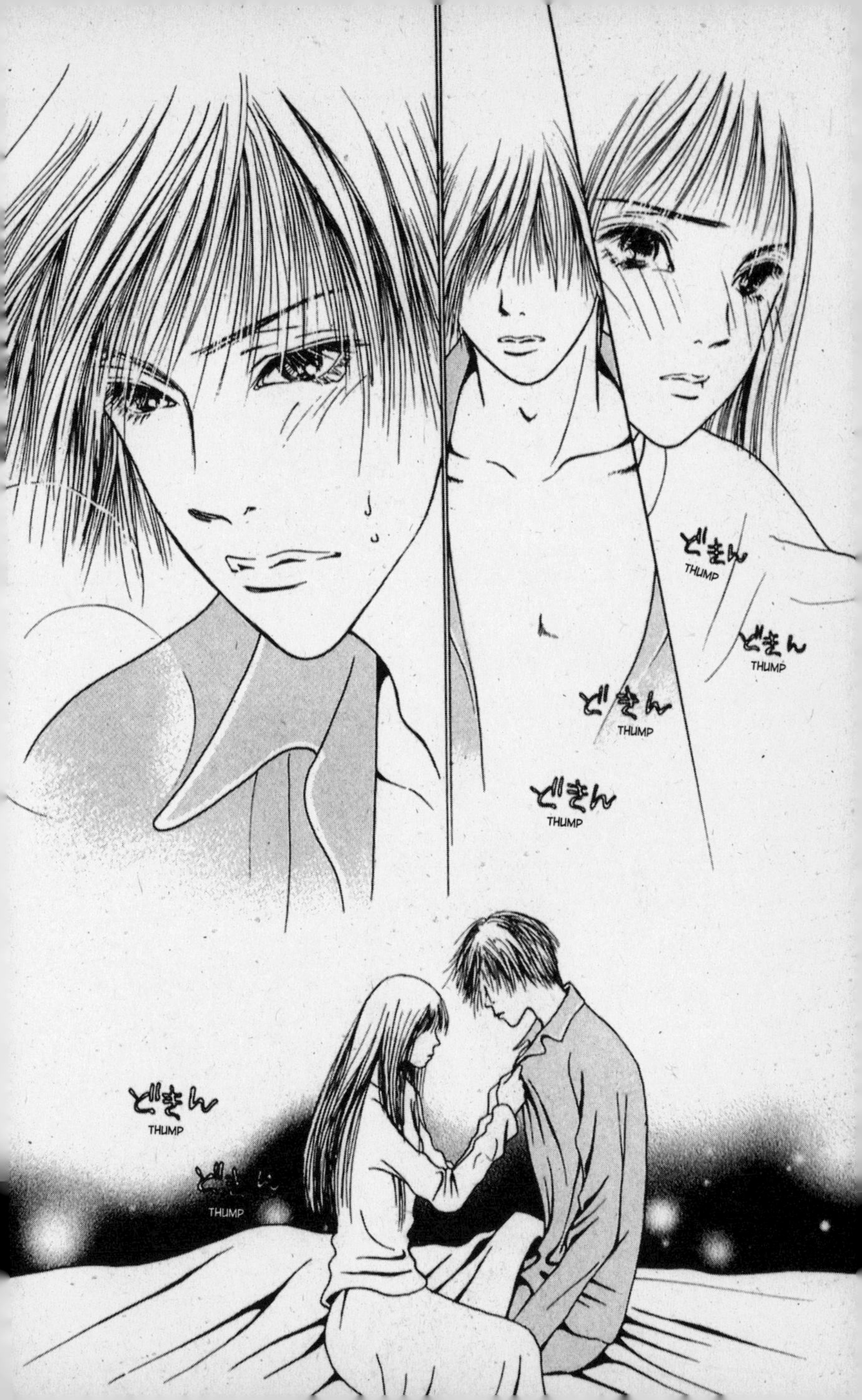
どきん
THUMP
どきん
THUMP
どきん
THUMP
どきん
THUMP
どきん
THUMP
THUMP

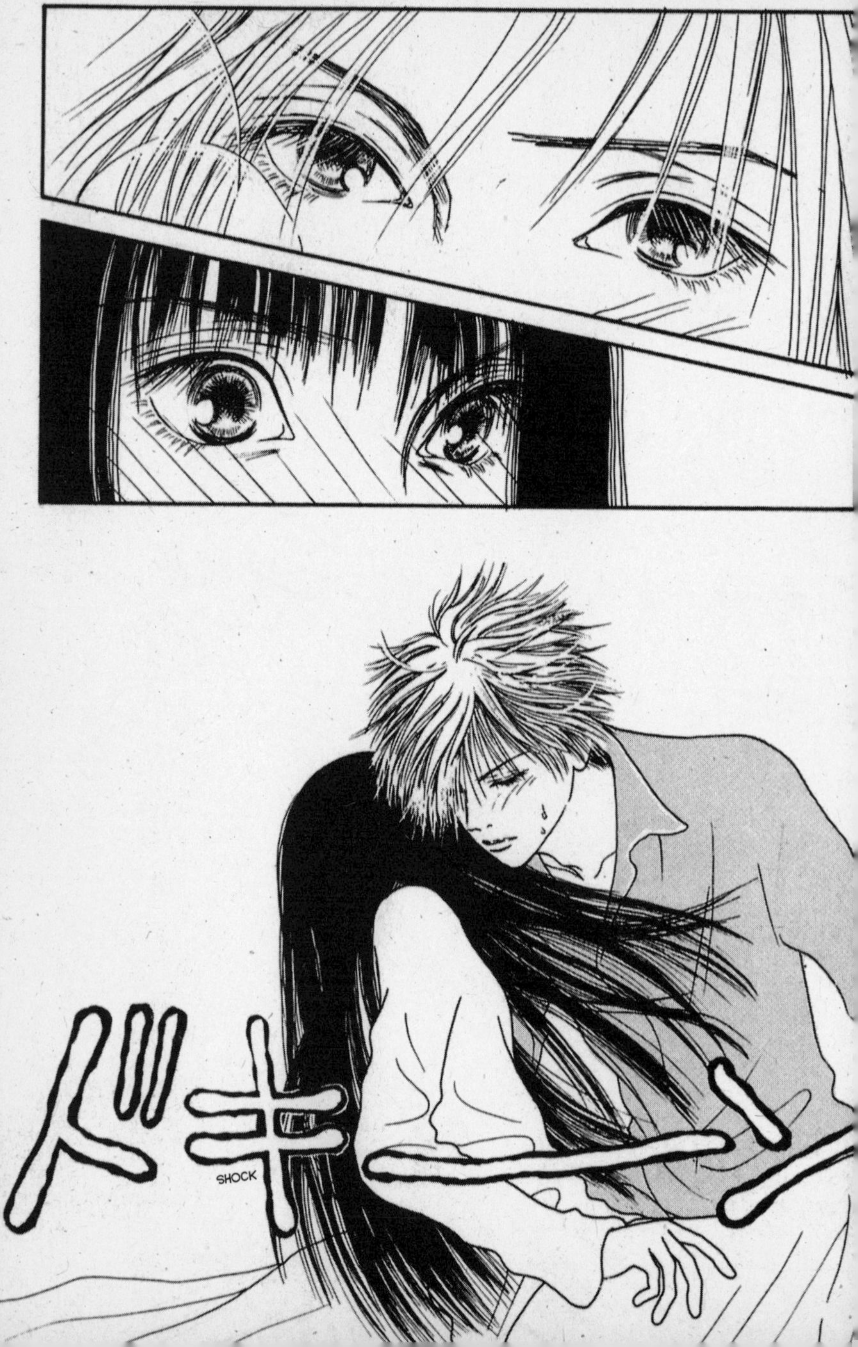
ドキーン
SHOCK

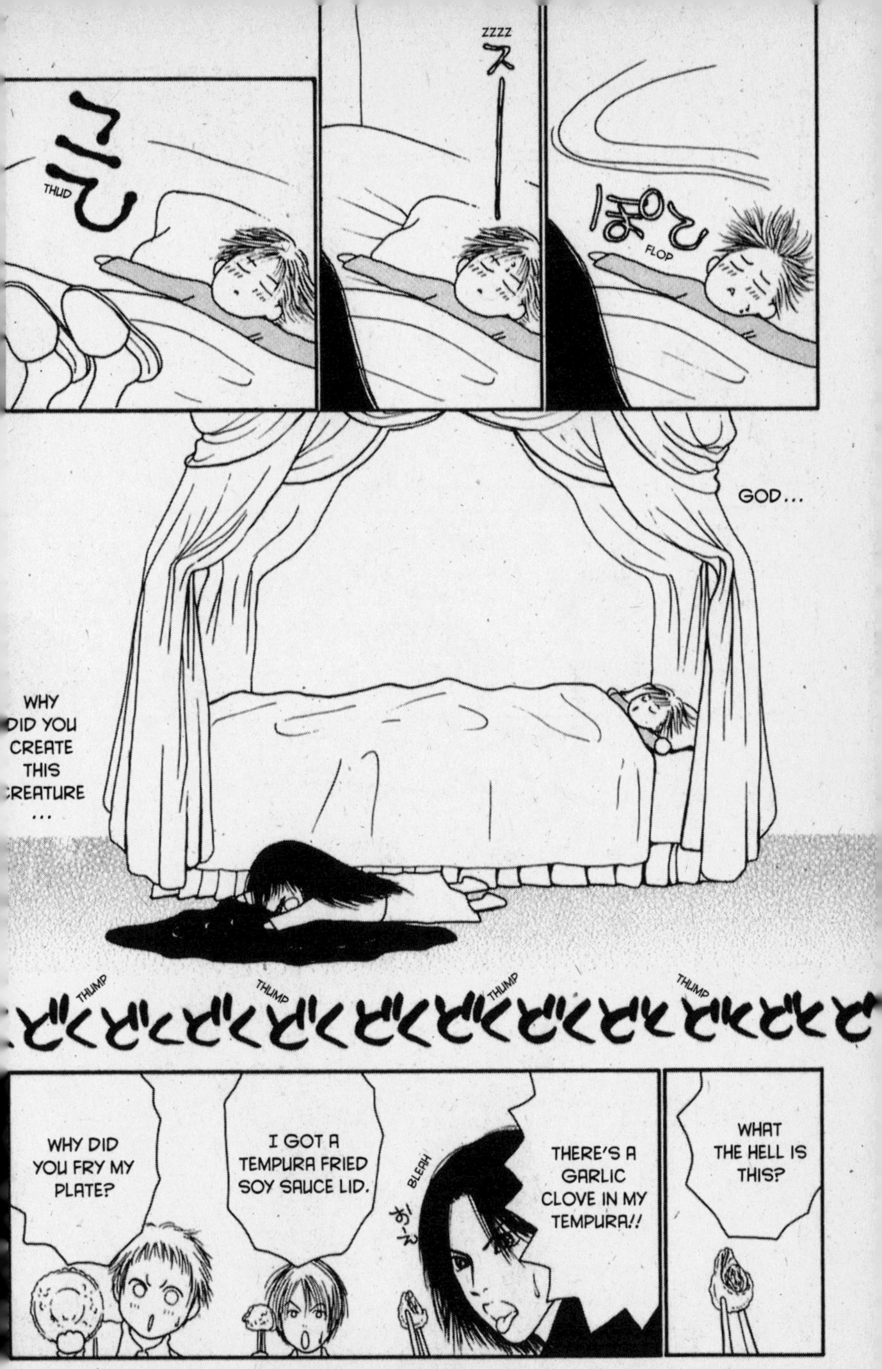
FLOP
ZZZZ
THUD
GOD...
WHY DID YOU CREATE THIS CREATURE ...
THUMP
THUMP
THUMP
THUMP
WHAT THE HELL IS THIS?
THERE'S A GARLIC CLOVE IN MY TEMPURA!!
BLEAH
I GOT A TEMPURA FRIED SOY SAUCE LID.
WHY DID YOU FRY MY PLATE?

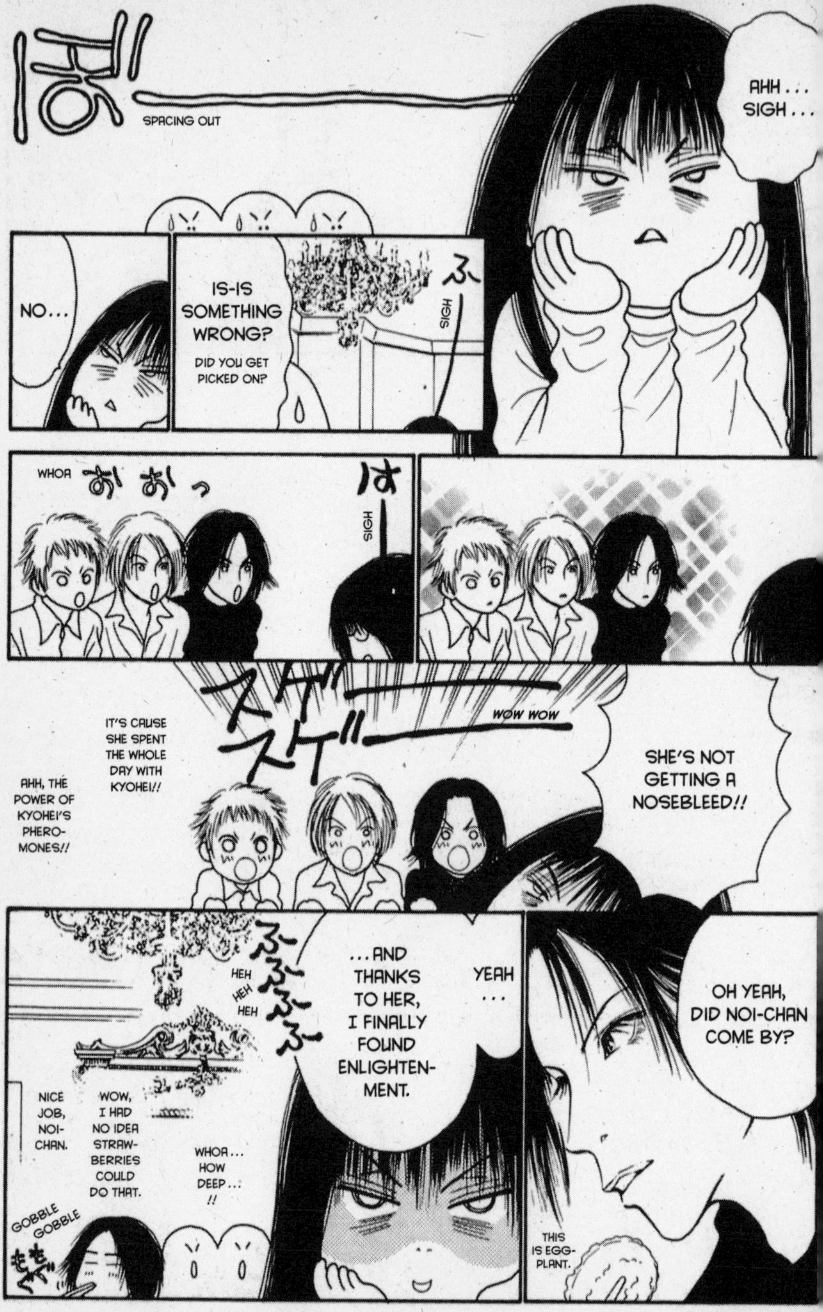
AHH... SIGH...
ぼ
SPACING OUT
ふ
SIGH
IS-IS SOMETHING WRONG?
DID YOU GET PICKED ON?
NO...
は
SIGH
おおっ
WHOA
SHE'S NOT GETTING A NOSEBLEED!!
スゲー スゲー
WOW WOW
IT'S CAUSE SHE SPENT THE WHOLE DAY WITH KYOHEI!!
AHH, THE POWER OF KYOHEI'S PHERO-MONES!!
OH YEAH, DID NOI-CHAN COME BY?
THIS IS EGG-PLANT.
YEAH...
...AND THANKS TO HER, I FINALLY FOUND ENLIGHTEN-MENT.
ふふふふふ
HEH HEH HEH
WHOA... HOW DEEP...!!
WOW, I HAD NO IDEA STRAW-BERRIES COULD DO THAT.
NICE JOB, NOI-CHAN.
GOBBLE GOBBLE

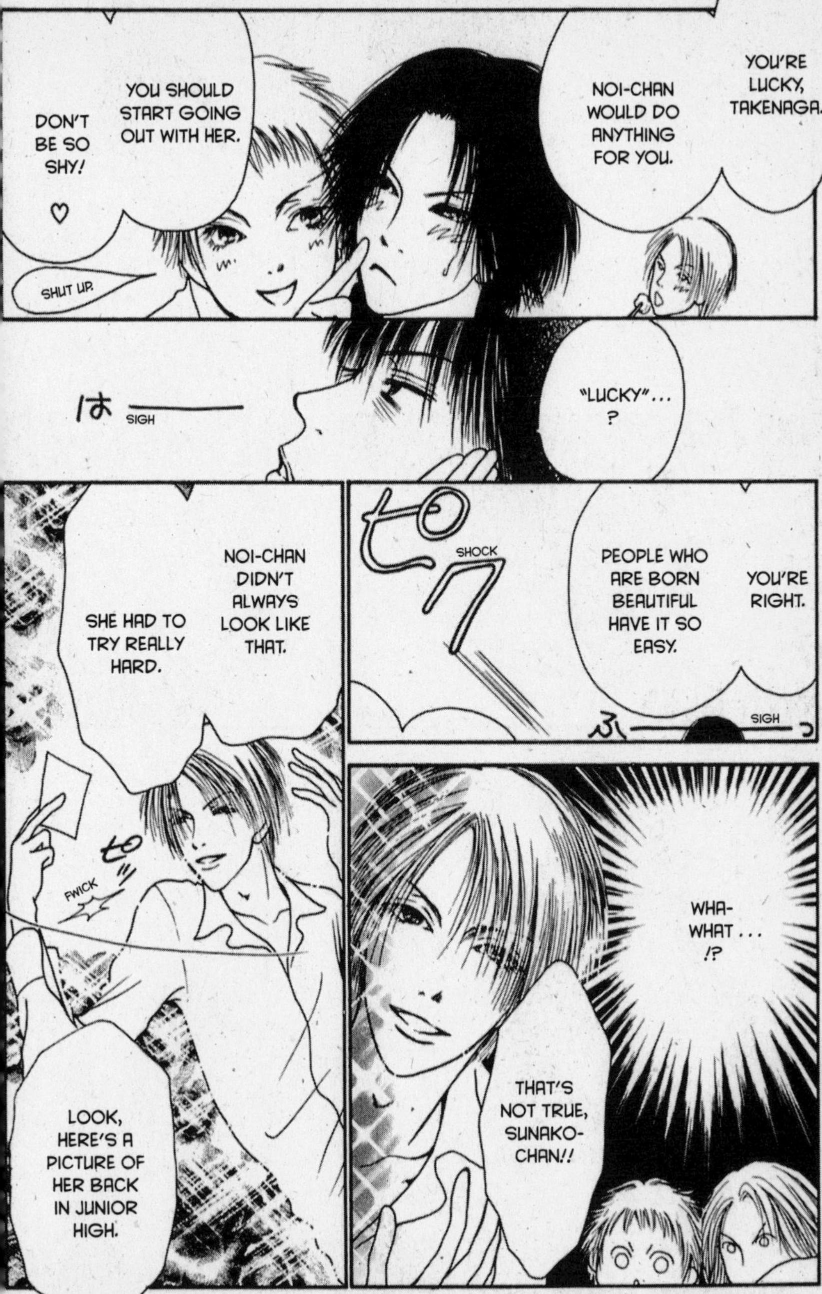
YOU'RE LUCKY, TAKENAGA.
NOI-CHAN WOULD DO ANYTHING FOR YOU.
YOU SHOULD START GOING OUT WITH HER.
DON'T BE SO SHY! ♡
SHUT UP.
"LUCKY"... ?
は SIGH
YOU'RE RIGHT.
PEOPLE WHO ARE BORN BEAUTIFUL HAVE IT SO EASY.
ふっ SIGH
SHOCK
WHA-WHAT... !?
THAT'S NOT TRUE, SUNAKO-CHAN!!
NOI-CHAN DIDN'T ALWAYS LOOK LIKE THAT.
SHE HAD TO TRY REALLY HARD.
FWICK
LOOK, HERE'S A PICTURE OF HER BACK IN JUNIOR HIGH.

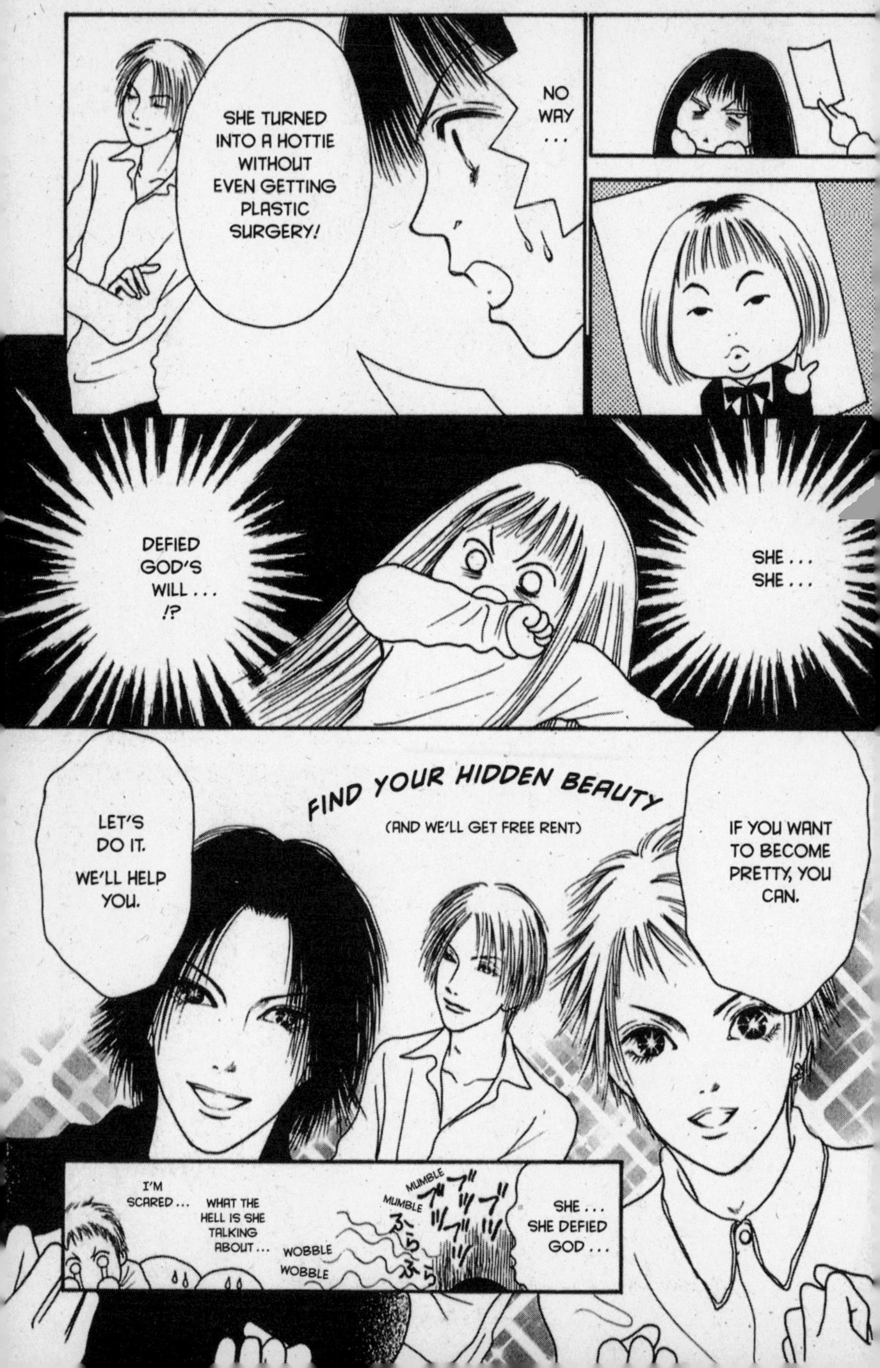
NO WAY . . .
SHE TURNED INTO A HOTTIE WITHOUT EVEN GETTING PLASTIC SURGERY!
SHE . . . SHE . . .
DEFIED GOD'S WILL . . . !?
IF YOU WANT TO BECOME PRETTY, YOU CAN.
FIND YOUR HIDDEN BEAUTY
(AND WE'LL GET FREE RENT)
LET'S DO IT.
WE'LL HELP YOU.
SHE . . . SHE DEFIED GOD . . .
MUMBLE MUMBLE
WOBBLE WOBBLE
WHAT THE HELL IS SHE TALKING ABOUT . . .
I'M SCARED . . .

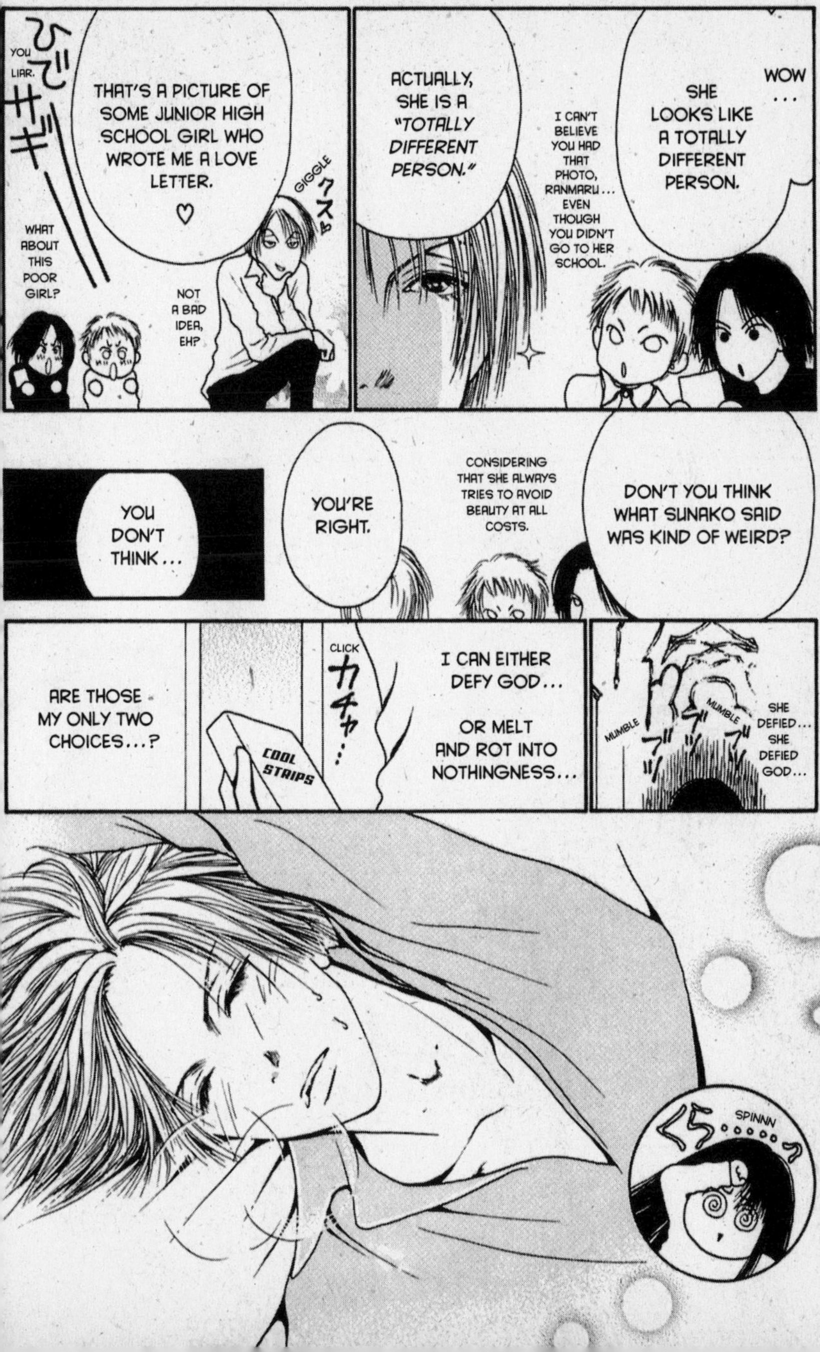
WOW . . .
SHE LOOKS LIKE A TOTALLY DIFFERENT PERSON.
I CAN'T BELIEVE YOU HAD THAT PHOTO, RANMARU... EVEN THOUGH YOU DIDN'T GO TO HER SCHOOL.
ACTUALLY, SHE IS A "TOTALLY DIFFERENT PERSON."
THAT'S A PICTURE OF SOME JUNIOR HIGH SCHOOL GIRL WHO WROTE ME A LOVE LETTER. ♡
GIGGLE
クス
NOT A BAD IDEA, EH?
YOU LIAR.
WHAT ABOUT THIS POOR GIRL?
DON'T YOU THINK WHAT SUNAKO SAID WAS KIND OF WEIRD?
CONSIDERING THAT SHE ALWAYS TRIES TO AVOID BEAUTY AT ALL COSTS.
YOU'RE RIGHT.
YOU DON'T THINK...
SHE DEFIED... SHE DEFIED GOD...
MUMBLE
MUMBLE
I CAN EITHER DEFY GOD...
OR MELT AND ROT INTO NOTHINGNESS...
CLICK
カチャ...
COOL STRIPS
ARE THOSE MY ONLY TWO CHOICES...?
SPINNN
くら

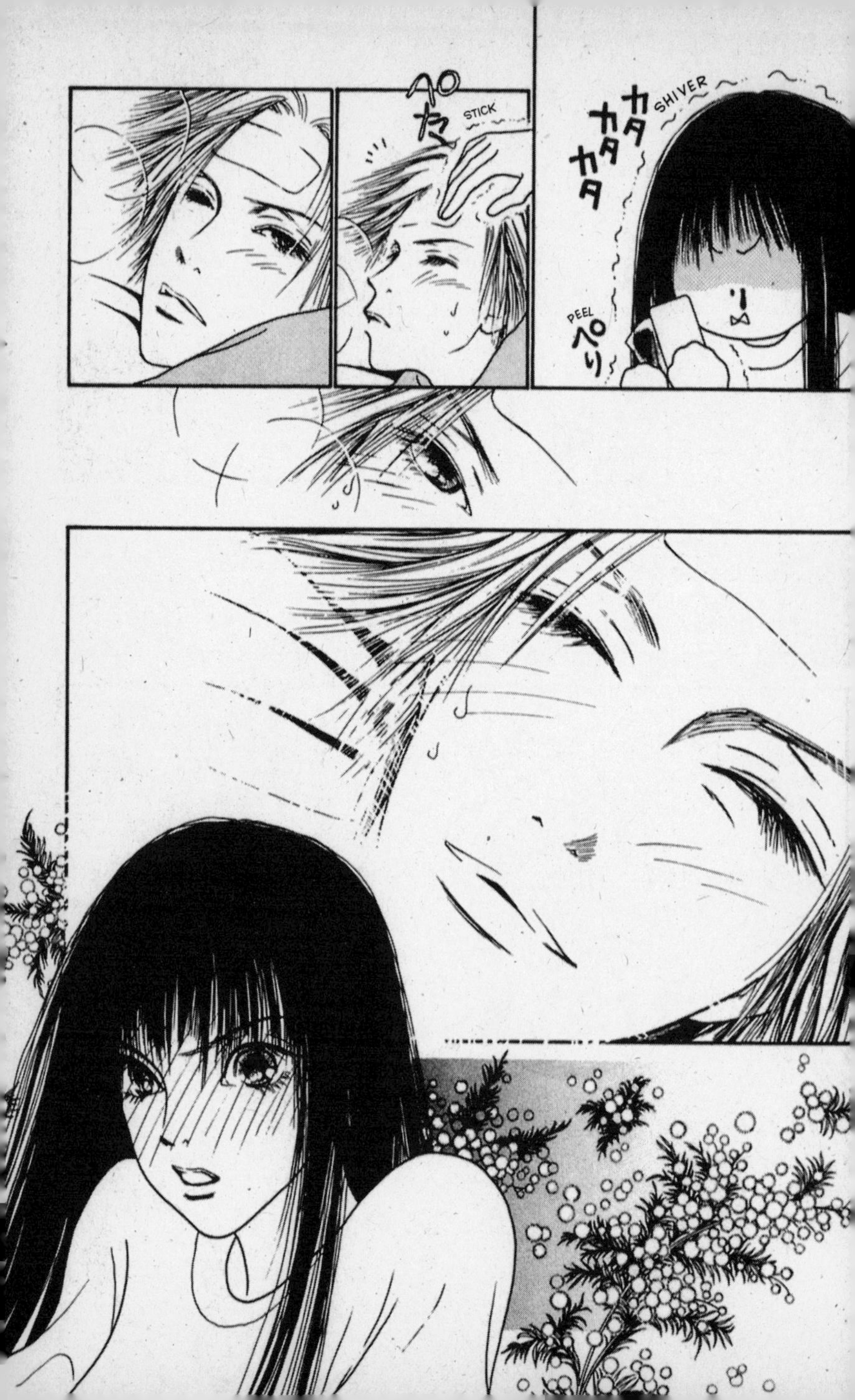
カタカタカタ
SHIVER
ぺり
PEEL
ぺた
STICK

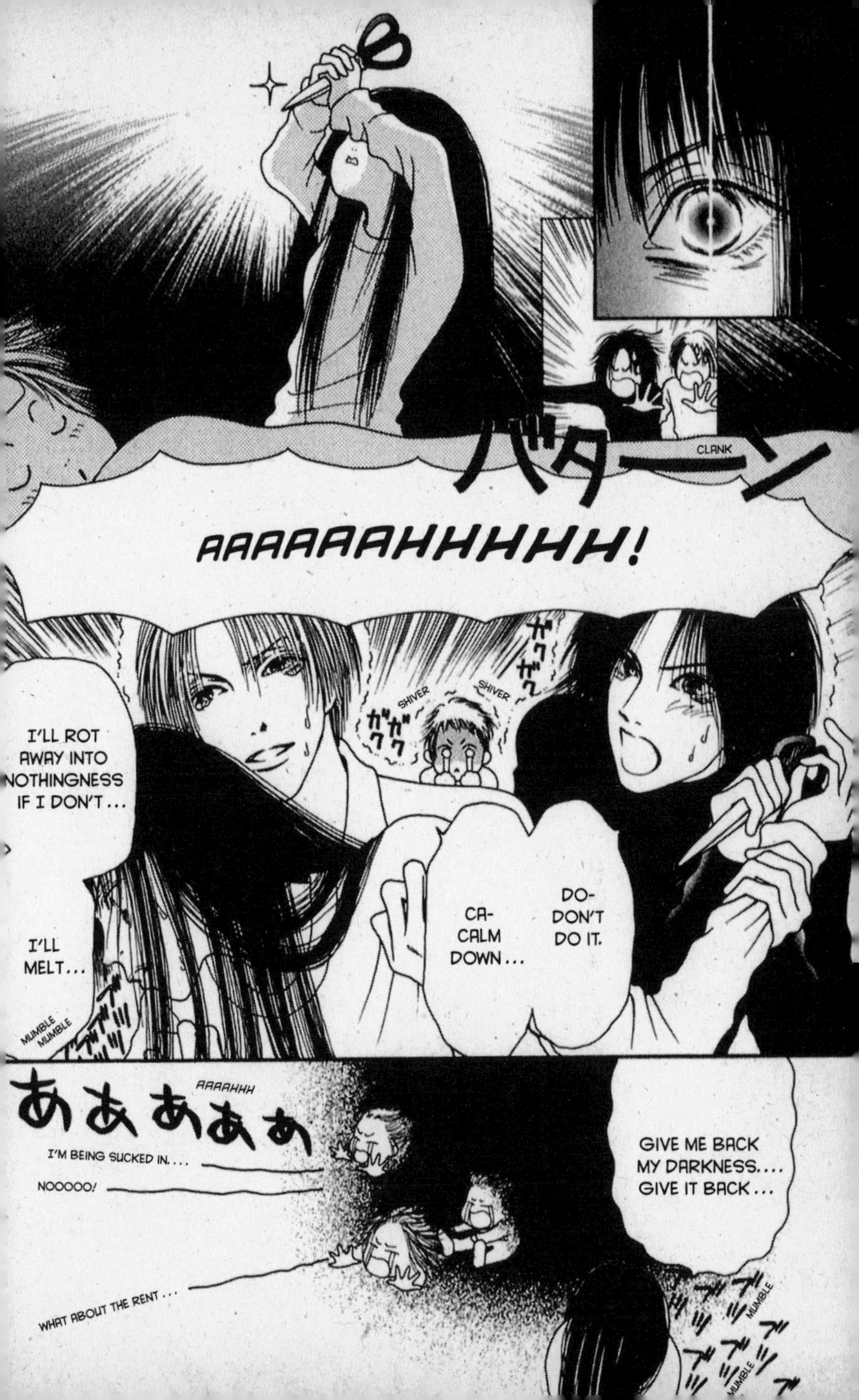

バターン
CLANK
AAAAAAHHHHHH!
ガクガク
SHIVER
SHIVER
ガクガク
DO- DON'T DO IT.
CA- CALM DOWN...
I'LL ROT AWAY INTO NOTHINGNESS IF I DON'T...
I'LL MELT...
MUMBLE MUMBLE
GIVE ME BACK MY DARKNESS.... GIVE IT BACK...
MUMBLE
MUMBLE
ああああああ
AAAAHHH
I'M BEING SUCKED IN....
NOOOOO!
WHAT ABOUT THE RENT ...

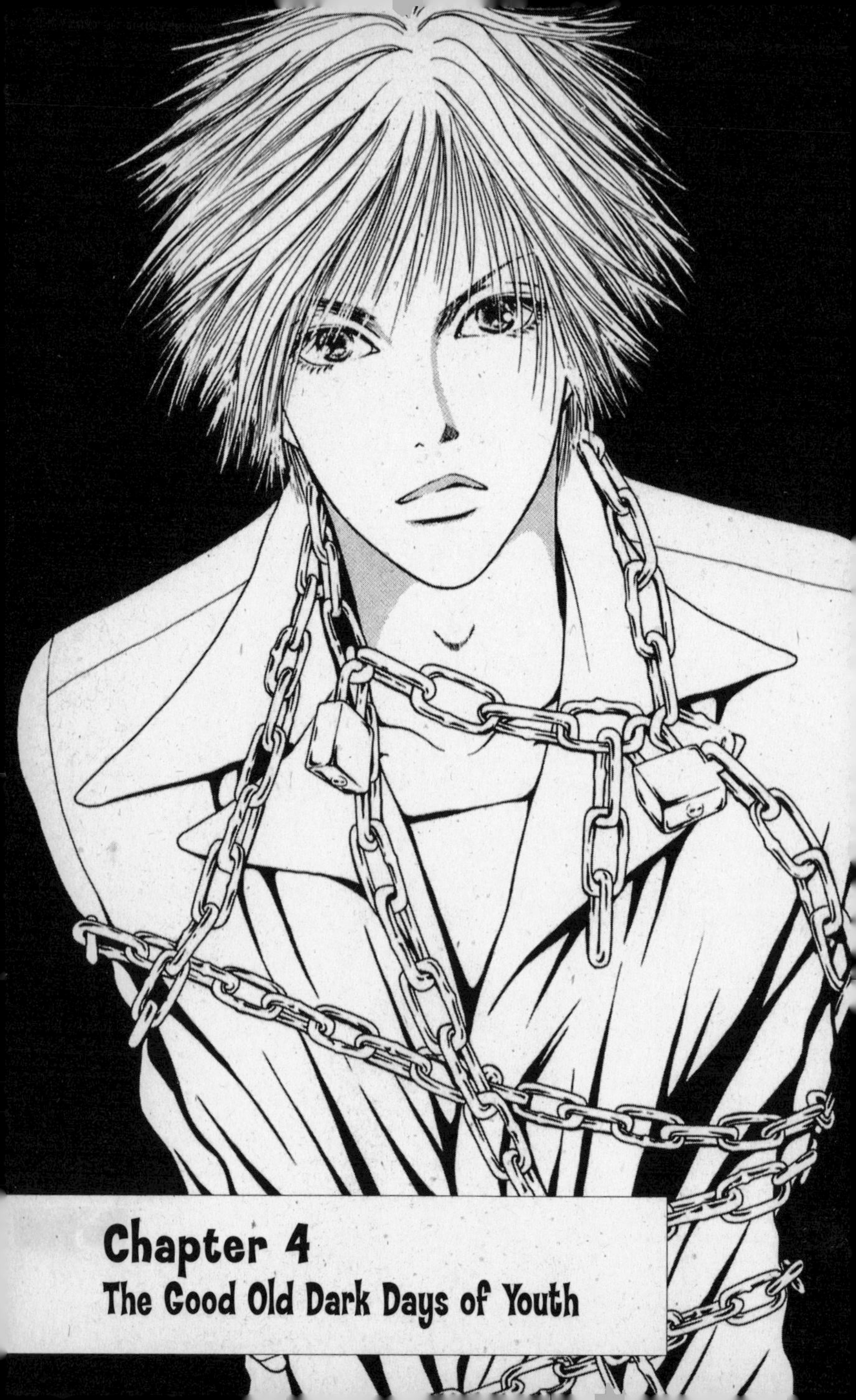
Chapter 4
The Good Old Dark Days of Youth

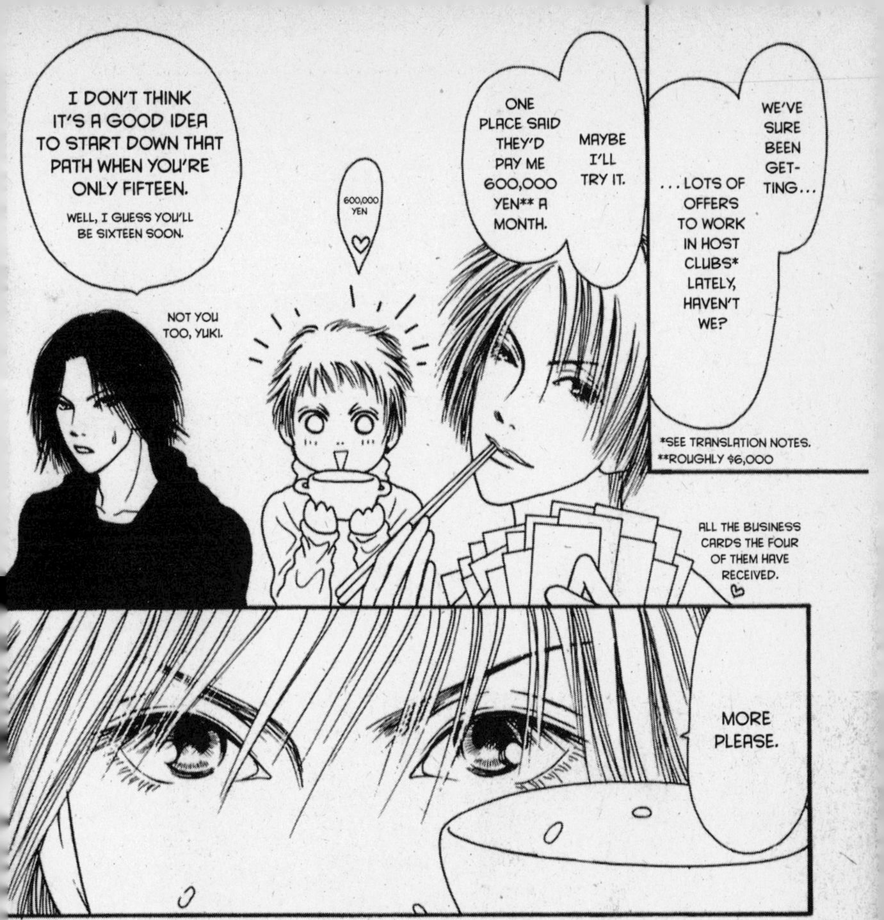
WE'VE SURE BEEN GETTING . . . LOTS OF OFFERS TO WORK IN HOST CLUBS* LATELY, HAVEN'T WE?
*SEE TRANSLATION NOTES.
**ROUGHLY $6,000
ONE PLACE SAID THEY'D PAY ME 600,000 YEN** A MONTH.
MAYBE I'LL TRY IT.
600,000 YEN ♡
I DON'T THINK IT'S A GOOD IDEA TO START DOWN THAT PATH WHEN YOU'RE ONLY FIFTEEN.
WELL, I GUESS YOU'LL BE SIXTEEN SOON.
NOT YOU TOO, YUKI.
ALL THE BUSINESS CARDS THE FOUR OF THEM HAVE RECEIVED. ♡
MORE PLEASE.

TAKENAGA ODA

HEIGHT 5'8??
WEIGHT 110 LBS??

HE LOOKS GENTLE AND CALM, BUT HE'S ACTUALLY PRETTY SPACEY.

HE'S THE ONLY ONE OF THE FOUR WHO WAS COMPLETELY MODELED AFTER A REAL PERSON. MARSHI-KUN, THE VOCALIST FOR THE INDY BAND "RISK."

HE'S SO HOT!

HE'S CUTE AND SWEET. HIS FACE IS ADORABLE. HIS VOICE IS TOO. (IT'S REALLY LOW AND SOUNDS COOL.)

I HOPE HE FINDS A CUTE GIRLFRIEND SOON. APPARENTLY, HE LIKES GIRLS WHO LOOK LIKE SARINA SUZUKI-CHAN.

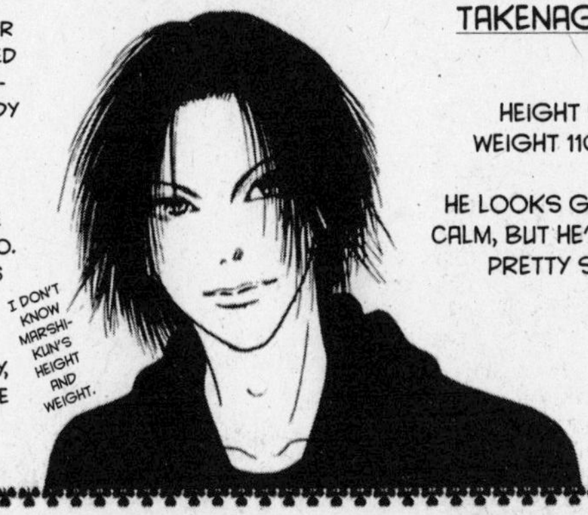
I DON'T KNOW MARSHI-KUN'S HEIGHT AND WEIGHT.

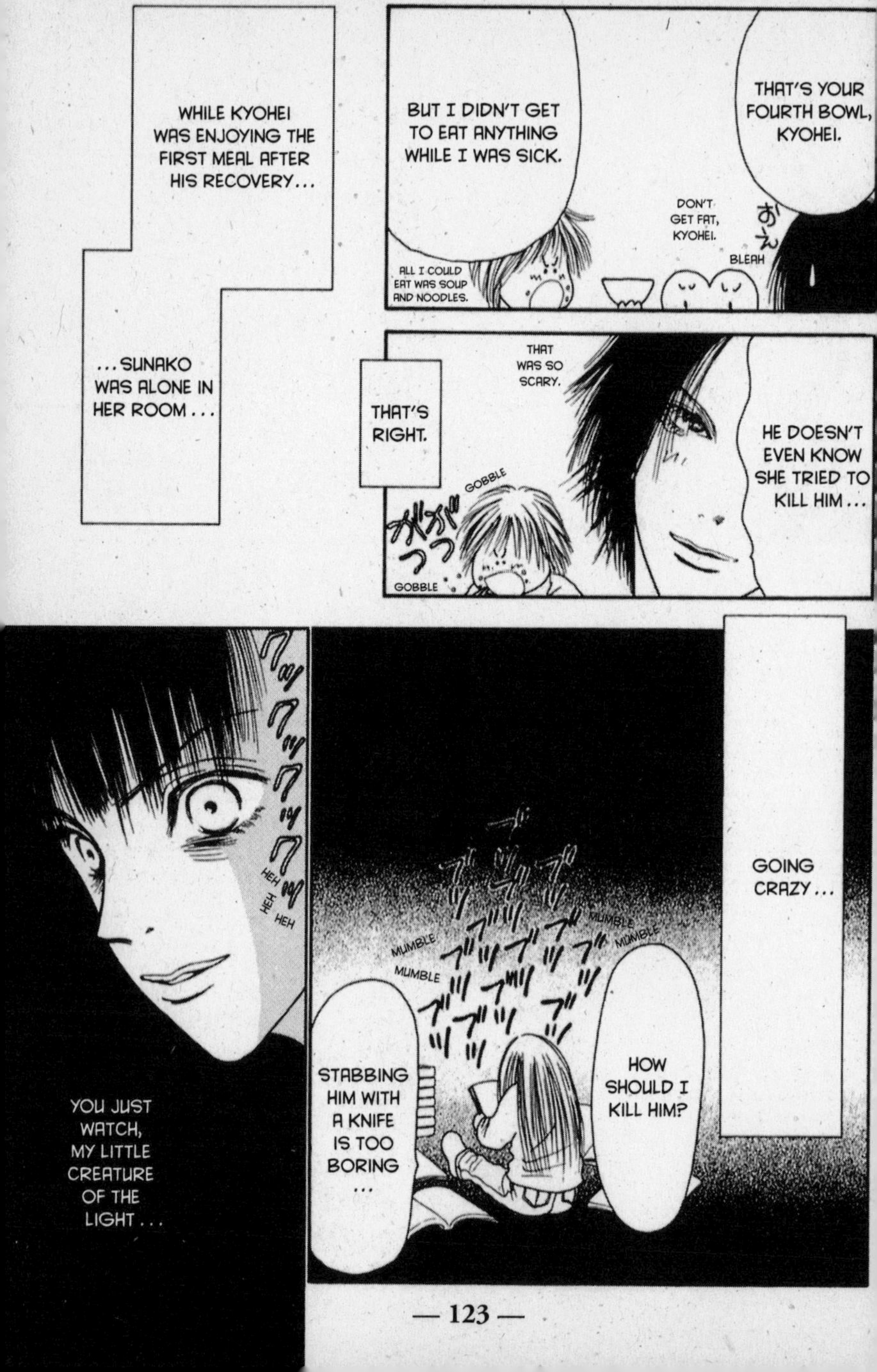
THAT'S YOUR FOURTH BOWL, KYOHEI.
おえ
BLEAH
DON'T GET FAT, KYOHEI.
BUT I DIDN'T GET TO EAT ANYTHING WHILE I WAS SICK.
ALL I COULD EAT WAS SOUP AND NOODLES.
HE DOESN'T EVEN KNOW SHE TRIED TO KILL HIM...
THAT WAS SO SCARY.
THAT'S RIGHT.
GOBBLE
ガツガツ
GOBBLE
WHILE KYOHEI WAS ENJOYING THE FIRST MEAL AFTER HIS RECOVERY...
...SUNAKO WAS ALONE IN HER ROOM...
GOING CRAZY...
HOW SHOULD I KILL HIM?
MUMBLE MUMBLE
MUMBLE MUMBLE
STABBING HIM WITH A KNIFE IS TOO BORING...
HEH HEH HEH
YOU JUST WATCH, MY LITTLE CREATURE OF THE LIGHT...

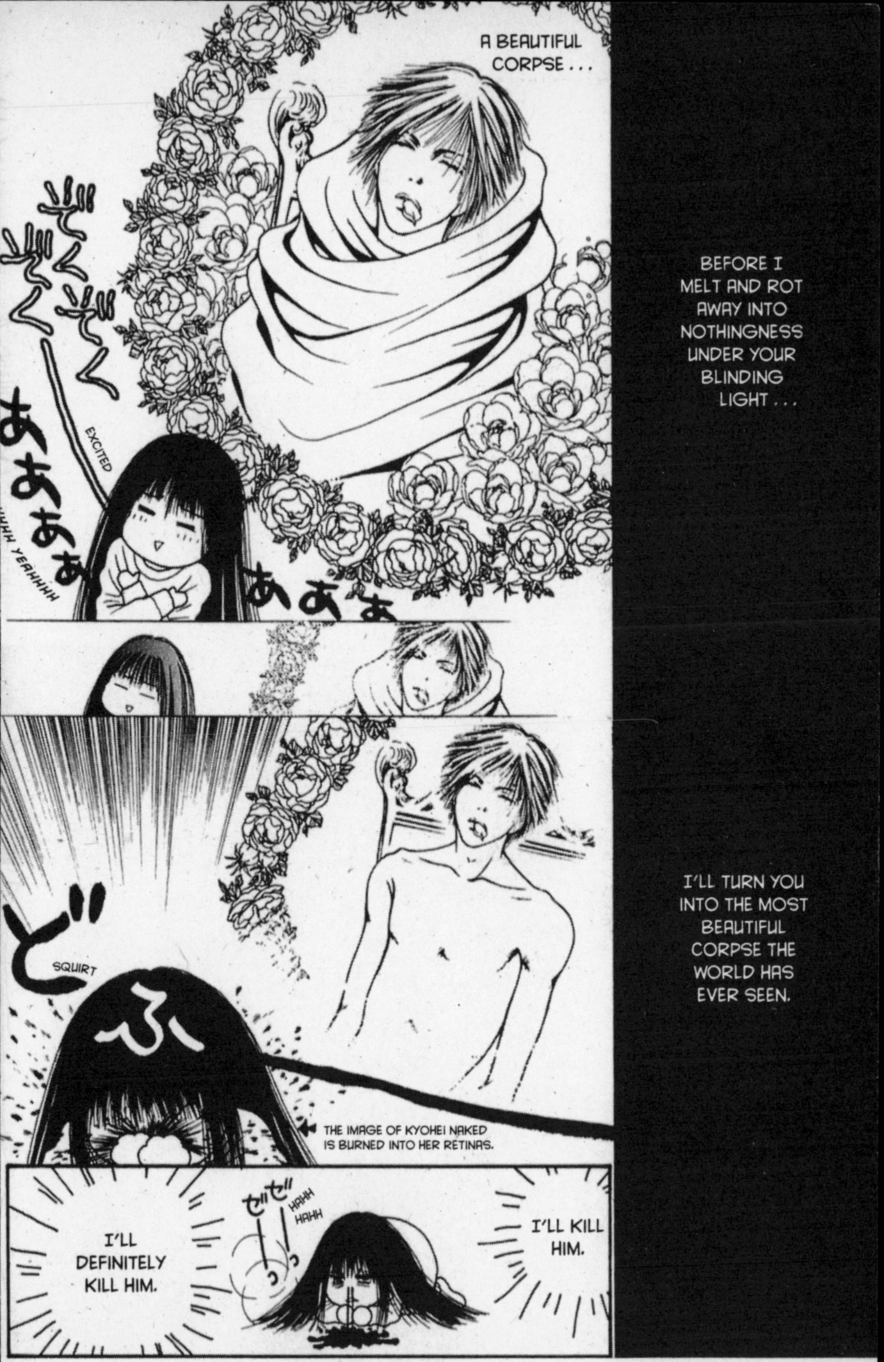
A BEAUTIFUL CORPSE . . .
BEFORE I MELT AND ROT AWAY INTO NOTHINGNESS UNDER YOUR BLINDING LIGHT . . .
ぞくぞく
ぞくぞく
EXCITED
あああぁ
あぁあ
HHHH YEAHHHH
I'LL TURN YOU INTO THE MOST BEAUTIFUL CORPSE THE WORLD HAS EVER SEEN.
ど
ふ
SQUIRT
THE IMAGE OF KYOHEI NAKED IS BURNED INTO HER RETINAS.
I'LL KILL HIM.
ぜぜ
HAHH HAHH
I'LL DEFINITELY KILL HIM.

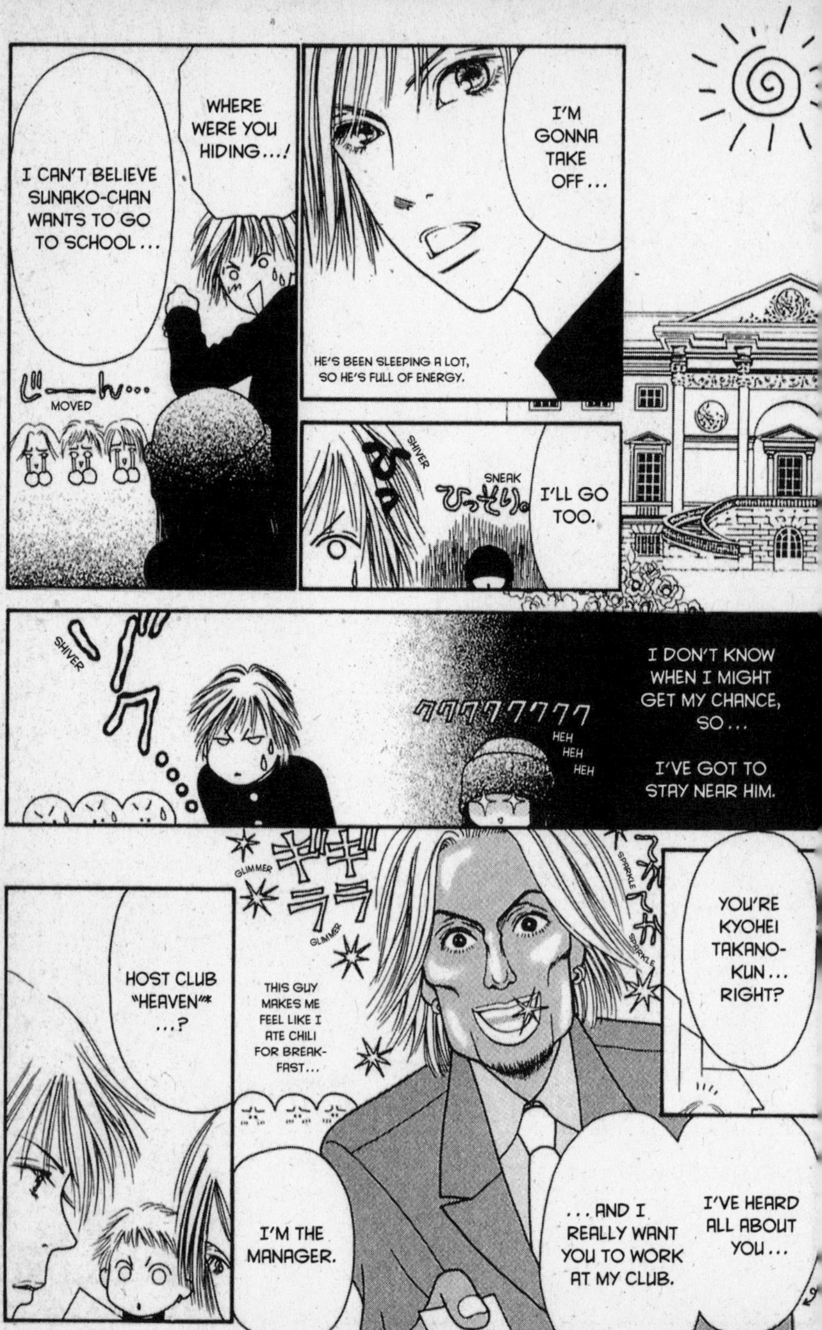
I'M GONNA TAKE OFF...
HE'S BEEN SLEEPING A LOT, SO HE'S FULL OF ENERGY.
I'LL GO TOO.
ひっそり。
SNEAK
SHIVER
WHERE WERE YOU HIDING...!
I CAN'T BELIEVE SUNAKO-CHAN WANTS TO GO TO SCHOOL...
じーーん...
MOVED
I DON'T KNOW WHEN I MIGHT GET MY CHANCE, SO...
I'VE GOT TO STAY NEAR HIM.
クククククククク
HEH HEH HEH
SHIVER
YOU'RE KYOHEI TAKANO-KUN... RIGHT?
SPARKLE
SPARKLE
GLIMMER
GLIMMER
I'VE HEARD ALL ABOUT YOU...
...AND I REALLY WANT YOU TO WORK AT MY CLUB.
I'M THE MANAGER.
THIS GUY MAKES ME FEEL LIKE I ATE CHILI FOR BREAK-FAST...
HOST CLUB "HEAVEN"* ...?

*IT'S FICTIONAL.

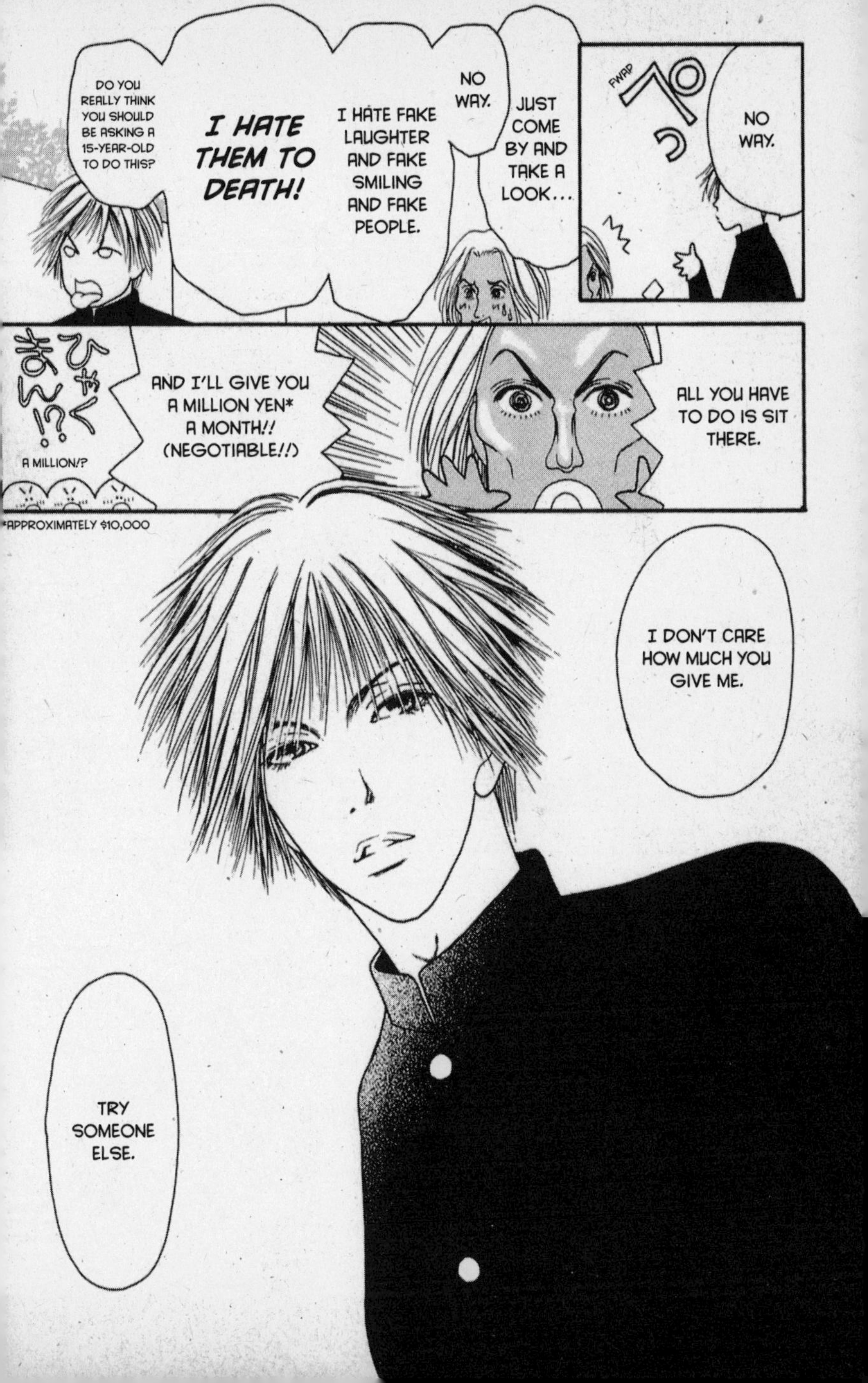
FWAP
NO WAY.
JUST COME BY AND TAKE A LOOK…
NO WAY.
I HATE FAKE LAUGHTER AND FAKE SMILING AND FAKE PEOPLE.
I HATE THEM TO DEATH!
DO YOU REALLY THINK YOU SHOULD BE ASKING A 15-YEAR-OLD TO DO THIS?
ALL YOU HAVE TO DO IS SIT THERE.
AND I'LL GIVE YOU A MILLION YEN* A MONTH!! (NEGOTIABLE!!)
ひゃくまん!?
A MILLION!?
*APPROXIMATELY $10,000
I DON'T CARE HOW MUCH YOU GIVE ME.
TRY SOMEONE ELSE.

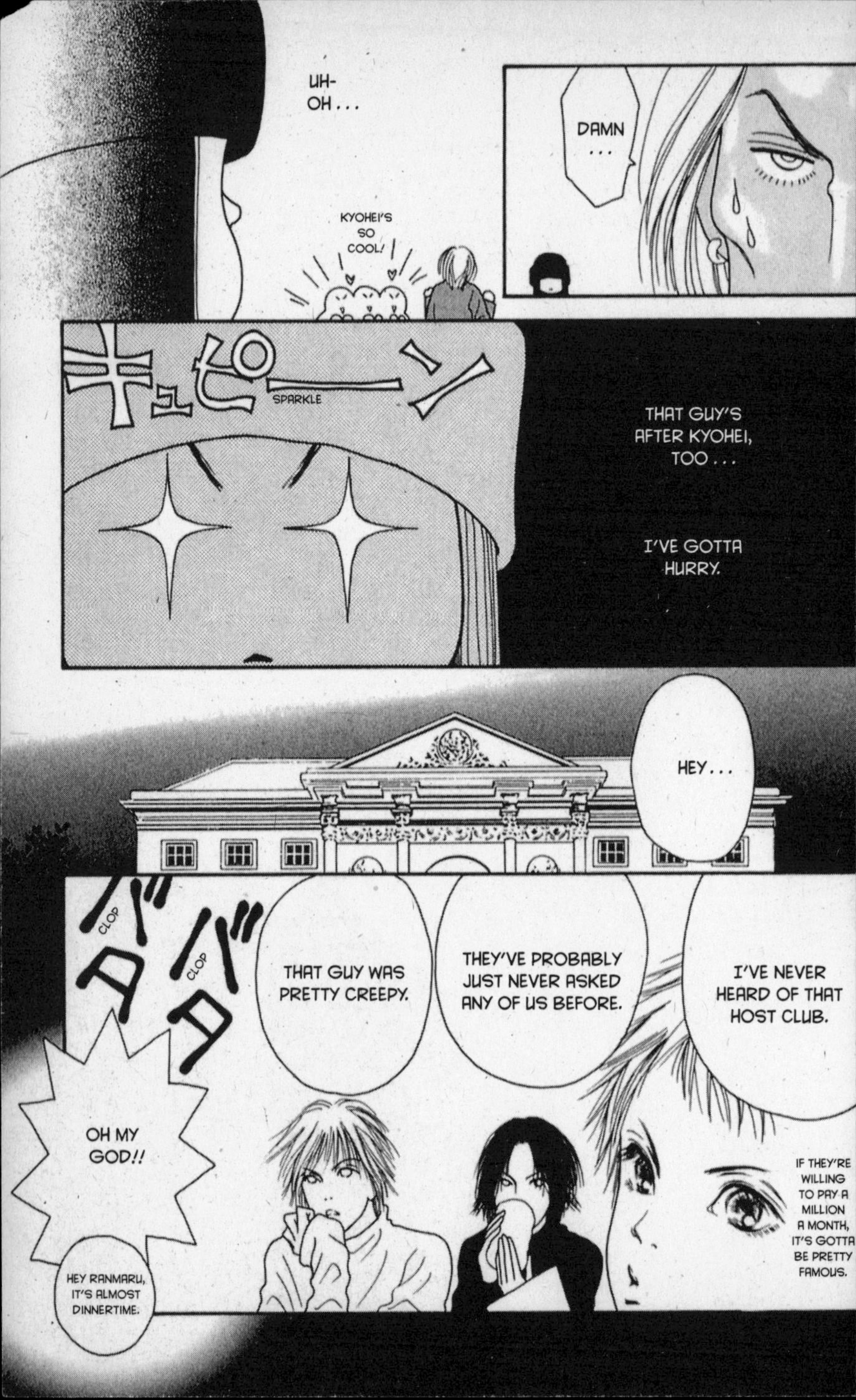
DAMN . . .
UH-OH . . .
KYOHEI'S SO COOL!
THAT GUY'S AFTER KYOHEI, TOO . . .
I'VE GOTTA HURRY.
キュピーン
SPARKLE
HEY . . .
I'VE NEVER HEARD OF THAT HOST CLUB.
IF THEY'RE WILLING TO PAY A MILLION A MONTH, IT'S GOTTA BE PRETTY FAMOUS.
THEY'VE PROBABLY JUST NEVER ASKED ANY OF US BEFORE.
THAT GUY WAS PRETTY CREEPY.
バタバタ
CLOP CLOP
OH MY GOD!!
HEY RANMARU, IT'S ALMOST DINNERTIME.

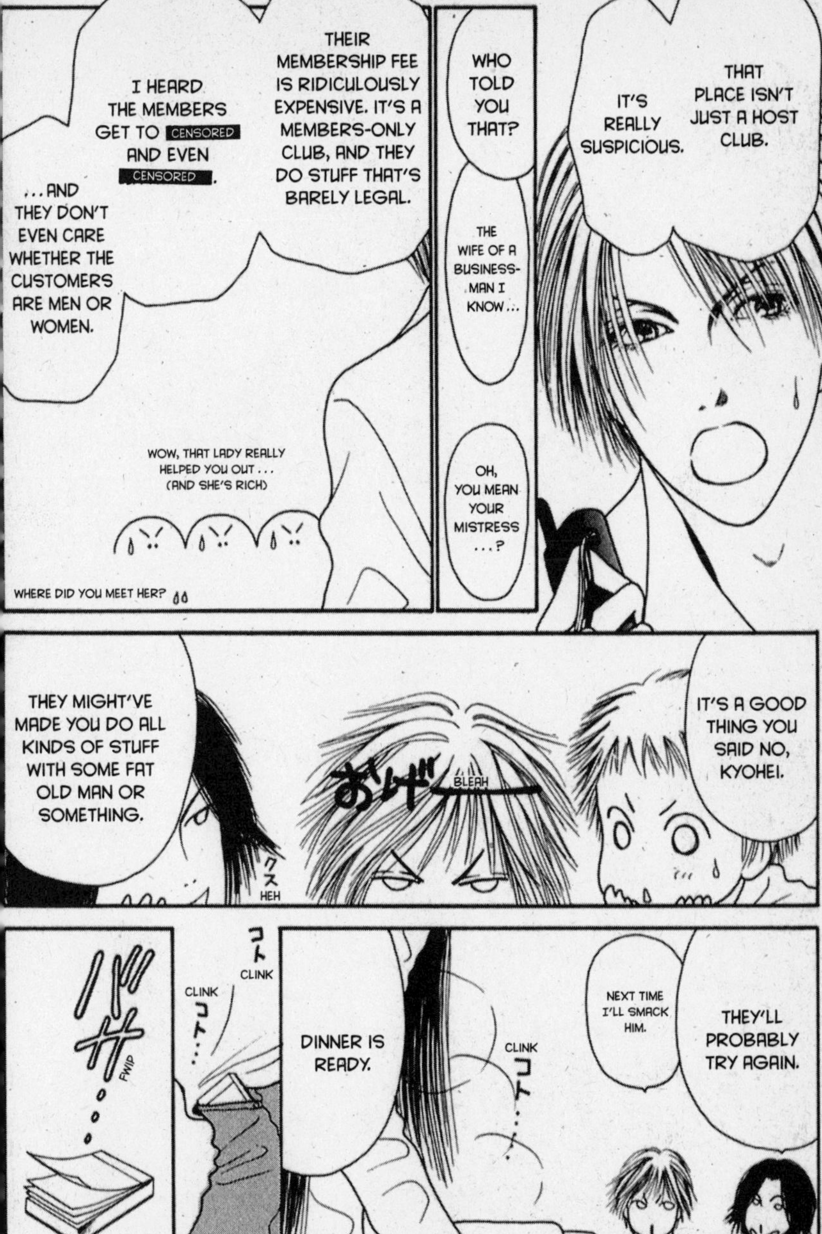
THAT PLACE ISN'T JUST A HOST CLUB.
IT'S REALLY SUSPICIOUS.
WHO TOLD YOU THAT?
THE WIFE OF A BUSINESS-MAN I KNOW...
OH, YOU MEAN YOUR MISTRESS...?
THEIR MEMBERSHIP FEE IS RIDICULOUSLY EXPENSIVE. IT'S A MEMBERS-ONLY CLUB, AND THEY DO STUFF THAT'S BARELY LEGAL.
I HEARD THE MEMBERS GET TO CENSORED AND EVEN CENSORED.
...AND THEY DON'T EVEN CARE WHETHER THE CUSTOMERS ARE MEN OR WOMEN.
WOW, THAT LADY REALLY HELPED YOU OUT... (AND SHE'S RICH)
WHERE DID YOU MEET HER?
IT'S A GOOD THING YOU SAID NO, KYOHEI.
おげー
BLEAH
THEY MIGHT'VE MADE YOU DO ALL KINDS OF STUFF WITH SOME FAT OLD MAN OR SOMETHING.
クス
HEH
THEY'LL PROBABLY TRY AGAIN.
NEXT TIME I'LL SMACK HIM.
CLINK
コト...
DINNER IS READY.
コト
CLINK
CLINK
コト...
バサ
FWIP

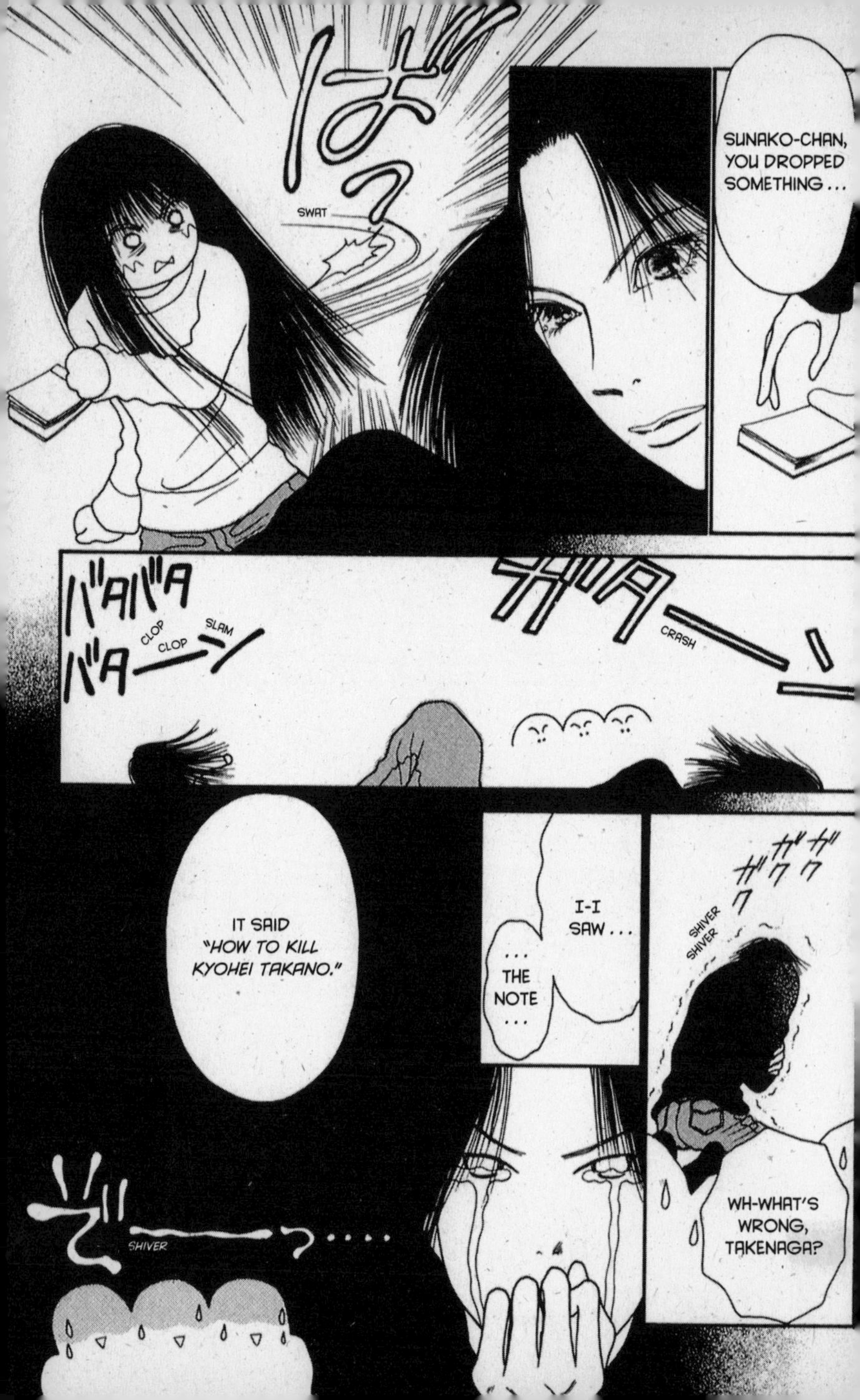
SUNAKO-CHAN, YOU DROPPED SOMETHING . . .
はっ
SWAT
ガタ——ン
CRASH
バタバタバタ——ン
CLOP CLOP
SLAM
WH-WHAT'S WRONG, TAKENAGA?
ガクガク
SHIVER SHIVER
I-I SAW . . .
. . . THE NOTE . . .
IT SAID "HOW TO KILL KYOHEI TAKANO."
ぞ——っ. . . .
SHIVER

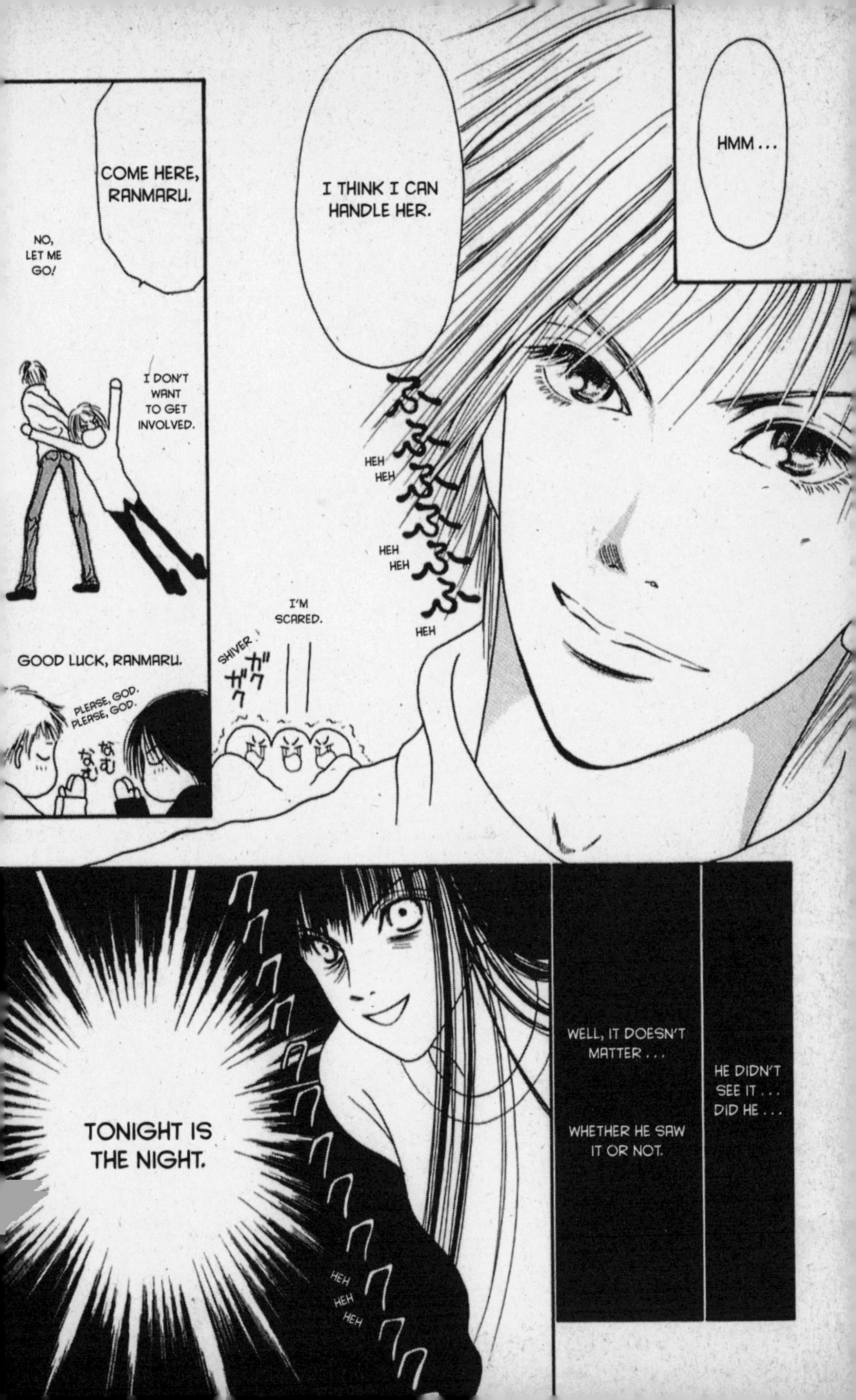
HMM . . .
I THINK I CAN HANDLE HER.
HEH HEH
HEH HEH
HEH
I'M SCARED.
SHIVER
COME HERE, RANMARU.
NO, LET ME GO!
I DON'T WANT TO GET INVOLVED.
GOOD LUCK, RANMARU.
PLEASE, GOD. PLEASE, GOD.
HE DIDN'T SEE IT . . . DID HE . . .
WELL, IT DOESN'T MATTER . . .
WHETHER HE SAW IT OR NOT.
TONIGHT IS THE NIGHT.
HEH HEH HEH

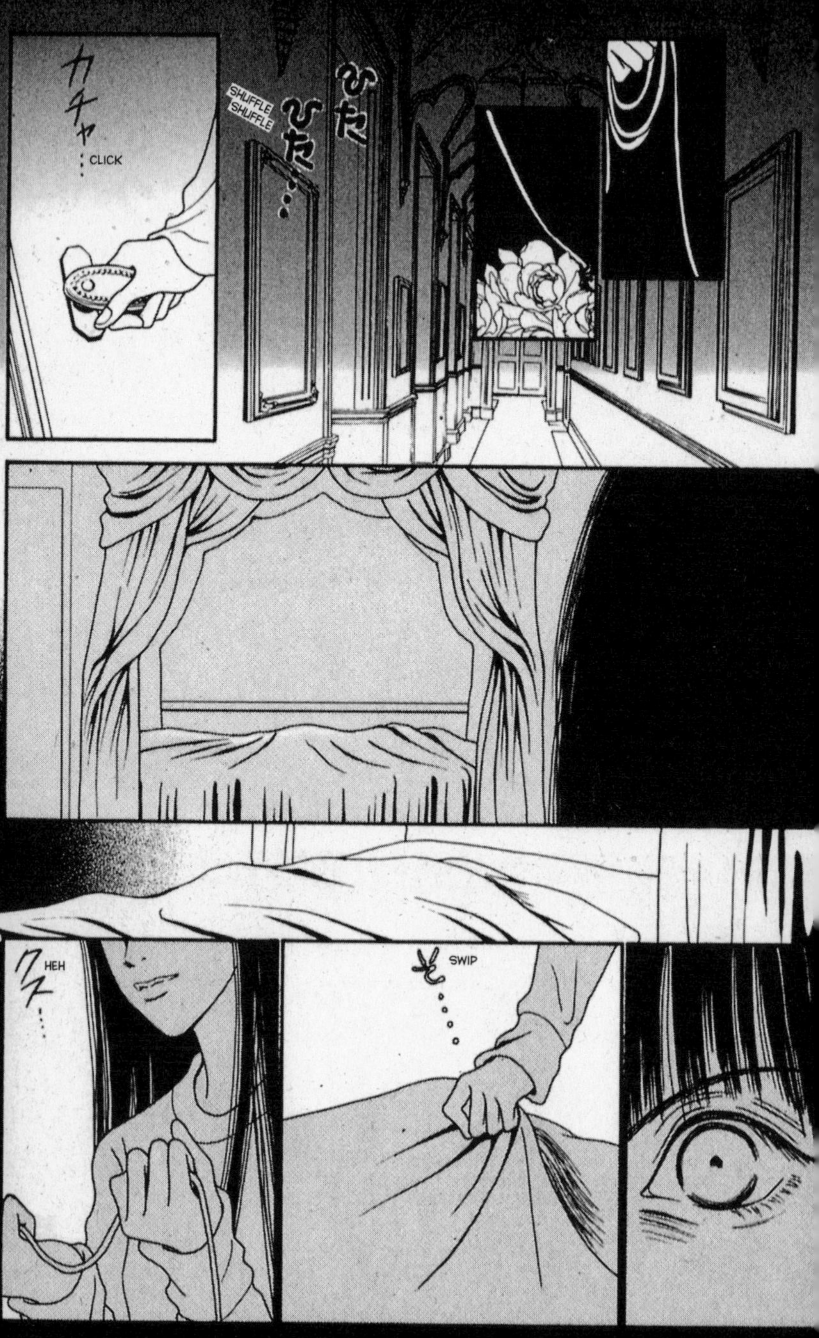

ひたひた…
SHUFFLE SHUFFLE
カチャ…
CLICK
SWIP
クス…
HEH

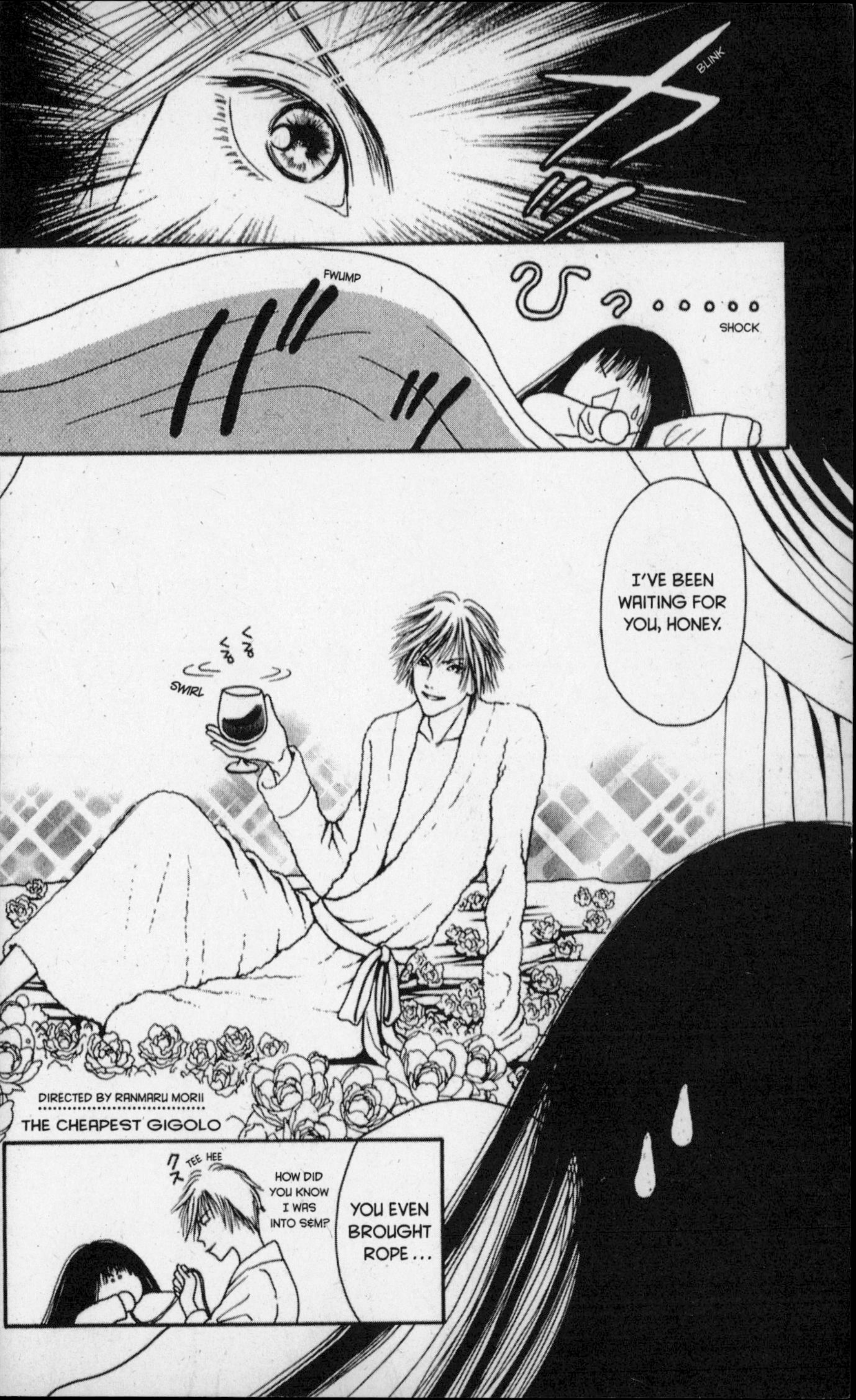
BLINK
SHOCK
FWUMP
I'VE BEEN WAITING FOR YOU, HONEY.
SWIRL
DIRECTED BY RANMARU MORII
THE CHEAPEST GIGOLO
YOU EVEN BROUGHT ROPE...
HOW DID YOU KNOW I WAS INTO S&M?
TEE HEE

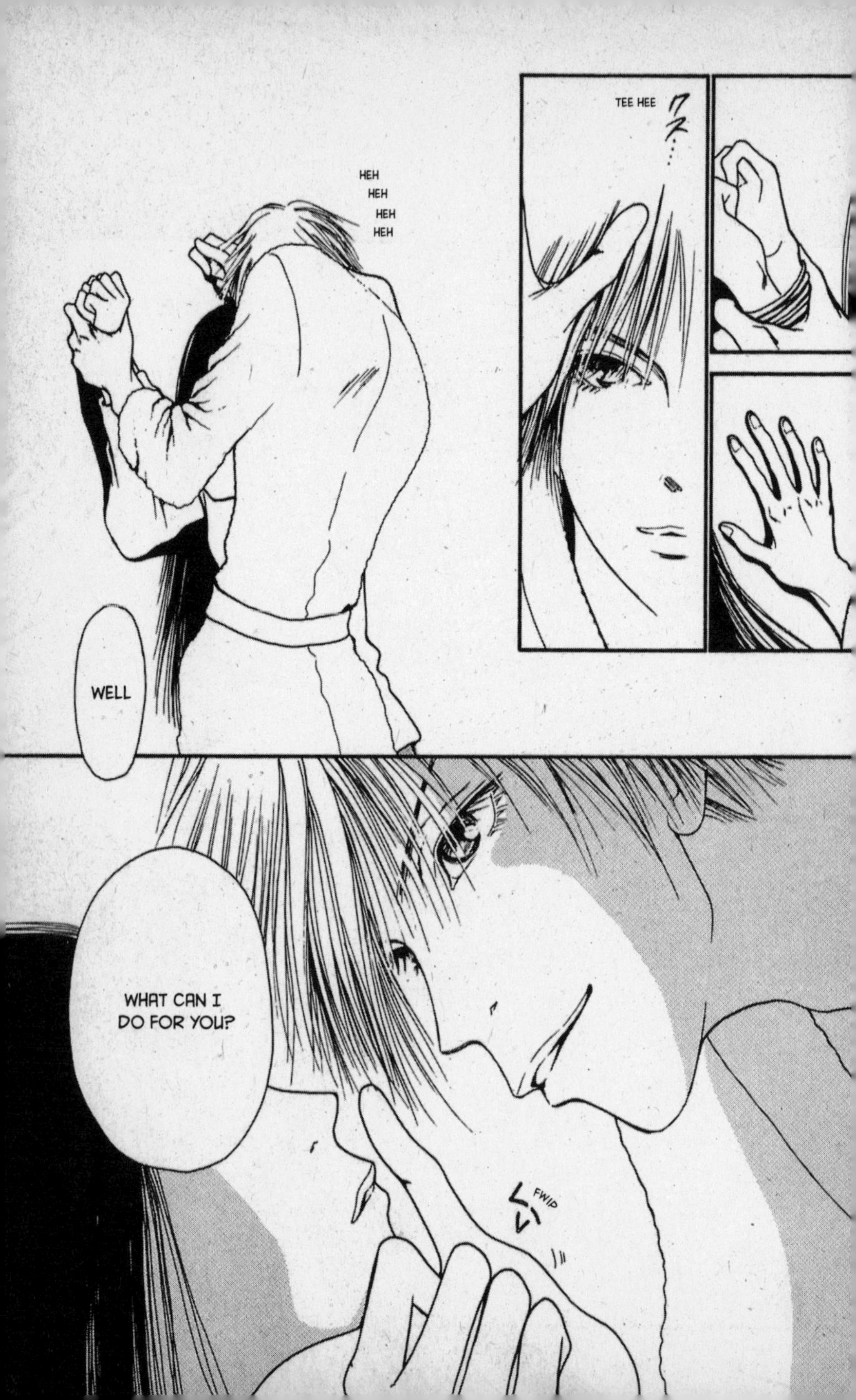
TEE HEE
HEH HEH HEH HEH
WELL
WHAT CAN I DO FOR YOU?
FWIP

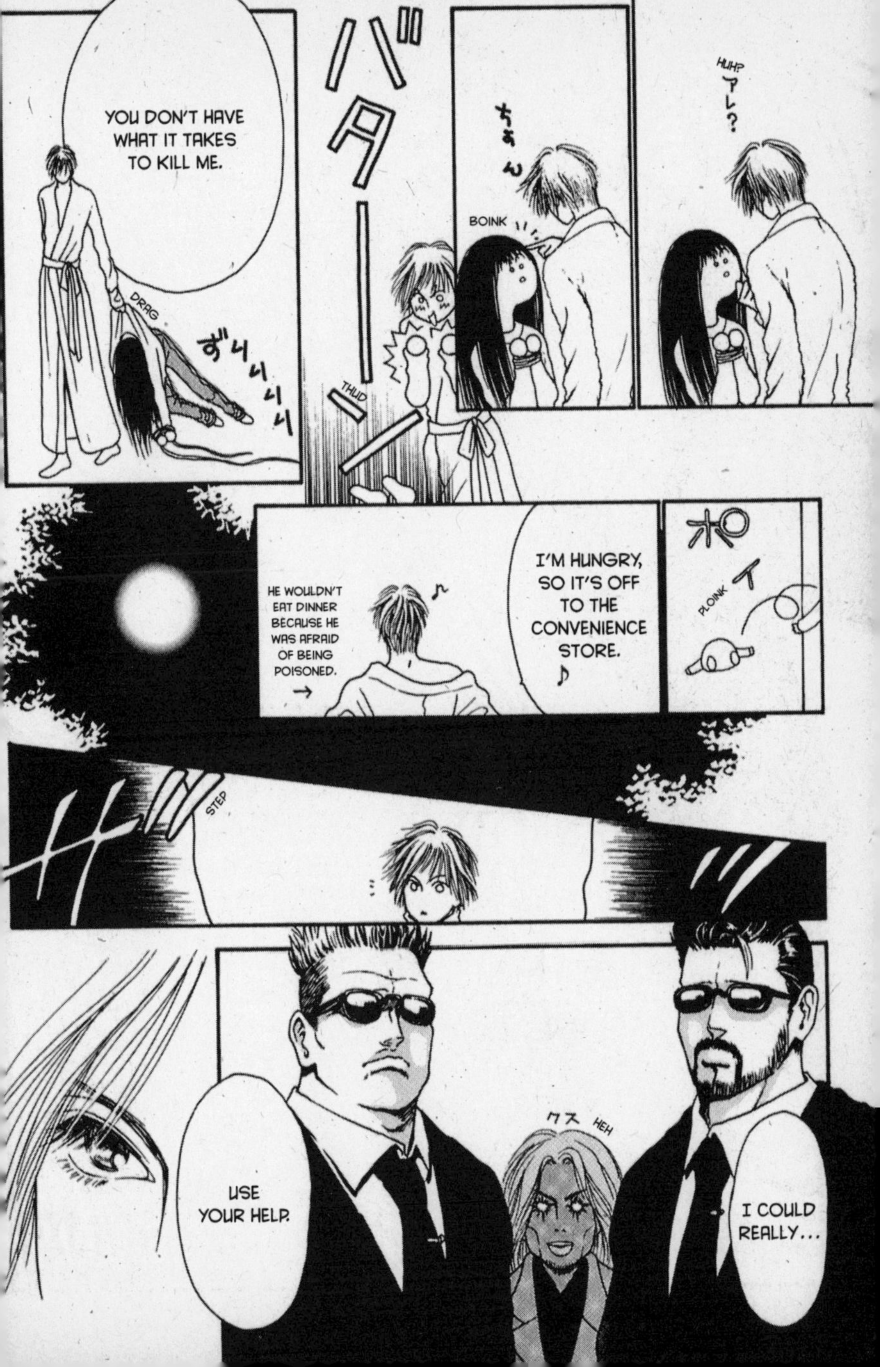
HUH?
アレ?
ちぇん
BOINK
バタ—
THUD
YOU DON'T HAVE WHAT IT TAKES TO KILL ME.
DRAG
ずいいいいい
ポイ
PLOINK
I'M HUNGRY, SO IT'S OFF TO THE CONVENIENCE STORE. ♪
HE WOULDN'T EAT DINNER BECAUSE HE WAS AFRAID OF BEING POISONED. →
STEP
I COULD REALLY...
クス
HEH
USE YOUR HELP.

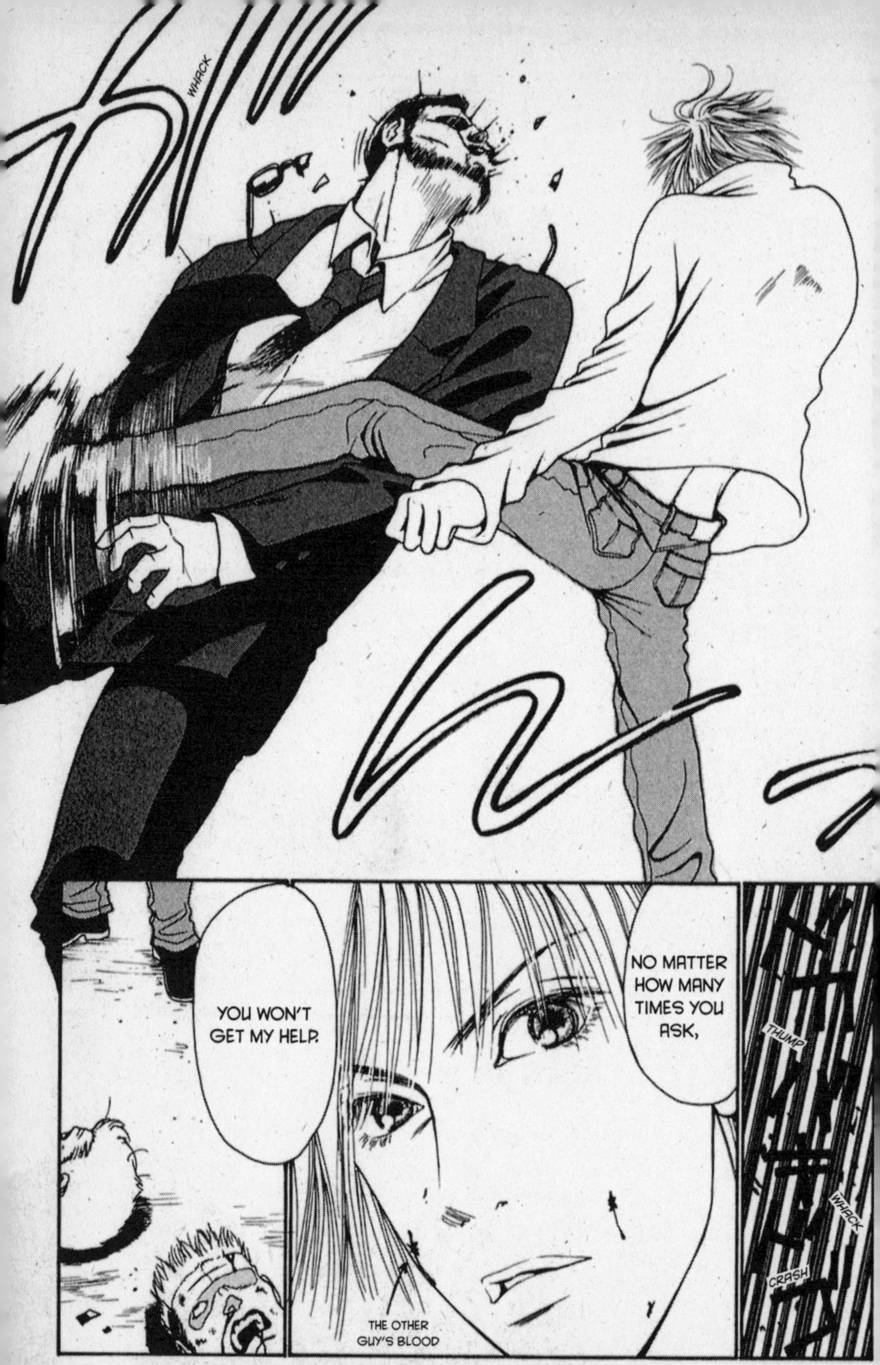
WHACK
THUMP
WHACK
CRASH
NO MATTER HOW MANY TIMES YOU ASK,
YOU WON'T GET MY HELP.
THE OTHER GUY'S BLOOD

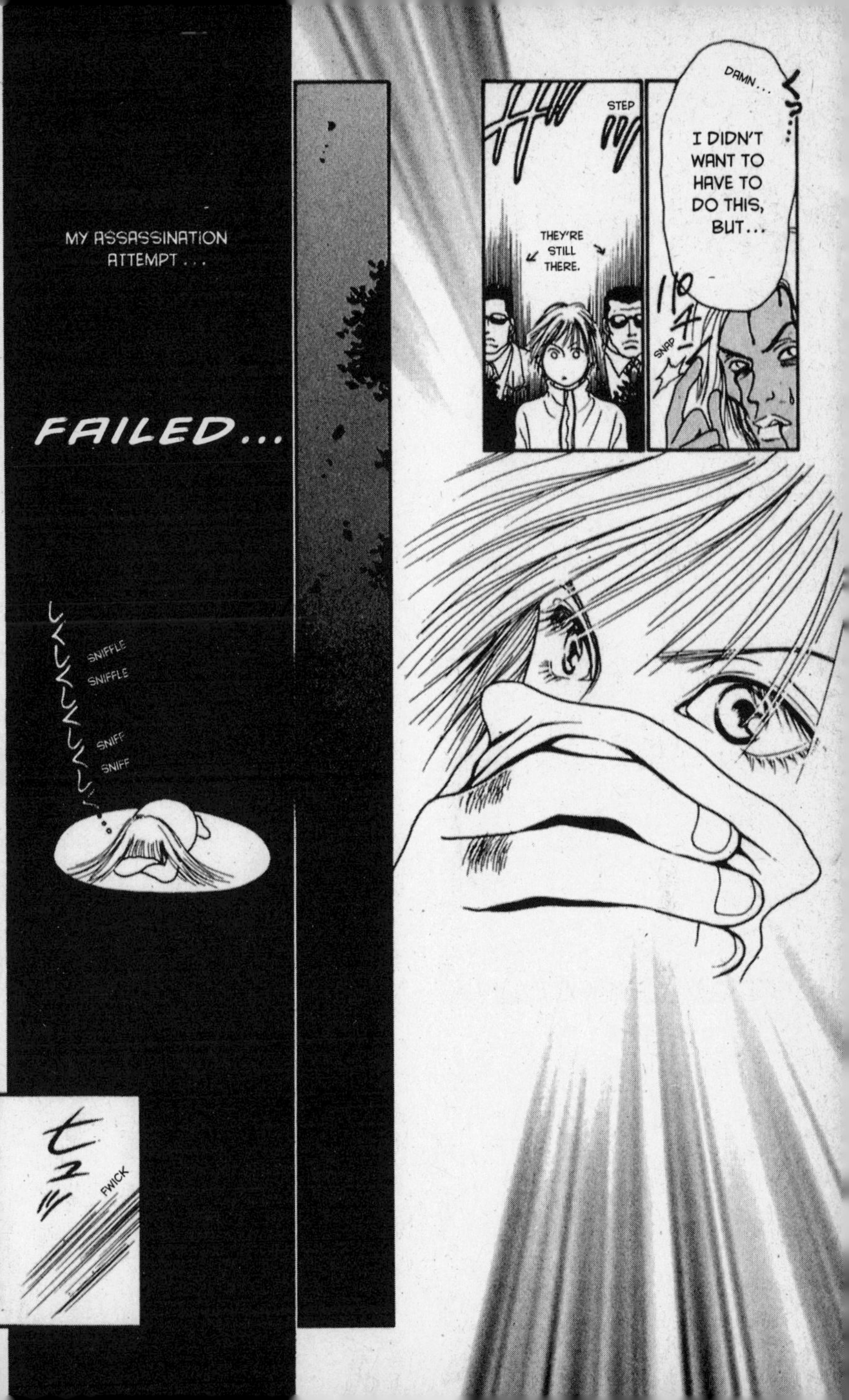
DAMN...
I DIDN'T WANT TO HAVE TO DO THIS, BUT...
SNAP
STEP
THEY'RE STILL THERE.
MY ASSASSINATION ATTEMPT...
FAILED...
SNIFFLE
SNIFFLE
SNIFF
SNIFF
FWICK

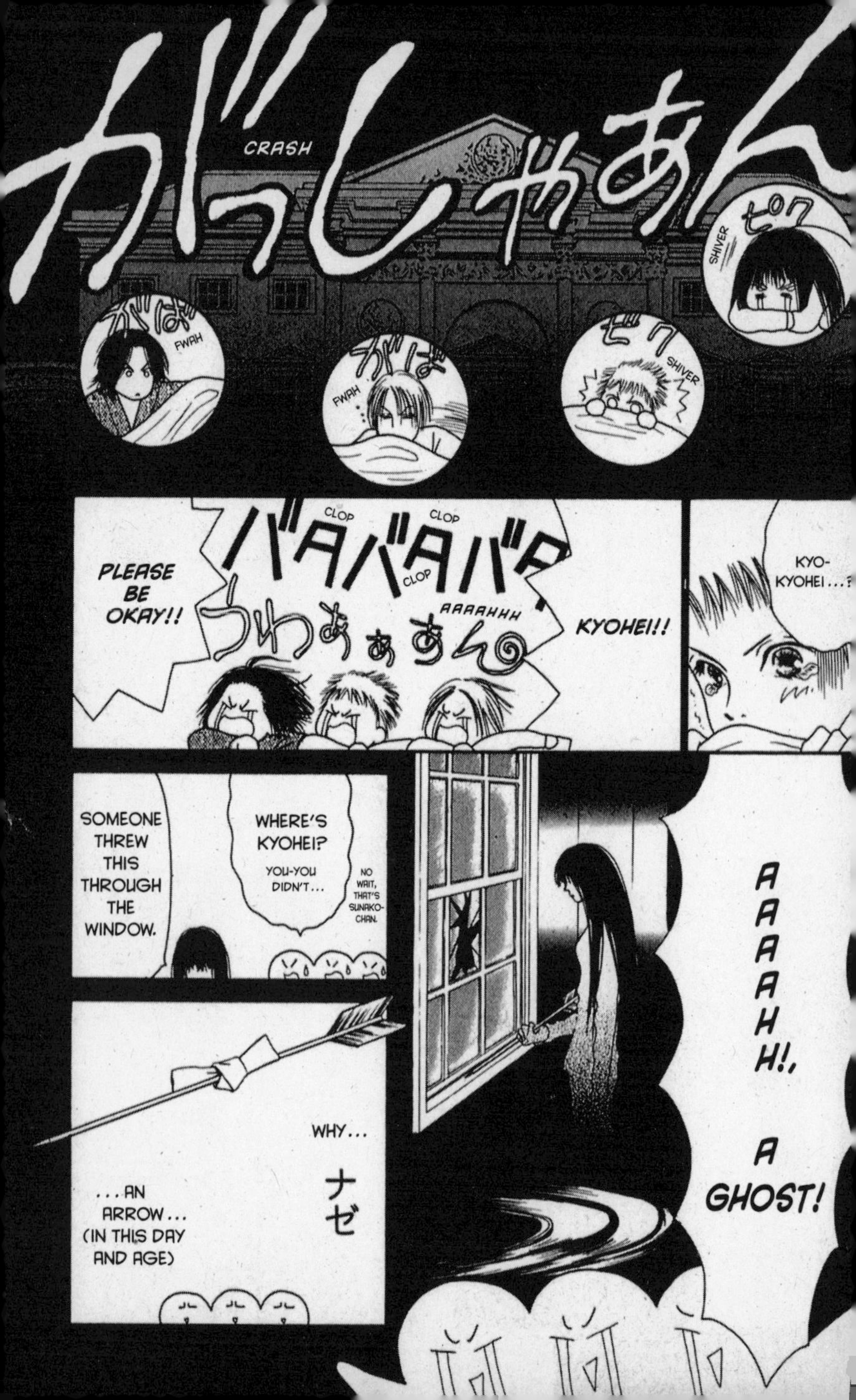

がしゃあん
CRASH
ぴくっ
SHIVER
ぞくっ
SHIVER
がばっ
FWAH
がばっ
FWAH
KYO-
KYOHEI...?
KYOHEI!!
バタバタバタ
CLOP
CLOP
CLOP
うわぁぁあん
AAAAHHH
PLEASE BE OKAY!!
AAAAAH!,
A GHOST!
WHERE'S KYOHEI?
SOMEONE THREW THIS THROUGH THE WINDOW.
YOU-YOU DIDN'T...
NO WAIT, THAT'S SUNAKO-CHAN.
WHY...
ナゼ
...AN ARROW... (IN THIS DAY AND AGE)

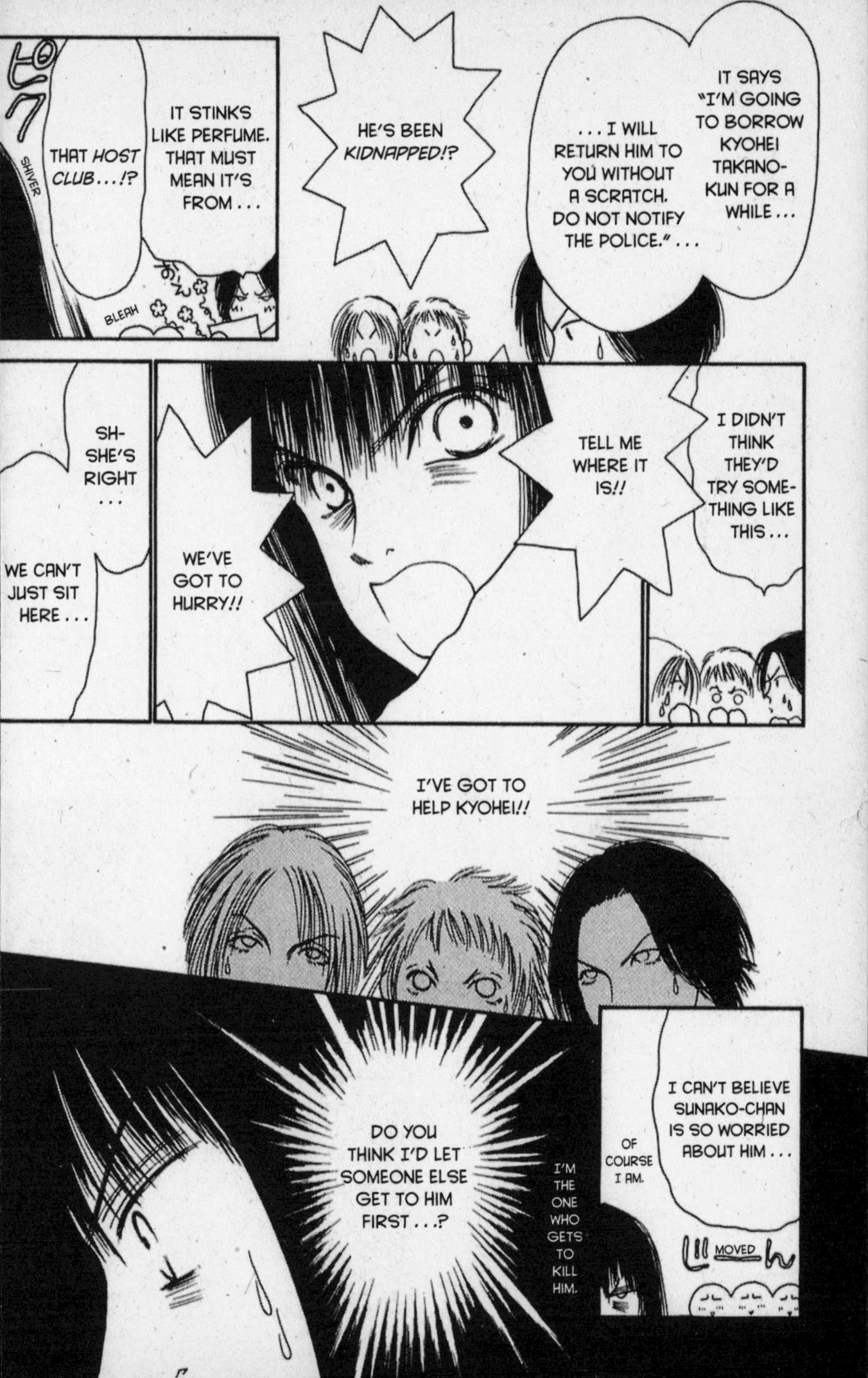
IT SAYS "I'M GOING TO BORROW KYOHEI TAKANO-KUN FOR A WHILE . . .
. . . I WILL RETURN HIM TO YOU WITHOUT A SCRATCH. DO NOT NOTIFY THE POLICE." . . .
HE'S BEEN *KIDNAPPED!?*
IT STINKS LIKE PERFUME. THAT MUST MEAN IT'S FROM . . .
THAT *HOST CLUB . . . !?*
SHIVER
BLEAH
I DIDN'T THINK THEY'D TRY SOMETHING LIKE THIS . . .
TELL ME WHERE IT IS!!
WE'VE GOT TO HURRY!!
SH-SHE'S RIGHT . . .
WE CAN'T JUST SIT HERE . . .
I'VE GOT TO HELP KYOHEI!!
I CAN'T BELIEVE SUNAKO-CHAN IS SO WORRIED ABOUT HIM . . .
MOVED
OF COURSE I AM.
I'M THE ONE WHO GETS TO KILL HIM.
DO YOU THINK I'D LET SOMEONE ELSE GET TO HIM FIRST . . . ?

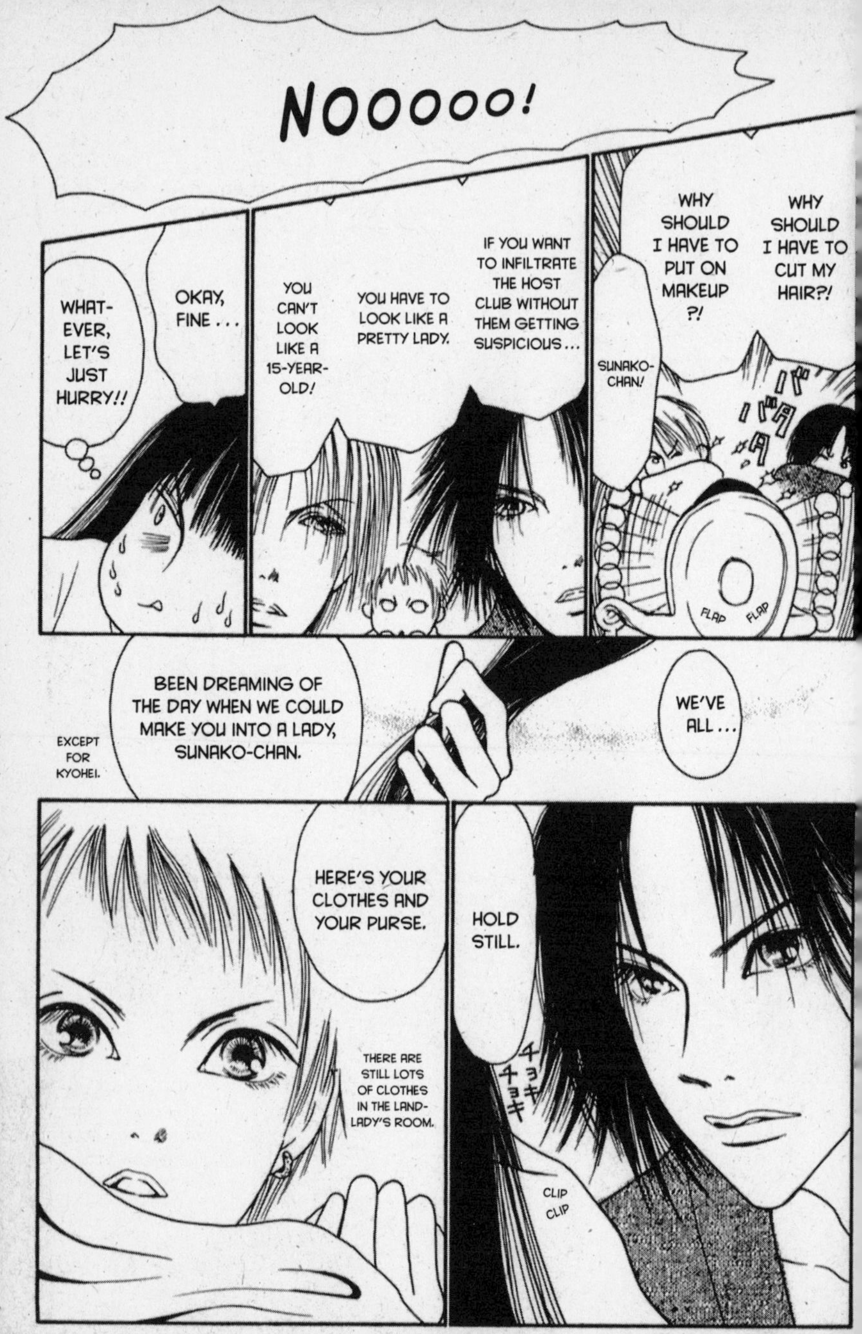
NOOOOO!
WHY SHOULD I HAVE TO CUT MY HAIR?!
WHY SHOULD I HAVE TO PUT ON MAKEUP ?!
SUNAKO-CHAN!
FLAP FLAP
IF YOU WANT TO INFILTRATE THE HOST CLUB WITHOUT THEM GETTING SUSPICIOUS . . .
YOU HAVE TO LOOK LIKE A PRETTY LADY.
YOU CAN'T LOOK LIKE A 15-YEAR-OLD!
OKAY, FINE . . .
WHATEVER, LET'S JUST HURRY!!
WE'VE ALL . . .
BEEN DREAMING OF THE DAY WHEN WE COULD MAKE YOU INTO A LADY, SUNAKO-CHAN.
EXCEPT FOR KYOHEI.
HOLD STILL.
チョキチョキ
CLIP CLIP
HERE'S YOUR CLOTHES AND YOUR PURSE.
THERE ARE STILL LOTS OF CLOTHES IN THE LANDLADY'S ROOM.

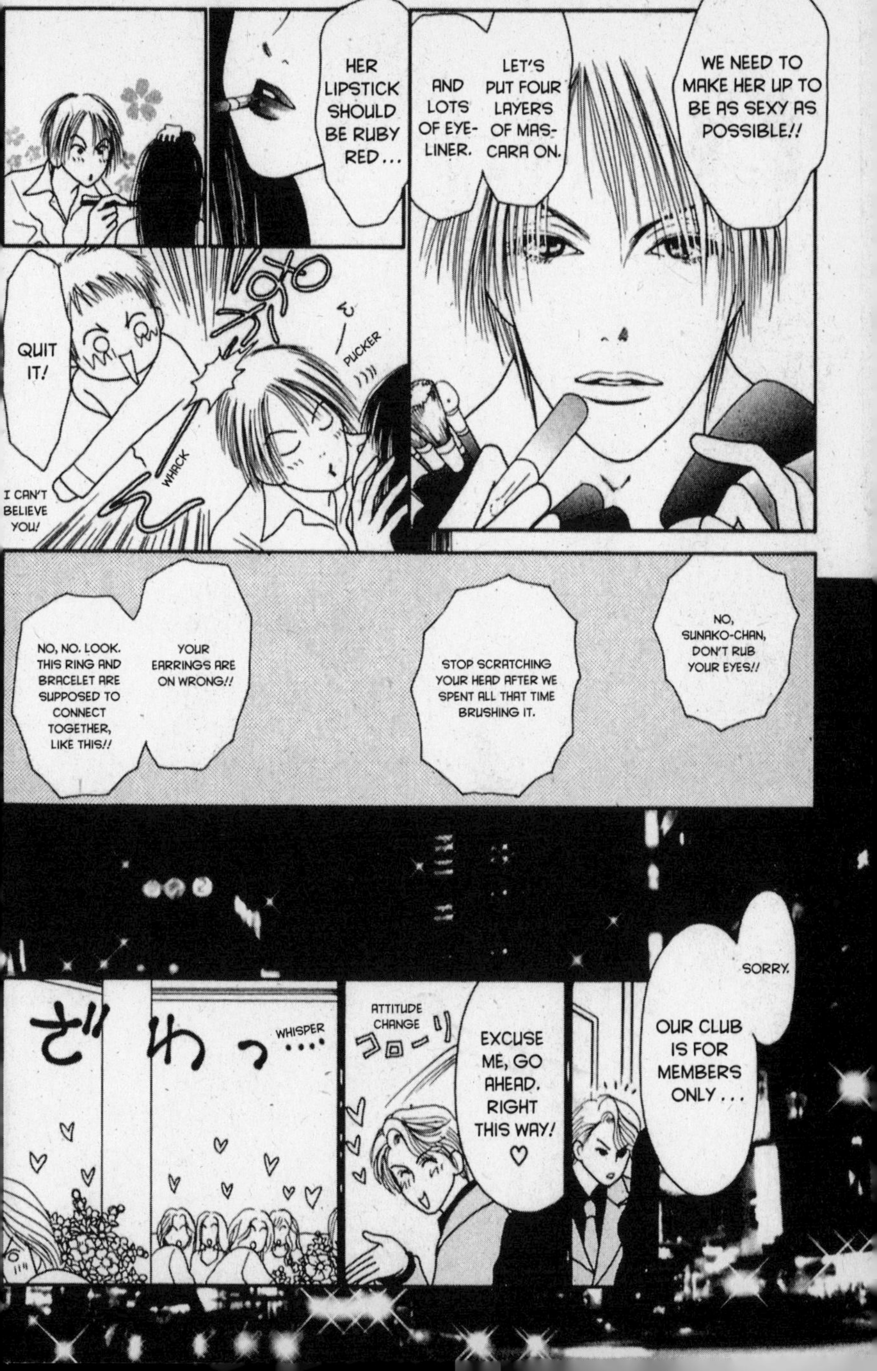
WE NEED TO MAKE HER UP TO BE AS SEXY AS POSSIBLE!!
LET'S PUT FOUR LAYERS OF MAS-CARA ON.
AND LOTS OF EYE-LINER.
HER LIPSTICK SHOULD BE RUBY RED...
PUCKER
QUIT IT!
WHACK
I CAN'T BELIEVE YOU!
NO, SUNAKO-CHAN, DON'T RUB YOUR EYES!!
STOP SCRATCHING YOUR HEAD AFTER WE SPENT ALL THAT TIME BRUSHING IT.
YOUR EARRINGS ARE ON WRONG!!
NO, NO. LOOK. THIS RING AND BRACELET ARE SUPPOSED TO CONNECT TOGETHER, LIKE THIS!!
SORRY.
OUR CLUB IS FOR MEMBERS ONLY...
EXCUSE ME, GO AHEAD. RIGHT THIS WAY!
コローリ
ATTITUDE CHANGE
ざわっ
WHISPER...

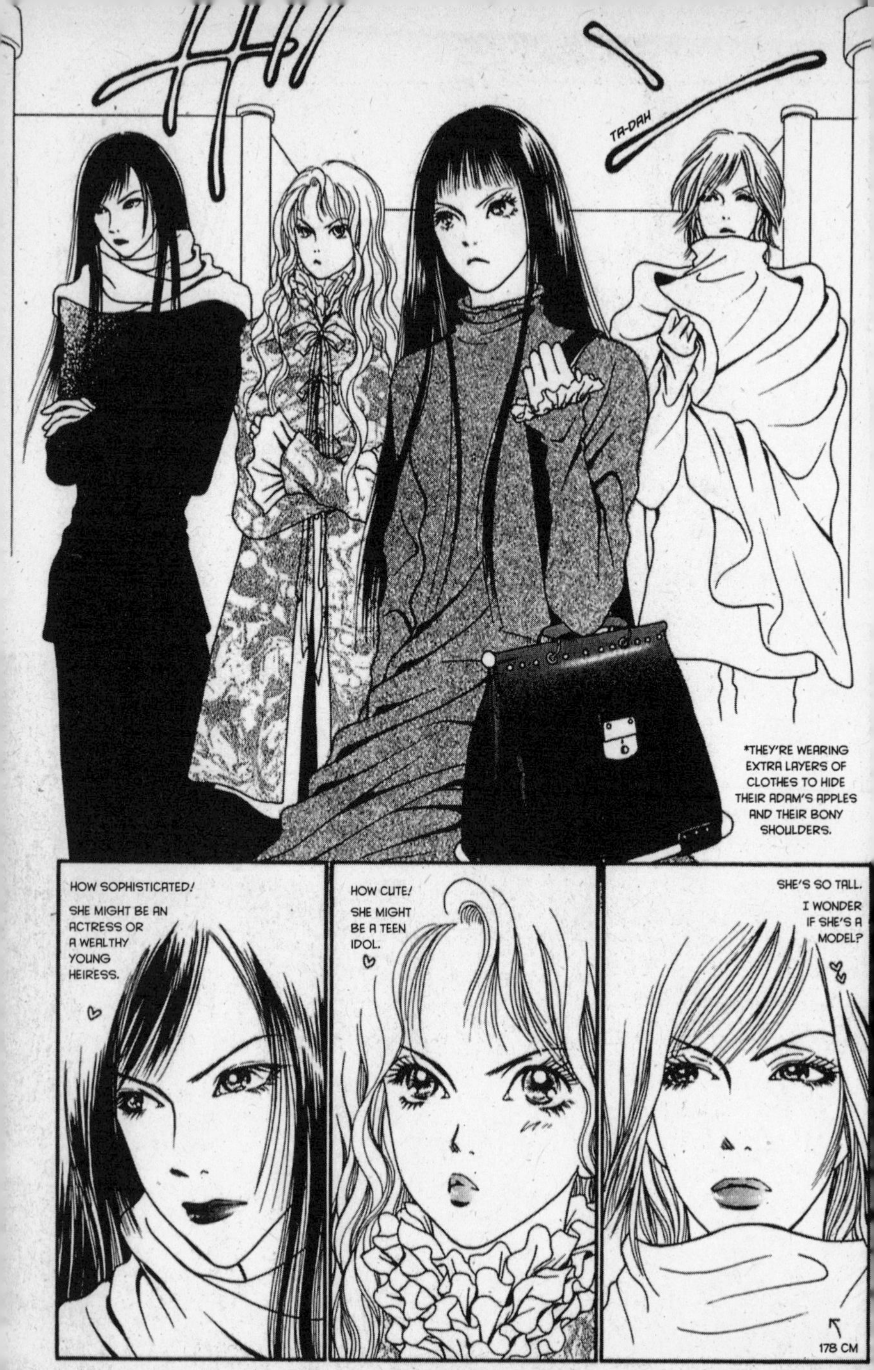
TA-DAH
*THEY'RE WEARING EXTRA LAYERS OF CLOTHES TO HIDE THEIR ADAM'S APPLES AND THEIR BONY SHOULDERS.
SHE'S SO TALL.
I WONDER IF SHE'S A MODEL?
178 CM
HOW CUTE!
SHE MIGHT BE A TEEN IDOL.
HOW SOPHISTICATED!
SHE MIGHT BE AN ACTRESS OR A WEALTHY YOUNG HEIRESS.

THE LANDLADY COLLECTS WIGS.

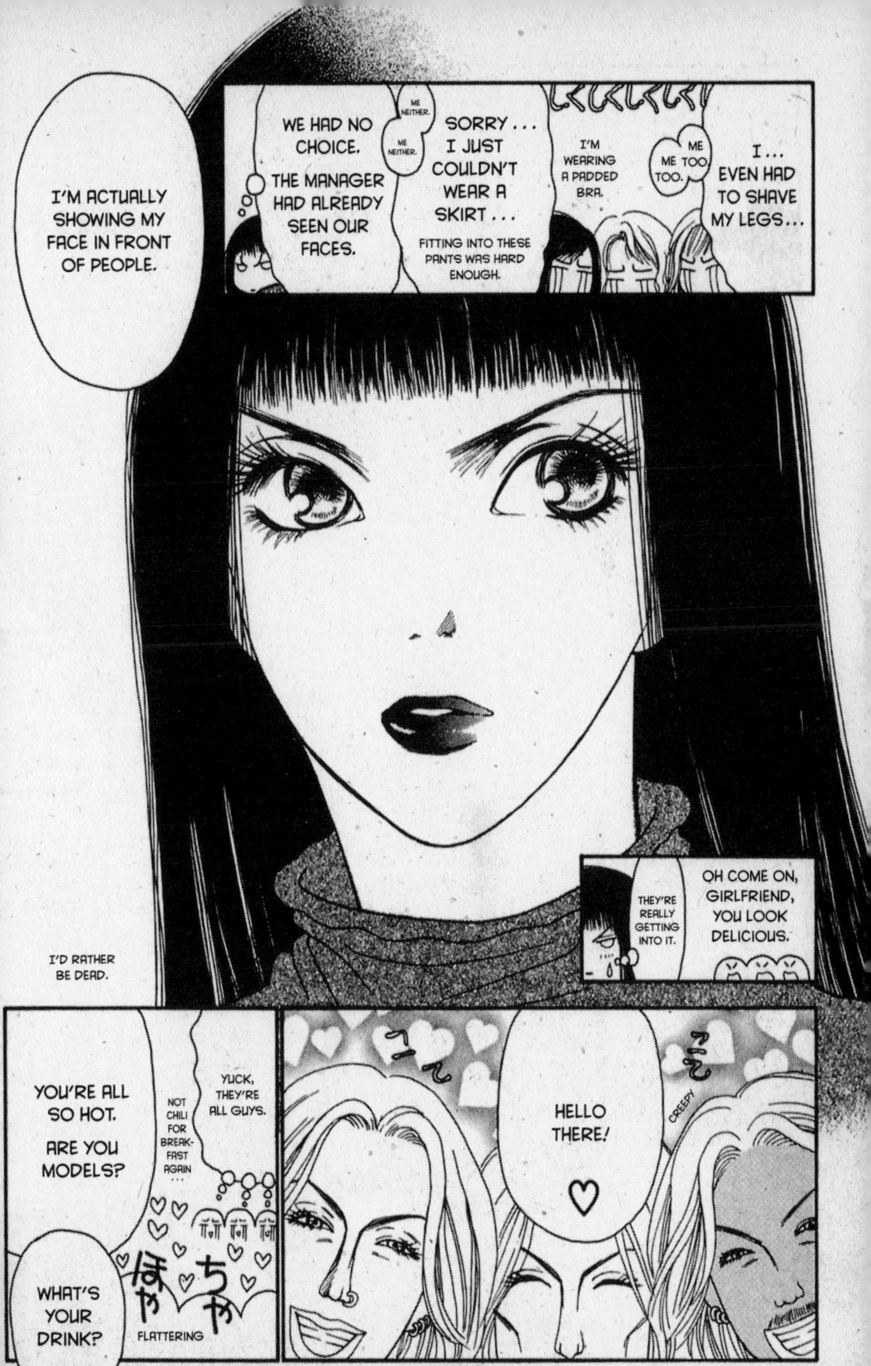
I... EVEN HAD TO SHAVE MY LEGS...
ME TOO.
ME TOO.
I'M WEARING A PADDED BRA.
SORRY... I JUST COULDN'T WEAR A SKIRT...
FITTING INTO THESE PANTS WAS HARD ENOUGH.
ME NEITHER.
ME NEITHER.
WE HAD NO CHOICE. THE MANAGER HAD ALREADY SEEN OUR FACES.
I'M ACTUALLY SHOWING MY FACE IN FRONT OF PEOPLE.
OH COME ON, GIRLFRIEND, YOU LOOK DELICIOUS.
THEY'RE REALLY GETTING INTO IT.
I'D RATHER BE DEAD.
CREEPY
HELLO THERE! ♡
YOU'RE ALL SO HOT. ARE YOU MODELS?
YUCK, THEY'RE ALL GUYS.
NOT CHILI FOR BREAKFAST AGAIN...
FLATTERING
WHAT'S YOUR DRINK?

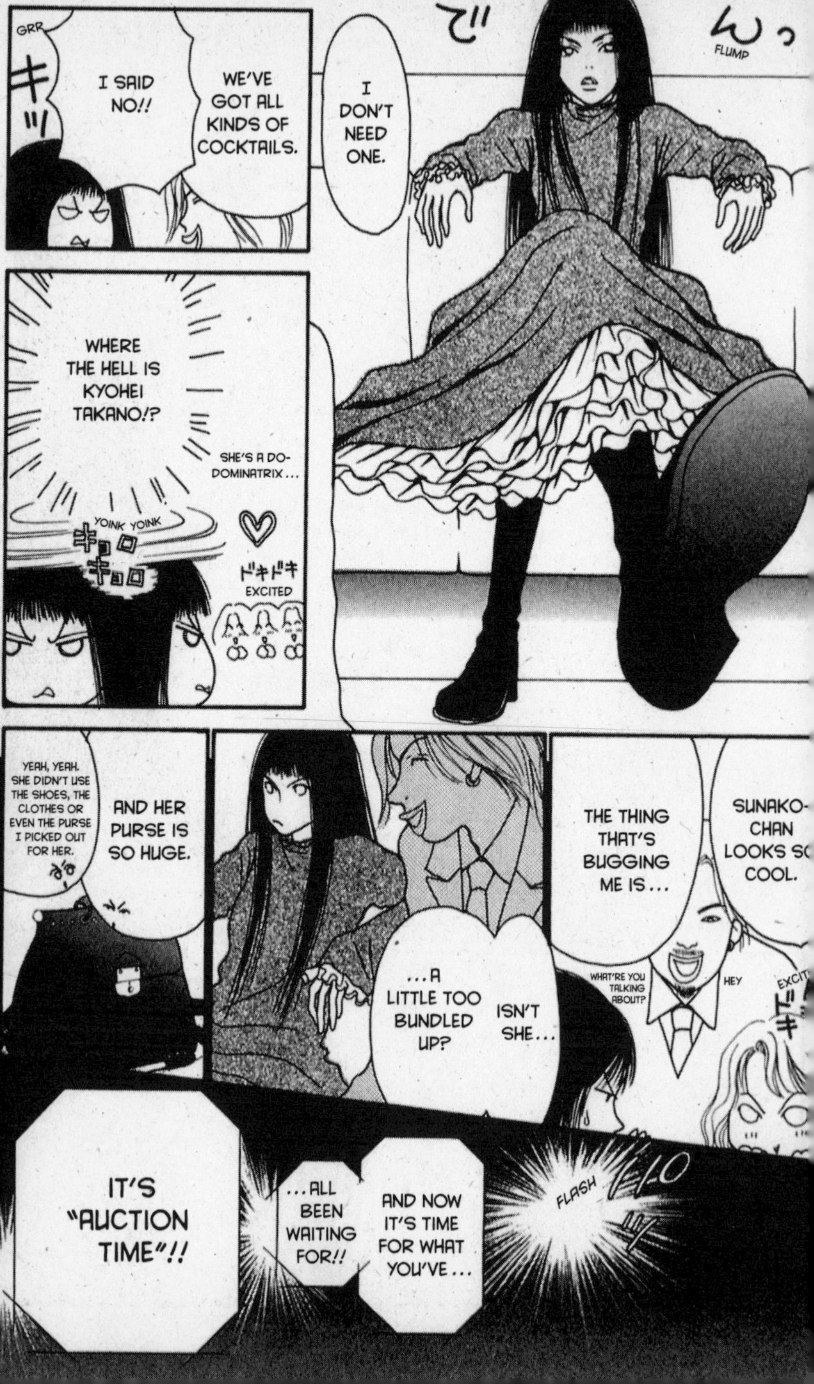
でんっ
FLUMP
I DON'T NEED ONE.
WE'VE GOT ALL KINDS OF COCKTAILS.
I SAID NO!!
GRR
WHERE THE HELL IS KYOHEI TAKANO!?
SHE'S A DO-DOMINATRIX...
YOINK YOINK
ドキドキ
EXCITED
SUNAKO-CHAN LOOKS SO COOL.
THE THING THAT'S BUGGING ME IS...
HEY
WHAT'RE YOU TALKING ABOUT?
ISN'T SHE...
...A LITTLE TOO BUNDLED UP?
AND HER PURSE IS SO HUGE.
YEAH, YEAH. SHE DIDN'T USE THE SHOES, THE CLOTHES OR EVEN THE PURSE I PICKED OUT FOR HER.
FLASH
AND NOW IT'S TIME FOR WHAT YOU'VE...
...ALL BEEN WAITING FOR!!
IT'S "AUCTION TIME"!!

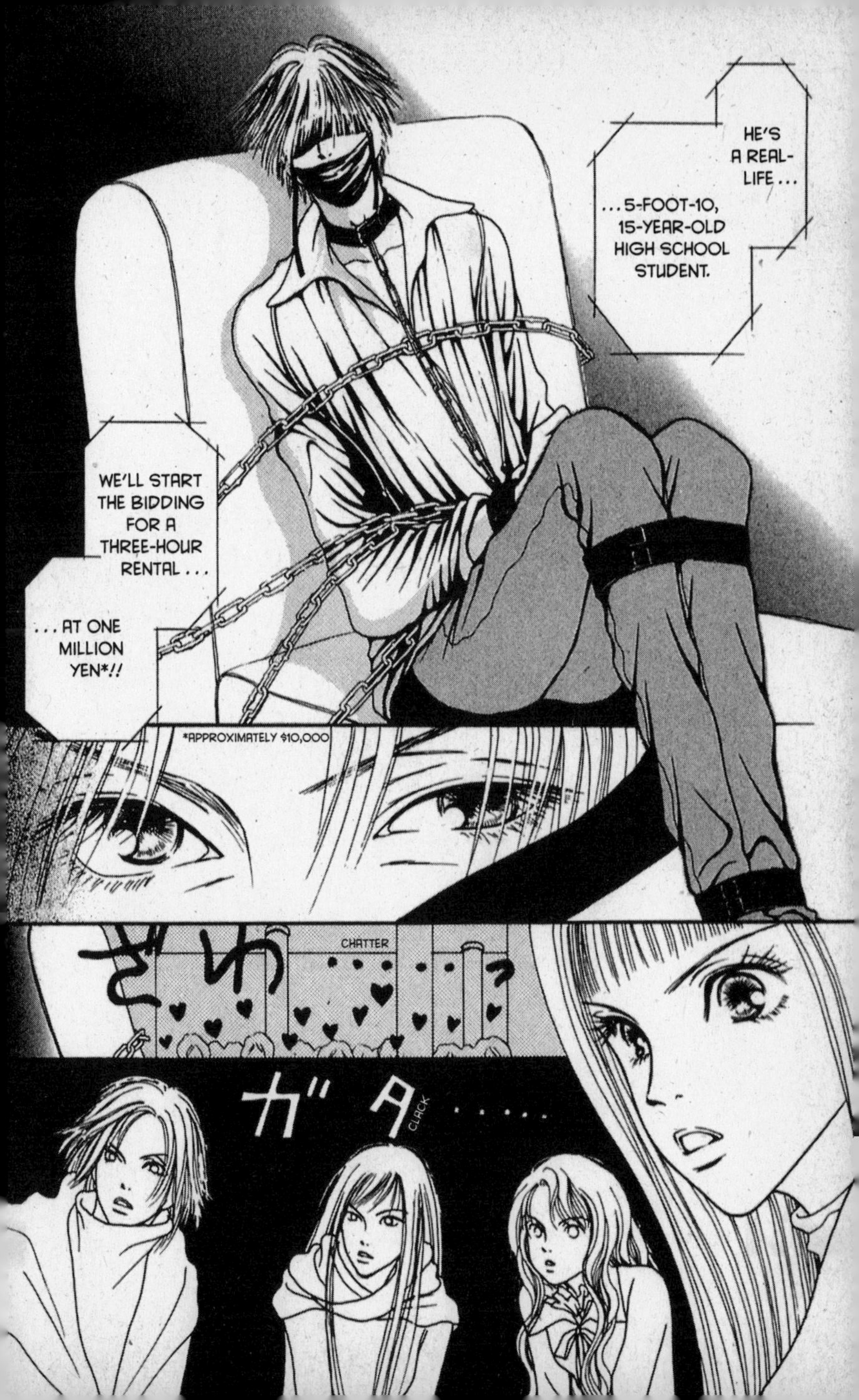
HE'S A REAL-LIFE . . .
. . . 5-FOOT-10, 15-YEAR-OLD HIGH SCHOOL STUDENT.
WE'LL START THE BIDDING FOR A THREE-HOUR RENTAL . . .
. . . AT ONE MILLION YEN*!!
*APPROXIMATELY $10,000
ざわ
CHATTER
ガタ
CLACK

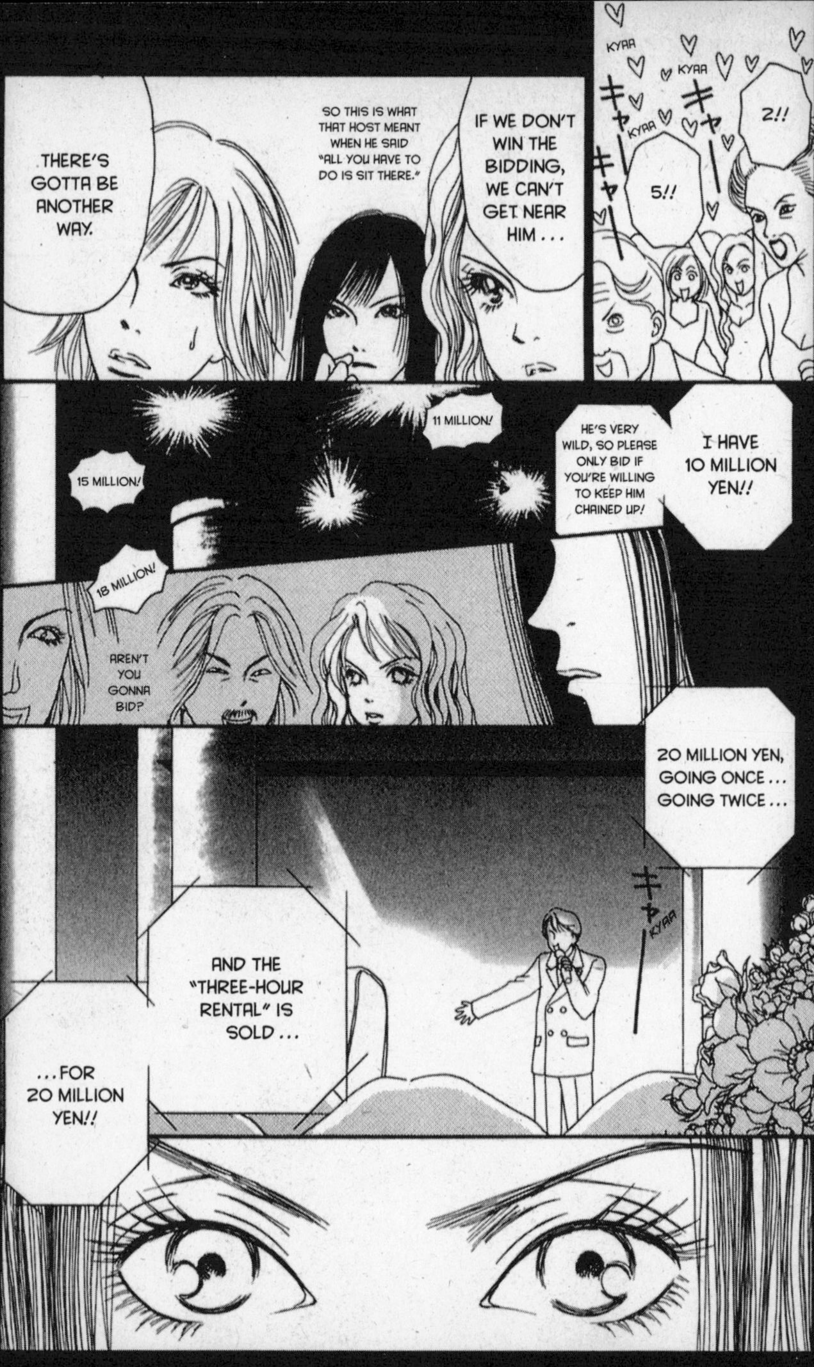
KYAA
KYAA
キャー
2!!
KYAA
キャー
キャー
5!!
IF WE DON'T WIN THE BIDDING, WE CAN'T GET NEAR HIM . . .
SO THIS IS WHAT THAT HOST MEANT WHEN HE SAID "ALL YOU HAVE TO DO IS SIT THERE."
THERE'S GOTTA BE ANOTHER WAY.
I HAVE 10 MILLION YEN!!
HE'S VERY WILD, SO PLEASE ONLY BID IF YOU'RE WILLING TO KEEP HIM CHAINED UP!
11 MILLION!
15 MILLION!
18 MILLION!
AREN'T YOU GONNA BID?
20 MILLION YEN, GOING ONCE . . . GOING TWICE . . .
キャー
KYAA
AND THE "THREE-HOUR RENTAL" IS SOLD . . .
. . . FOR 20 MILLION YEN!!

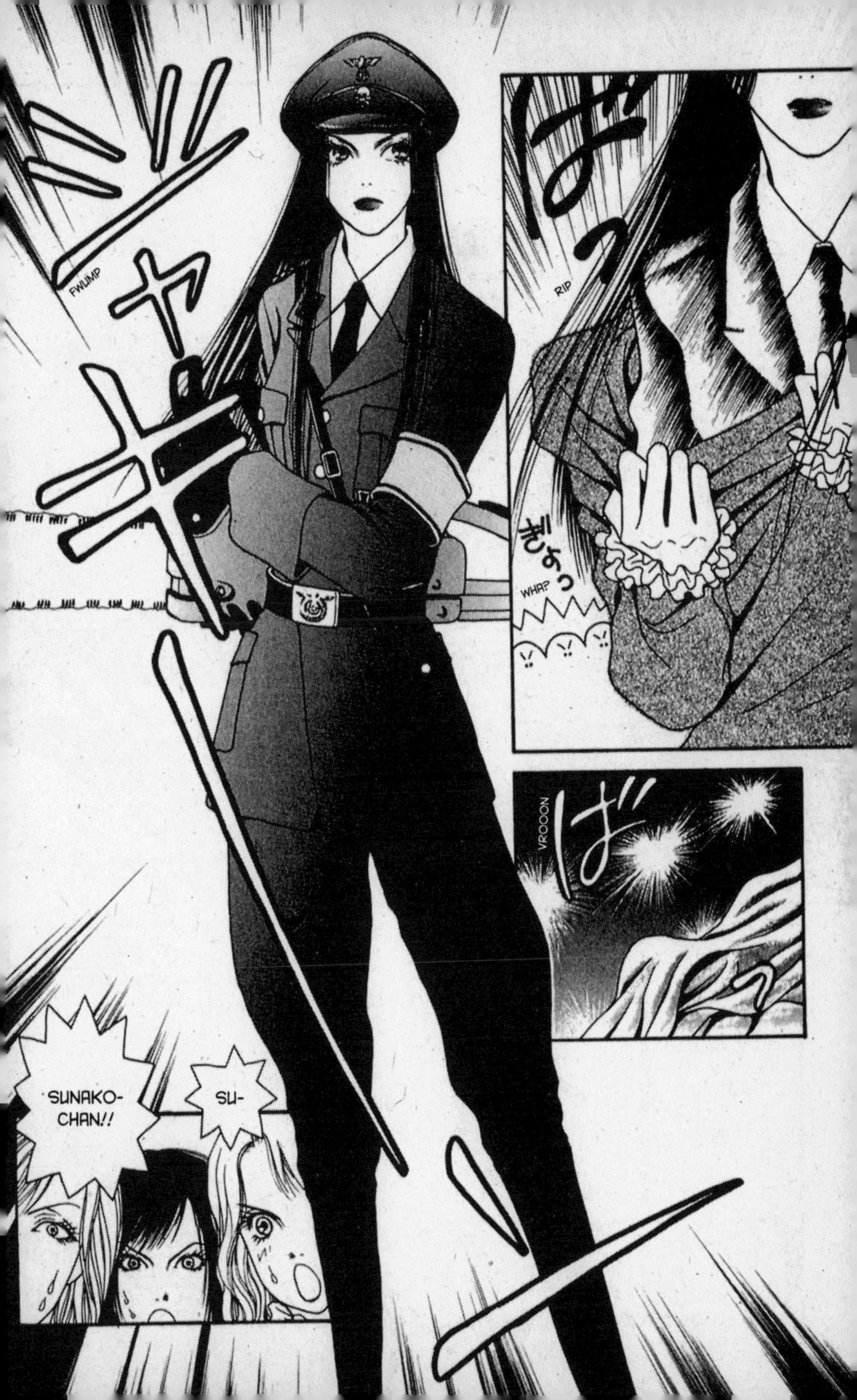
RIP
WHA?
VROOON
FWUMP
SU-
SUNAKO-CHAN!!

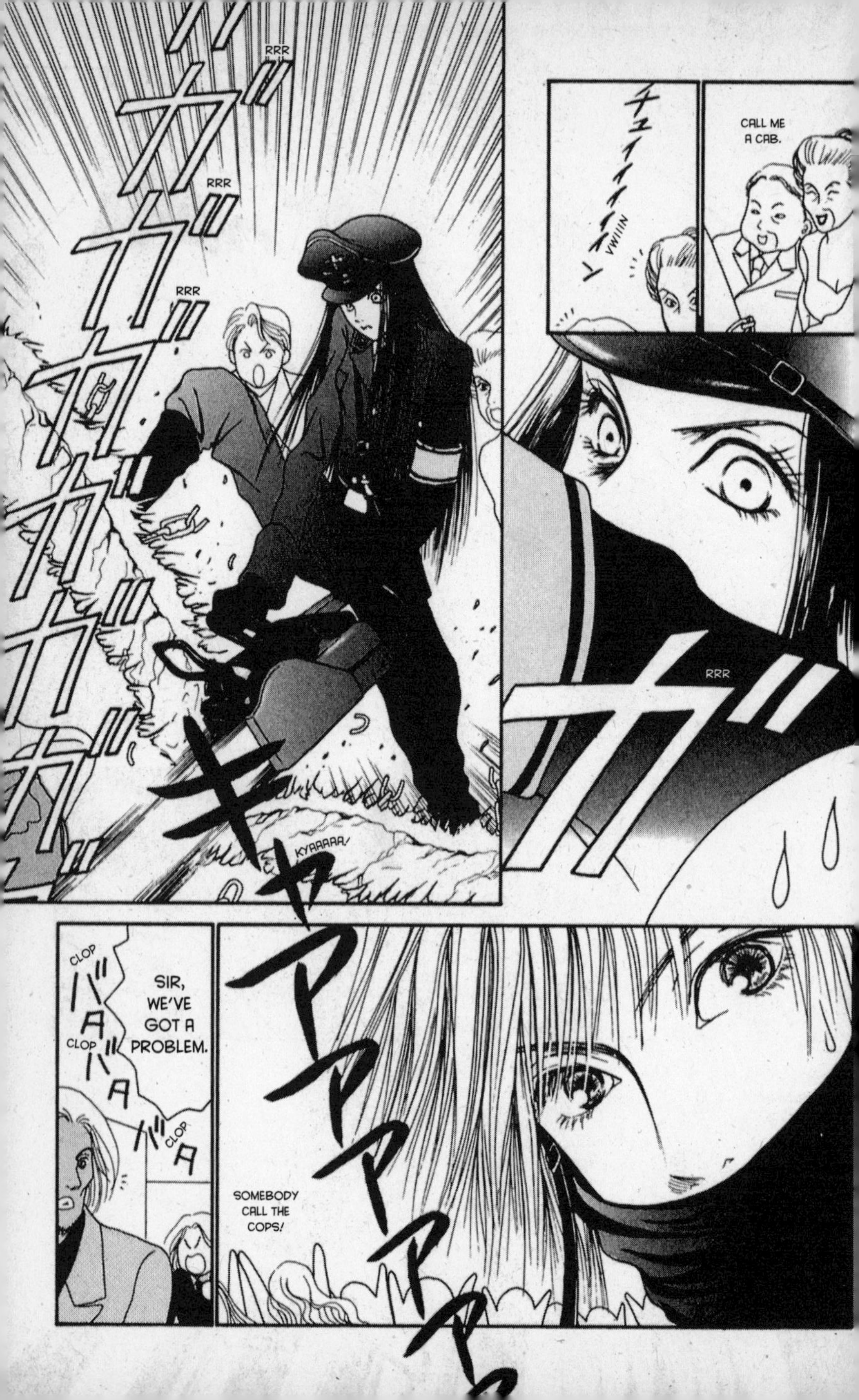
CALL ME A CAB.
VWIIIN
RRR
RRR
RRR
RRR
KYAAAAA!
SOMEBODY CALL THE COPS!
SIR, WE'VE GOT A PROBLEM.
CLOP
CLOP
CLOP

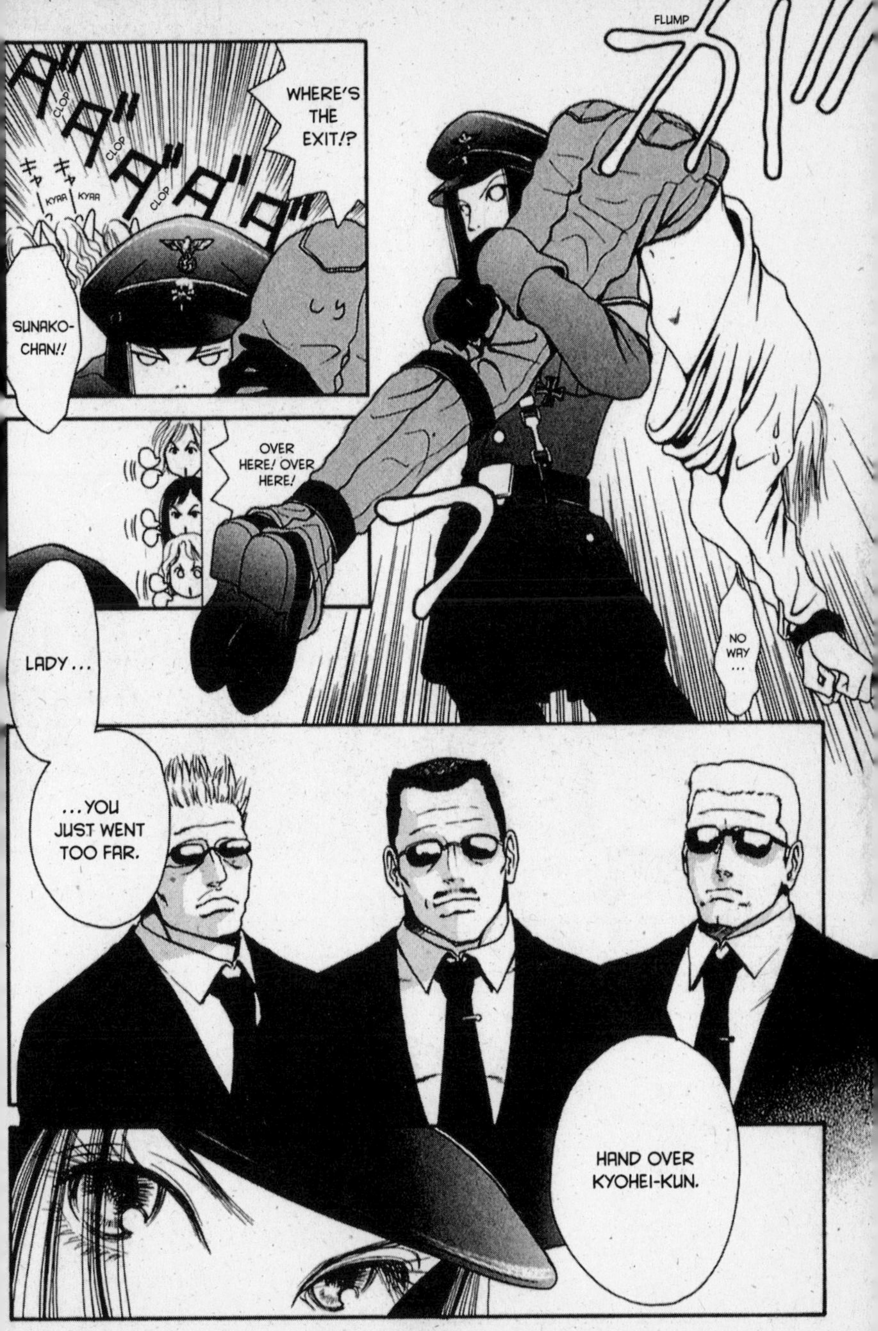
FLUMP
NO WAY...
WHERE'S THE EXIT!?
CLOP CLOP CLOP
KYRA KYRA
SUNAKO-CHAN!!
OVER HERE! OVER HERE!
LADY...
...YOU JUST WENT TOO FAR.
HAND OVER KYOHEI-KUN.

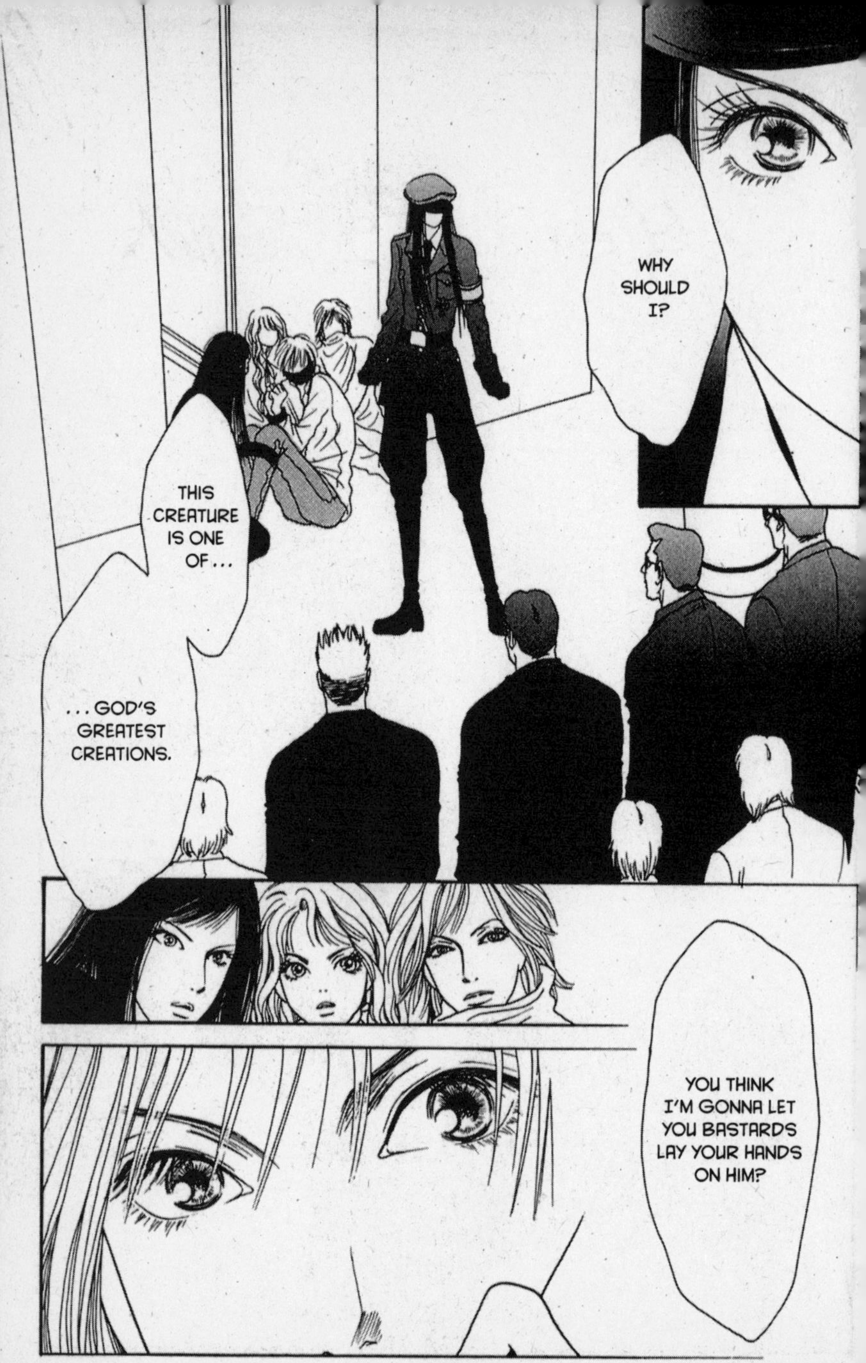
WHY SHOULD I?
THIS CREATURE IS ONE OF . . .
. . . GOD'S GREATEST CREATIONS.
YOU THINK I'M GONNA LET YOU BASTARDS LAY YOUR HANDS ON HIM?

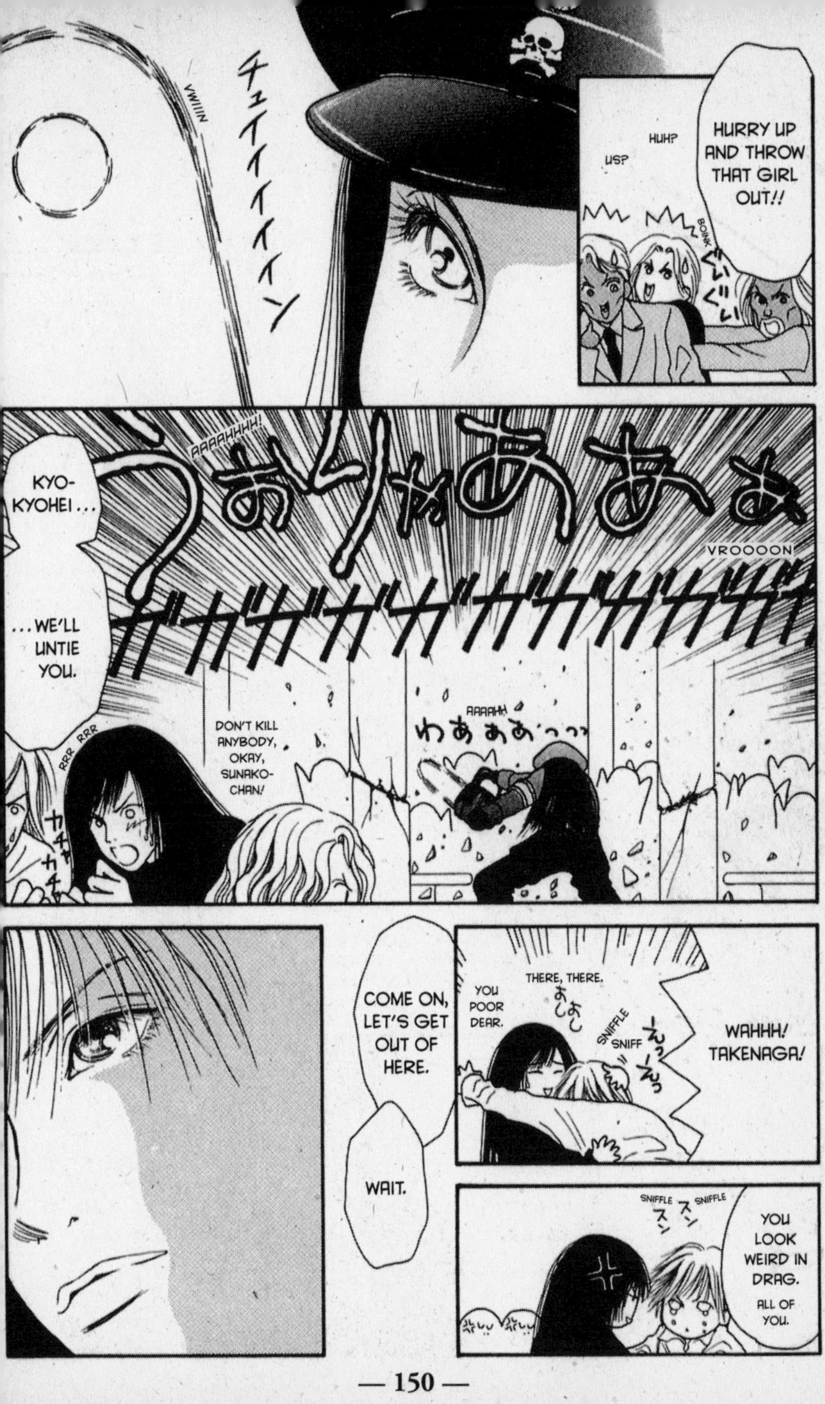
HURRY UP AND THROW THAT GIRL OUT!!
HUH?
US?
BOINK
ぐいぐい
チェイイイイイン
VWIIIN
うぉりゃあああ
AAAAHHHH!
VROOOON
KYO-KYOHEI...
...WE'LL UNTIE YOU.
DON'T KILL ANYBODY, OKAY, SUNAKO-CHAN!
わあああっっ
AAAAHH!
RRR RRR
WAHHH! TAKENAGA!
THERE, THERE.
YOU POOR DEAR.
SNIFFLE SNIFF
YOU LOOK WEIRD IN DRAG.
ALL OF YOU.
SNIFFLE SNIFFLE
COME ON, LET'S GET OUT OF HERE.
WAIT.

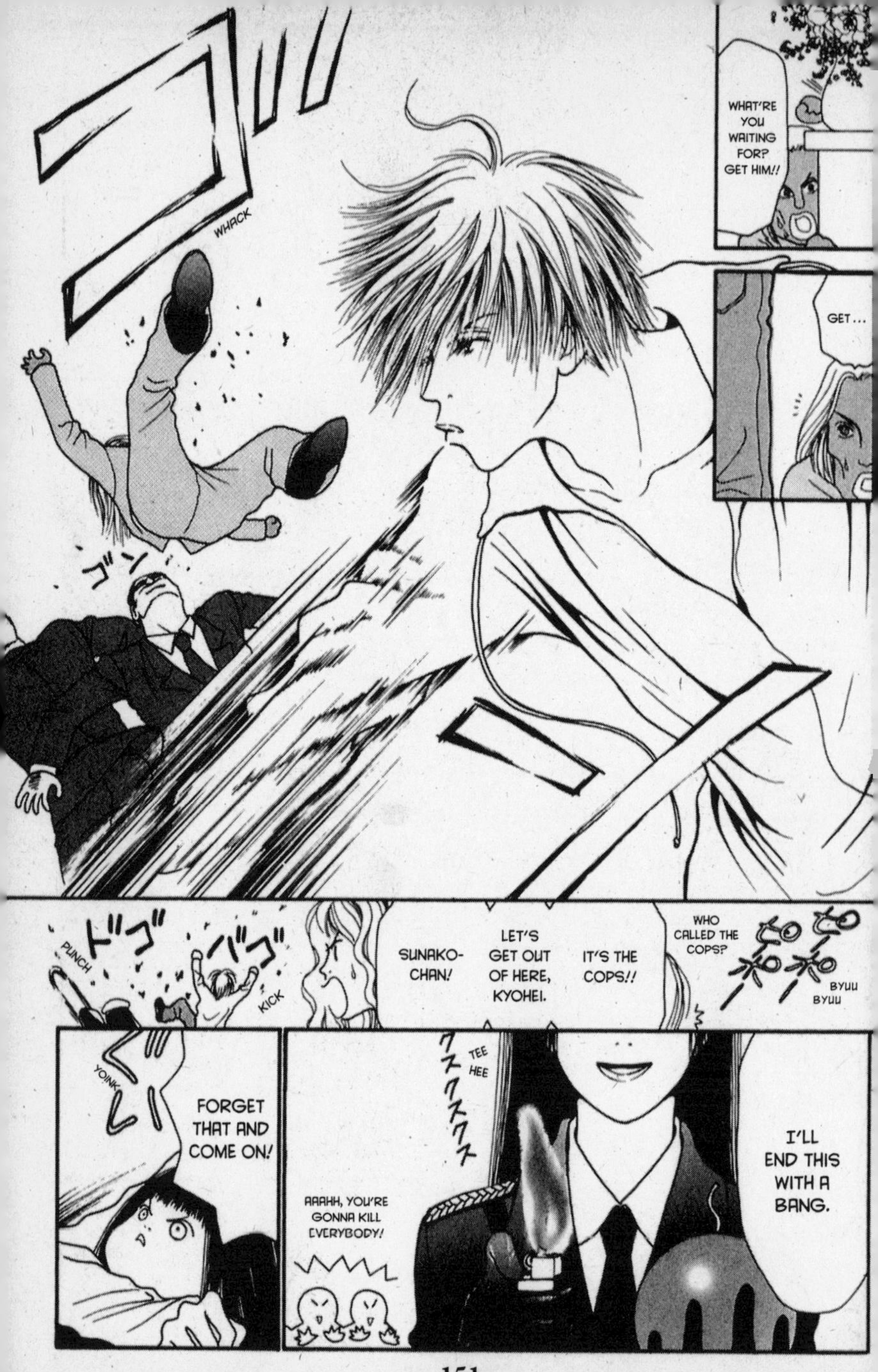
WHAT'RE YOU WAITING FOR? GET HIM!!
GET...
WHACK
ゴン
WHO CALLED THE COPS?
BYUU BYUU
IT'S THE COPS!!
LET'S GET OUT OF HERE, KYOHEI.
SUNAKO-CHAN!
バゴ
KICK
ドゴ
PUNCH
I'LL END THIS WITH A BANG.
TEE HEE
AAAHH, YOU'RE GONNA KILL EVERYBODY!
YOINK
FORGET THAT AND COME ON!

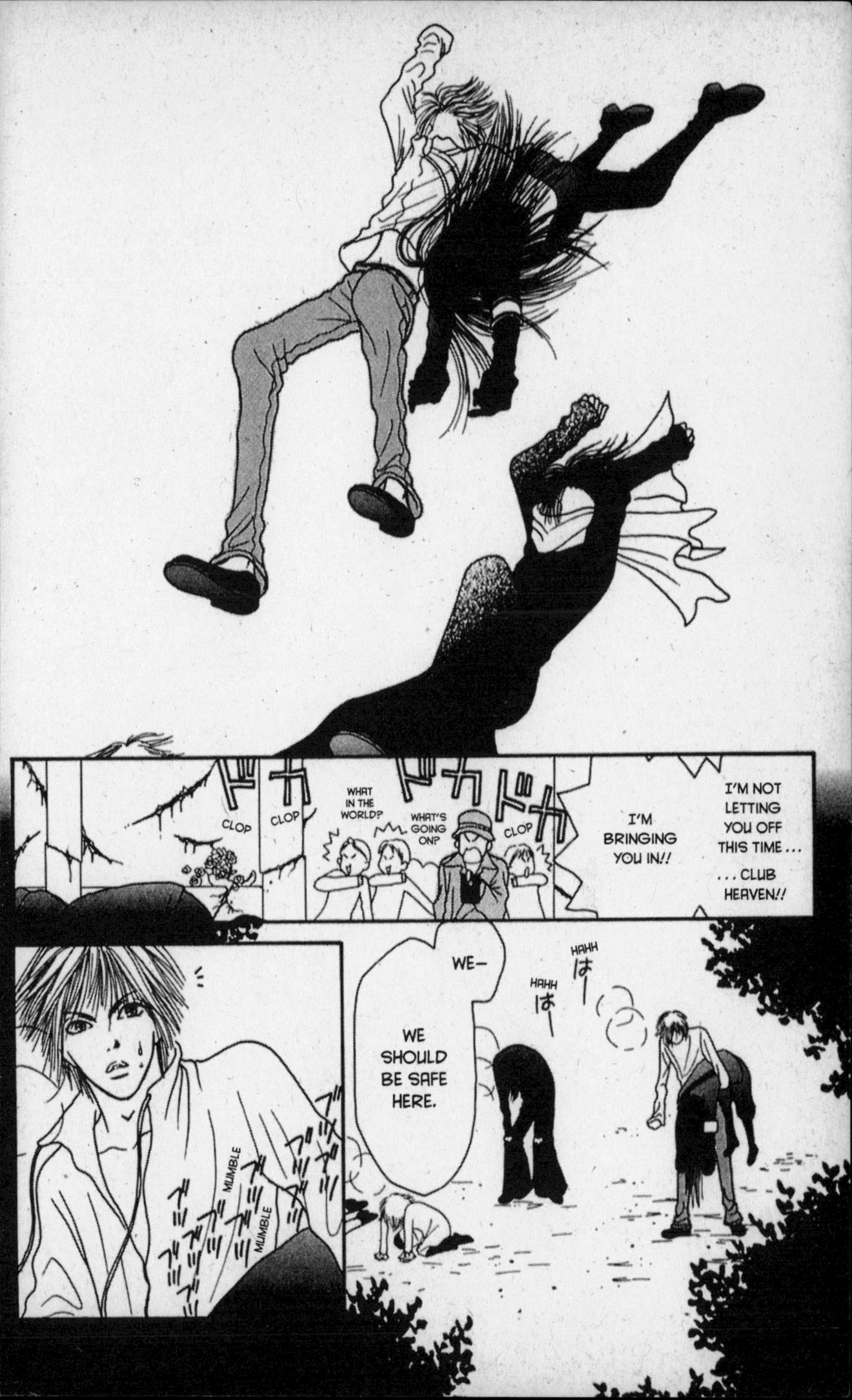
I'M NOT LETTING YOU OFF THIS TIME . . .
. . . CLUB HEAVEN!!
I'M BRINGING YOU IN!!
CLOP
WHAT'S GOING ON?
WHAT IN THE WORLD?
CLOP
CLOP
HAHH
HAHH
WE—
WE SHOULD BE SAFE HERE.
MUMBLE
MUMBLE

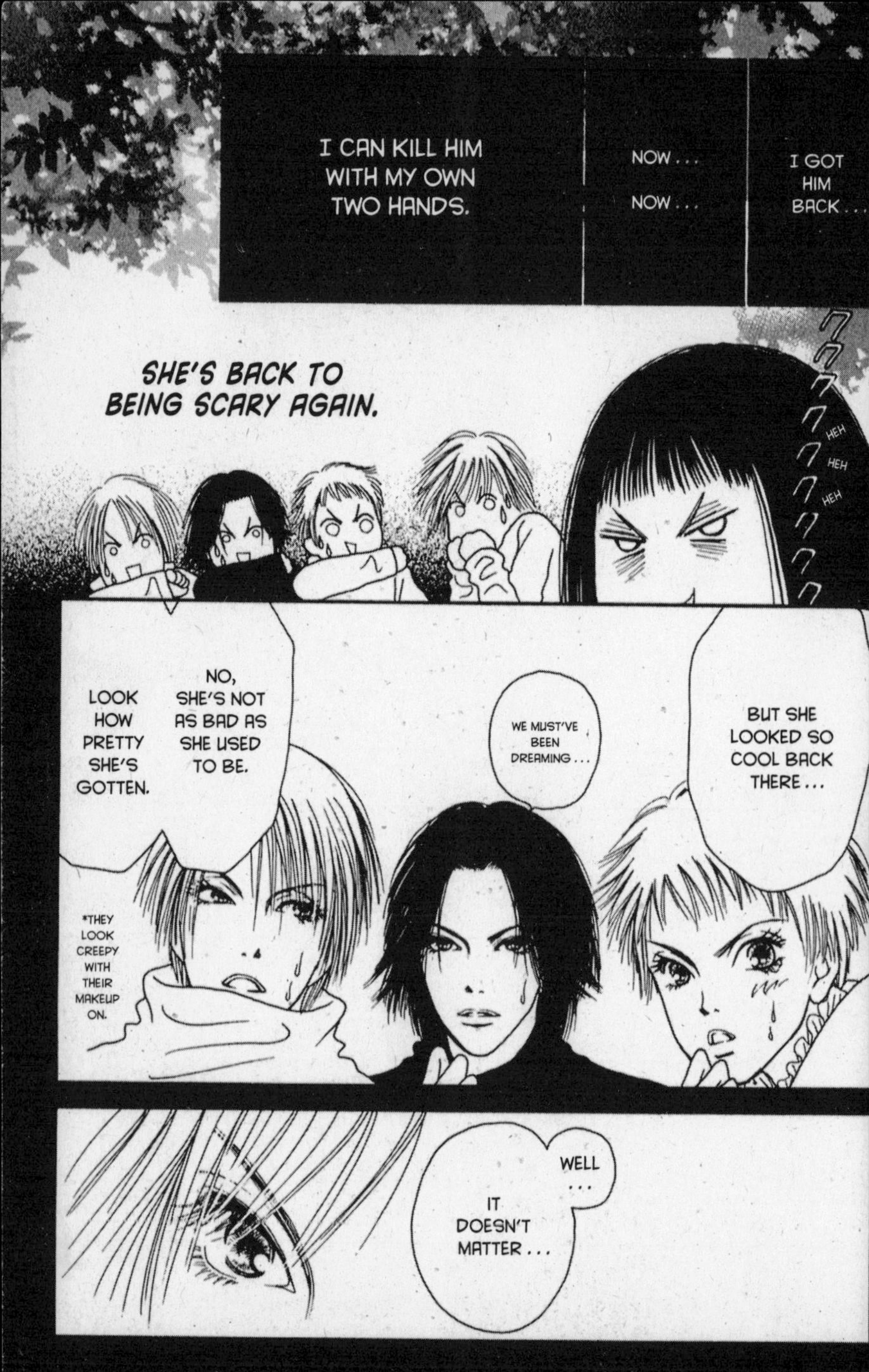
I GOT HIM BACK...
NOW... NOW...
I CAN KILL HIM WITH MY OWN TWO HANDS.
HEH HEH HEH
SHE'S BACK TO BEING SCARY AGAIN.
BUT SHE LOOKED SO COOL BACK THERE...
WE MUST'VE BEEN DREAMING...
NO, SHE'S NOT AS BAD AS SHE USED TO BE.
LOOK HOW PRETTY SHE'S GOTTEN.
*THEY LOOK CREEPY WITH THEIR MAKEUP ON.
WELL...
IT DOESN'T MATTER...

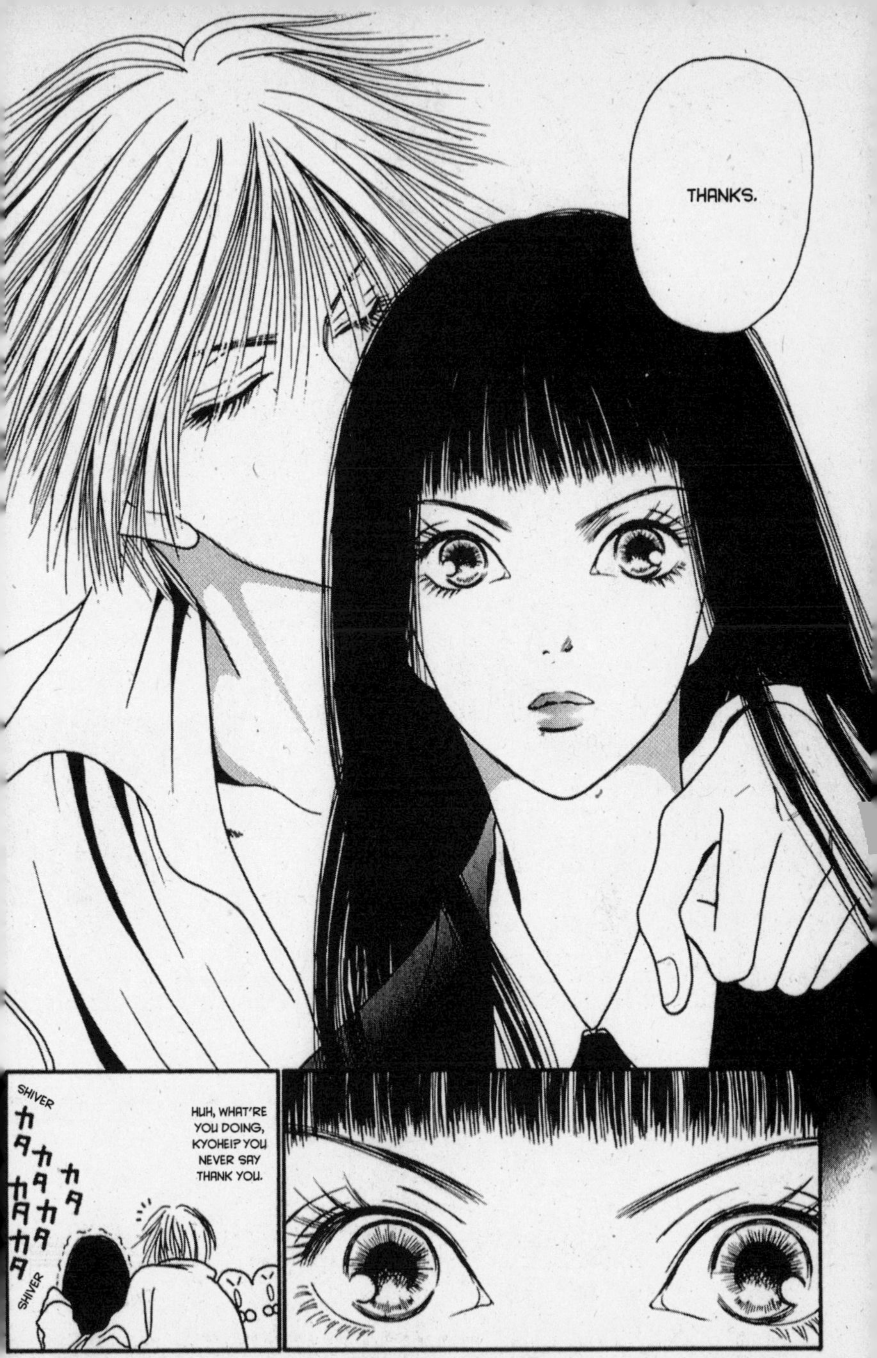
THANKS.
HUH, WHAT'RE YOU DOING, KYOHEI? YOU NEVER SAY THANK YOU.
SHIVER
カタカタカタカタカタカタ
SHIVER

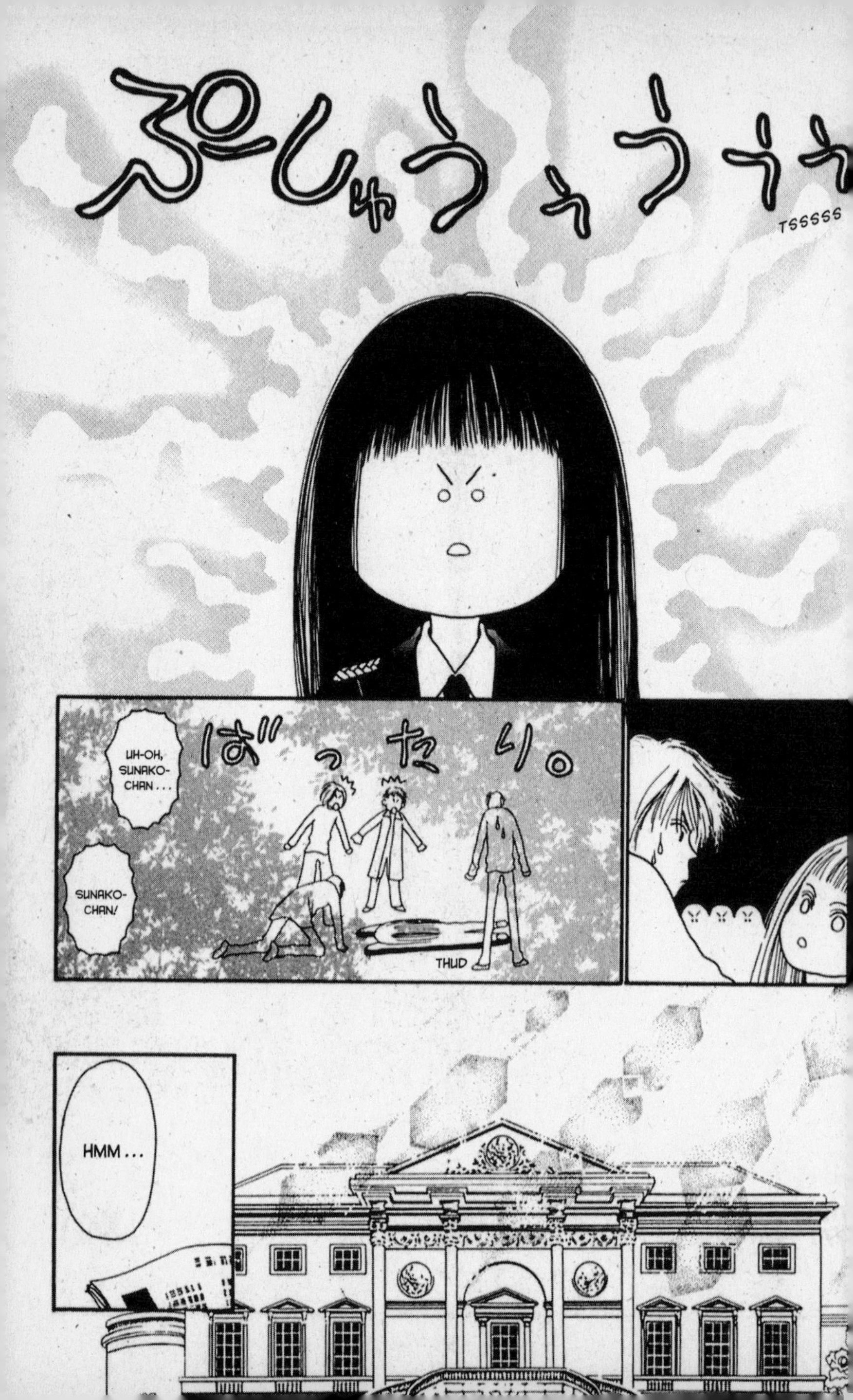
TSSSSS
ばったり。
UH-OH, SUNAKO-CHAN...
SUNAKO-CHAN!
THUD
HMM...

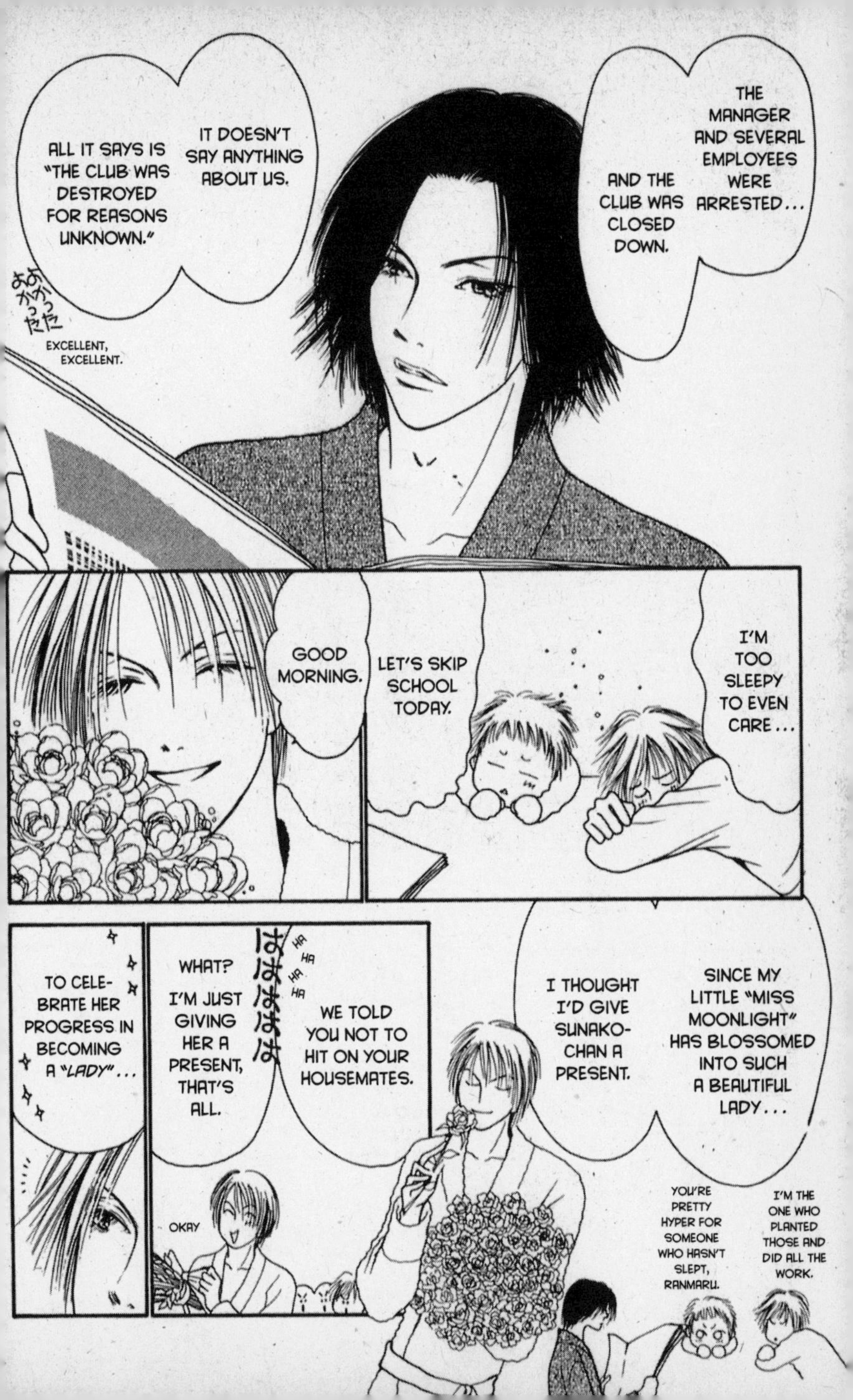
THE MANAGER AND SEVERAL EMPLOYEES WERE ARRESTED...
AND THE CLUB WAS CLOSED DOWN.
IT DOESN'T SAY ANYTHING ABOUT US.
ALL IT SAYS IS "THE CLUB WAS DESTROYED FOR REASONS UNKNOWN."
EXCELLENT, EXCELLENT.
I'M TOO SLEEPY TO EVEN CARE...
LET'S SKIP SCHOOL TODAY.
GOOD MORNING.
SINCE MY LITTLE "MISS MOONLIGHT" HAS BLOSSOMED INTO SUCH A BEAUTIFUL LADY...
I THOUGHT I'D GIVE SUNAKO-CHAN A PRESENT.
I'M THE ONE WHO PLANTED THOSE AND DID ALL THE WORK.
YOU'RE PRETTY HYPER FOR SOMEONE WHO HASN'T SLEPT, RANMARU.
WE TOLD YOU NOT TO HIT ON YOUR HOUSEMATES.
ははははは
HA HA HA HA
WHAT? I'M JUST GIVING HER A PRESENT, THAT'S ALL.
OKAY
TO CELEBRATE HER PROGRESS IN BECOMING A "LADY"...

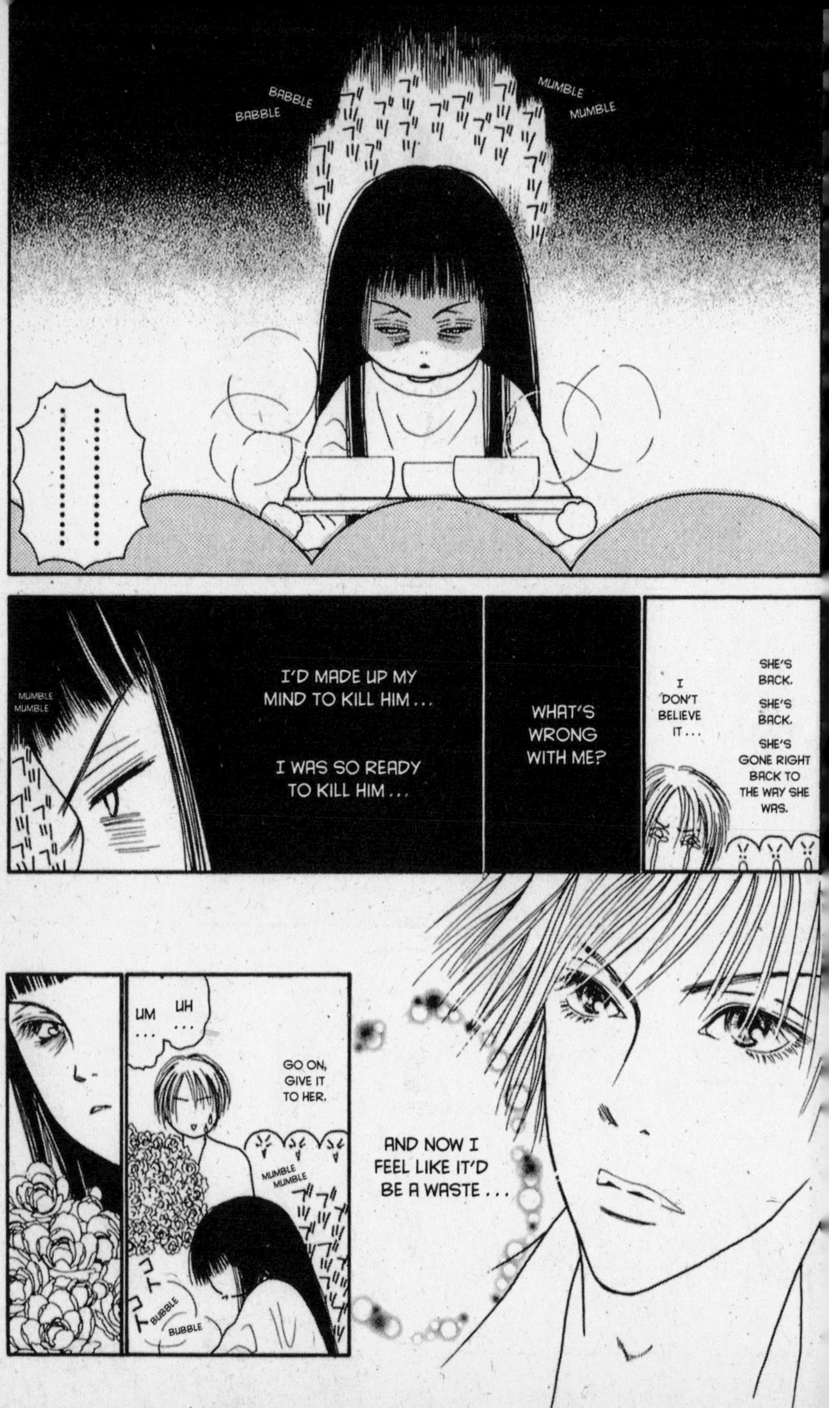
MUMBLE
MUMBLE
BABBLE
BABBLE
. . . . . .
SHE'S BACK.
SHE'S BACK.
SHE'S GONE RIGHT BACK TO THE WAY SHE WAS.
I DON'T BELIEVE IT...
WHAT'S WRONG WITH ME?
I'D MADE UP MY MIND TO KILL HIM...
I WAS SO READY TO KILL HIM...
MUMBLE MUMBLE
AND NOW I FEEL LIKE IT'D BE A WASTE...
GO ON, GIVE IT TO HER.
UH...
UM...
MUMBLE MUMBLE
BUBBLE
BUBBLE

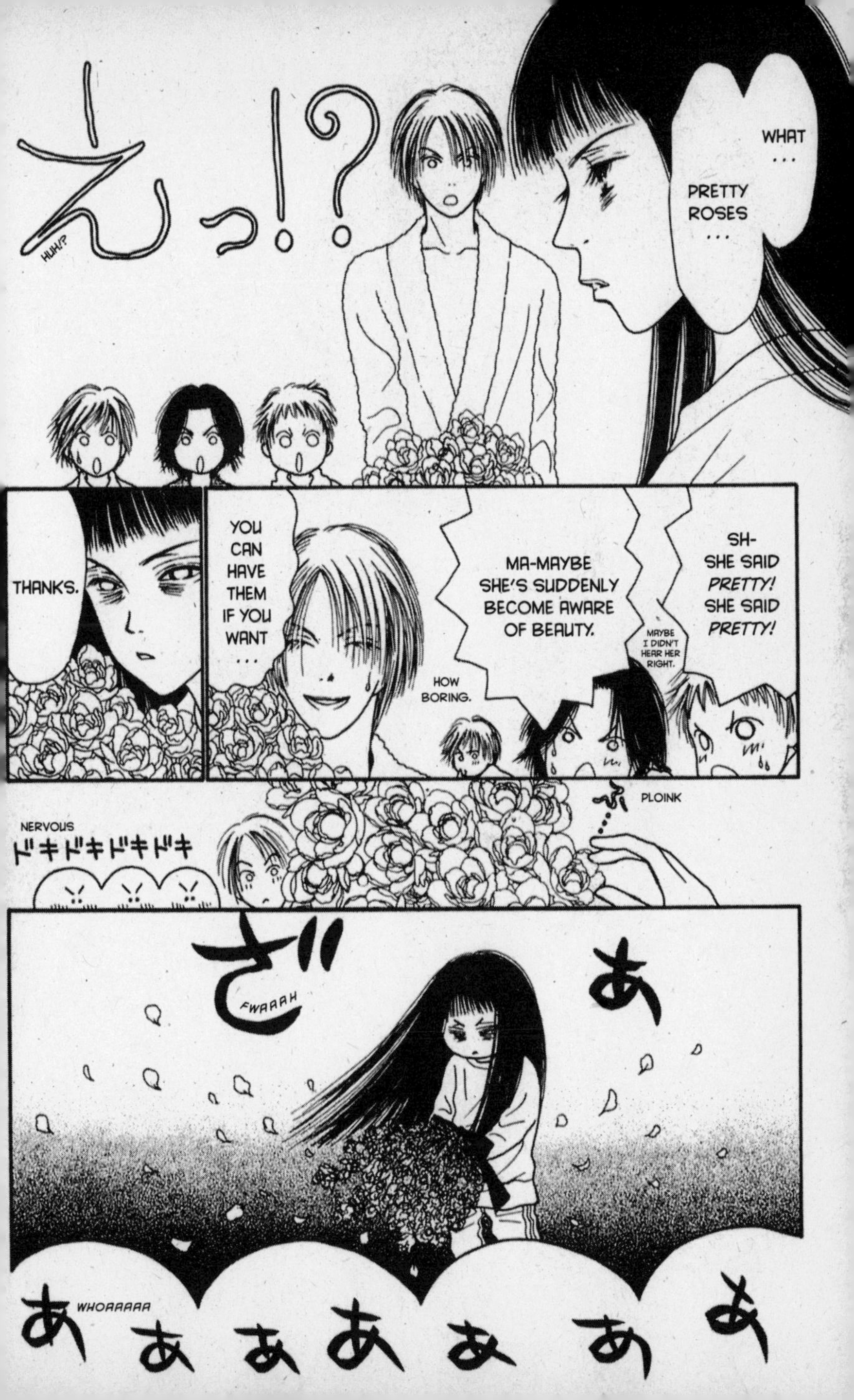
WHAT ... PRETTY ROSES ...
えっ!?
HUH!?
SH- SHE SAID PRETTY! SHE SAID PRETTY!
MAYBE I DIDN'T HEAR HER RIGHT.
MA-MAYBE SHE'S SUDDENLY BECOME AWARE OF BEAUTY.
HOW BORING.
YOU CAN HAVE THEM IF YOU WANT ...
THANKS.
ぷ
PLOINK
NERVOUS
ドキドキドキドキ
ざあ
FWAAAH
ああああああああ
WHOAAAAAA

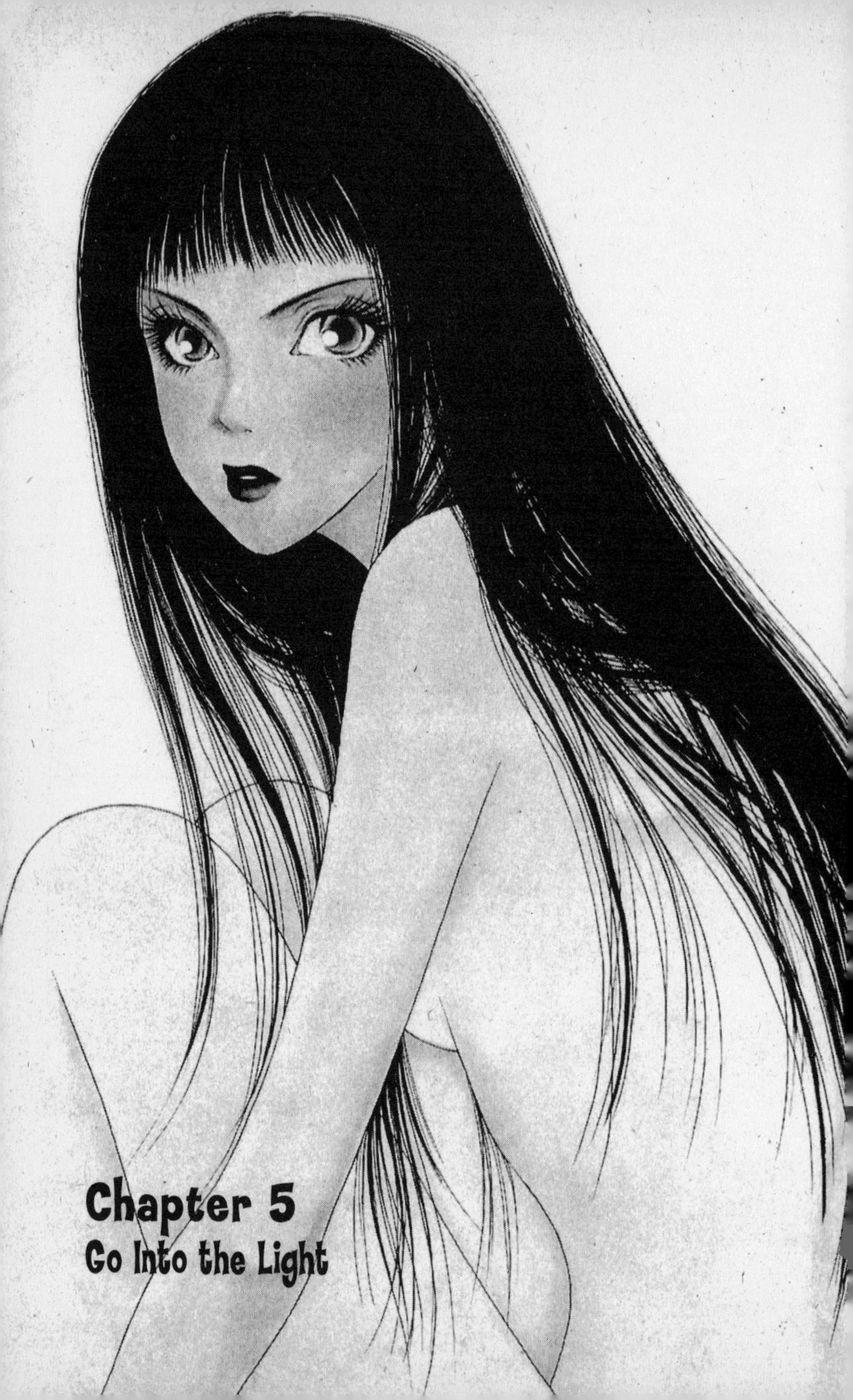

Chapter 5
Go Into the Light

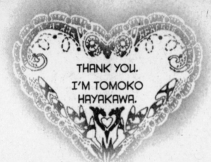

THANK YOU.
I'M TOMOKO HAYAKAWA.

THANK YOU FOR YOUR LETTERS.

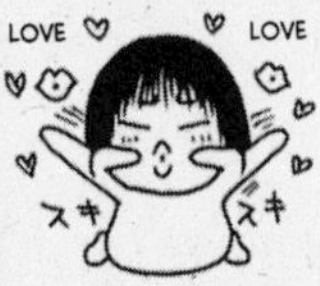
LOVE
LOVE
スキ
スキ

I LOVE YOU ALL!

THANK YOU FOR BUYING KODANSHA COMICS.

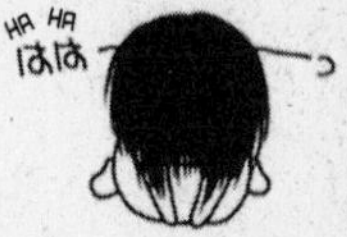
HA HA
はは

THANK YOU VERY MUCH.

THIS IS VOLUME ONE. SINCE IT'S CALLED VOLUME ONE, THAT MUST MEAN THERE'S ALSO A VOLUME TWO. AND IT'S ALL THANKS TO YOU GUYS. THANK YOU. I'D LIKE TO THANK MY EDITOR AND EVERYBODY IN THE EDITING DEPARTMENT.

AMAZING.
OBVIOUS, BUT STILL AMAZING.

THIS IS THE ONLY BONUS PAGE IN THIS VOLUME. I WANTED TO INCLUDE SOME PHOTOS OF MY FAVORITE BANDS . . . BUT THERE'S NOT ENOUGH ROOM. NOOOO! INSTEAD, THERE'S A LOT OF MANGA. ♥ OKAY?

"RISK"
THEY'RE IN THE KODANSHA COMIC "KIREI NA OTOKONOKO" [THE CUTE GUY]

"SHOCKING LEMON."
I'LL WRITE ABOUT THEM SOMETIME SOON.

"AFTER EFFECT."
I'LL INCLUDE THEM TOO. (I HAVEN'T MENTIONED THEM YET, BUT I WAS PLANNING ON INCLUDING THEM.)

"RISK" VOCALIST MARSHI-KUN.
I'LL BE WAITING FOR YOU BACKSTAGE.

"SHOCKING LEMON" VOCALIST, OGINO-KUN.
I GOT TO TALK TO HIM A WHILE BACK AND IT WAS REALLY FUN. I HOPE WE GET TO TALK AGAIN.

"AFTER EFFECT" BASSIST, BANSAKU-KUN.
I'LL GO SEE YOU IN CONCERT SOON. SORRY, I HAVEN'T GONE YET.

I CAN'T BELIEVE THAT'S HIS REAL NAME . . . HOW CUTE.

I WENT BACKSTAGE AT A "PIERROT" SHOW, BUT I DIDN'T GET TO TALK TO ANYONE. THANKS TO TOSHIBA EMI AND HAMANO-SAMA.

I CAN'T INCLUDE A "GROUPIE DIARY" THIS TIME CAUSE I HAVEN'T BEEN BACKSTAGE AT ALL LATELY.

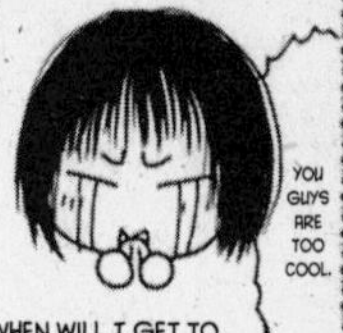
YOU GUYS ARE TOO COOL.

SIGH, WHEN WILL I GET TO MEET KIYOHARU, THE MAN OF MY DREAMS . . .

SPECIAL THANKS

TO THE FOLLOWING:

SHO HIROSE-SAMA ♥ . . . THANKS FOR EVERYTHING. I HOPE YOU'LL HELP ME AGAIN IF YOU HAVE TIME. GOOD LUCK WITH YOUR MANGA.

HANA-CHAN ♥ . . . YOU GENIUS, HANAOKA. GOOD LUCK WITH YOUR MANGA.

MAMA ♥ . . . YOU HELPED ME WITH THE COLORING WHEN I WENT HOME. YOU AND DADDY ALWAYS LOOK SO IN LOVE.

THANKS TO - CHITOSE SAKURA-SAMA, TATSU-CHAN, NOBUMASA-KUN, TOBECCHI, KUMI, YUU-CHAN, KYOUHEI-KUN, MAKORIN.

MASASHI-ONIICHAMA (MY COUSIN) . . . THANKS FOR THE INFO ON "MILITARY WEAR."

SHIGE-CHAN . . . THANKS FOR ALL THE CLIPPINGS ABOUT KIYOHARU. ♥♥♥ I LOVE YOU. ♥♥♥

KENTARO . . . THANKS FOR THE INFO ON THE "CHAINSAWS" ♥.

RYO-CHAN . . . THANKS FOR THE COPIES OF THE KIYOHARU STUFF. ♥

MACHIKO SAKURAI ♥, MIZUHO AIMOTO ♥, THANKS FOR EVERYTHING.

LET ME APOLOGIZE AHEAD OF TIME TO ANYONE I LEFT OUT . . .

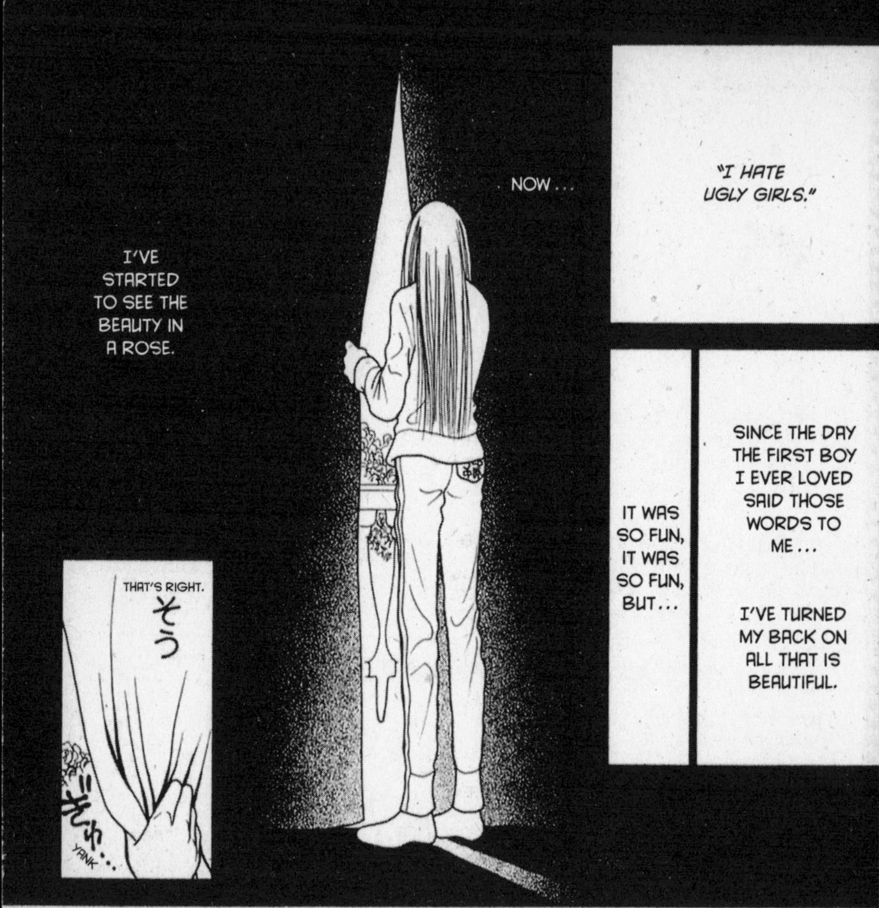
"I HATE UGLY GIRLS."
SINCE THE DAY THE FIRST BOY I EVER LOVED SAID THOSE WORDS TO ME...
I'VE TURNED MY BACK ON ALL THAT IS BEAUTIFUL.
IT WAS SO FUN, IT WAS SO FUN, BUT...
NOW...
I'VE STARTED TO SEE THE BEAUTY IN A ROSE.
THAT'S RIGHT.
そう
YANK...

RANMARU MORII

HEIGHT 5'10?
WEIGHT 122 LBS.

HE LOVES GIRLS. HE'S VERY EXPERIENCED. NICKNAME: THE HOUSE-WIFE'S DREAM BOY.

HE GETS A RASH WHEN HE SEES AN UGLY GIRL.

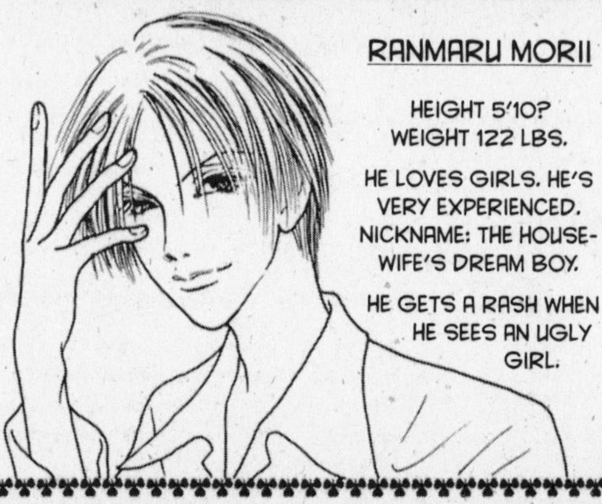

MY FIRST-EVER "LADIES' MAN" CHARACTER. AT FIRST I WANTED HIM TO BE A GUY WHO "KNOWS HOW TO HANDLE A LADY." BUT SOMEHOW HE BECAME LIKE "PRINCE MICHY"... MAYBE THAT HAPPENED BECAUSE I LIKE PRINCE MICHY SO MUCH. I GOT HIS NAME FROM THE HISTORICALLY FAMOUS, HANDSOME YOUNG MAN, RANMARU MORI. I HARDLY EVEN CHANGED IT. I SUCK AT THINKING UP NAMES...

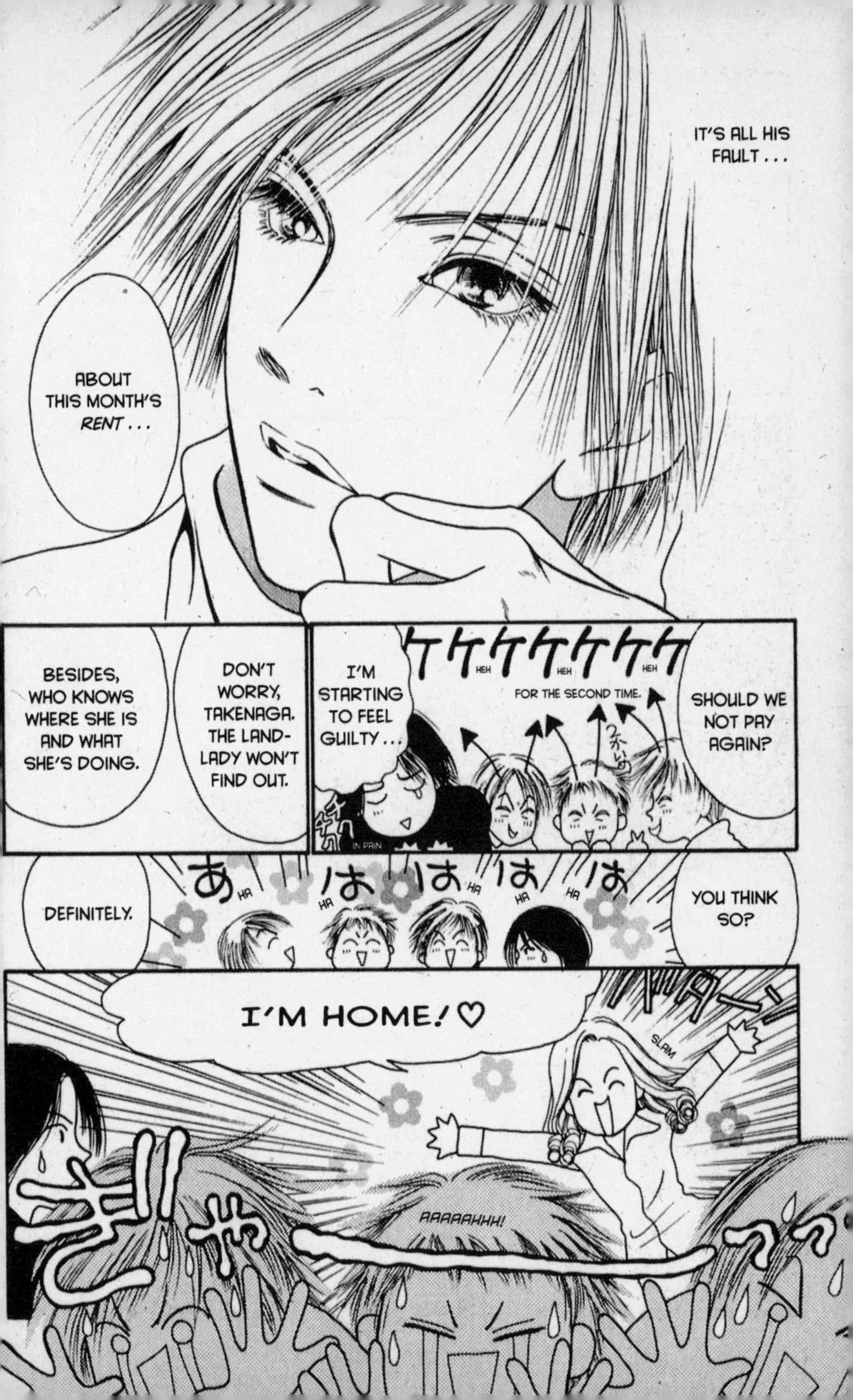
IT'S ALL HIS FAULT . . .
ABOUT THIS MONTH'S *RENT* . . .
SHOULD WE NOT PAY AGAIN?
HEH HEH HEH
FOR THE SECOND TIME.
I'M STARTING TO FEEL GUILTY . . .
IN PAIN
DON'T WORRY, TAKENAGA. THE LAND-LADY WON'T FIND OUT.
BESIDES, WHO KNOWS WHERE SHE IS AND WHAT SHE'S DOING.
YOU THINK SO?
HA HA HA HA HA
DEFINITELY.
SLAM
I'M HOME! ♡
AAAAAHHH!

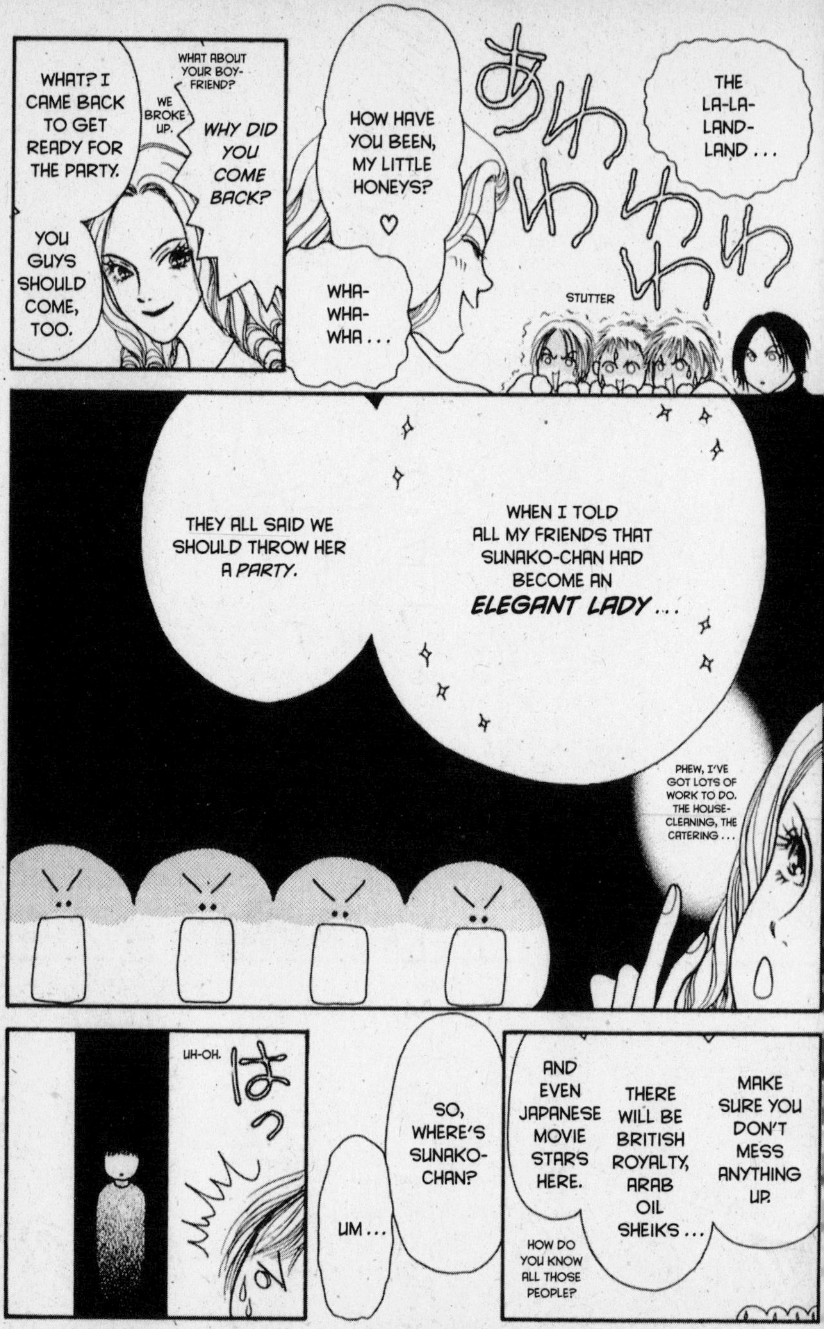
THE LA-LA-LAND-LAND . . .
あわわわわわ
STUTTER
HOW HAVE YOU BEEN, MY LITTLE HONEYS? ♡
WHA-WHA-WHA . . .
WHY DID YOU COME BACK?
WHAT ABOUT YOUR BOY-FRIEND?
WE BROKE UP.
WHAT? I CAME BACK TO GET READY FOR THE PARTY.
YOU GUYS SHOULD COME, TOO.
WHEN I TOLD ALL MY FRIENDS THAT SUNAKO-CHAN HAD BECOME AN ELEGANT LADY . . .
THEY ALL SAID WE SHOULD THROW HER A PARTY.
PHEW, I'VE GOT LOTS OF WORK TO DO. THE HOUSE-CLEANING, THE CATERING . . .
MAKE SURE YOU DON'T MESS ANYTHING UP.
THERE WILL BE BRITISH ROYALTY, ARAB OIL SHEIKS . . .
AND EVEN JAPANESE MOVIE STARS HERE.
HOW DO YOU KNOW ALL THOSE PEOPLE?
SO, WHERE'S SUNAKO-CHAN?
UM . . .
UH-OH.
はっ

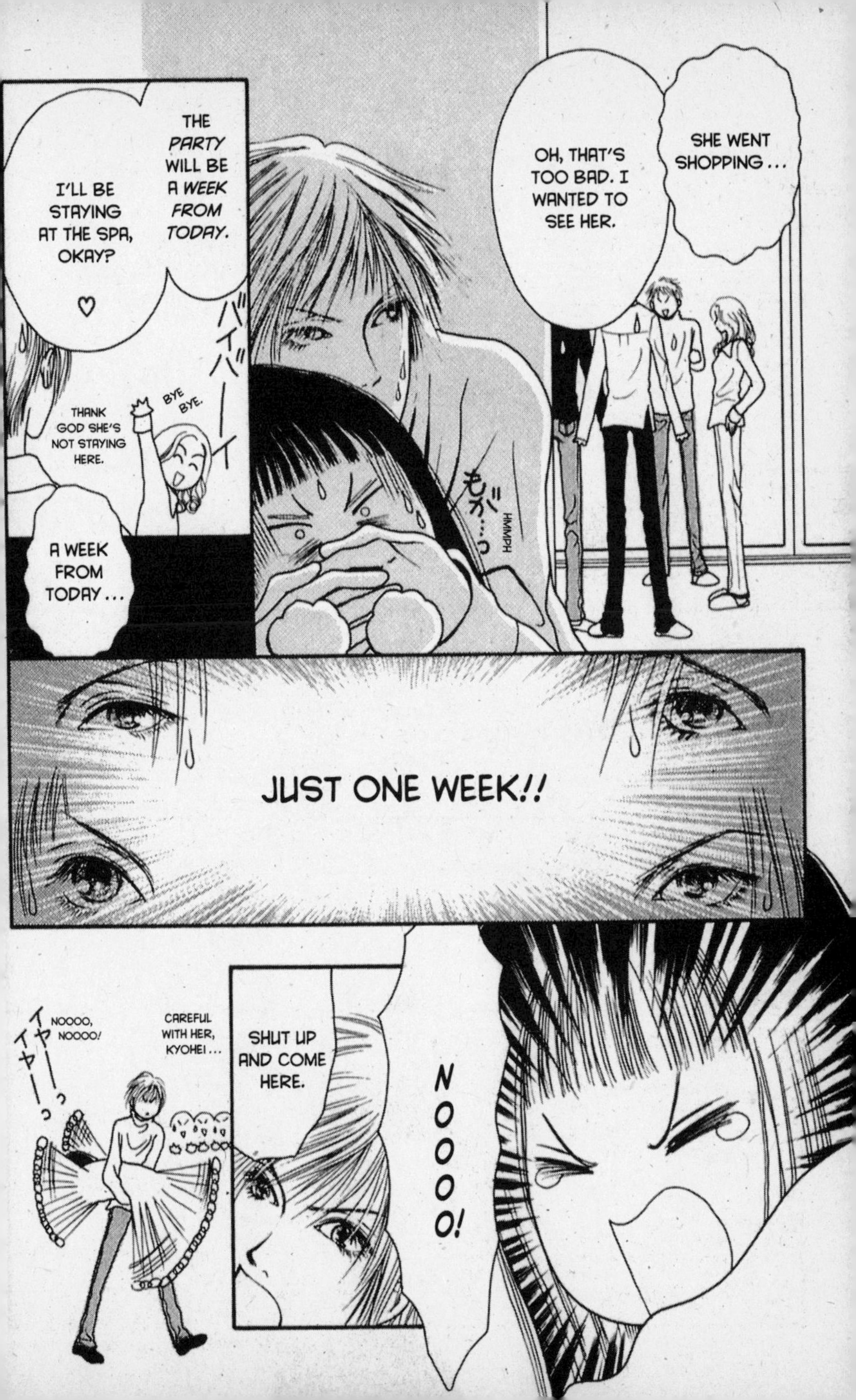
SHE WENT SHOPPING . . .
OH, THAT'S TOO BAD. I WANTED TO SEE HER.
もが…っ
HMMPH
THE *PARTY* WILL BE A *WEEK FROM TODAY*.
I'LL BE STAYING AT THE SPA, OKAY? ♡
バイバーイ
BYE BYE.
THANK GOD SHE'S NOT STAYING HERE.
A WEEK FROM TODAY . . .
JUST ONE WEEK!!
NOOOO!
SHUT UP AND COME HERE.
CAREFUL WITH HER, KYOHEI . . .
イヤーイヤーっ
NOOOO, NOOOO!

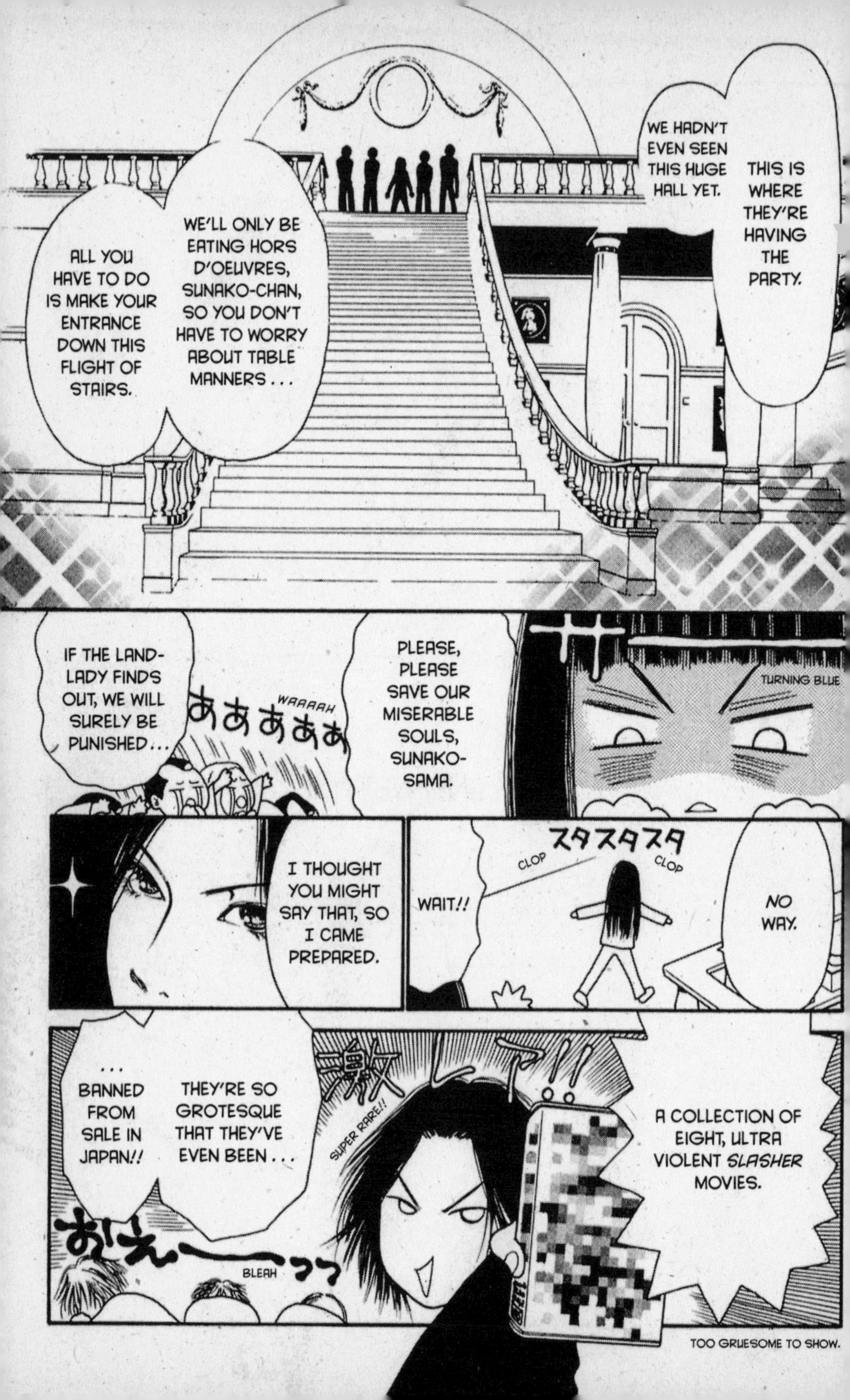
THIS IS WHERE THEY'RE HAVING THE PARTY.
WE HADN'T EVEN SEEN THIS HUGE HALL YET.
WE'LL ONLY BE EATING HORS D'OEUVRES, SUNAKO-CHAN, SO YOU DON'T HAVE TO WORRY ABOUT TABLE MANNERS . . .
ALL YOU HAVE TO DO IS MAKE YOUR ENTRANCE DOWN THIS FLIGHT OF STAIRS.
TURNING BLUE
PLEASE, PLEASE SAVE OUR MISERABLE SOULS, SUNAKO-SAMA.
ああああ
WAAAAAH
IF THE LAND-LADY FINDS OUT, WE WILL SURELY BE PUNISHED . . .
NO WAY.
スタスタスタ
CLOP CLOP
WAIT!!
I THOUGHT YOU MIGHT SAY THAT, SO I CAME PREPARED.
A COLLECTION OF EIGHT, ULTRA VIOLENT *SLASHER* MOVIES.
激レア!!
SUPER RARE!!
THEY'RE SO GROTESQUE THAT THEY'VE EVEN BEEN . . .
. . . BANNED FROM SALE IN JAPAN!!
おえーっ
BLEAH
TOO GRUESOME TO SHOW.

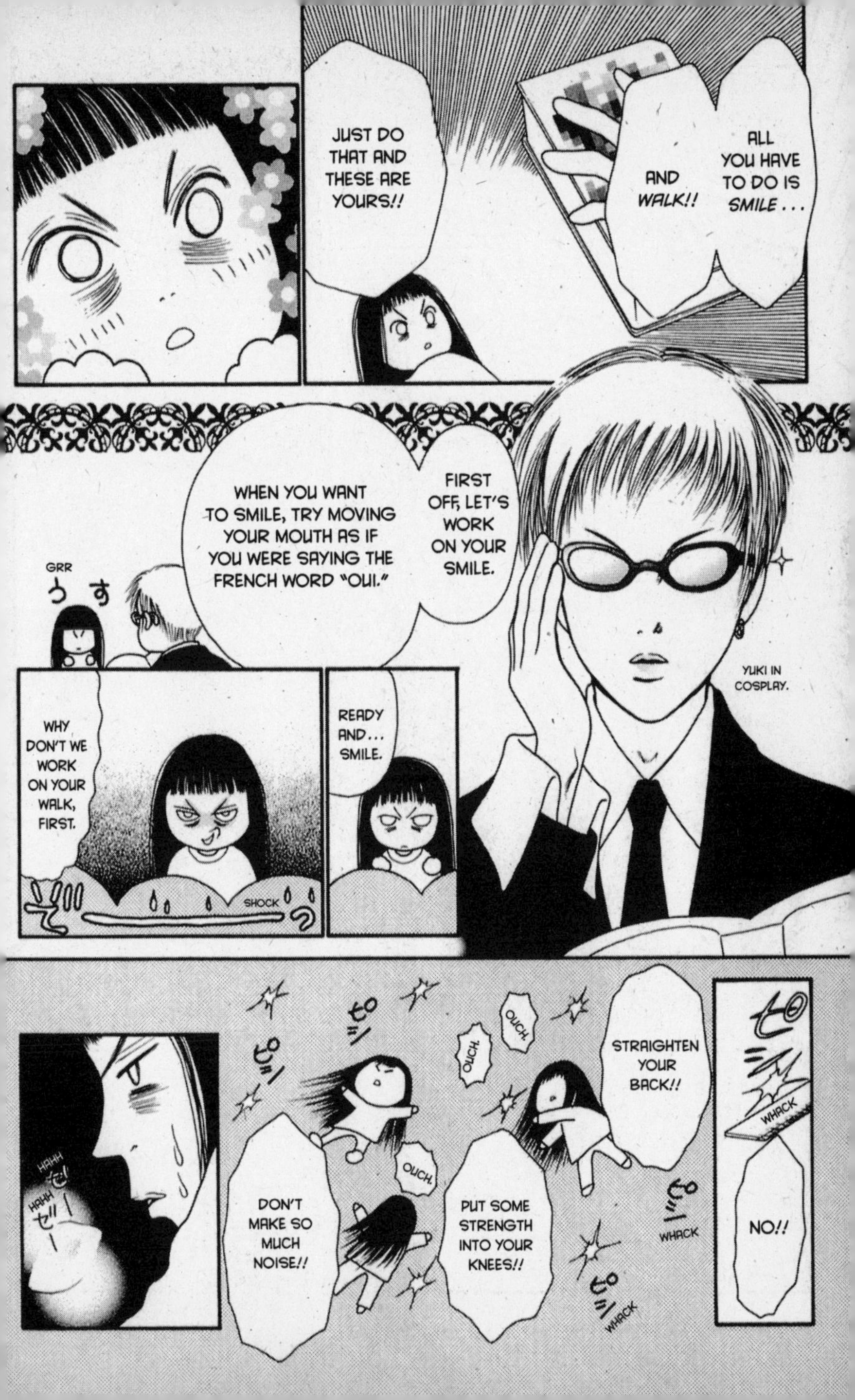
ALL YOU HAVE TO DO IS *SMILE* . . .
AND *WALK!!*
JUST DO THAT AND THESE ARE YOURS!!
FIRST OFF, LET'S WORK ON YOUR SMILE.
WHEN YOU WANT TO SMILE, TRY MOVING YOUR MOUTH AS IF YOU WERE SAYING THE FRENCH WORD "OUI."
GRR
うす
YUKI IN COSPLAY.
READY AND . . . SMILE.
WHY DON'T WE WORK ON YOUR WALK, FIRST.
SHOCK
WHACK
NO!!
STRAIGHTEN YOUR BACK!!
OUCH.
OUCH.
WHACK
PUT SOME STRENGTH INTO YOUR KNEES!!
OUCH.
WHACK
DON'T MAKE SO MUCH NOISE!!
HAHH
HAHH

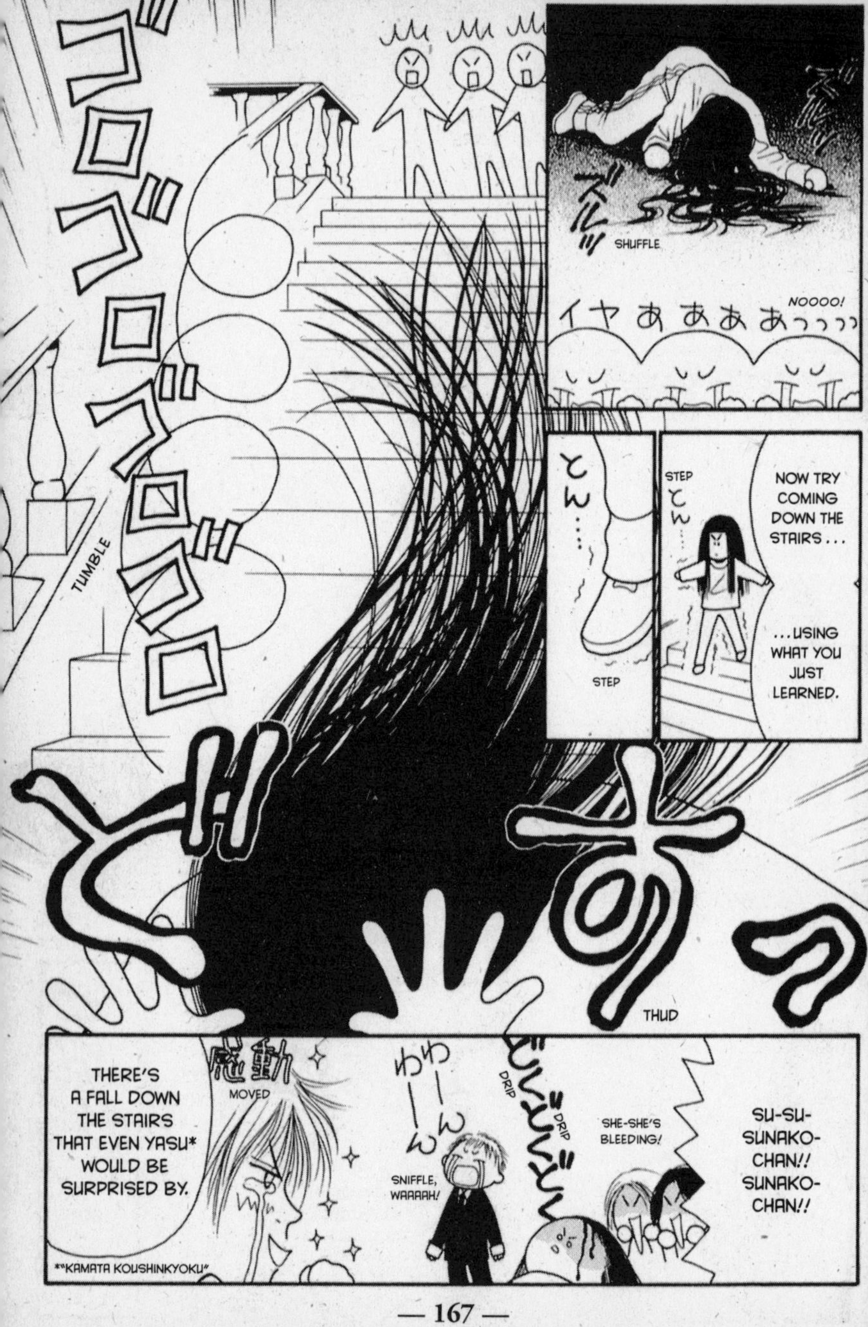
ズル
SHUFFLE
イヤあああああっっっ
NOOOO!
NOW TRY COMING DOWN THE STAIRS . . .
. . . USING WHAT YOU JUST LEARNED.
とん
STEP
とん . . .
STEP
ゴロゴロゴロゴロ
TUMBLE
どすっ
THUD
SU-SU-SUNAKO-CHAN!! SUNAKO-CHAN!!
SHE-SHE'S BLEEDING!
どくどく
DRIP
DRIP
わーん
SNIFFLE, WAAAAH!
感動
MOVED
THERE'S A FALL DOWN THE STAIRS THAT EVEN YASU* WOULD BE SURPRISED BY.
*"KAMATA KOUSHINKYOKU"

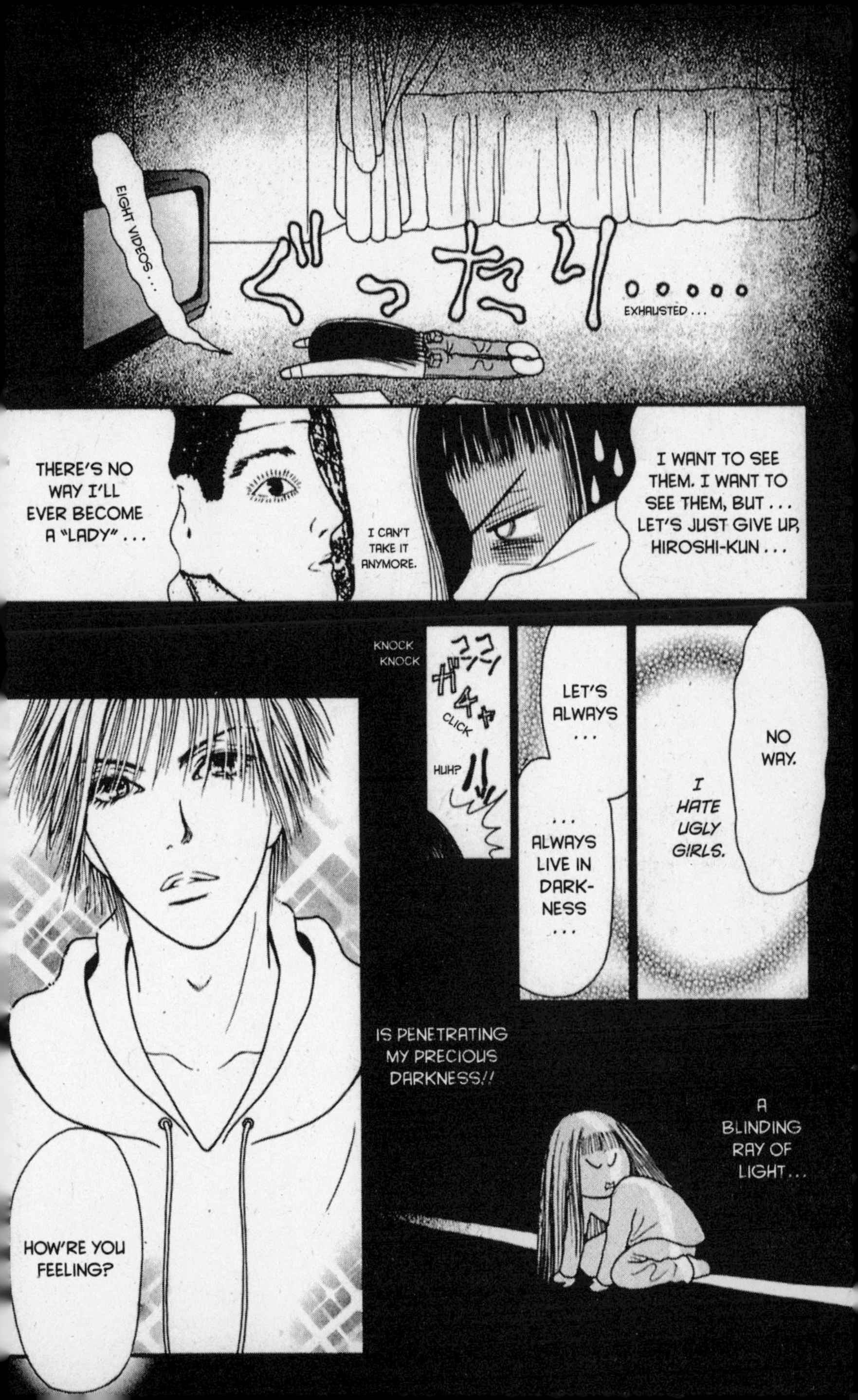
ぐったり
EXHAUSTED . . .
EIGHT VIDEOS . . .
I WANT TO SEE THEM. I WANT TO SEE THEM, BUT . . . LET'S JUST GIVE UP, HIROSHI-KUN . . .
I CAN'T TAKE IT ANYMORE.
THERE'S NO WAY I'LL EVER BECOME A "LADY" . . .
NO WAY.
I HATE UGLY GIRLS.
LET'S ALWAYS . . .
. . . ALWAYS LIVE IN DARKNESS . . .
KNOCK KNOCK
CLICK
HUH?
A BLINDING RAY OF LIGHT . . .
IS PENETRATING MY PRECIOUS DARKNESS!!
HOW'RE YOU FEELING?

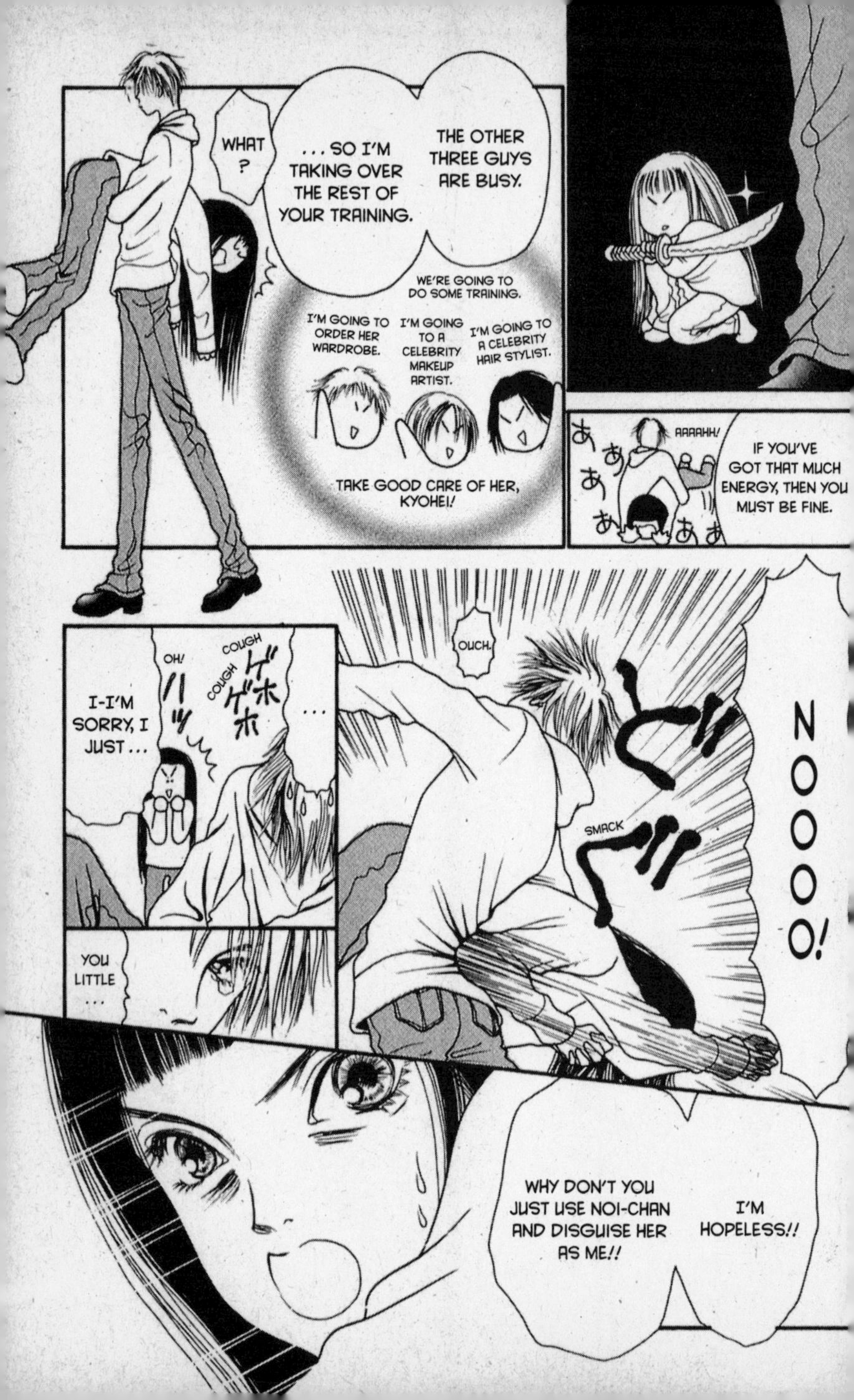
AAAAHH!
IF YOU'VE GOT THAT MUCH ENERGY, THEN YOU MUST BE FINE.
THE OTHER THREE GUYS ARE BUSY.
. . . SO I'M TAKING OVER THE REST OF YOUR TRAINING.
WHAT?
WE'RE GOING TO DO SOME TRAINING.
I'M GOING TO A CELEBRITY HAIR STYLIST.
I'M GOING TO A CELEBRITY MAKEUP ARTIST.
I'M GOING TO ORDER HER WARDROBE.
TAKE GOOD CARE OF HER, KYOHEI!
NOOOO!
SMACK
OUCH.
. . .
COUGH
COUGH
ゲホゲホ
OH!
ハッ
I-I'M SORRY, I JUST . . .
YOU LITTLE . . .
I'M HOPELESS!!
WHY DON'T YOU JUST USE NOI-CHAN AND DISGUISE HER AS ME!!

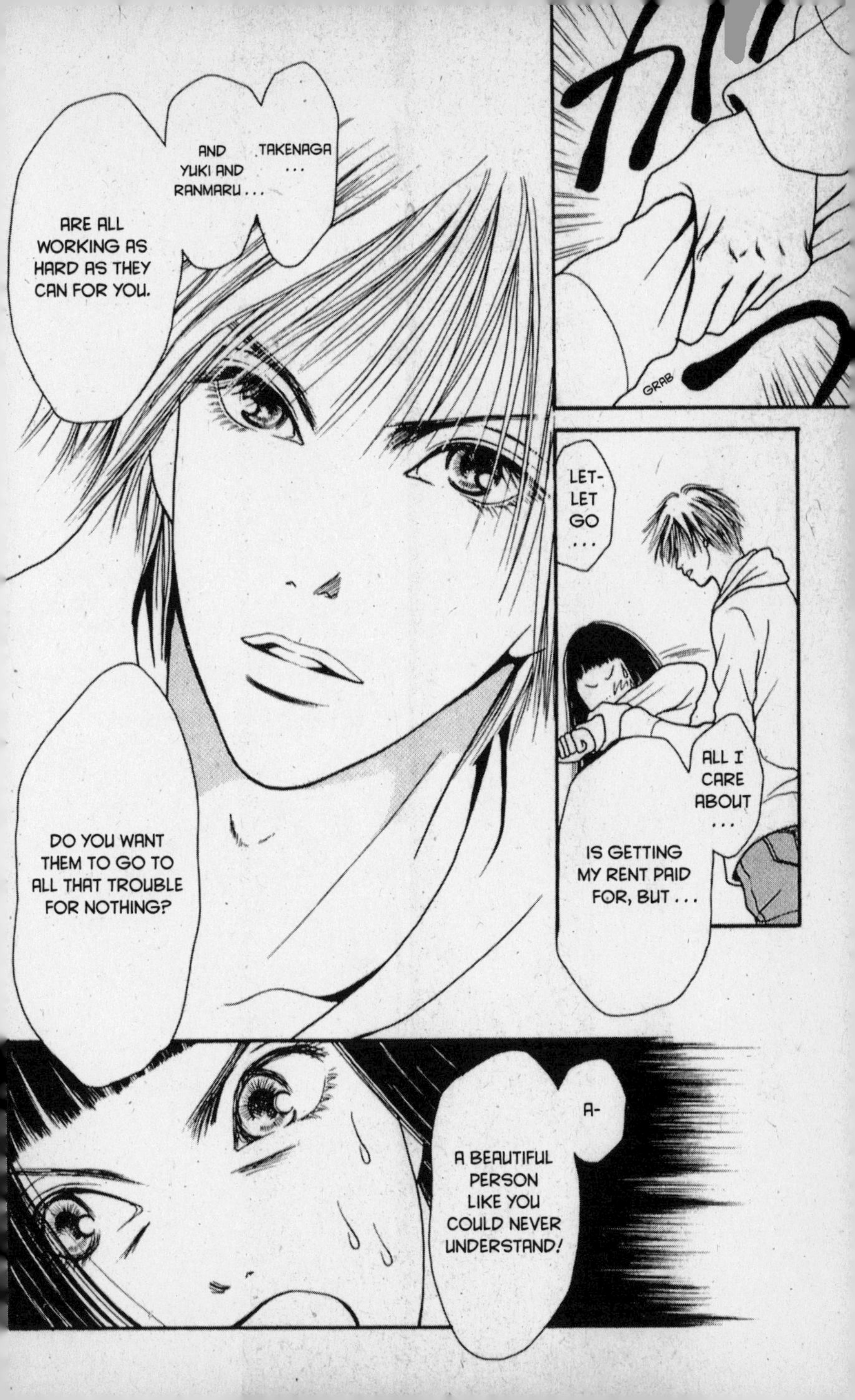
GRAB
LET- LET GO . . .
ALL I CARE ABOUT . . .
IS GETTING MY RENT PAID FOR, BUT . . .
TAKENAGA . . .
AND YUKI AND RANMARU . . .
ARE ALL WORKING AS HARD AS THEY CAN FOR YOU.
DO YOU WANT THEM TO GO TO ALL THAT TROUBLE FOR NOTHING?
A-
A BEAUTIFUL PERSON LIKE YOU COULD NEVER UNDERSTAND!

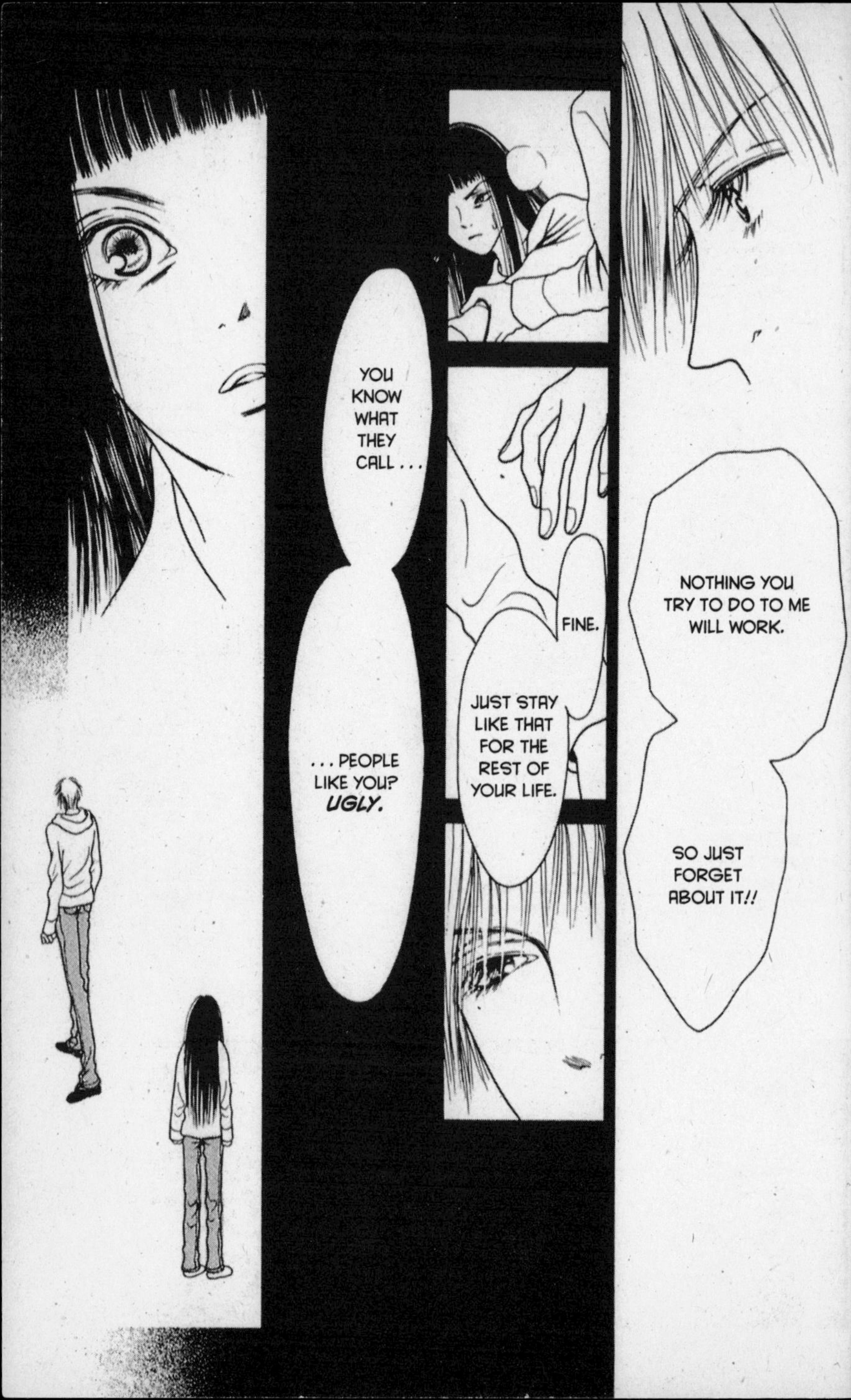
NOTHING YOU TRY TO DO TO ME WILL WORK.
SO JUST FORGET ABOUT IT!!
FINE.
JUST STAY LIKE THAT FOR THE REST OF YOUR LIFE.
YOU KNOW WHAT THEY CALL . . .
. . . PEOPLE LIKE YOU? *UGLY.*

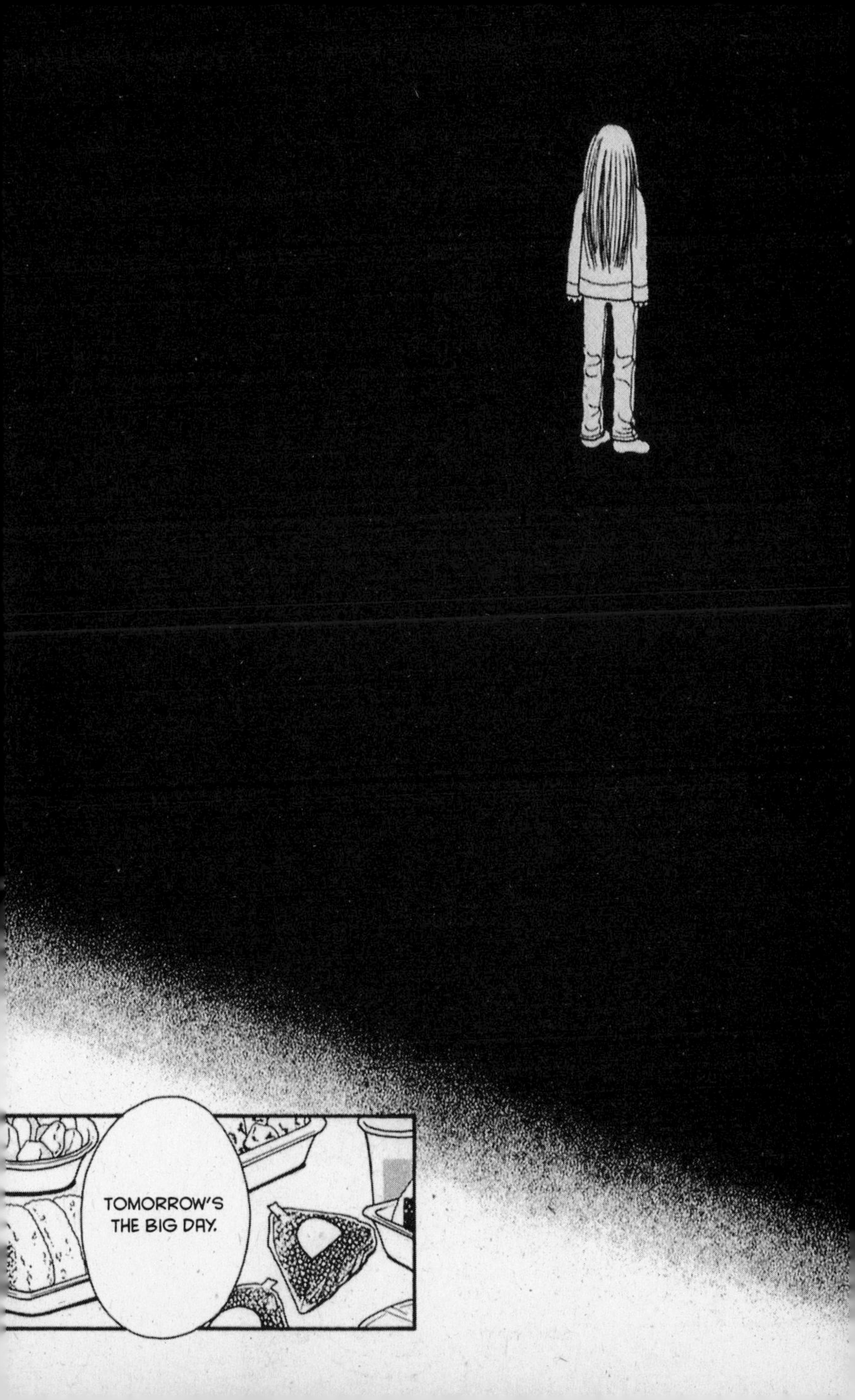
TOMORROW'S THE BIG DAY.

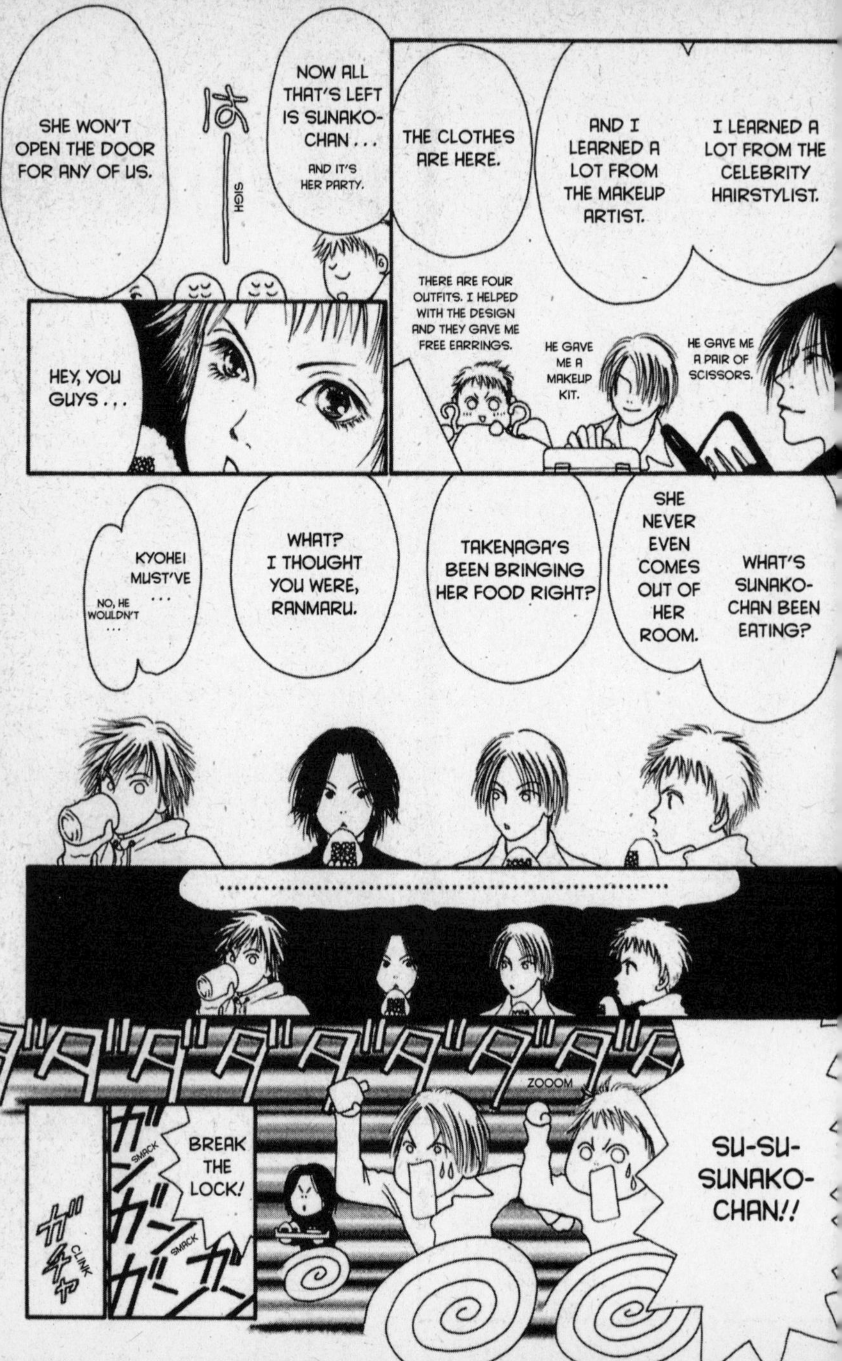
I LEARNED A LOT FROM THE CELEBRITY HAIRSTYLIST.
AND I LEARNED A LOT FROM THE MAKEUP ARTIST.
THE CLOTHES ARE HERE.
HE GAVE ME A PAIR OF SCISSORS.
HE GAVE ME A MAKEUP KIT.
THERE ARE FOUR OUTFITS. I HELPED WITH THE DESIGN AND THEY GAVE ME FREE EARRINGS.
NOW ALL THAT'S LEFT IS SUNAKO-CHAN . . .
AND IT'S HER PARTY.
SIGH
SHE WON'T OPEN THE DOOR FOR ANY OF US.
HEY, YOU GUYS . . .
WHAT'S SUNAKO-CHAN BEEN EATING?
SHE NEVER EVEN COMES OUT OF HER ROOM.
TAKENAGA'S BEEN BRINGING HER FOOD RIGHT?
WHAT? I THOUGHT YOU WERE, RANMARU.
KYOHEI MUST'VE . . .
NO, HE WOULDN'T . . .
....
ZOOOM
SU-SU-SUNAKO-CHAN!!
BREAK THE LOCK!
SMACK
SMACK
CLINK

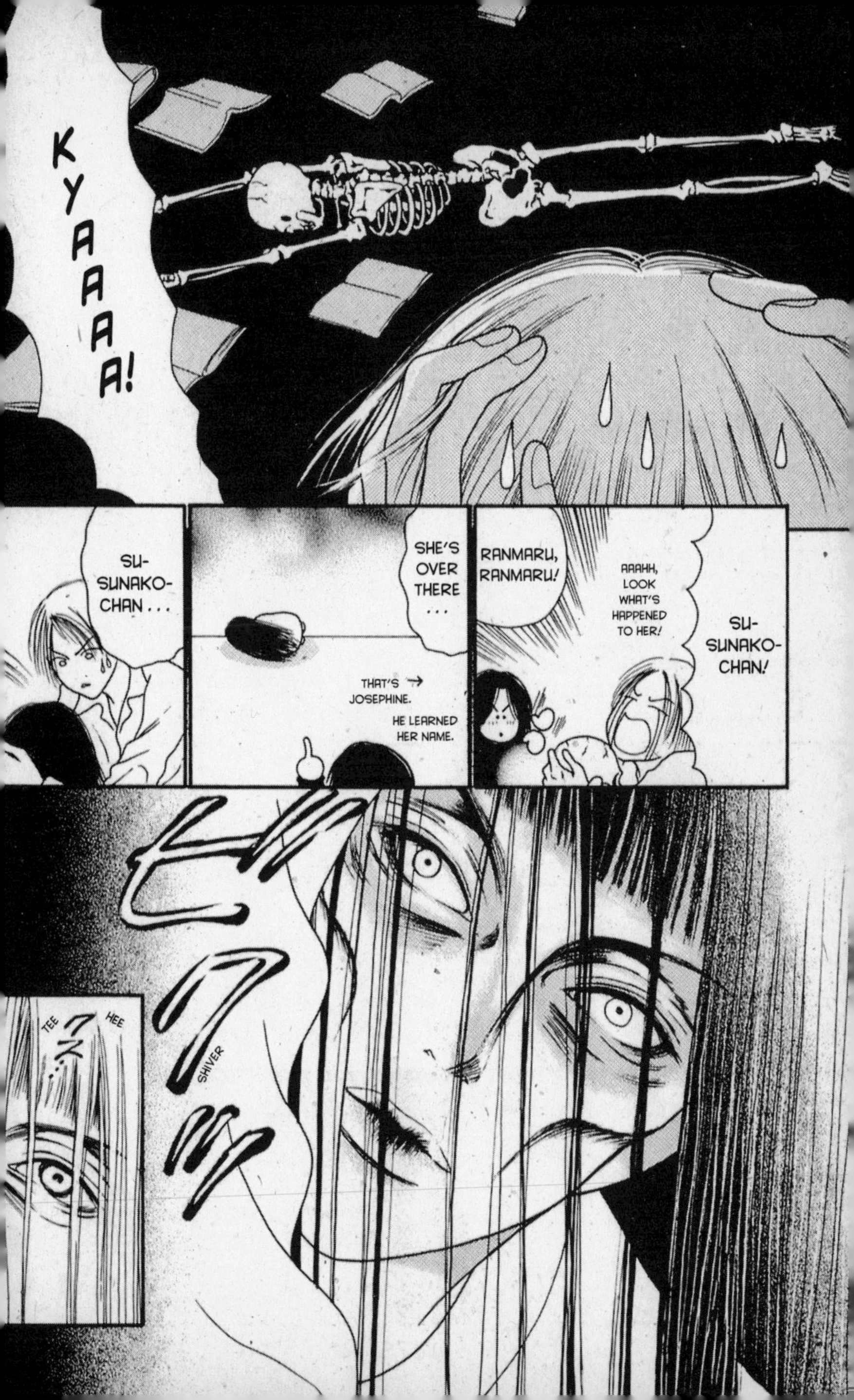
KYAAAA!
SU-SUNAKO-CHAN!
AAAHH, LOOK WHAT'S HAPPENED TO HER!
RANMARU, RANMARU!
SHE'S OVER THERE . . .
THAT'S → JOSEPHINE.
HE LEARNED HER NAME.
SU-SUNAKO-CHAN . . .
SHIVER
TEE HEE

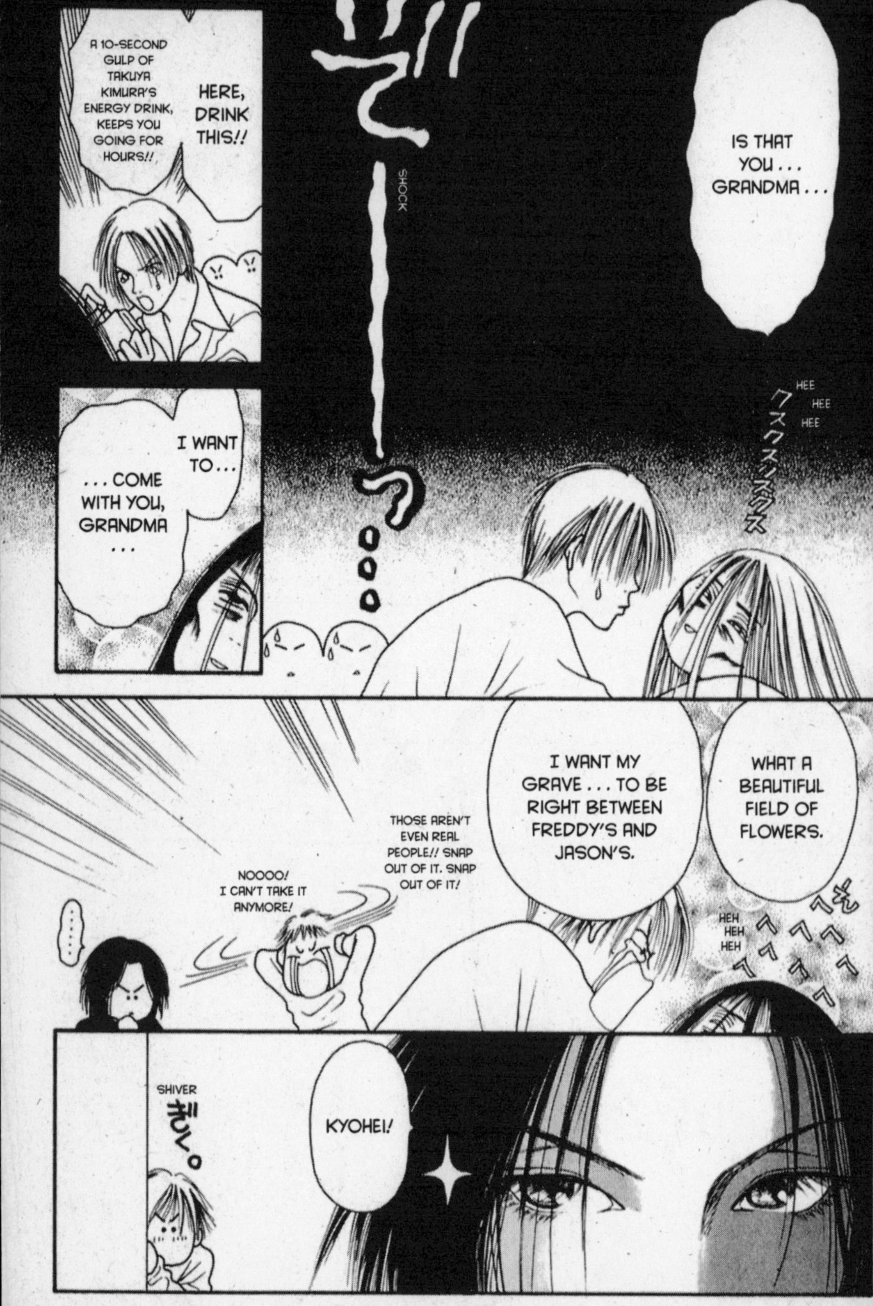
IS THAT YOU . . . GRANDMA . . .
SHOCK
HEE HEE HEE
HERE, DRINK THIS!!
A 10-SECOND GULP OF TAKUYA KIMURA'S ENERGY DRINK, KEEPS YOU GOING FOR HOURS!!
I WANT TO . . .
. . . COME WITH YOU, GRANDMA . . .
WHAT A BEAUTIFUL FIELD OF FLOWERS.
I WANT MY GRAVE . . . TO BE RIGHT BETWEEN FREDDY'S AND JASON'S.
HEH HEH HEH
THOSE AREN'T EVEN REAL PEOPLE!! SNAP OUT OF IT. SNAP OUT OF IT!
NOOOO! I CAN'T TAKE IT ANYMORE!
. . . . . .
KYOHEI!
SHIVER

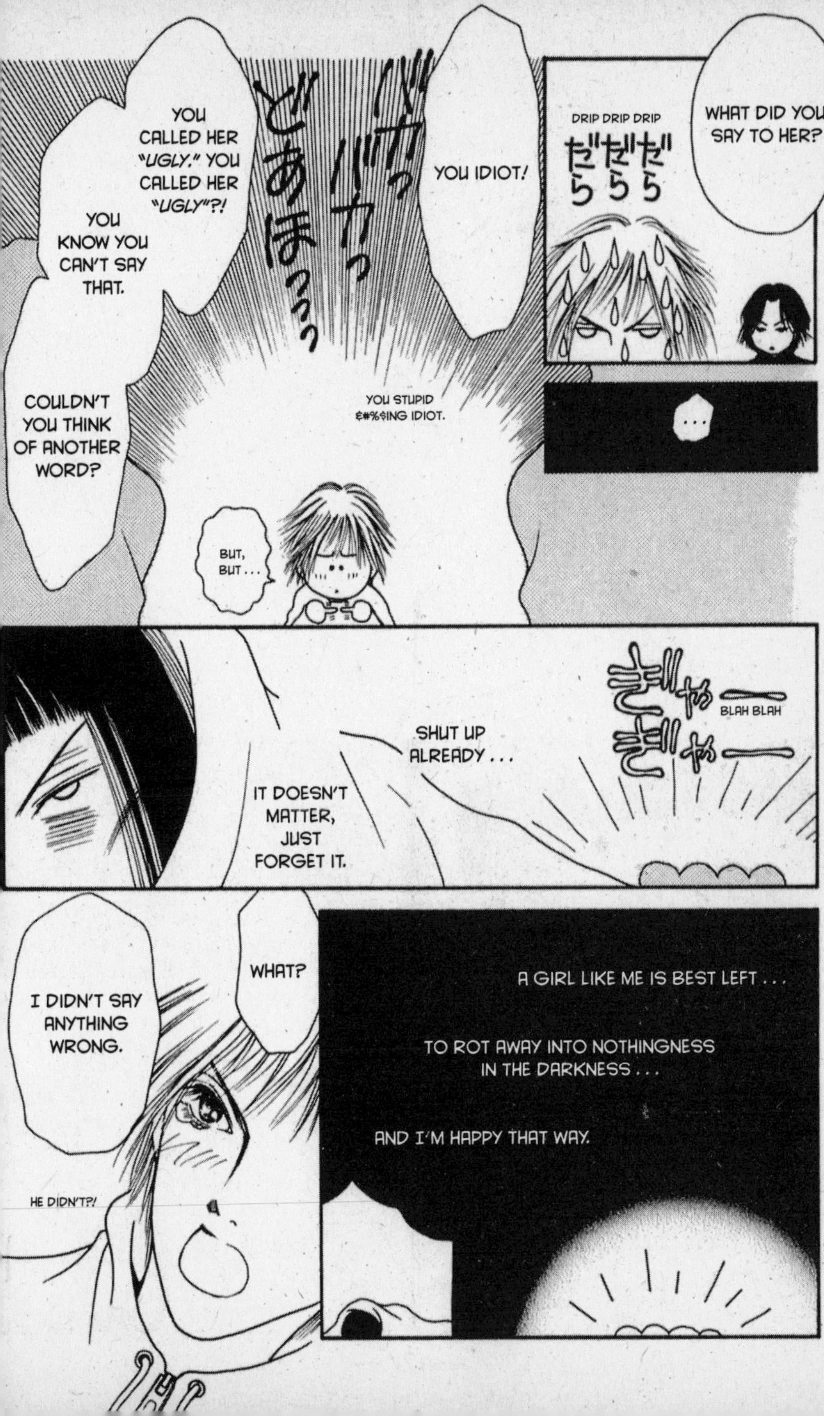
WHAT DID YOU SAY TO HER?
だらだらだら
DRIP DRIP DRIP
. . .
YOU IDIOT!
バカッバカッどあほっっっ
YOU STUPID $#%$ING IDIOT.
YOU CALLED HER "UGLY." YOU CALLED HER "UGLY"?!
YOU KNOW YOU CAN'T SAY THAT.
COULDN'T YOU THINK OF ANOTHER WORD?
BUT, BUT . . .
ぎゃーぎゃー
BLAH BLAH
SHUT UP ALREADY . . .
IT DOESN'T MATTER, JUST FORGET IT.
A GIRL LIKE ME IS BEST LEFT . . .
TO ROT AWAY INTO NOTHINGNESS IN THE DARKNESS . . .
AND I'M HAPPY THAT WAY.
WHAT?
I DIDN'T SAY ANYTHING WRONG.
HE DIDN'T?!

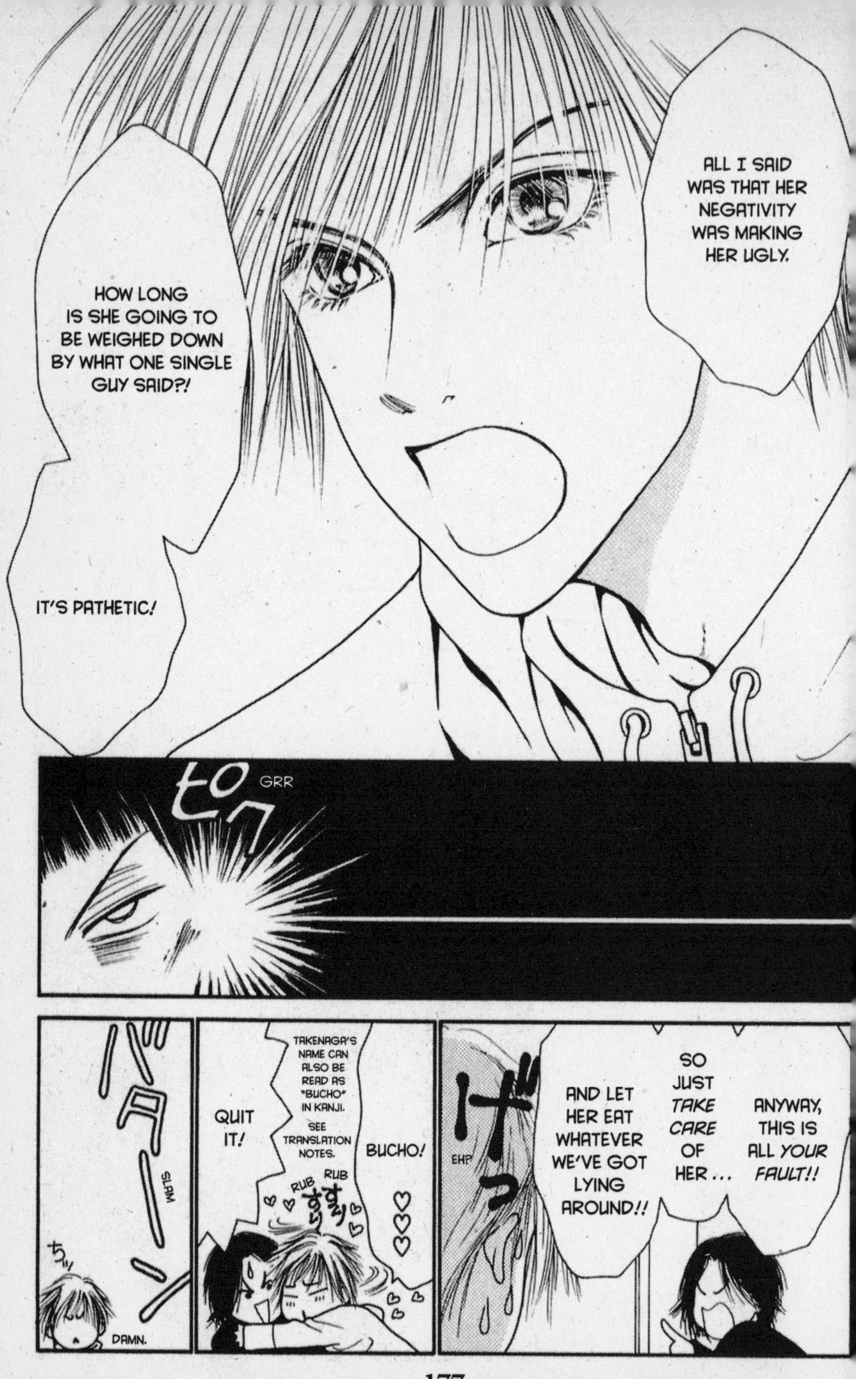
ALL I SAID WAS THAT HER NEGATIVITY WAS MAKING HER UGLY.
HOW LONG IS SHE GOING TO BE WEIGHED DOWN BY WHAT ONE SINGLE GUY SAID?!
IT'S PATHETIC!
GRR
ANYWAY, THIS IS ALL *YOUR FAULT!!*
SO JUST *TAKE CARE* OF HER...
AND LET HER EAT WHATEVER WE'VE GOT LYING AROUND!!
EH?
BUCHO!
TAKENAGA'S NAME CAN ALSO BE READ AS "BUCHO" IN KANJI.
SEE TRANSLATION NOTES.
QUIT IT!
RUB RUB
SLAM
DAMN.

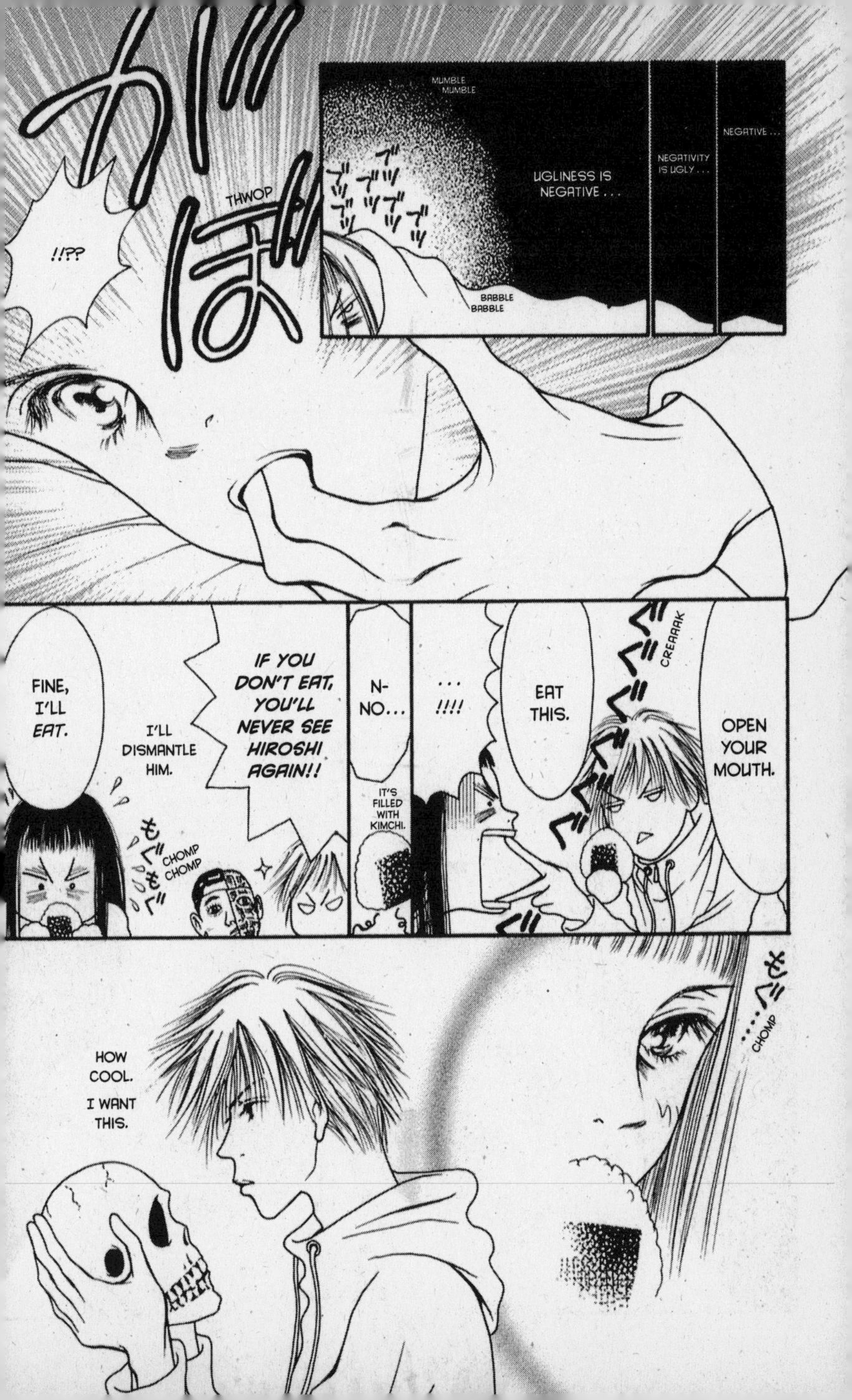
NEGATIVE . . .
NEGATIVITY IS UGLY . . .
UGLINESS IS NEGATIVE . . .
MUMBLE MUMBLE
BABBLE BABBLE
THWOP
!!??
OPEN YOUR MOUTH.
CREAAAK
EAT THIS.
. . . !!!!
N-NO . . .
IT'S FILLED WITH KIMCHI.
IF YOU DON'T EAT, YOU'LL NEVER SEE HIROSHI AGAIN!!
I'LL DISMANTLE HIM.
CHOMP CHOMP
FINE, I'LL EAT.
. . . . CHOMP
HOW COOL.
I WANT THIS.

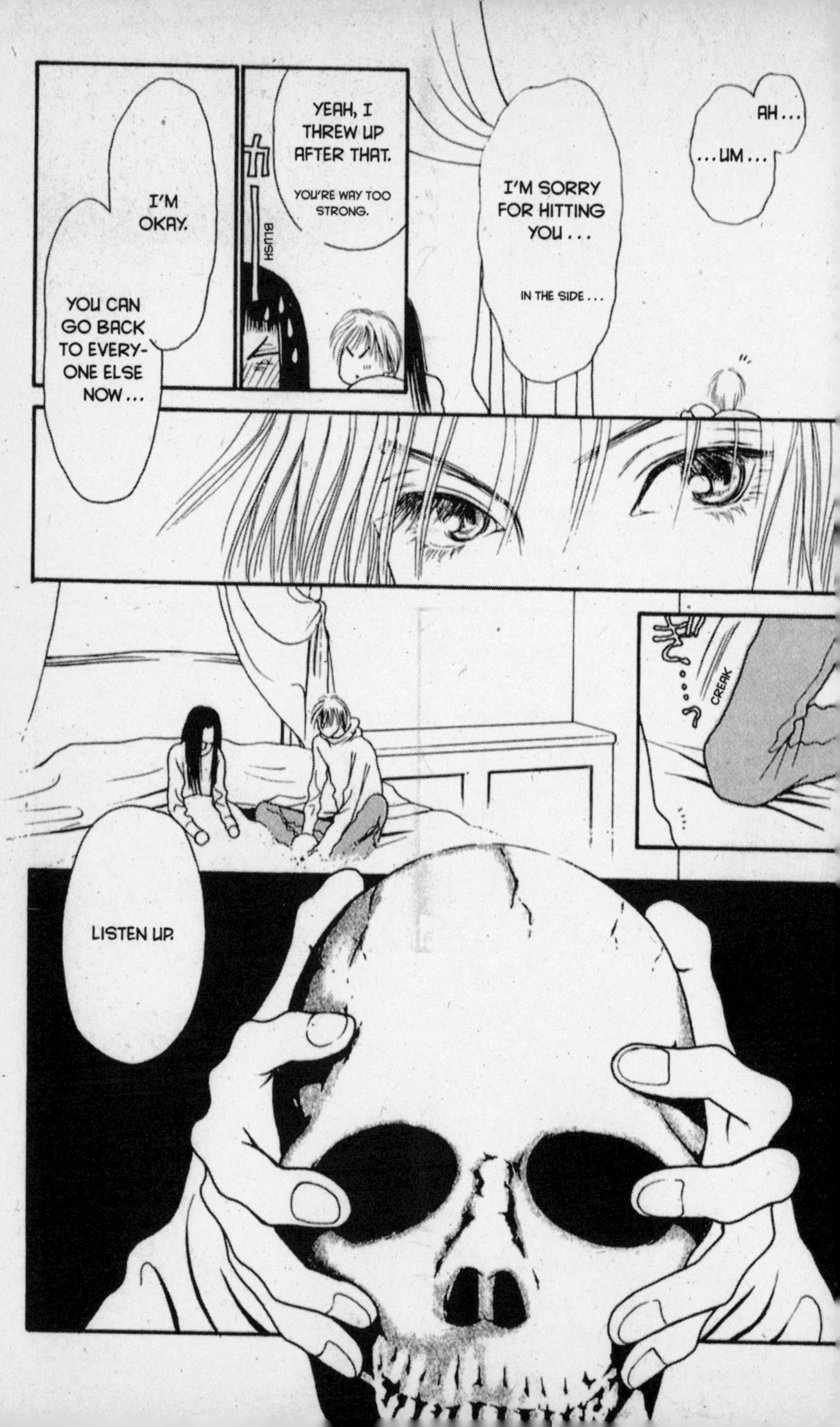
AH...
...UM...
I'M SORRY FOR HITTING YOU...
IN THE SIDE...
YEAH, I THREW UP AFTER THAT.
YOU'RE WAY TOO STRONG.
BLUSH
I'M OKAY.
YOU CAN GO BACK TO EVERY-ONE ELSE NOW...
CREAK
LISTEN UP.

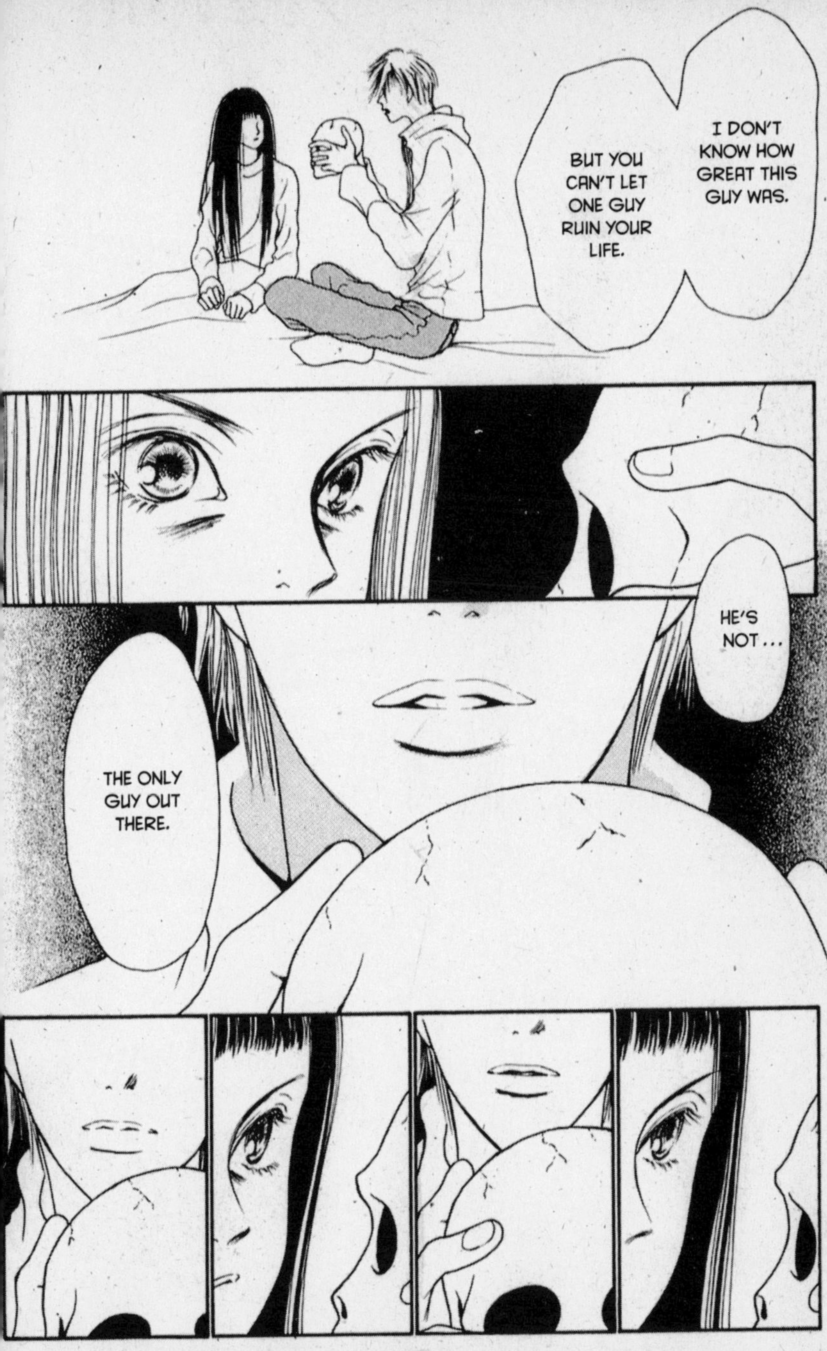
I DON'T KNOW HOW GREAT THIS GUY WAS.
BUT YOU CAN'T LET ONE GUY RUIN YOUR LIFE.
HE'S NOT...
THE ONLY GUY OUT THERE.

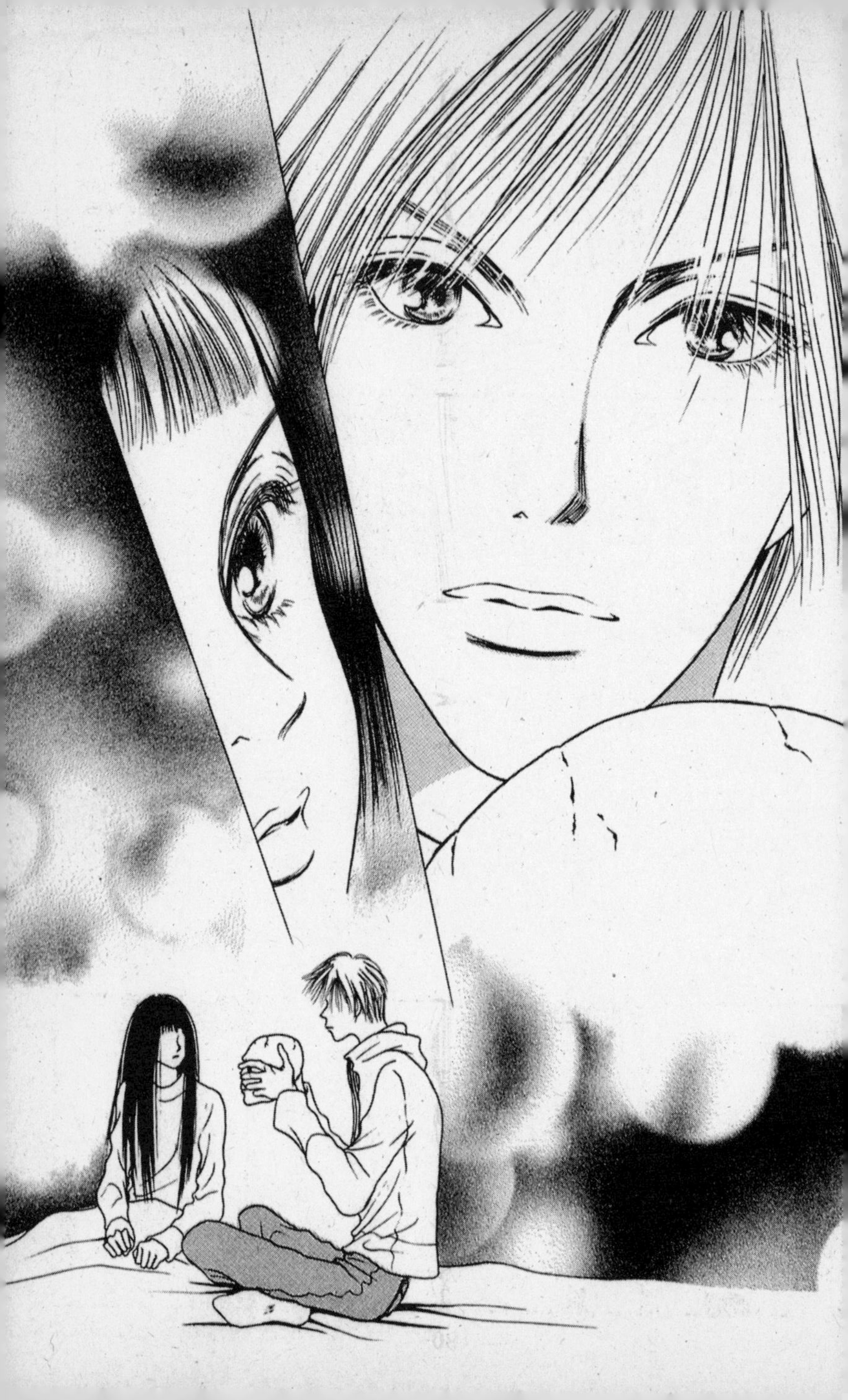

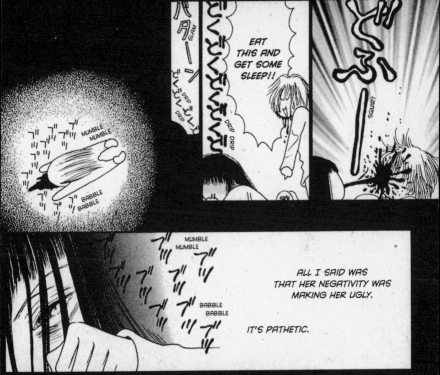

SQUIRT
EAT THIS AND GET SOME SLEEP!!
DRIP DRIP
SLAM
DRIP DRIP
MUMBLE MUMBLE
BABBLE BABBLE
ALL I SAID WAS THAT HER NEGATIVITY WAS MAKING HER UGLY.
IT'S PATHETIC.
MUMBLE MUMBLE
BABBLE BABBLE
HE'S NOT THE ONLY GUY OUT THERE.
OUT THERE . . .
OUT THERE . . .
FLASH

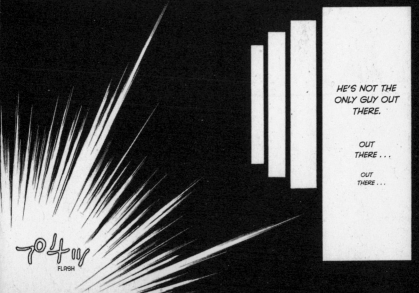

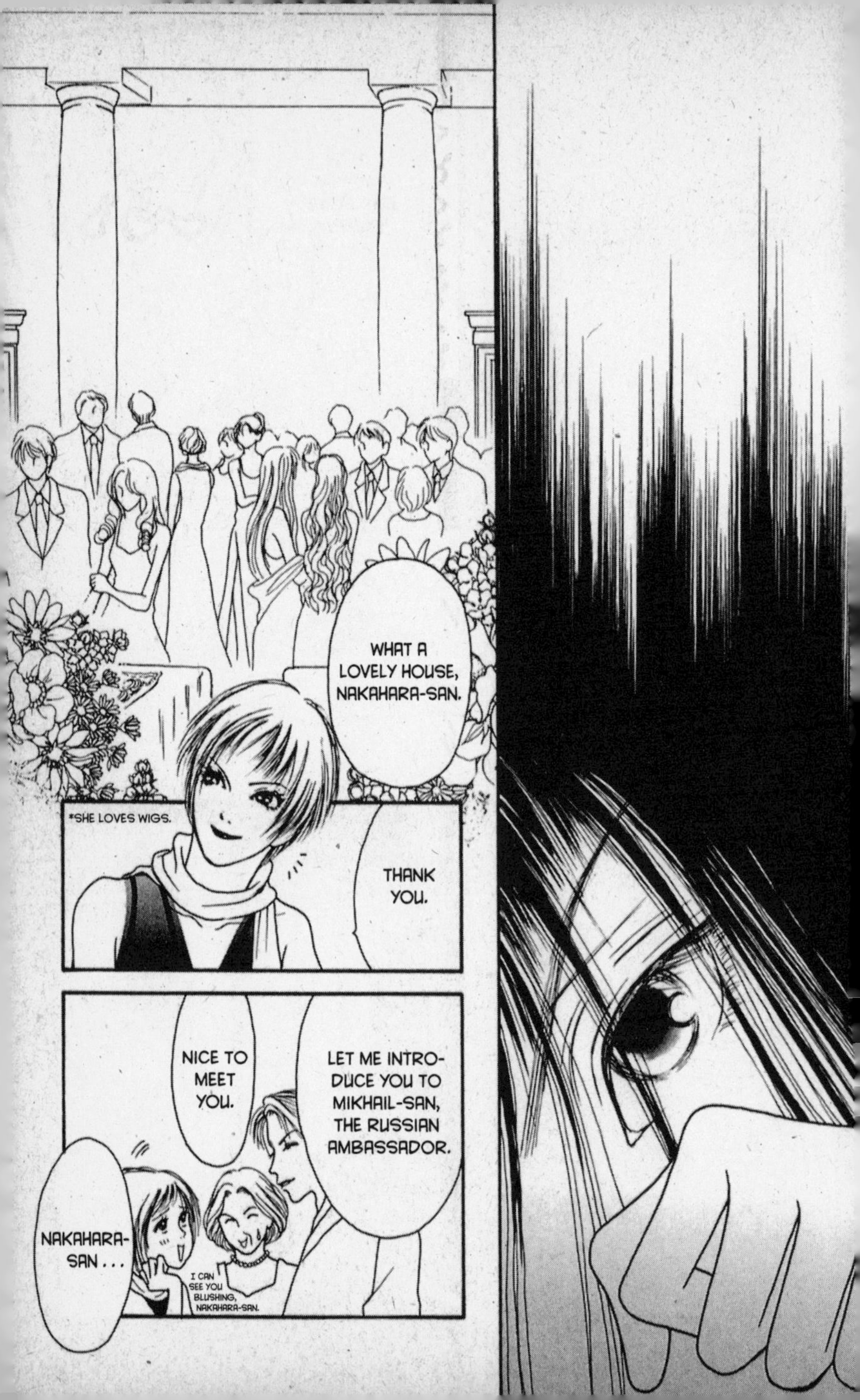
WHAT A LOVELY HOUSE, NAKAHARA-SAN.
*SHE LOVES WIGS.
THANK YOU.
LET ME INTRO-DUCE YOU TO MIKHAIL-SAN, THE RUSSIAN AMBASSADOR.
NICE TO MEET YOU.
NAKAHARA-SAN . . .
I CAN SEE YOU BLUSHING, NAKAHARA-SAN.

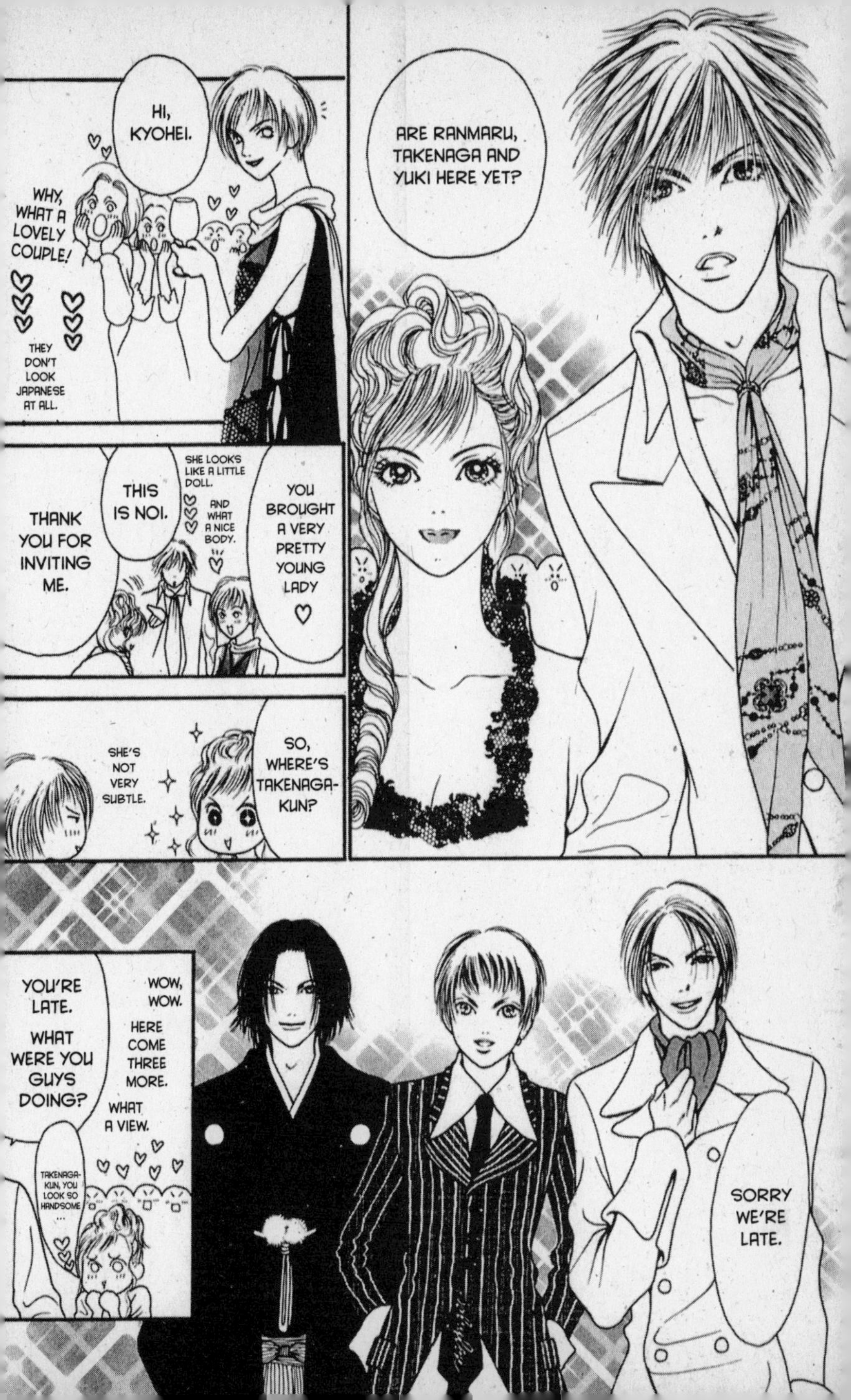
ARE RANMARU, TAKENAGA AND YUKI HERE YET?
HI, KYOHEI.
WHY, WHAT A LOVELY COUPLE!
THEY DON'T LOOK JAPANESE AT ALL.
YOU BROUGHT A VERY PRETTY YOUNG LADY
SHE LOOKS LIKE A LITTLE DOLL.
AND WHAT A NICE BODY.
THIS IS NOI.
THANK YOU FOR INVITING ME.
SO, WHERE'S TAKENAGA-KUN?
SHE'S NOT VERY SUBTLE.
SORRY WE'RE LATE.
WOW, WOW.
HERE COME THREE MORE.
WHAT A VIEW.
YOU'RE LATE. WHAT WERE YOU GUYS DOING?
TAKENAGA-KUN, YOU LOOK SO HANDSOME ...

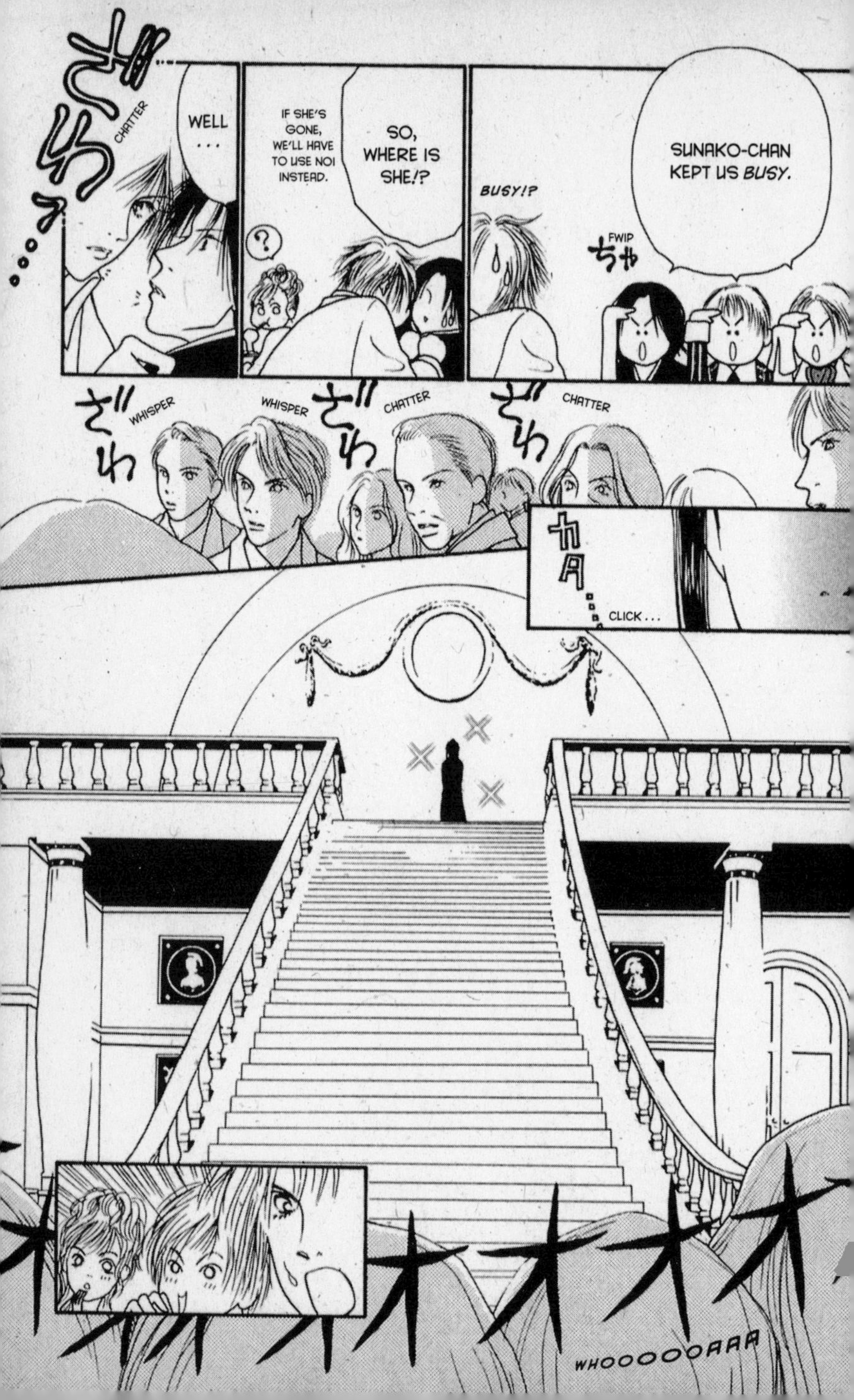

SUNAKO-CHAN KEPT US BUSY.
ちゃ
FWIP
BUSY!?
SO, WHERE IS SHE!?
IF SHE'S GONE, WE'LL HAVE TO USE NOI INSTEAD.
WELL . . .
CHATTER
ざわ
CHATTER
ざわ
CHATTER
ざわ
WHISPER
WHISPER
CLICK . . .
WHOOOOOAAA

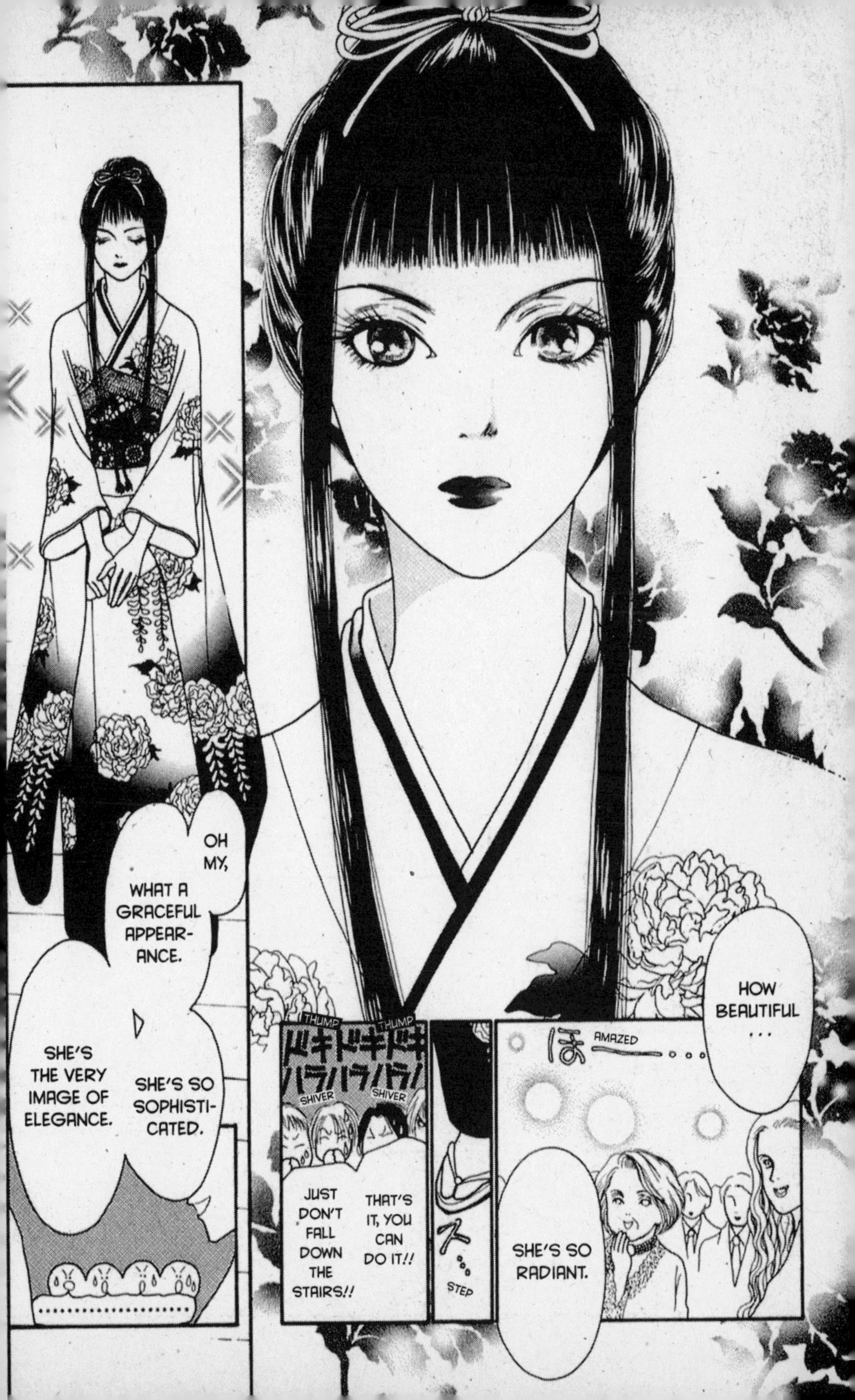
ほー AMAZED
HOW BEAUTIFUL...
SHE'S SO RADIANT.
STEP
ドキドキドキ THUMP THUMP
ハラハラハラ SHIVER SHIVER
THAT'S IT, YOU CAN DO IT!!
JUST DON'T FALL DOWN THE STAIRS!!
OH MY,
WHAT A GRACEFUL APPEARANCE.
SHE'S SO SOPHISTICATED.
SHE'S THE VERY IMAGE OF ELEGANCE.
....

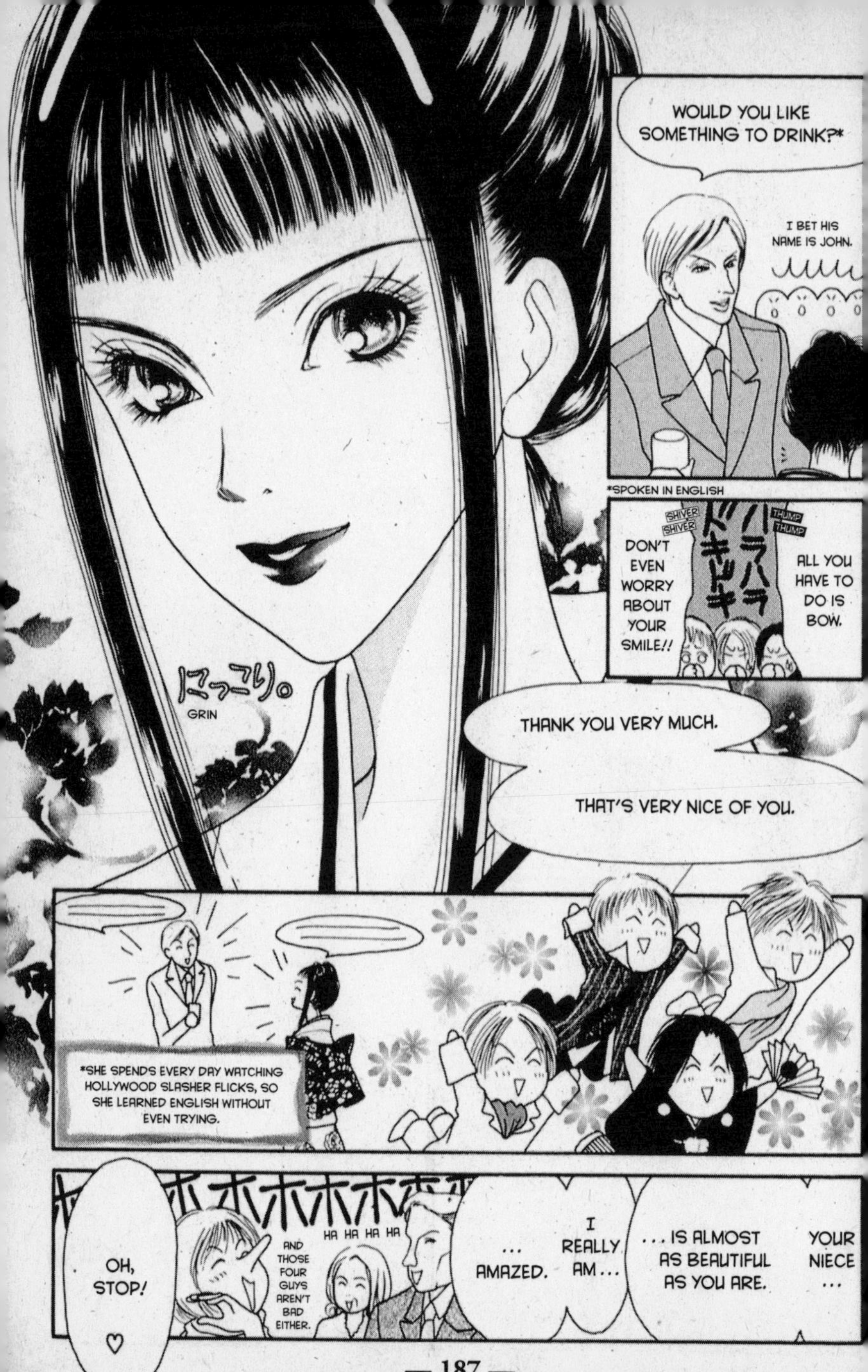
WOULD YOU LIKE SOMETHING TO DRINK?*
I BET HIS NAME IS JOHN.
*SPOKEN IN ENGLISH
ハラハラ
ドキドキ
THUMP THUMP
SHIVER SHIVER
ALL YOU HAVE TO DO IS BOW.
DON'T EVEN WORRY ABOUT YOUR SMILE!!
THANK YOU VERY MUCH.
THAT'S VERY NICE OF YOU.
にっこり。
GRIN
*SHE SPENDS EVERY DAY WATCHING HOLLYWOOD SLASHER FLICKS, SO SHE LEARNED ENGLISH WITHOUT EVEN TRYING.
YOUR NIECE ...
... IS ALMOST AS BEAUTIFUL AS YOU ARE.
I REALLY AM ...
... AMAZED.
HA HA HA HA
AND THOSE FOUR GUYS AREN'T BAD EITHER.
OH, STOP! ♡

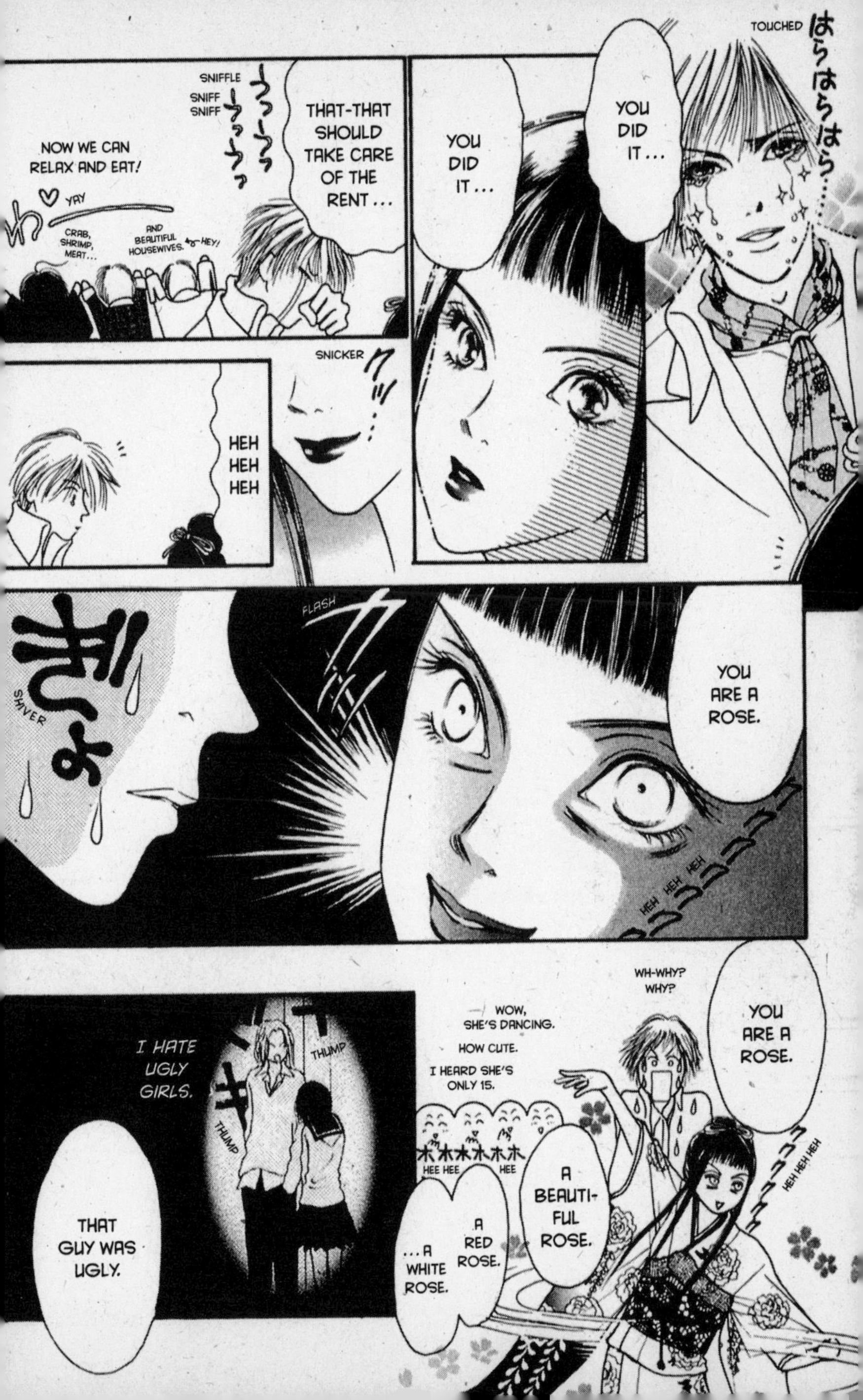
TOUCHED
はらはら
YOU DID IT...
YOU DID IT...
THAT-THAT SHOULD TAKE CARE OF THE RENT...
SNIFFLE
SNIFF SNIFF
NOW WE CAN RELAX AND EAT!
YAY
CRAB, SHRIMP, MEAT...
AND BEAUTIFUL HOUSEWIVES.
HEY!
SNICKER
HEH HEH HEH
YOU ARE A ROSE.
HEH HEH HEH
FLASH
SHIVER
YOU ARE A ROSE.
WH-WHY? WHY?
HEH HEH HEH
A BEAUTIFUL ROSE.
WOW, SHE'S DANCING.
HOW CUTE.
I HEARD SHE'S ONLY 15.
HEE HEE HEE
A RED ROSE.
...A WHITE ROSE.
THUMP
I HATE UGLY GIRLS.
THUMP
THAT GUY WAS UGLY.

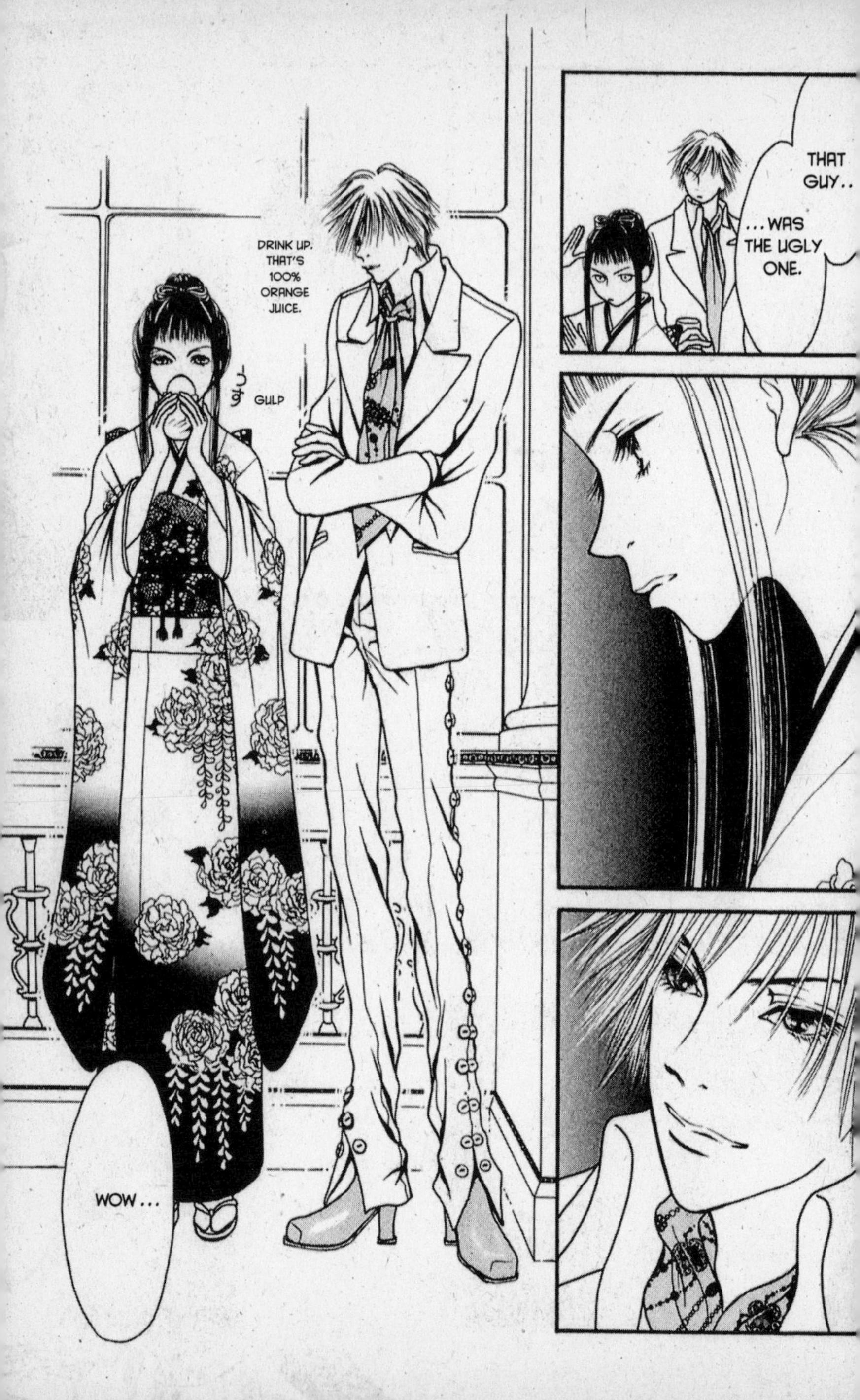
THAT GUY..
...WAS THE UGLY ONE.
DRINK UP. THAT'S 100% ORANGE JUICE.
GULP
WOW...

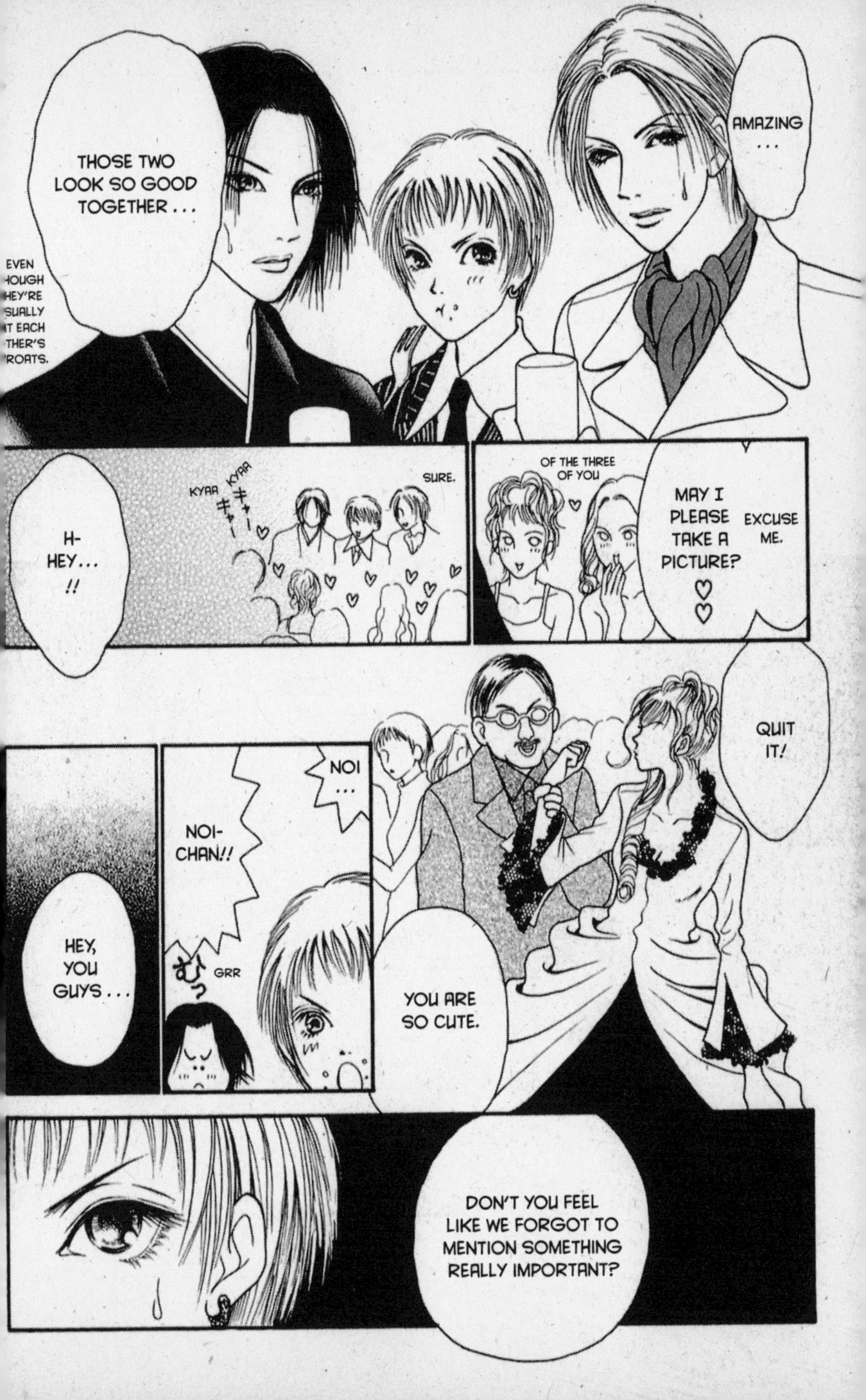
AMAZING . . .
THOSE TWO LOOK SO GOOD TOGETHER . . .
EVEN HOUGH HEY'RE SUALLY T EACH THER'S ROATS.
EXCUSE ME.
MAY I PLEASE TAKE A PICTURE? ♡ ♡
OF THE THREE OF YOU ♡
SURE.
キャーキャー KYAA KYAA
H- HEY . . . !!
QUIT IT!
YOU ARE SO CUTE.
NOI . . .
NOI- CHAN!!
むっ GRR
HEY, YOU GUYS . . .
DON'T YOU FEEL LIKE WE FORGOT TO MENTION SOMETHING REALLY IMPORTANT?

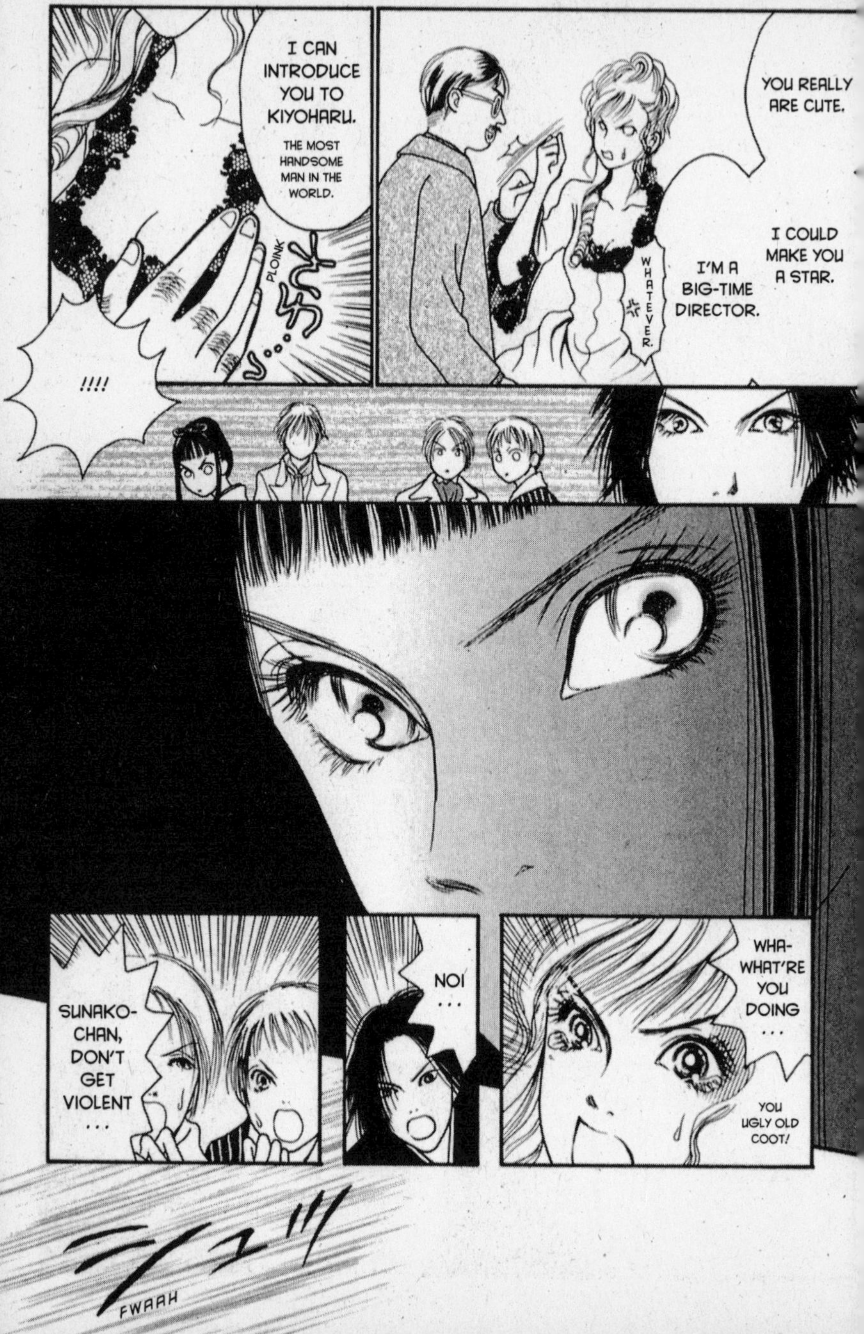
YOU REALLY ARE CUTE.
I COULD MAKE YOU A STAR.
I'M A BIG-TIME DIRECTOR.
WHATEVER.
I CAN INTRODUCE YOU TO KIYOHARU.
THE MOST HANDSOME MAN IN THE WORLD.
PLOINK
!!!!
WHA-WHAT'RE YOU DOING . . .
YOU UGLY OLD COOT!
NOI . . .
SUNAKO-CHAN, DON'T GET VIOLENT . . .
FWAAH

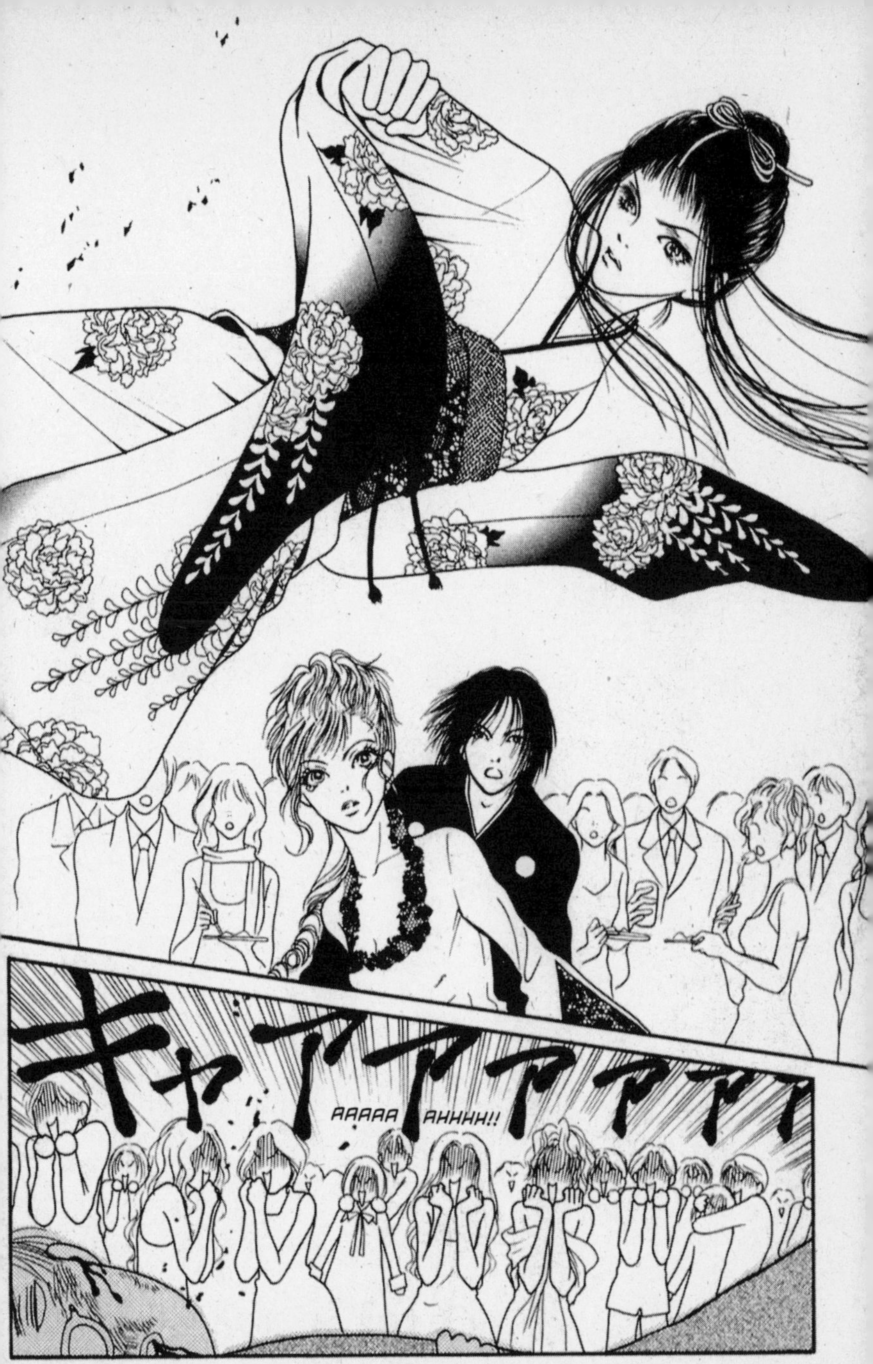
キャアアアアア
AAAAA AHHHH!!

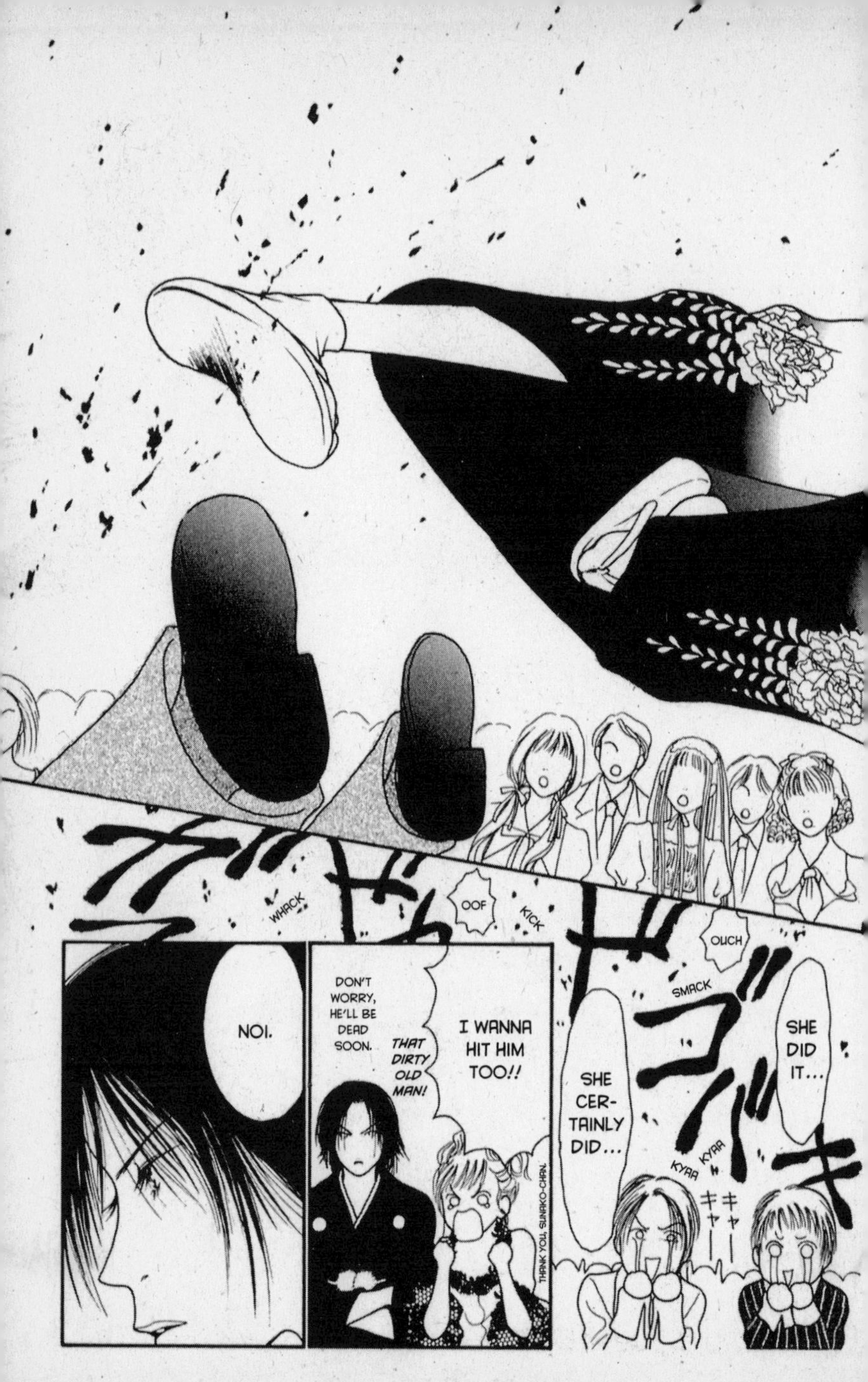

OUCH
SMACK
KICK
OOF
WHACK
SHE DID IT...
KYAA KYAA
キャーキャー
SHE CER-TAINLY DID...
I WANNA HIT HIM TOO!!
THAT DIRTY OLD MAN!
DON'T WORRY, HE'LL BE DEAD SOON.
THANK YOU, SUNAKO-CHAN.
NOI.

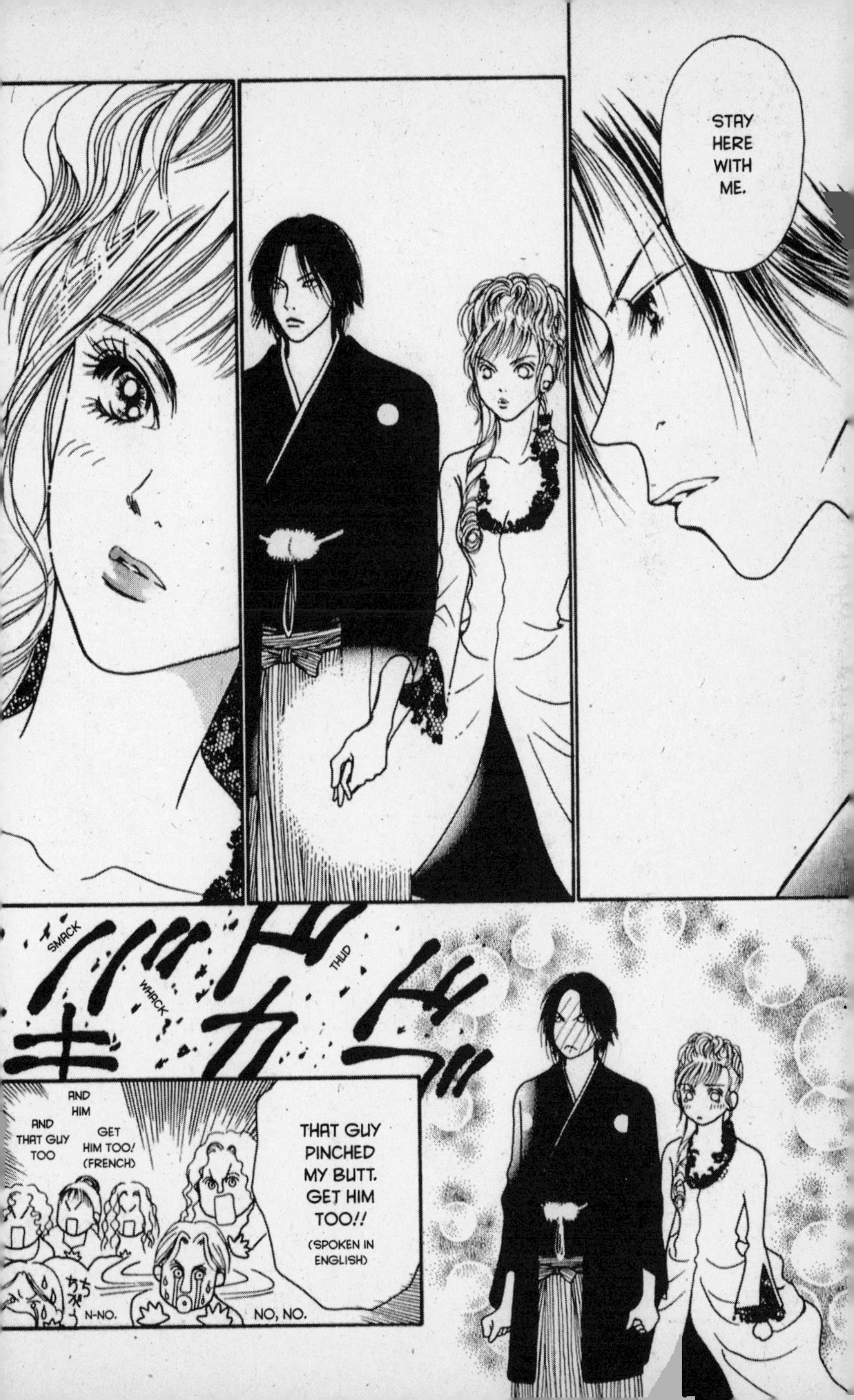
STAY HERE WITH ME.
THUD
WHACK
SMACK
THAT GUY PINCHED MY BUTT. GET HIM TOO!!
(SPOKEN IN ENGLISH)
GET HIM TOO! (FRENCH)
AND HIM
AND THAT GUY TOO
NO, NO.
N-NO.

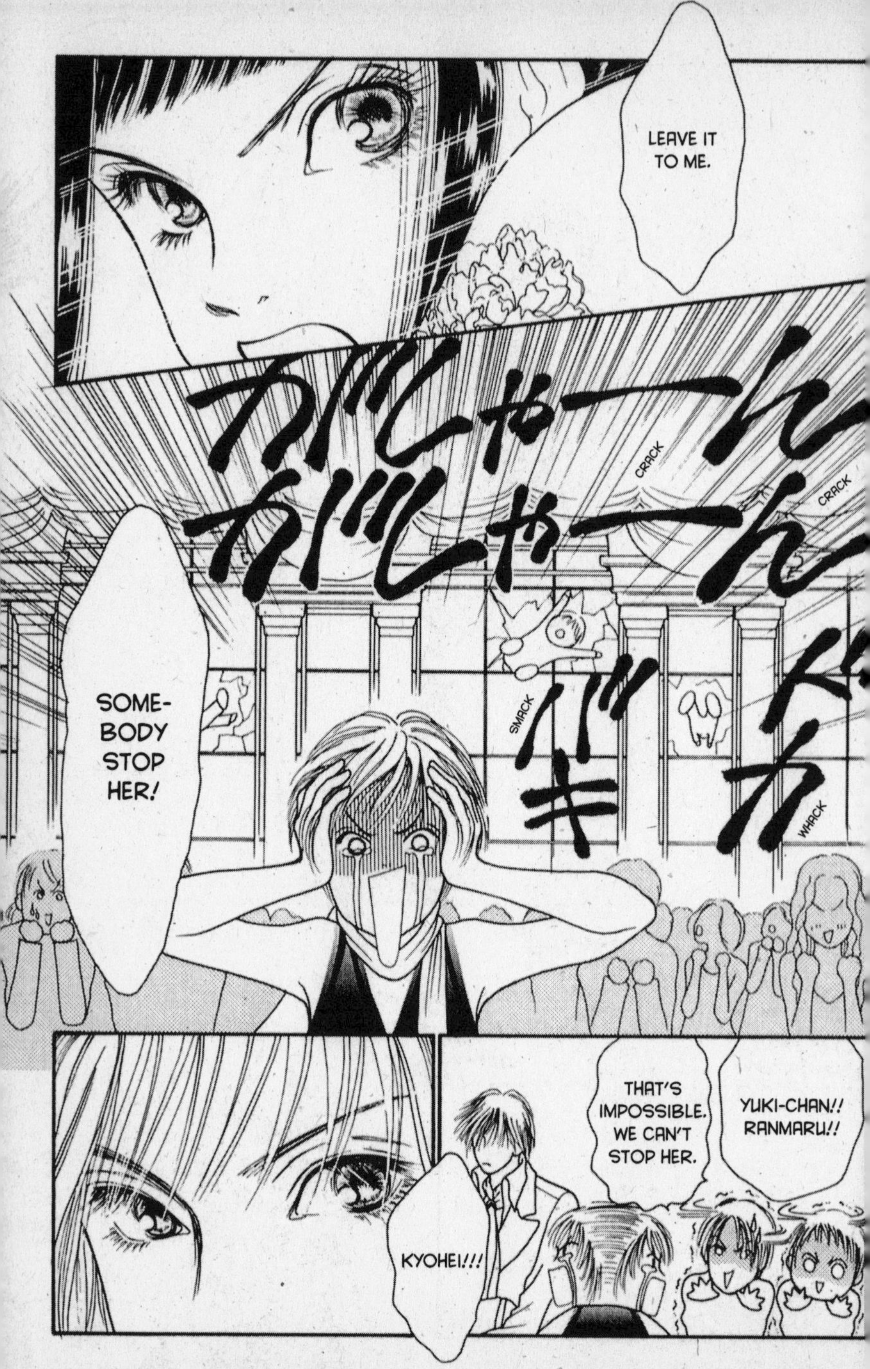
LEAVE IT TO ME.
がしゃーん
CRACK
がしゃーん
CRACK
ドカ
WHACK
バキ
SMACK
SOME-BODY STOP HER!
YUKI-CHAN!! RANMARU!!
THAT'S IMPOSSIBLE. WE CAN'T STOP HER.
KYOHEI!!!

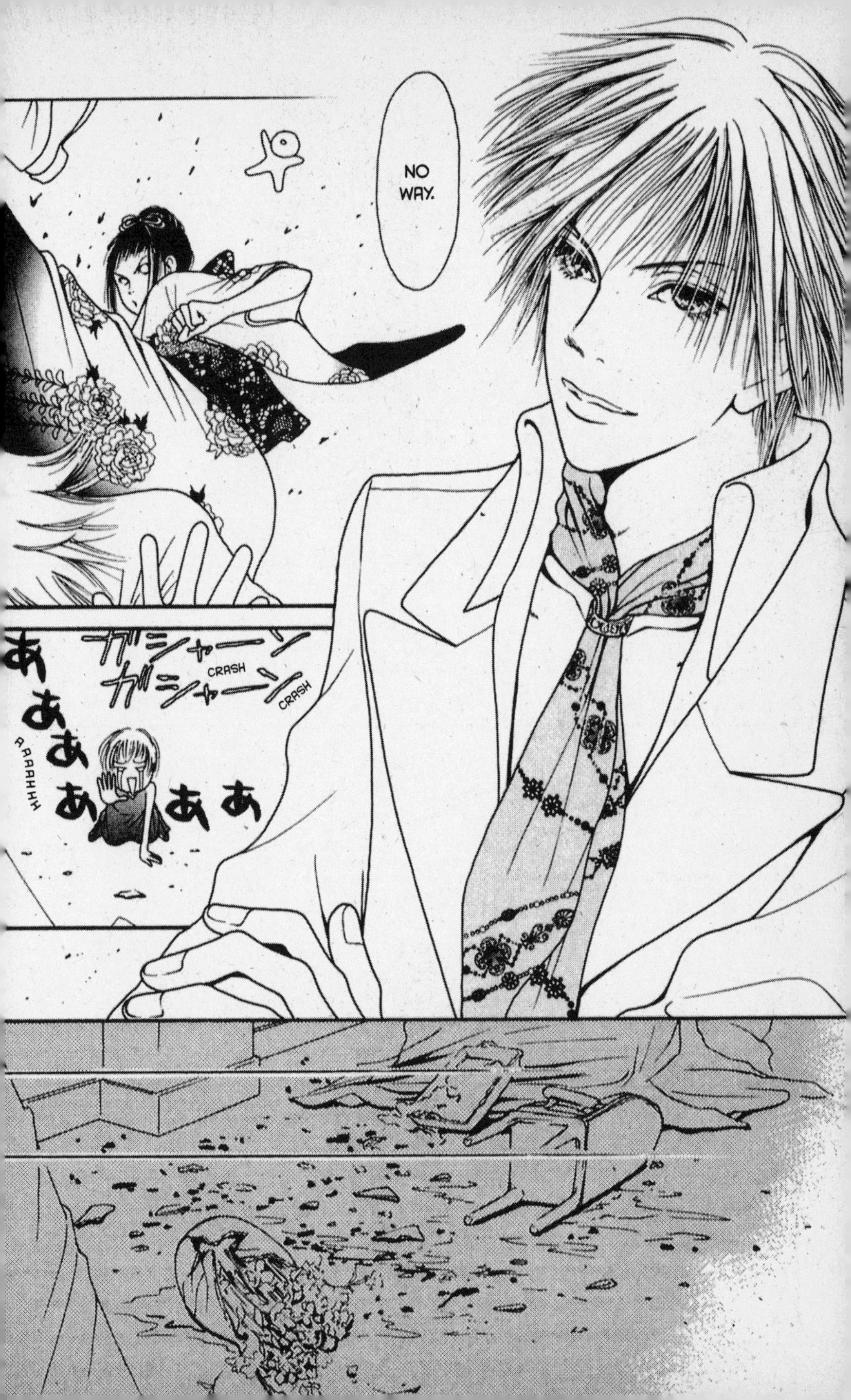
NO WAY.
ガシャーン CRASH
ガシャーン CRASH
ああああああ
AAAAHHHH

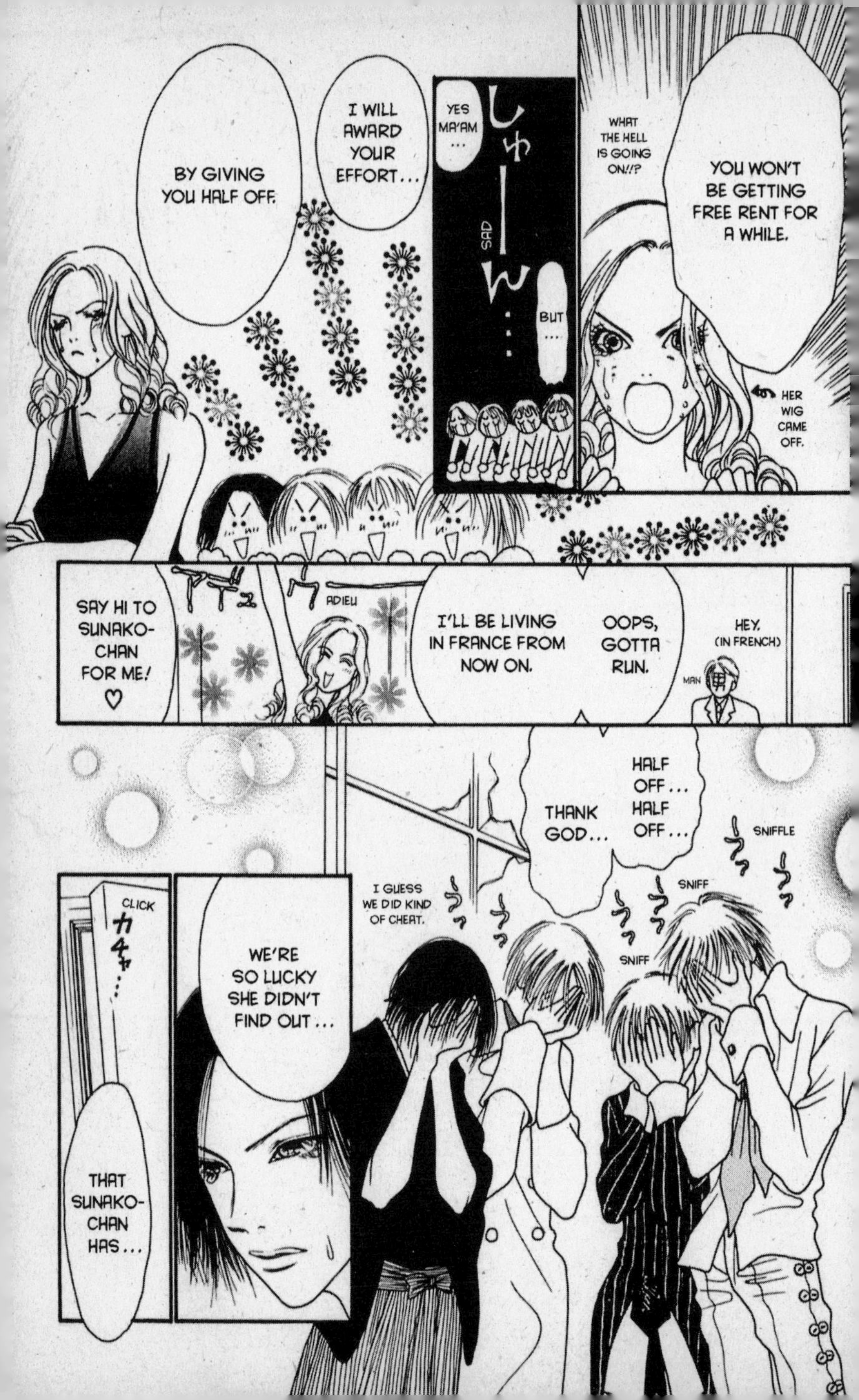
WHAT THE HELL IS GOING ON!!?
YOU WON'T BE GETTING FREE RENT FOR A WHILE.
HER WIG CAME OFF.
しゅーん…
SAD
YES MA'AM …
BUT …
I WILL AWARD YOUR EFFORT…
BY GIVING YOU HALF OFF.
HEY. (IN FRENCH)
MAN
OOPS, GOTTA RUN.
I'LL BE LIVING IN FRANCE FROM NOW ON.
アデュー
ADIEU
SAY HI TO SUNAKO-CHAN FOR ME! ♡
HALF OFF… HALF OFF…
THANK GOD…
SNIFFLE
SNIFF
SNIFF
I GUESS WE DID KIND OF CHEAT.
WE'RE SO LUCKY SHE DIDN'T FIND OUT…
カチャ…
CLICK
THAT SUNAKO-CHAN HAS…

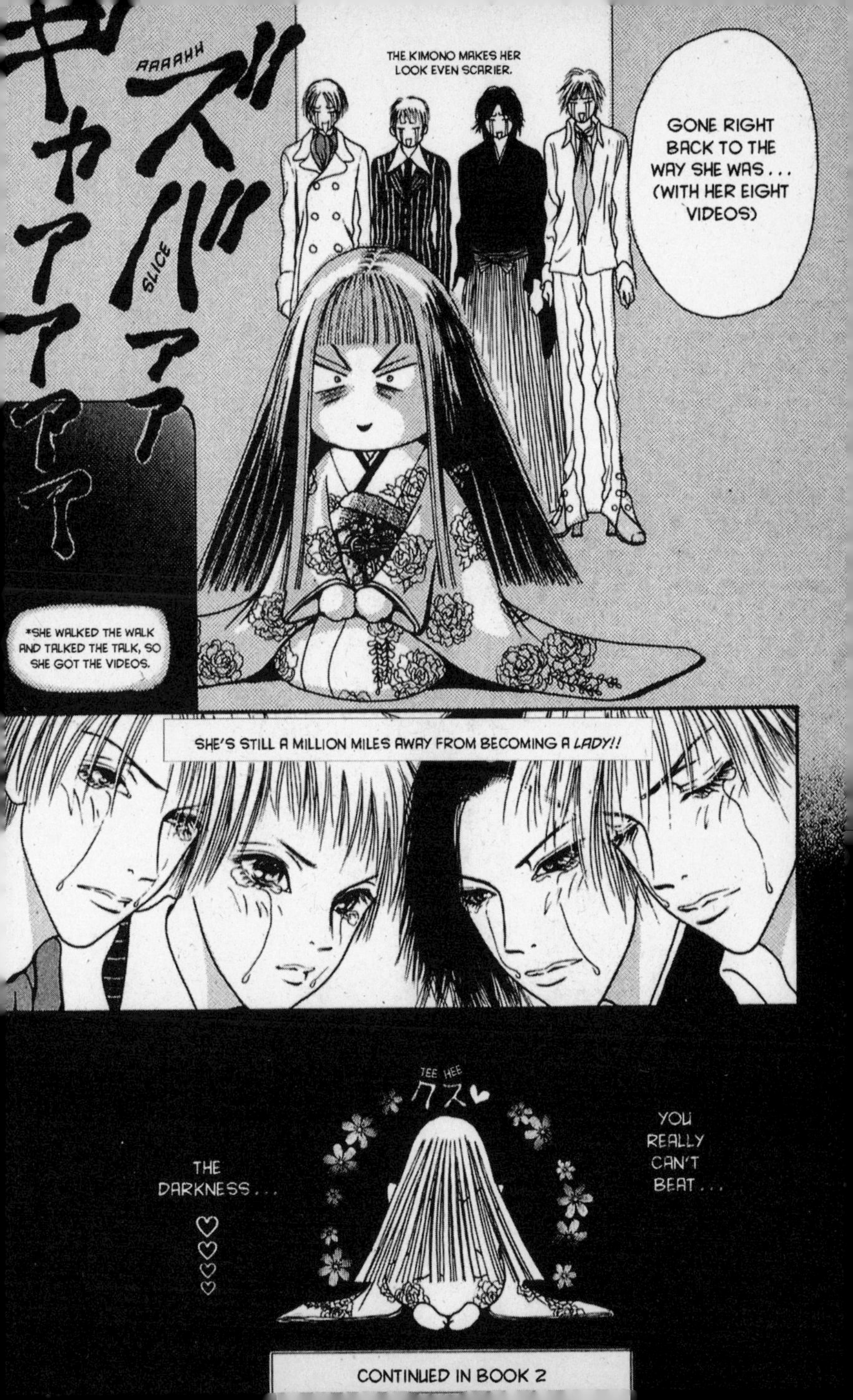

GONE RIGHT BACK TO THE WAY SHE WAS . . . (WITH HER EIGHT VIDEOS)
THE KIMONO MAKES HER LOOK EVEN SCARIER.
SLICE
AAAAHH
*SHE WALKED THE WALK AND TALKED THE TALK, SO SHE GOT THE VIDEOS.
SHE'S STILL A MILLION MILES AWAY FROM BECOMING A LADY!!
TEE HEE
クス♥
YOU REALLY CAN'T BEAT . . .
THE DARKNESS . . .
CONTINUED IN BOOK 2

WELL,

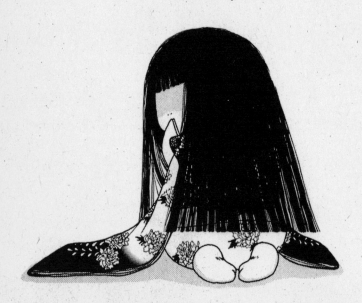

I'LL SEE YOU IN BOOK 2!

About the Creator

Born: March 4. Zodiac sign: Pisces. Blood group: AB.

Since her debut as a manga creator, Tomoko Hayakawa has worked on many shojo titles with the theme of romantic love—only to realize that she could write about other subjects as well. She decided to pack her newest story with the things she likes most, which led to her current, enormously popular series, *The Wallflower (Yamato Nadeshiko)*.

Her favorite things are: Tim Burton's *The Nightmare Before Christmas*, Jean-Paul Gaultier, and samurai dramas on TV. Her hobbies are collecting items with skull designs and watching *bishonen* (beautiful boys). her dream is to build a mansion like the one that the Addams family live in. Her favorite pastime is to lie around at home with her cat, Ten (whose full name is Tennosuke).

Translation Notes

Japanese is a tricky language for most Westerners, and translation is often more art than science. For your edification and reading pleasure, here are notes on some of the places where we could have gone in a different direction in our translation of the work, or where a Japanese cultural reference is used.

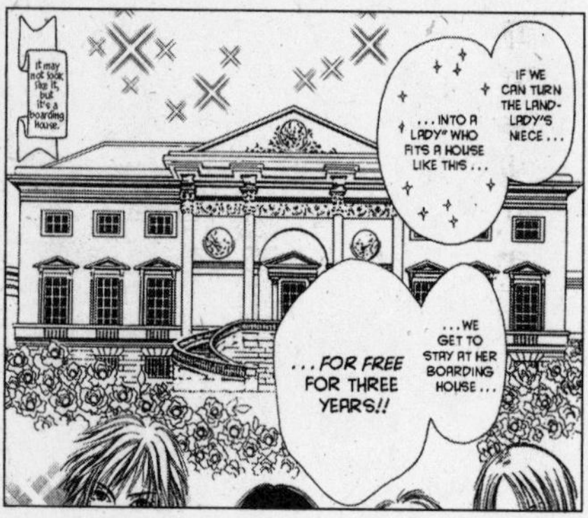

IF WE CAN TURN THE LAND-LADY'S NIECE...
...INTO A LADY" WHO FITS A HOUSE LIKE THIS...
...WE GET TO STAY AT HER BOARDING HOUSE...
...FOR FREE FOR THREE YEARS!!
It may not look like it, but it's a boarding house.

The Boarding House (page 4)

The Japanese term used for boarding house is *geshuku*. *Geshuku* are much more common in Japan than in America. *Geshuku* are commonly used by students who are going to school away from home. Meals are usually provided.

Daiei (page 7)

Daiei is a department store/grocery store chain in Japan. It's the equivalent of Kmart and equally uncool.

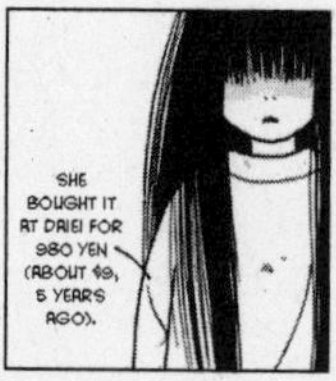

SHE BOUGHT IT AT DAIEI FOR 980 YEN (ABOUT $9, 5 YEARS AGO).

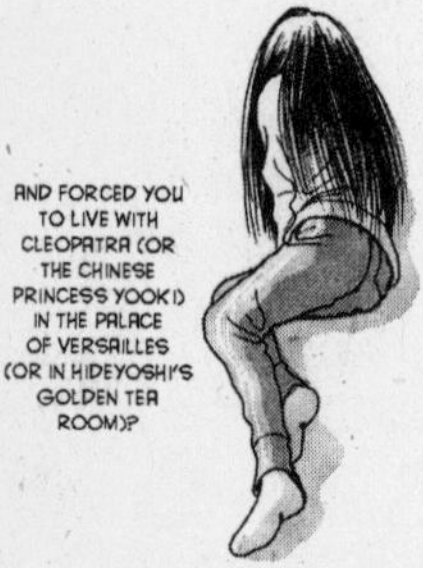

AND FORCED YOU TO LIVE WITH CLEOPATRA (OR THE CHINESE PRINCESS YOOKI) IN THE PALACE OF VERSAILLES (OR IN HIDEYOSHI'S GOLDEN TEA ROOM)?

Hideyoshi Toyotomi (page 21)

Hideyoshi Toyotomi is a historical ruler of Japan. Considered by many to be the most significant figure in Japanese history, Hideyoshi ruled Japan from 1590 to 1598. Renowned for lavishing his considerable wealth on the imperial court and on lords throughout the nation of Japan, he was declared a Shinto deity after his death and given the title of Hokoku, or "Wealth of the Nation."

Underground Tunnels (page 23)

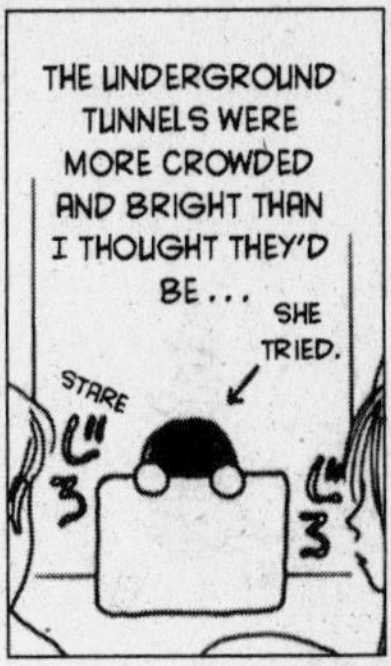
THE UNDERGROUND TUNNELS WERE MORE CROWDED AND BRIGHT THAN I THOUGHT THEY'D BE...
SHE TRIED.
STARE

Underground tunnels are walkways that run beneath Japanese subway and train stations. They often serve the purpose of connecting two or more stations and subway lines and are full of shops and restaurants. At night they are populated by the homeless. When the narrator says "she tried," she means she tried to sleep on cardboard with the other homeless people.

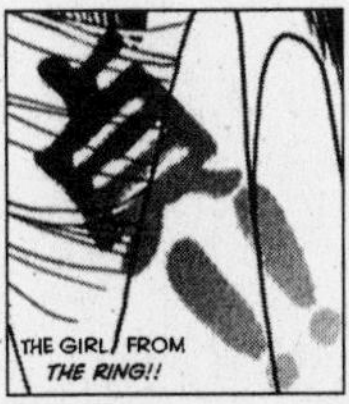
THE GIRL FROM *THE RING!!*

Sada!! (page 24)

The kanji Sada refers to the female name *Sadako*, the girl from the movie *Ringu*, which was remade in the U.S. as *The Ring*.

Tacky! (page 46)

This is probably a reference to the singer Tacky from the J-Pop group Tacky & Tsubasa.

Class B (page 54)

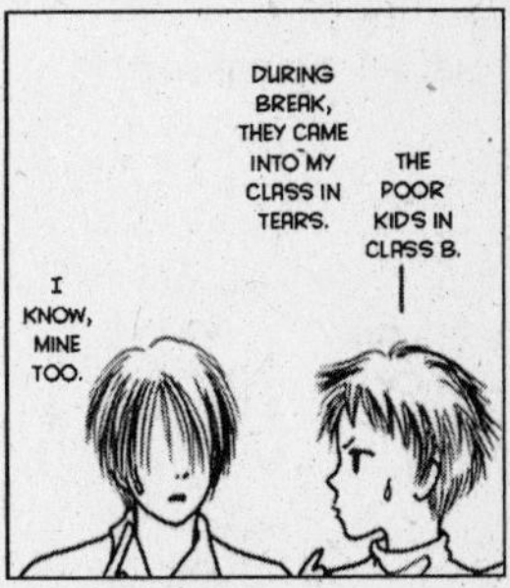
DURING BREAK, THEY CAME INTO MY CLASS IN TEARS.
THE POOR KIDS IN CLASS B.
I KNOW, MINE TOO.

In secondary school in Japan, each grade of students is broken down into several classes. The classes are often categorized by letters or numbers.

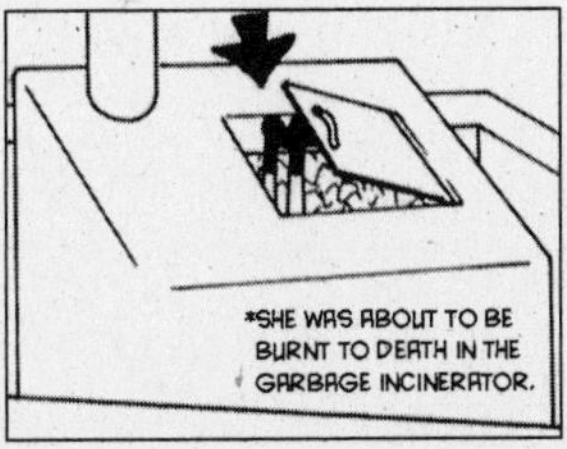
*SHE WAS ABOUT TO BE BURNT TO DEATH IN THE GARBAGE INCINERATOR.

Hiding in the Incinerator (page 57)

She's hiding in the garbage incinerator. Since Japan has few landfills, garbage is usually burned.

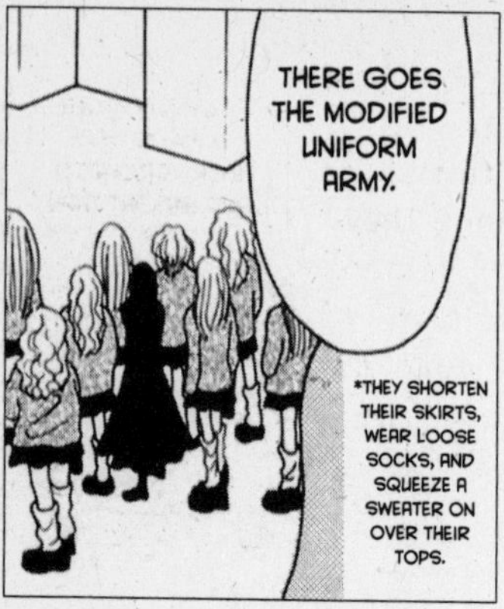
THERE GOES THE MODIFIED UNIFORM ARMY.
*THEY SHORTEN THEIR SKIRTS, WEAR LOOSE SOCKS, AND SQUEEZE A SWEATER ON OVER THEIR TOPS.

Short Skirts, Loose Socks (page 71)

In Japan, some students try to rebel by altering their school uniforms and showing as much skin as they can get away with. Loose socks are puffy white socks, which are worn high up on the shins. Some girls even use glue to keep them up.

Kiyoharu (page 84)

Kiyoharu, the man Tomoko Hayakawa modeled Yukinojo after, was the vocalist for the now defunct band "Kuroyume."

Punch Perm (page 92)

In Japanese, Noi actually says she saw a guy with a "punch-perm" say hi. A "punch-perm" is a hairstyle that is generally associated with the Japanese mafia (the yakuza).

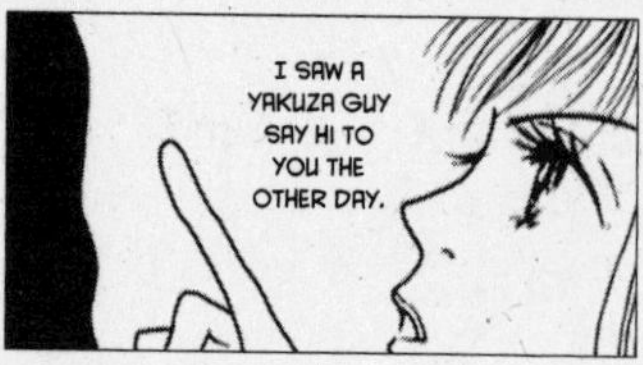
I SAW A YAKUZA GUY SAY HI TO YOU THE OTHER DAY.

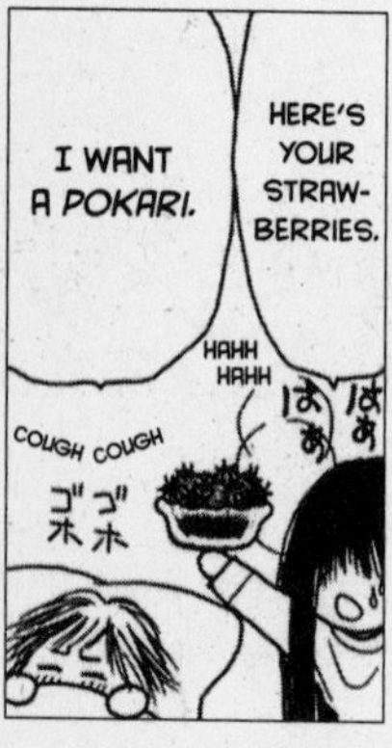
HERE'S YOUR STRAW-BERRIES.
I WANT A *POKARI.*
HAHH HAHH
はぁ はぁ
COUGH COUGH
ゴホゴホ

Pokari (page 102)

Pokari Sweat is a famous Japanese soft drink. It tastes, in your humble editor's opinion, a lot like Gatorade.

Kyohei's "Soup" (page 103)

In the original Japanese text, Kyohei actually says make me some *okayu*. *Okayu* is a rice porridge that's often eaten when one suffers from a cold or flu. It's the Japanese equivalent of chicken soup.

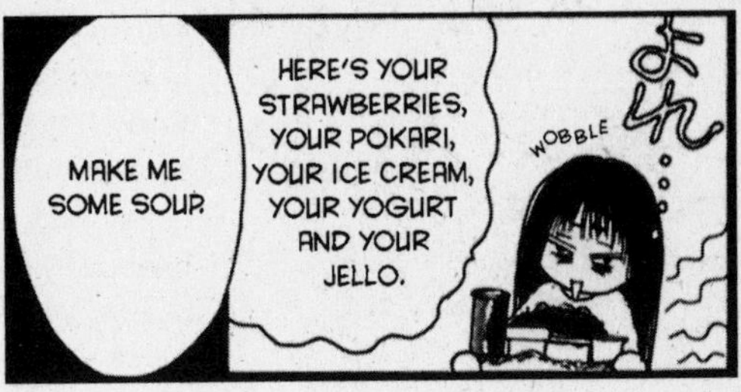
よれ
WOBBLE
HERE'S YOUR STRAWBERRIES, YOUR POKARI, YOUR ICE CREAM, YOUR YOGURT AND YOUR JELLO.
MAKE ME SOME SOUP.

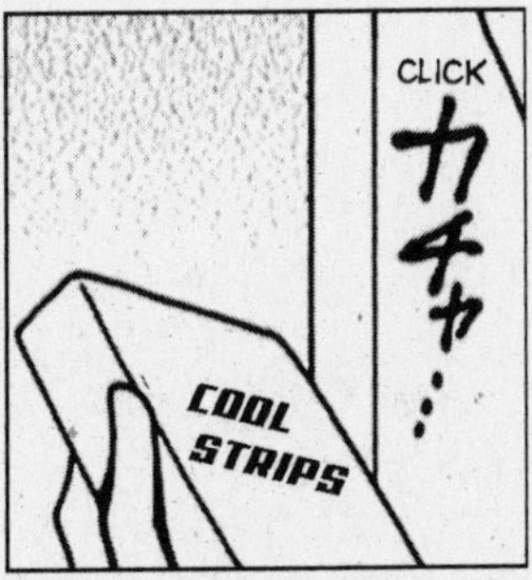
CLICK
カチャ..
COOL STRIPS

Cool Strips (page 118)

Cool Strips are miniature ice packs that you can stick on your body.

Host Clubs (page 122)

Japan is full of host and hostess clubs in which patrons pay a hefty price to drink alcohol while talking to the sexy hosts or hostesses. The workers make huge amounts of money and often get a cut of the payments for the overpriced drinks their clients buy. Club scouts stand in front of busy shops and train stations and give their cards to sexy potential employees.

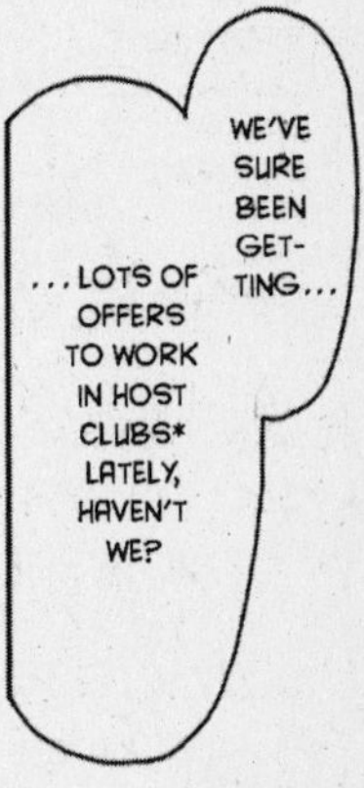
WE'VE SURE BEEN GETTING...
...LOTS OF OFFERS TO WORK IN HOST CLUBS* LATELY, HAVEN'T WE?

Sarina Suzuki (page 122)

Sarina Suzuki is a popular Japanese actress.

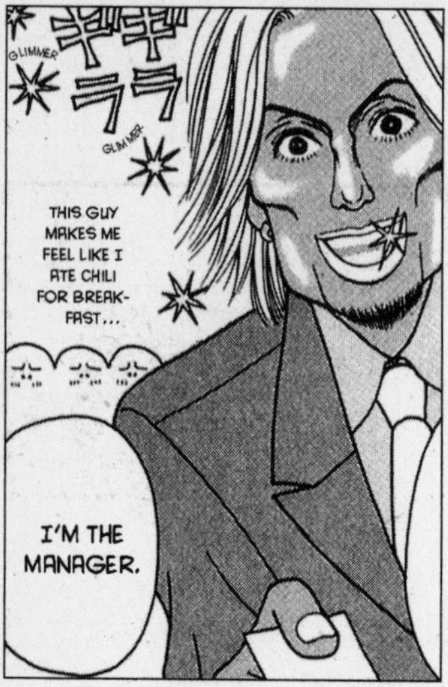
GLIMMER
GLIMMER
THIS GUY MAKES ME FEEL LIKE I ATE CHILI FOR BREAK-FAST...
I'M THE MANAGER.

Chili Tonkatsu (page 125)
The guys actually say *asappara kara tonkatsu kutta kibun*. Which literally means "I feel like I ate tonkatsu first thing in the morning." Tonkatsu is a breaded, fried pork cutlet. The translator used "chili" because he thought it was the most accurate way to communicate this feeling to American readers. A second reference to this joke occurs on page 142.

Prince Michy (page 161)
Prince Michy is a Japanese musician and actor.

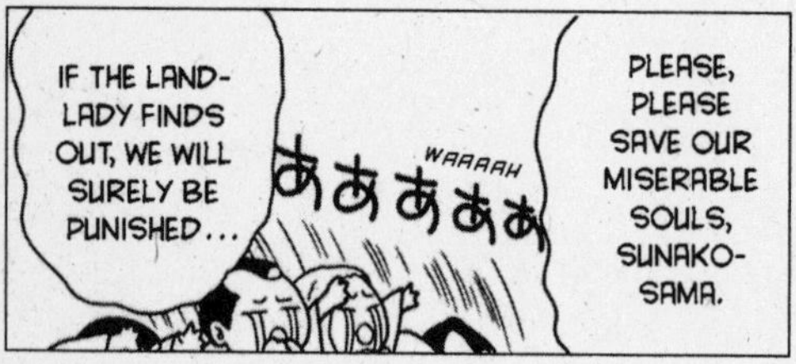
PLEASE, PLEASE SAVE OUR MISERABLE SOULS, SUNAKO-SAMA.
WAAAAH
ああああ
IF THE LAND-LADY FINDS OUT, WE WILL SURELY BE PUNISHED...

Save Our Souls (page 165)
The guy's dialogue parodies Japanese samurai-period-piece dramas, hence the samurai-style top knots in this panel.

Kamata Koushinkyoku (page 167)
Kamata Koushinkyoku is a movie, and Yasu is most likely a character from that film.

Takuya Kimura (page 175)
Takuya Kimura is a Japanese boy-band star and actor. He once did a Japanese commercial for an energy drink.

Bucho (page 177)

Japanese names are made up of kanji characters which can have several readings/ pronunciations. Here Kyohei uses an alternative reading of Takenaga's name. *Bucho* can also mean department head or boss, so this is a pun.

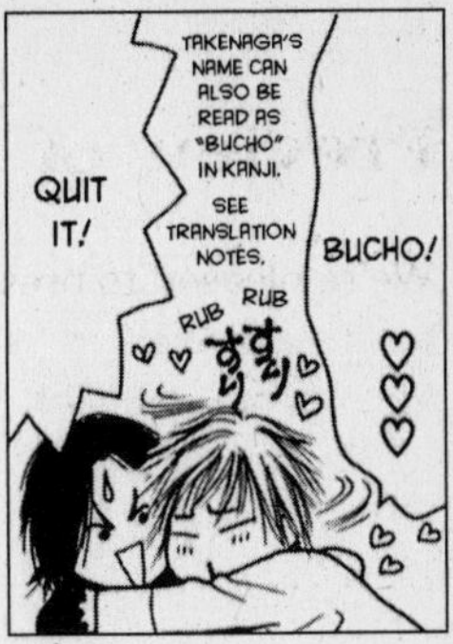
BUCHO!
TAKENAGA'S NAME CAN ALSO BE READ AS "BUCHO" IN KANJI. SEE TRANSLATION NOTES.
RUB RUB
すりすり
QUIT IT!

Preview of Volume 2

We're pleased to present you a preview from Volume 2. This volume will be available in English on December 28, 2004, but for now you'll have to make do with Japanese!

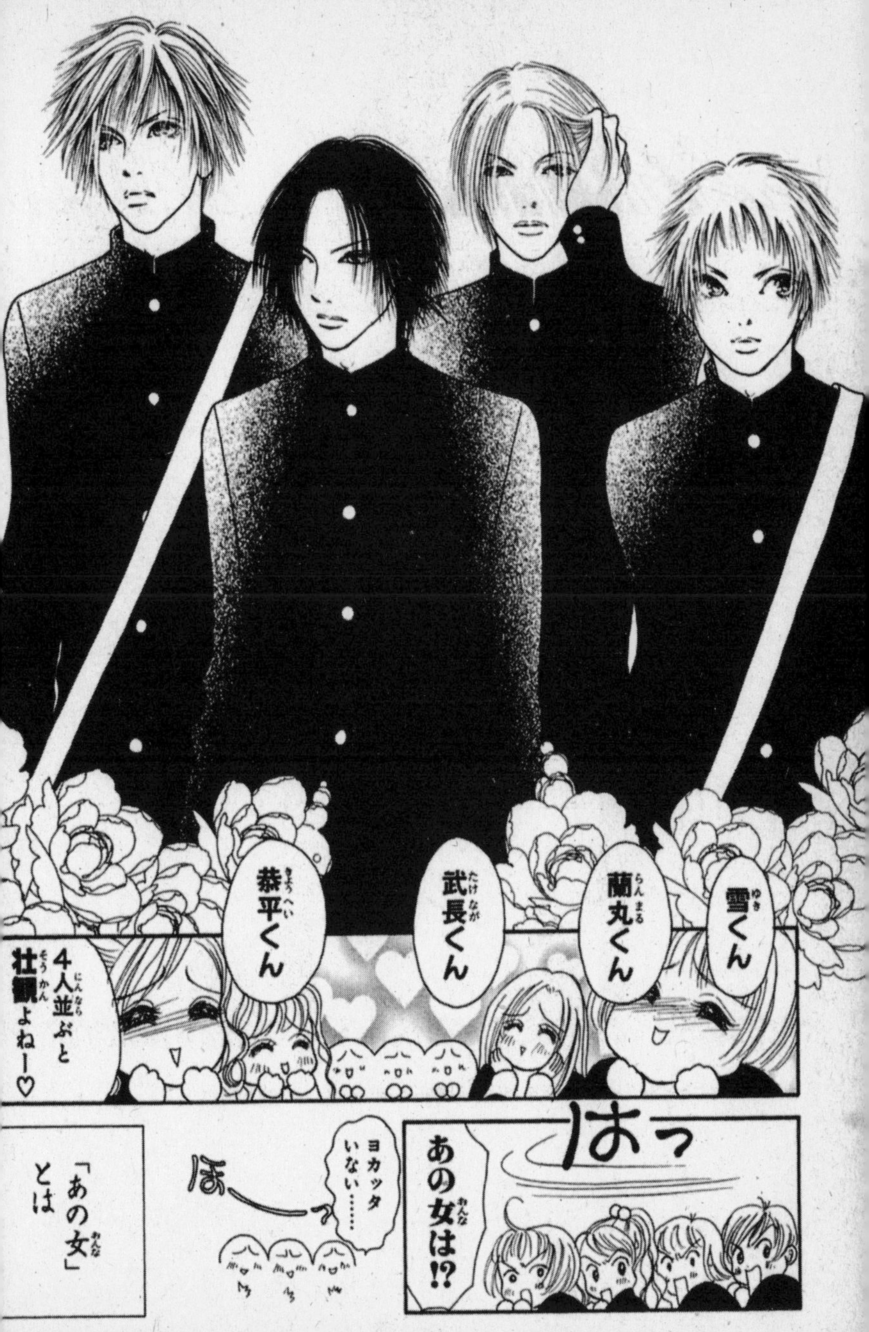
雪くん
蘭丸くん
武長くん
恭平くん
4人並ぶと壮観よねー♡
はっ
あの女は!?
ほーっ
ヨカッタいない……
「あの女」とは

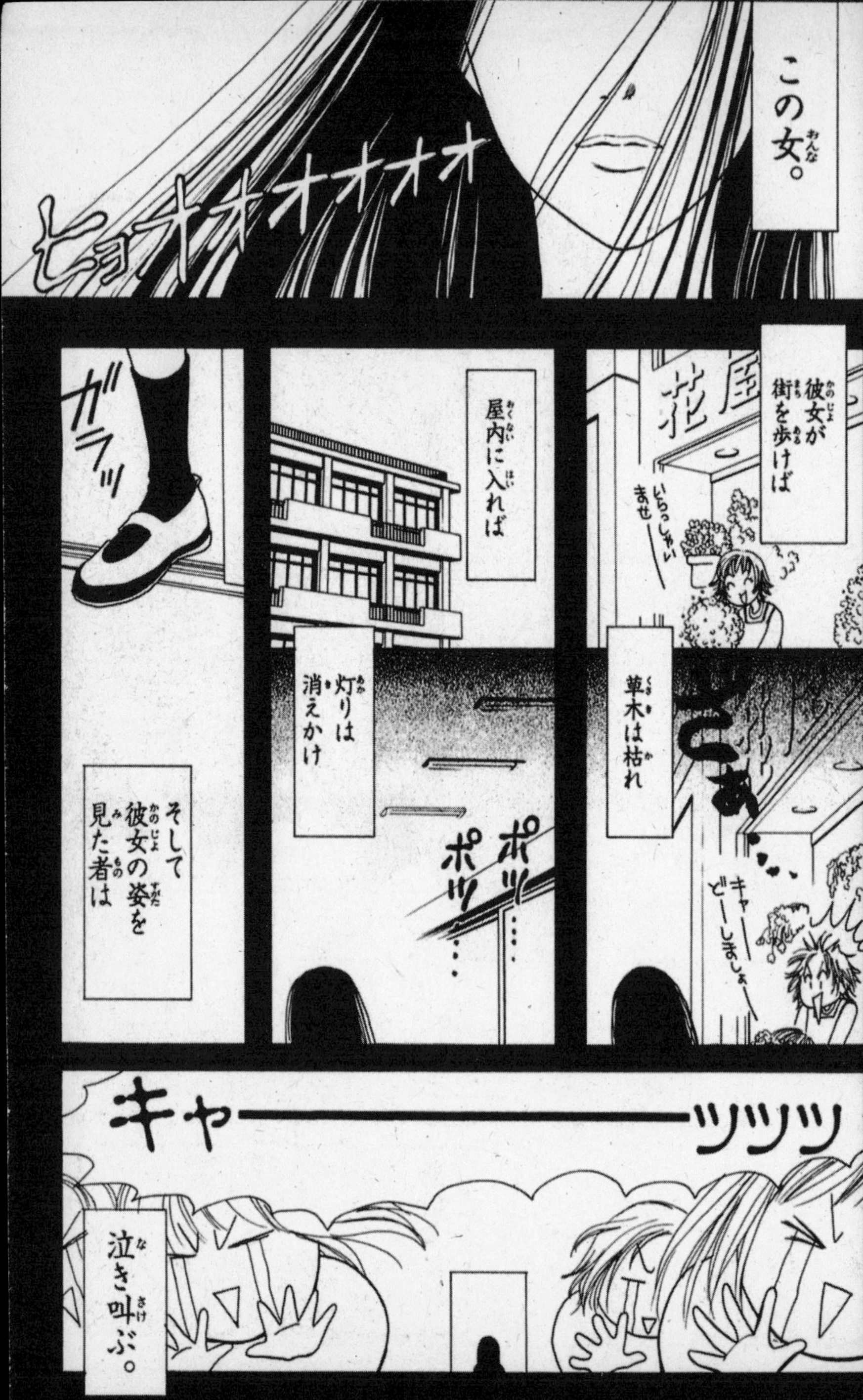
この女。
ヒョオオオオオオ
彼女が街を歩けば
いらっしゃいませー
華木は枯れ
キャーどーしましょー
屋内に入れば
灯りは消えかけ
ポツ……
ポツ……
ガラッ
そして彼女の姿を見た者は
キャーーーーッツツ
泣き叫ぶ。

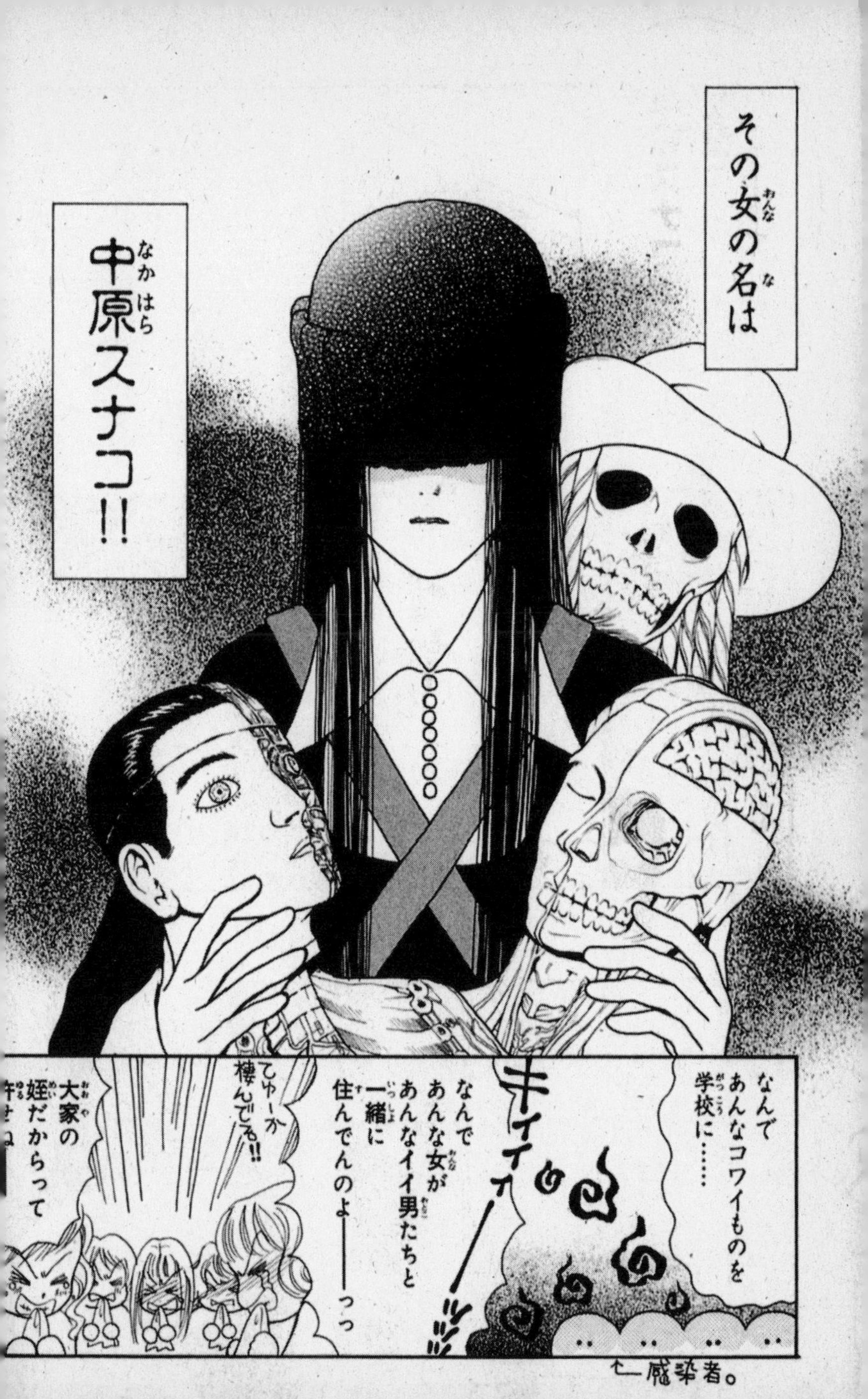
その女の名は
中原スナコ!!
なんであんなコワイものを学校に……
キイイイーー
なんであんな女があんなイイ男たちと一緒に住んでんのよーーーっっ
てゆーか棲んでる!!
大家の姪だからって
←感染者。

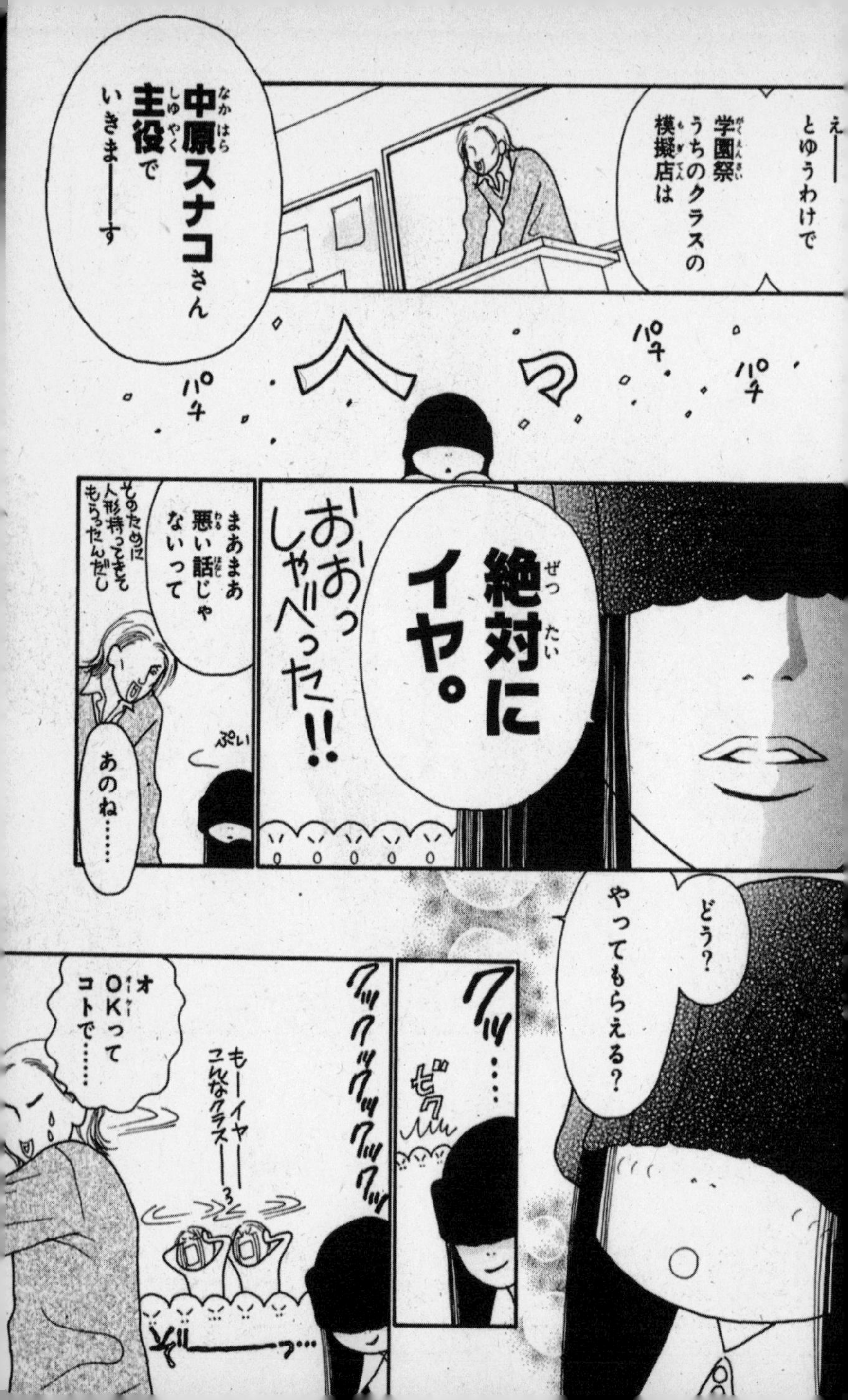

え──
とゆうわけで
学園祭
うちのクラスの
模擬店は
中原スナコさん
主役で
いきま───す
パチ
パチ
パチ
へっ
絶対に
イヤ。
おおっ
しゃべった!!
まあまあ
悪い話じゃ
ないって
そのために
人形持ってきて
もらったんだし
ぷい
あのね……
どう？
やってもらえる？
ワッ…
ビク
ワッワッワッワッワッ
もーイヤー
こんなクラスー
オ
OKって
コトで……
ぞぉ───っ…

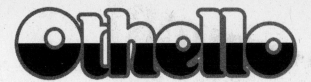

VOLUME 1

BY SATOMI IKEZAWA

High school girls Yaya and Nana couldn't be more different. Yaya's always being picked on—her friends call her "Yaya the cry-ya! Yaya the misfi-ya!" Nana isn't afraid of anything—she exposes Yaya's "friends" as slime-balls, doles out punishment, and does it all with style.

Is there anything that terminally shy Yaya and butt-kicking Nana have in common? Well, for one thing, they're the same person . . .

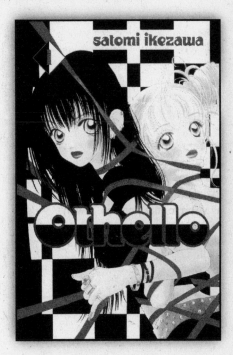

Volume 1 on sale now!

VOLUME 2: On sale December 28, 2004 • **VOLUME 3:** On sale March 29, 2005

For more information and to sign up for Del Rey's manga e-newsletter, visit www.delreymanga.com

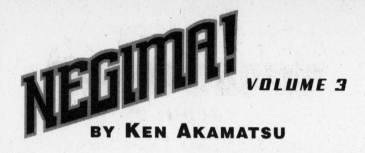

NEGIMA! VOLUME 3

BY KEN AKAMATSU

There is a vampire stalking the night! Normally ten-year-old teacher/magician Negi Springfield would have no problem dispatching such a villain, but this vampire has a magic-enhancing partner, and worse, the vampire is a student in his own class! Now Nagi must find a partner of his own, but with a class full of beautiful girls all vying for the position, it won't be an easy task. Add in Negi's old friend, a skirt-chasing, wise-cracking weasel from Wales, and the nice, orderly chaos of Negi's life turns into a hilarious melee of sirens and sorcery!

3
NEGIMA!
MAGISTER NEGI MAGI
by
KEN AKAMATSU
CREATOR OF LOVE HINA!

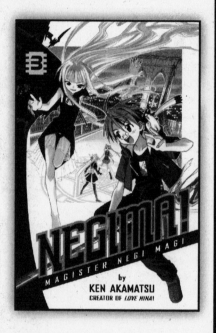

VOLUME 3: On sale October 12, 2004 • VOLUME 4: On sale December 28 2004

For more information and to sign up for Del Rey's manga e-newsletter, visit www.delreymanga.com

TSUBASA
VOLUME 3
BY CLAMP

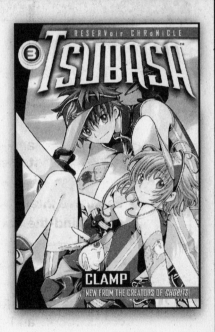

Sakura is awake, but she remembers almost nothing— certainly not Syaoran, who has sacrificed everything to help her. Accompanied by the happy-go-lucky Fai, the intense Kurogane, and the strikingly odd creature Mokona Modoki, Sakura and Syaoran make their way into a new universe where a traveling magician has suddenly become frighteningly powerful and is terrorizing an entire town. Only a few independent-minded stragglers remain to battle for control of their own lives. Fai, the lone magician in the group, traded his magical powers to the dimension witch, xxxHOLiC's Yûko, before the journey started. Without a weapon with which to fight, can the extraordinary group of friends defeat a master magician who can control the Earth's elements?

VOLUME 3: On sale October 26, 2004 • VOLUME 4: On sale January 25, 2005

For more information and to sign up for Del Rey's manga e-newsletter, visit www.delreymanga.com

TOMARE!

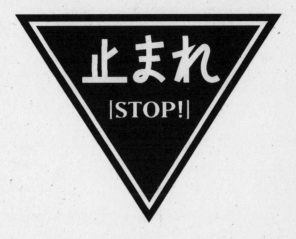

|STOP!|

You're going the wrong way!

Manga is a completely different type of reading experience.

To start at the *beginning*, go to the *end*!

That's right! Authentic manga is read the traditional Japanese way—from right to left. Exactly the *opposite* of how American books are read. It's easy to follow: Just go to the other end of the book, and read each page—and each panel—from right side to left side, starting at the top right. Now you're experiencing manga as it was meant to be!